Also by Elysia Whisler

Rescue You
Forever Home

ELYSIA WHISLER

becoming family

mira

mira™

Recycling programs
for this product may
not exist in your area.

ISBN-13: 978-0-7783-8646-9

Becoming Family

For questions and comments about the quality of this book, please contact us
at CustomerService@Harlequin.com.

Mira
22 Adelaide St. West, 41st Floor
Toronto, Ontario M5H 4E3, Canada
BookClubbish.com

Printed in U.S.A.

For my parents.

You did good.

becoming family

one

Tabitha's radar was lit before the woman even entered the store. The way she whipped into the parking space, killed the engine at a crooked angle and jangled the bell over the shop door like it was being throttled. Tabitha had just taken a bite of the Really Big Cookie—a birthday indulgence bought at the community college cafeteria—when the woman marched right up to the front counter and, without so much as hello, slapped down some pictures. "My father's old Harley has been sitting in the barn for decades," she declared, out of breath. "And I'm determined to get it going."

Tabitha closed up her Journal of Invincibility—*I am not afraid; I was born to do this. ~Joan of Arc*—and tucked it behind the counter, like a mother protecting her young. The woman went on for a bit, while Tabitha tried to chew and swallow her treat. When she was done ranting, she stood there in silence. Eventually, she shook her head. "Don't you know anything about motorcycles?" Big-breasted, big-hipped, big personality, big, brassy red hair, the customer rested her elbow on the counter and leaned against it, settling in.

"Not much, no." A hunk of cookie fell from Tabitha's lips and landed on the front of her Triple M Classics employee T-shirt. She hastily brushed it away and gestured to the shelves that lined the rear of the shop. "I just ring up the merchandise. Keep tabs on the floor when the mechanics are in the back." She closed her eyes and rubbed her temples, but that just prompted images from school this morning, which she didn't want in her head. Still, with her eyes closed, Tabitha sensed that this wasn't really about the motorcycle. The woman was upset, possibly grieving. The motorcycle meant something to her and she wanted quick answers because she was searching for a way to ease her pain. Tabitha opened her eyes again, looked past the woman and settled her gaze on Trinity, the little black rescue pit bull who always made her feel better.

"Then get the mechanic. Or, better yet, get the owner. Where's Delaney Monroe?"

"She's on an errand." Tabitha kept her gaze on Trinity, who lay near the stairs that led to Delaney's apartment. She was catching some zees in the dog bed intended for Delaney's dog, Wyatt. For about the third time that day Tabitha thought, *What am I doing here? I'm not cut out for this.*

"Delaney Monroe is who I came to see," the woman pressed. "I heard she's an expert on classic bikes. If you work in a bike shop, you should know about bikes. I don't have time for this." She straightened up and planted her hands on her hips.

"Delaney's out. Maybe I can help."

Tabitha turned to the sound of Nora's raspy voice.

"I'm Nora. One of the mechanics." Delaney's mom had come out of the back room, wiping grease from her fingers with a shop rag. She had a cigarette tucked behind her ear, right where her temples were starting to gray. The rest of her hair was silky black and tied back in a ponytail. Nora was a small woman with a slight build, but the way she carried herself, she might as well have been six feet tall. She wore blue jeans and the same Triple M Classics T-shirt and she locked her fearless, almond-shaped eyes into the irritated gaze of the customer. "Whatcha got?" She nodded at the photographs.

The woman pushed them across the countertop. "This has been in my father's barn for ages. He recently passed and I'm not sure if it's worth fixing up."

Nora went silent while she leafed through the pictures. "An old Harley Panhead," she murmured. "Sweet. Do you know the year? Looks like a '49."

"Yes. How did you know that?"

Tabitha felt a shift in the air as the woman's demeanor changed, her anger melting away, relief softening her shoulders and her scrunched-up mouth. Crisis averted.

"The window on a Panhead is only '48 to '65. The emblem on the gas tank in this shot tells me it's a '49." Nora tapped the top photo with her grease-stained finger.

The woman stuck out her hand, a huge grin on her face. "Nelly Washington. Nice to meet you."

"Nora." Nora glanced at Nelly's hand but didn't touch her. "My girl owns this place."

"I've heard good things."

"Damn straight you heard good things. My girl's the best."

Nelly gave off a deep belly laugh and used the humor as an excuse to withdraw her unrequited handshake. "Can she fix it up? Make it run?"

Like a cowgirl walking into a saloon in an old Western, Delaney pushed open the shop door at that moment. The bell jangled as she strode inside, motorcycle boots thunking over the floor, helmet in her gloved hand. Delaney was taller than her mother by several inches, had the same slender build and dark hair, but in a pixie cut. Wyatt, the wandering white pit bull with the brown eye patch, trotted in next to her, still wearing his Doggles. Delaney slipped the eye protection off her motorcycle-riding companion. Wyatt spotted Trinity on his dog bed and raced over to play. He leaned on his front paws, butt in the air, tail wagging, then jumped backward and spun. When that didn't work, he danced all around her, flipping his head and poking his muzzle in the air. Trinity, unmoved, looked to Tabitha for instruction.

"Break, Trinity," Tabitha said, and the dogs were soon twining necks like ponies.

Nora waved at her daughter and shrugged at Nelly. "You'll need to bring the bike in. See what's up. Is it dry?"

"Been in the shed. Covered up." Nelly's gaze went to Delaney as she neared.

"She means did you drain the carburetor and gas tank," Delaney clarified, settling her helmet on the counter. "Before you stored it."

"Oh." Nelly's face went straight. "I don't know, actually. My father is the one who stored it. Once his arthritis got too bad for him to ride."

"That'll make a difference," Delaney continued, like she'd been in on the conversation from the beginning. "That, and how straight the bike was when it was put up." She glanced at the photos. "A '49 Panhead. Cool. Bring it in. We'll take a look."

"I will definitely do that. Thank you. My father recently passed away. He used to take me on rides on that bike when I was a little girl." Nelly's voice grew faraway, wistful. "We'd go to the general store and he'd buy me a grape soda. I loved feeling the wind in my hair." Nelly waved a hand. "This was before helmet laws. Anyway." The reminiscent look in Nelly's eyes slid away and she sniffed deeply. "Are you Delaney?"

"Yes, ma'am. Don't worry. I've never met a Panhead I can't get going."

Tabitha stuffed the rest of the cookie in her mouth and tried to sneak away, her lack of motorcycle knowledge no longer an issue. Her shift was over, she was exhausted and she was ready to go home.

"Get back here, Steele." Delaney grasped the hem of Tabitha's shirt and pulled her back gently. "You need to take down this lady's information. The more you listen, the more you'll learn. Pretty soon you'll know a Harley Panhead on sight." Delaney nodded at Tabitha. "She's still learning."

"She seems like a nice young lady." Nelly was all smiles now, like their earlier interaction had never happened.

After Tabitha filled out a capture sheet with Nelly Washington's information, and the woman had left the shop in an entirely different mood than the one she'd barged in with, Delaney turned to her and said, "What's going on, Steele? You look ready to lie on the floor and call your dog for Smoosh Time."

Smoosh Time was Delaney's slang for the deep pressure therapy Trinity was trained to provide if Tabitha was having a panic attack. It was affectionate rather than sarcastic. Unused to affection, Tabitha liked it and had taken to calling the therapy Smoosh Time herself. Smoosh Time actually sounded really good about now. But Trinity was still on break, chasing Wyatt around the perimeter of the shop. "It's been a long day."

"Massage school getting you down?"

"Old Nelly was kinda rough on her," Nora offered. She slipped the cigarette from behind her ear and stuck it between her lips.

"That's why she's learning as much as she can." Delaney

tapped the capture sheet. "That's all you can do, Steele. I don't expect you to become a mechanic, unless you want to, but you soak in everything you can while you're here." She glanced at her mother. "Don't you dare light that in here, Nora."

Nora pulled it from her lips and rolled her eyes. "I'm not. It's just a prop, okay?"

"How many days has it been?" After some hemming and hawing Delaney clarified, "For real."

"Half a day," Nora admitted. "I'd gone two days and then I caved this morning. It's so hard not to smoke after I eat. Maybe I need to stop eating."

Delaney shook her head. "You gotta be tough, Nora. Like Tabitha here."

"I'm not tough." Tabitha had been enjoying watching the mother-daughter pair interact, despite how rough her day had been so far. They made her wonder what her relationship with her birth mother would've been like, if she'd known her. Tabitha's relationship with Auntie El—the woman who'd raised her and the only mother Tabitha had ever known— was as old-fashioned as it got. Yes, ma'am, No, ma'am, please and thank you, respect your elders and all boundaries clearly drawn and rarely crossed. There was none of this role reversal or sarcastic banter. Life certainly hadn't been easy, and Tabitha had been handed absolutely nothing. If that didn't make her tough, nothing would. "Tough is just not my nature."

Sensitive was Tabitha's nature, for good or bad. The armor she lacked had never been very useful, not until she joined the navy and her main job in Afghanistan was to protect her chaplain from harm. She'd been pretty good at smelling trouble, hearing things nobody else heard, seeing things nobody else saw. Some had even jokingly called her Radar, after the character from *M*A*S*H*. It made her good at her job, despite the fact that she hadn't been able to prevent the IED that had got her chaplain hurt, and despite the fact that the skill was kind of useless, and often counterintuitive, in everyday life.

"You're tough-ish, Tabitha," Nora agreed. "Which means you got potential. Just gotta stand up for yourself with lippy women like Nelly."

"Spill it, Steele." Delaney shot her mother a silencing look. "What's going on?"

"You were right, Sarge," Tabitha admitted. She hadn't planned on discussing her day, but there was just something about Delaney, the woman she'd met at Camp Leatherneck years ago. The woman who'd helped her keep her head straight during that awful day when an IED had taken out her convoy. "It's massage school."

"What about it?"

"It's the student exchanges." Tabitha drew a deep breath. "We have to swap with our classmates once a week to practice the strokes we learn in class. At first, I was doing really well. Everyone loved my massages and said that I just had that magic touch. But then…well… I'm doing something wrong. I'm not…massaging right." Tabitha bit down on her lower lip.

"How can you not massage right?" Nora spoke around the unlit cigarette dangling from her lips. "Aren't you just squirting lotion on each other? How hard can that be?"

"No. We're not just squirting lotion. It's a lot more than that." Tabitha was used to Nora's directness at this point, and did her best to not let Delaney's mother get under her skin. "You have to learn all the bones and muscles and physiology. Plus all the strokes. There's a lot of science. You have to learn about how the body moves and how everything works together. And then you have to massage in such a way that you're helping people. And right now, I'm not helping anyone." Just like she hadn't been able to help Nelly Washington with her Panhead. Tabitha wasn't helping anyone, anywhere.

She was an impostor in every aspect of her own life.

Nora pulled a Zippo from her pocket and flipped it open. "How do you know?" She ran her thumb over the wheel, making a clicking sound with the lighting mechanism without actually bringing the flame to life.

"I'm…" Tabitha sighed and faced the blank expressions of the women. "I'm giving the men erections."

A round of silence passed.

"I've done it three times now, to three different men. So it's not like a one-off. I'm doing something wrong."

"Man," Delaney said, shaking her head. "It's always the quiet ones."

Wyatt gave off a loud woof and everyone burst into laughter.

"Well." Nora stuck the cigarette behind her ear and jammed the lighter in the front pocket of her jeans. "Au contraire, but I bet those men think you're doing something right."

"We're definitely not supposed to get erections," Tabitha insisted. All three men had reacted differently. Todd—young, indifferent, thought massage therapy would be an easy career field—had pretended it didn't happen. Frank—in his forties, quiet, deliberate—had been embarrassed and would no longer make eye contact with Tabitha in class. Corbin—a loud twentysomething who called everyone *dude*—had eyed his own erection with detached interest and announced, "You're doing something wrong, dude."

Delaney shook her head. "Men are just like that. The wind blows and their dicks get hard. I wouldn't be so down on yourself."

"I already struggle with the science. Like right now we're learning all the bones, with all their divots and ridges and stuff. It's excruciating and not coming easily to me," Tabitha said. "And now I'm screwing up the massages. I'm starting to think I'm just not cut out for it." *Just like I'm not cut out for this bike shop*, she didn't add. She already knew Delaney had given her the job out of pity. No need to shine a spotlight.

"Sounds like the bones *are* coming easily to you," Nora muttered as she collected today's paperwork from the counter and started to file it away. "You'll be the most requested massage girl in the county. I don't see what the big problem is."

Delaney stifled a laugh. "Don't listen to her. Ask Red about it later. We have the Halloween party, remember?"

The party. Tabitha died a little inside. "Right. The party. Tonight." But Delaney was right. Tonight she could ask Constance, "Red" for short, the famous massager of humans and dogs alike, about the erections. See what advice she had to give. She'd been the one to talk Tabitha into massage school in the first place, claiming Tabitha had a gift for connecting with people. She was connecting, all right. Just not in the way she meant to.

Delaney grinned and slapped her on the shoulder. "Go home and get some Smoosh Time with your dog, Steele. Rest up. We'll figure out the boners later."

The house was quiet when Tabitha got home. The kitchen was empty, devoid of supper smells, like shepherd's pie or chicken and dumplings—two of Tabitha's favorites, one of which she was sure Auntie El would've fixed for her birthday. Auntie's crossword lay on the table, half-done, and her glasses rested in the little wooden holder Tabitha had bought her at a craft festival one Christmas.

"Auntie El?" Tabitha moved through the rooms, calling her name. "Auntie?"

Tabitha found the door to the den—converted to Auntie El's bedroom a few years ago when she decided she was done climbing stairs on a daily basis—ajar. She poked her head in and saw Auntie El asleep on the bed, atop the covers, television running on a game show at low volume, curtains drawn to keep out most of the sunlight. Her chest rose and fell deeply. Tabitha backed out and pulled the door almost shut.

Well, it wasn't like she was a five-year-old and needed to be entertained with a moon bounce and a piñata. Not that Tabitha had ever got those things on any birthday, but Auntie El usually at least made that chicken and dumplings and a pan of brownies with her age drawn in cheap tube icing.

Tabitha sighed. No big deal. She'd just have a sandwich before she got ready for the Halloween party. Auntie El loved to cook, and loved even more to make sure Tabitha ate good, healthy food, but lately she'd been cooking a little less and napping a lot more. She'd been eating less, too, now that Tabitha thought about it. Though Auntie El had never been a small woman, her clothes had been fitting a bit looser these past few months.

Tabitha stood outside the bedroom door, closed her eyes and listened to the silence. She could hear a clock ticking from the living room. The neighbor's dog was yapping in the yard. Auntie El's television program was ending, the theme song playing while the audience cheered. Tabitha opened her eyes again and brushed aside the gnawing feeling in her gut.

She went up to her room, pulled her Dorothy costume out of her closet and tossed it on the bed. There was still a chance to back out of going to this party. Who would really care if she was there or not? But then Tabitha thought about spending the evening sitting on the couch with her dog, worrying whether or not everything was okay with Auntie El.

She stripped off her clothes and took the gingham dress from the hanger. Might as well put on another costume. Navy chaplain's assistant. Massage student. Motorcycle shop cashier. Dorothy. Auntie El's adopted daughter.

They were all costumes in Tabitha's world. Just Tabitha, pretending to be someone else for a while. Putting on hats, sliding on skins, hiding inside her perpetual Halloween of various identities.

Because Tabitha wasn't, technically, Auntie El's kin. Auntie El had raised her from infancy but Tabitha's birth mother had left her with Reverend Stokes when she was nothing but a few days old. The reverend had found Tabitha behind the altar, in the bottom half of an old pet carrier, wrapped in blankets. "I was worried you were ill, or worse," Reverend Stokes said, every time he told the story. "Because you were so quiet. But when I unwrapped the blankets, you peeked out at me with wide-open eyes. You made no fuss. You were just peacefully waiting for me to find you. Like a little angel."

Tabitha had never been a crier. Not because she was tough, but because she just didn't like to draw attention to herself. Auntie El had taken her home as a foster, and even though she had three other foster kids at various ages at the time, Tabitha was the only one who had stayed on with Auntie El forever.

Tabitha eyed herself in the mirror in the Dorothy dress. Her slender build—*a hundred pounds with rocks in your pockets*, as Reverend Stokes liked to say—didn't really fill out the dress like Judy Garland had, but Tabitha thought her brown skin made the blue-and-white gingham pop. She wasn't going to bother putting her black curls into braids, but the ruby-red slippers would leave no doubt who she was supposed to be. Which left Tabitha wondering, as she often did, who she really was. Not who her parents were—despite her earlier thoughts on what her relationship with her birth mother might've been like, Tabitha had never put much stock into who had given her up. They had their reasons and Tabitha certainly wasn't going to go looking for the people who left her in a dog crate at church. But she did sometimes wonder what her actual, real birthday was. If she was really born on Halloween—the best approximate date given by the doctor who examined her as an abandoned infant—or if she was born somewhere around Halloween. Tabitha's money was on Halloween because both that date and the fact that she was left behind the altar had defined early on who she was going to be. A quiet, abandoned question mark, trying not to make a fuss. Tabitha already knew she was no Wonder Woman. Dorothy—unassuming, soft-spoken and very lost—suited her just fine.

Maybe, like the character, it would take a tornado to shake her world.

two

That old beagle might fool everyone else, but Hobbs knew when he was being judged. Humphrey lay on his dog bed, pretending to be aloof, hiding behind the cataracts in his eyes. His gaze followed Hobbs across the gym as he took his personal training client, Serena, from the rack to the floor and back again, running her through a variety of gymnastics and plyometrics over the course of an hour.

"Keep it up!" Hobbs shouted over the music. "Stand all the way up on that box! No bent knees!"

Serena locked out her knees after her feet landed, her glutes tightening with the effort. She paused at the top, sucking air, a sheen of sweat glistening over her forehead, her ponytail ragged from all the running, jumping and swinging on the rig.

Stop judging, Hobbs mentally willed Humphrey. *I can't help it if she wore tiny little shorts for her personal training session. I'm not staring. I'm just* not *not looking.*

The little beagle huffed out his jowls and settled his head between his paws, but his eyes stayed open, bright and alert.

"C'mon!" Hobbs shouted. "You've got thirty seconds left! Open the tank and give it all you got!"

Serena stepped up her pace, racing from the box to the rig and flinging herself into her final set of toes-to-bars attempts.

"Three…two…one…time!" Hobbs yelled.

Serena sank to the floor, on her back, forearm over her eyes, gasping for air. Hobbs took down the music a few notches. He left ZZ Top's "Legs" playing at a low hum—turning off such a classic would be a crime—and entered notes for Serena's workout on his spreadsheet. She had a ninety-day block of private lessons scheduled, either in the early morning before her shift in DC, where she worked for one federal agency or another, or on Saturday afternoon, like today.

On his way back to see if she'd recovered, Hobbs stopped by Humphrey's bed, squatted down and reached out slowly, hoping today would be the day that Rhett's old rescue beagle would let someone outside his tight-knit circle pet him.

Humphrey got a glint in his rheumy eyes and reared back, away from Hobbs's thick fingers.

"Not today, huh?" Hobbs shrugged. "You don't know what you're missing, old boy. My petting game is pretty on point."

"That so?"

Hobbs looked over his shoulder to see Serena standing there, the shine mopped from her face and a smile on her lips. She was a tall woman, could look Hobbs dead in the eye when he rose to his feet, and had the confidence of someone who'd been told she was beautiful all her life. She was pretty enough, with thick brown hair and dark, warm eyes. Definitely hot, the way she moved like she knew everyone was watching and didn't really care, even though she enjoyed the attention. But she was a little too into herself to be attractive to Hobbs, the way she made everything about her, from her job to her personal training to the extracurricular activities she talked about all the time, the hiking and the wine tastings and the nightclubbing with girlfriends. Hobbs got the feeling that her world had never had to revolve around anyone but herself, which was fine. That simplified things, and Hobbs definitely liked to keep things simple.

"I'd like to hear more about this petting game," Serena continued, with no attempt to disguise her flirting. "Will you be at the Halloween party tonight?"

"It's required." Hobbs had been wondering if Serena chose him for one-on-one training because he was the main PT guy or if she'd had ulterior motives. Looked like she wasn't making much of a secret of her interest, which Hobbs had picked up on during a few of the regular class sessions. "So, yes, I'll be there."

"Great." Serena took a sip from her water bottle. Hot pink and covered in flowers. "See you then." With a grin, she was gone.

Hobbs figured he should be more excited about that prospect. Serena was single, in her early thirties, successful, fit, no kids. He should be all over that. Instead, he kept glancing at his phone, his mood diving down a notch every time there was a new notification.

Victor again.

Hobbs's older brother had tried to call him no less than a dozen times since last night. Hobbs had ignored each one. A sane person would get the hint, give up and send a text message. Or give up altogether. Not Victor. Victor was still the same kid who'd found a way to bully Hobbs out of his stocking chocolate every single Christmas. They'd get a net baggie full of chocolate coins in gold foil and Victor would pig all his down in one day. Hobbs, more patient, would ration his out. After that, the game was on. Victor came after Hobbs with bets, dares, deals, anything to get his hands on Hobbs's coins. No matter how hard he tried to dodge him, Victor found a way and always got the larger share of his little brother's chocolate before the week was out.

"Not going to work anymore," Hobbs said, and clicked off his phone. "You can call till the cows come home and I'm not going to answer it."

His next client walked through the door at that moment, saving him from feeling guilty. Jim was a powerlifter, training to compete in the next meet in January. This would be a much different session than the one with Serena. Jim was quiet and methodical and didn't talk much. Hobbs switched the music from Jock Jams to thrash metal and got Jim set up for bench press and related strength exercises. They exchanged hellos and slipped right into the work, the hour progressing steadily. By the time they were done, Hobbs had forgotten all about Victor and the phone calls. That was, until he packed everything up and headed home for dinner. He plugged his phone into his car, and when the screen lit up he saw there was a new text waiting. From Victor.

Hobbs sighed and tried to decide whether to look at it now or after he ate. It wasn't like Victor's attempts to get in touch with him, when the most they ever did was exchange pleasantries over the holidays, could be good. So Hobbs could either ruin his dinner anticipating the message or ruin his dinner with whatever he read once he opened the text. Hobbs was a rip-the-bandage-off kind of guy, so he clicked the text open.

Call me. It's about Pops.

Yep. Dinner was ruined.

The drops of orange light were like little candle flames bursting inside the cold October air. The tree's giant dome would otherwise have been cloaked in nightfall, but Tabitha spied it from the road, her eye caught as soon as she strode up the walk. She peered inside the overhang of pendulous branches, spellbound by what looked like a million pulsing firefly hearts. A cat skeleton climbed the trunk and a human one hung from the thicker apex of an inner branch. Below them both, on the ground, was a dog skeleton, jaw unhinged in a silent bark. A ghoul, hung from a higher branch, flitted in the breeze.

"Trick or treat."

Tabitha turned to the voice—a young girl in shredded clothes and face paint. She clasped a bulging pillowcase. Tabitha parted her lips to speak.

"A doggy!" The girl's face split into a smile as she spied Trinity, calm, patiently waiting out Tabitha's obsession with the tree, sitting on the lawn near her ruby-red slippers. "Is she supposed to be Toto?" The girl looked Tabitha up and down, taking in the shoes and the blue-and-white gingham dress.

"Sure," Tabitha lied.

The girl scrunched her nose. "Toto didn't wear a vest."

"This is true." Trinity, in her camo service vest, had no hints of Toto whatsoever. Not even a basket. "She's a working dog. Dressing her up didn't seem right."

The girl shrugged. "She's cute. And your shoes are cool."

"Thanks. I like your costume, too." Tabitha didn't know what the girl was supposed to be. She looked like some kind of zombie Barbie, if that was a thing, with shredded bright colors and eerie face paint. Kids were so creative these days. When Tabitha was young they just cut up sheets or put in those plastic fangs that made your saliva pool. "Are you a zombie Barbie?"

"What's a zombie Barbie?"

"I don't know." Tabitha shook her head. Awkward, even with kids.

After a long pause the girl said, "Don't you have any candy?"

"Oh." Tabitha laughed and pointed at the front door. "Ring the bell. I don't live here."

The girl's eyes shifted to the front porch. The glass door revealed a group of women already inside—they'd gathered for the car pool over to the Halloween party at the gym. They milled between the rooms inside, all clad in costumes. "Why are you standing out here in the dark?" The girl looked the tree up and down, perhaps as impressed as Tabitha by the size, the great sweeping umbrella of lit-up branches, the careful placement of fake skeletons.

"That's a good question." *I'm already late,* she didn't add. *I got stopped by the tree. I wouldn't mind living under this tree.* No use saying things like that, unless she wanted to scare the poor kid for real. "I'll go up with you." Tabitha nodded at the door. This was the first time she'd ever been to Clementine's house, even though they'd been gym buddies for about six months. She wouldn't have pegged Clementine as a Halloween person, but this display was something else.

Braver than Tabitha, the girl rang the bell. Some time went by before Clementine appeared, clasping a plastic cauldron. She pushed open the door and the women's voices filled the night. Clementine, dressed up like a marathon runner, complete with what looked like an official Marine Corps Marathon race bib from some years past, smiled at them both.

"Trick or treat." The girl opened her pillowcase.

"Cool costume."

"Thanks. I'm a clown who's been murdered."

Tabitha could totally see that now.

Clementine didn't miss a beat. "Specific," she said, and dropped in a candy bar.

"Thankyoubye!" The girl closed the bag as soon as the candy bar hit, was two steps away before she turned back and added, "'Bye, Toto!" She stooped down, ignored the service vest and gave two pats to Trinity's head before she skipped away, past the tree and over to a woman who'd been waiting patiently under a streetlight, clicking on her phone. The neighborhood was on the classy side, with large homes situated on lots at least an acre wide. Rather than a steady throng of trick-or-treaters, kids moved in groups trained by flashlight beams, chattering in the distance.

"Get in here, birthday girl." Clementine ushered Tabitha and Trinity inside. "You're late." The storm door closed behind them, locking out the night and the far-off cries of kids hyped on adrenaline and sugar.

"Not on purpose or anything." Tabitha was surrounded by a different sort of energy now: happy women, ready for a Saturday night party. Trinity stood by her side, unbothered, but Tabitha wished she could go back to the tree and hide under its umbrella of branches.

Clementine grinned at the lie. "Not at all like you rushing into the gym seconds before the class starts, every single time."

"I've gotten a lot better." Six months ago, Tabitha had sat in her car with Trinity, outside the gym, unsure if she'd ever muster the courage to go in.

"This is true." Clementine patted her arm. Her nails were neither long nor short, neatly manicured and painted a pumpkin orange with a little black spiderweb on her thumb. Tabitha wondered how Clementine managed to keep her nails so pretty when she was slinging weights around the gym three days a week and unpacking cartons in her running shop all day long.

From somewhere in the house, a dog barked. It was yappy, like it came from a little thing.

"That's Roscoe," Clementine said, tilting her head toward a stairway that led up. "I put him in the spare room for now.

He's half-blind and wigs out around other dogs. Lily's latest rescue from the shelter. He was going to be put down today."

"Aw." Tabitha frowned. "Poor guy."

"She's got someone lined up to adopt him. It's just going to take another week." Clementine shrugged, like she'd been through it a million times. "He'll calm down in a minute."

"I love your tree." Tabitha motioned to the front door. "What is it?"

"That—" Clementine gave her blond ponytail a toss "—is a European weeping hornbeam. Tyler planted it when we moved in fifteen years ago. Just a tiny thing back then." Her voice dropped, a wave of sadness crossing her petite features, then disappearing so fast Tabitha wondered if she'd imagined it.

"The lights and skeletons are so cool."

"Lily did the decorating," Clementine said. "Halloween is her favorite holiday. If it were left up to me, there'd just be a happy jack-o'-lantern on the porch, not skeletons crawling around."

Tabitha followed Clementine into the kitchen, warm and smelling of baked goods. The sight made her edges soften. A small group of women—all of whom she'd grown to trust—clustered around the table. They smiled and waved and greeted her at once. Right in the center of the table was a giant sheet cake, covered in candles, that screamed *Happy Boo-Day, Tabitha* in orange frosting. Only once she saw that cake did she let herself admit just how disappointed she'd been that Auntie El had skipped the birthday dinner and brownies. She hadn't woken before Tabitha left and Tabitha had decided to leave her be.

Tabitha scanned the room for the elusive Lily. Clementine talked about her sixteen-year-old daughter all the time, mostly about her escapades while on the job at the local animal shelter, but Tabitha had never met her, had no idea what she looked like, for that matter. She pictured a younger version of Clementine—tiny, blonde, athletic build, bright green eyes.

"Lily's not here." Clementine must've read her mind. "Out hanging with friends."

"You're late to your own birthday party," Sunny scolded, then slugged a glass of red wine. She owned Pittie Place— the dog rescue that had saved Trinity. Tonight she sported a set of cat's ears atop her long, straight blond hair and a black leotard with a tail attached.

"I didn't know there was a birthday party." Tabitha suddenly felt lit up inside. Maybe this day wasn't going to be totally horrible after all. The agreement had been for the five gym friends—Tabitha, Clementine, Delaney, Sunny and Red—to meet up at Clementine's, the designated driver, to ride over to Semper Fit together for the Halloween party. If anyone had too much to drink, then they would crash here later instead of driving home. Nobody had said anything about surprising her for her birthday. With a cake. "I can't believe you made me a cake."

"Sunny made it," Clementine said.

Sunny snorted. "Sunny bought it. Because Delaney said you had a bad day. And the last thing a sweet lady like you deserves for her birthday is something I baked." As the room rippled with laughter, Sunny turned her attention to Trinity. "There she is. There's my good girl." She squatted down. "The most badass of *The Matrix* litter. Look what a good worker you are."

"Go see Sunny," Tabitha told the pittie, who waited patiently.

Sunny opened her arms and Trinity went to her, her whole bottom wagging. Sunny's hands rested on the dog's back as she laid her muzzle on Sunny's shoulder. As Sunny stroked her fur, the other women made a collective "Ahhhh" sound at the cuteness of it all.

After Sunny planted a kiss on Trinity's head, and Trinity had taken her place again by Tabitha's side, Clementine flicked a grill lighter to life and used the long nose to carefully light all thirty candles. Sunny closed her eyes and faked a snore, which made everyone laugh.

"All right, birthday girl," Clementine said after the last candle was lit. She snapped off the kitchen lights. "Make a wish."

Tabitha faced the instantly quiet room. The smiling faces of the four other women flickered behind the flames, reminding her of the lights on the weeping hornbeam out front. It was Halloween, a Saturday night and a rare blue full moon. Tabitha was thirty years old today. It seemed like a special moment. She white-knuckled the edge of the table and closed her eyes. Despite having survived a war zone, she felt her pulse rise and her breathing go shallow. She said a few silent words, which might've counted as a prayer.

Then she opened her eyes and blew.

All thirty candles went out, leaving behind a waft of smoke in the dark, the smell of wax and cheers from the women. Tabitha released any remaining breath into a sigh of satisfaction.

Just as Clementine turned on her kitchen lights, one of the extinguished candles burst back into flame. Tabitha's heart sank. "Oh, no," she said, then, hopefully, "Did you buy those trick candles?"

"No." Clementine pinched the wick and the candle went out, for good this time. A wriggle of smoke snaked into the air. "I think those are mean."

"Darn." Tabitha worried her lower lip with her teeth. "If they were trick candles, it wouldn't count." She reached down and stroked Trinity's head. The mini pittie had sensed Tabitha's shift in mood and pressed closer, her warm, furry shoulder a comfort against Tabitha's leg.

"Don't worry about it, Steele." Delaney, relaxed, leaning back in a kitchen chair, forearm draped over one knee, hand clasped around the neck of a water bottle, shook her head. "It's just a superstition." She fanned away the smoke of thirty extinguished birthday candles. "My wish would've been that Clementine hadn't actually used thirty candles. Damn fire hazard."

Ah, to be as cool and irreverent as Sergeant Monroe. Even retired, Delaney was a marine, through and through. Tabitha forced a laugh. She didn't want to believe in superstitions; she found herself doing it on autopilot. Avoiding stepping on cracks, even though she had no mother's back to break, knocking on wood, even though so many surfaces were superficial these days. Superstitions were bred by uncertainty. Nobody with Delaney's brand of confidence bothered taking the time to throw salt over her shoulder.

"What'd you wish for?" Sunny nodded at the cake. The hazy aftermath that hovered over the chocolate frosting made it look a little like a graveyard. Which wasn't inappropriate, considering the holiday. Sunny was another one who would never bother with superstitions—she'd simply rescue all the black cats crossing her path, take them home, feed them and find them loving families.

As though on cue, the doorbell rang. "Be right back." Clementine grabbed up her cauldron.

"She can't tell you what she wished for, Sunny," Red chided, sounding every bit like the older sister of the pair. "Or it won't come true." Red wore a flowing dress, cascading headdress with coins across the forehead, bangle bracelets and heavy makeup. She even had a tiny crystal ball in front of her on the table. Tabitha was quite sure she'd never seen the practical-minded massage therapist wear any makeup whatsoever. The black liner made her bright blue eyes pop and the red lipstick highlighted the fullness of her mouth.

"It won't come true, anyway," Tabitha said. "I didn't blow them all out."

"There's another way to look at this." Red pushed a lock of strawberry hair behind her ear. "You did, initially, get all the candles. So it counts."

"But one came back to life." Sunny planted her elbows on the table, palms up in a shrug. "It's iffy."

Delaney polished off her water and lofted the empty bottle into the trash, halfway across the room. She was the only one not wearing a costume, other than she'd smeared a red hand-print down the front of her white T-shirt, making it look like someone who was dying had grabbed on to her before they slid to the floor and expired. The rest of her attire was typical Sergeant Monroe: baggy jeans suitable for riding a motorcycle, boots, hair brushed back to frame her pretty face and startling, honey-colored eyes. "That would be a matter for the Superstition Gods. They probably need some time to deliberate."

"What'd you wish for?" Sunny pressed. She wiggled her eyebrows suggestively and sipped at her refilled glass of pinot.

"I wished that I was as badass as all of you," Tabitha admitted, just as Red had parted her lips to shush her baby sister for a second time. Now that the candle had been wonky, and the wish was suspect, Tabitha just wanted it out in the open. Other than Delaney, she hadn't known these ladies long, but she trusted them. Felt connected to them. Which was saying something, because it wasn't like she'd had a lot of birthday parties in her life. "I've made a lot of progress recently." The room went quiet, maybe too quiet, but Tabitha pressed on. "Helped train Trinity as a service dog." She glanced down at the pittie, who'd relaxed on the tile floor. "Joined the gym. Got a job. Started school. But today was rough. Today I felt like I'm just fooling my way through." She caught Red's eye and held it. "You all are so strong and confident. And I'm so…" Tabitha trailed off, hands gesturing helplessly over her Dorothy dress just as Clementine came back into the kitchen, clasping her cauldron of miniature chocolate bars. She spied Delaney's water bottle stuck between the hinged trash lid, gasped, pulled it out and dropped it into her recycle bin.

"You're stronger than you think, Tabitha," Sunny said. "We can all see it."

"I've been telling her that," Delaney joined in. "Besides, Steele, all you have to do is learn how to ride a motorcycle and you'll never doubt yourself again. Trust me." Delaney grinned and snagged a candy bar from Clementine's cauldron, while Clementine was busy pulling all thirty candles from the cake and sucking the frosting off each one.

"I've never even *ridden* a motorcycle," Tabitha lamented.

"Running." Clementine spoke around a candle. "Join my running group and fall in love with a new sport. That'll make you feel strong."

Tabitha wrinkled her nose. "Doubtful." Despite how much she loved her gym, she struggled at everything. Running. Gymnastics. Lifting.

"You're all knees and elbows," Coach Rhett had declared one day in his bold baritone. He'd been watching her try to snatch a barbell, his narrowed eyes taking in Tabitha's skinny legs and caving knees. "We need to fatten you up. With muscles."

Red offered a soft, knowing smile, which peeked out from behind her fire-engine lipstick like a secret. "Let's forget about the wish and start slicing this cake up." She glanced at her phone. "Rhett's regretting opening up the gym for a party. Things are getting wild over there."

Right. The party. Tabitha had forgotten about the party.

She was so proud of herself for dressing up, driving out here, making a wish in front of people, she'd forgotten that she actually had to *attend* a Halloween party. She drowned her trepidation in the huge slice of chocolate cake Clementine thrust into her hands, and by the time they'd all finished, her jitters had been doused with sugar.

"All right, ladies." Clementine drew a jacket over her running clothes and held up her keys. "Let's go have some fun."

They all piled into Clementine's SUV, Tabitha climbing in the farthest seats in the back with Trinity. She was going along for the fun, even though she had no plans to drink excessively. Safety in numbers, and this night shouldn't be so bad. Though Tabitha had to admit, she'd feel a lot more comfortable right now if she hadn't put her wish out in the universe like that. *I wish I could be as confident and strong as this group of badass ladies. And that includes my dog.*

Because that was true. Even Trinity was more badass than Tabitha.

Red climbed in beside her, nestled her crystal ball in her lap and gave it a rub. "The ball tells me you need my ear."

Tabitha waited until they were under way and the other women were all talking and singing along with the music before she peeked around Trinity's furry shoulder and said, "I think massage school was a mistake."

Red's expression didn't change. "Why?"

"Aside from doing poorly on most of my quizzes, I'm giving all the men in my class erections."

The interior of the SUV went silent. Clementine even turned the music down.

"Brava," Sunny quipped.

"That's pretty normal, right?" Clementine peeked in the rearview mirror. "That can be a normal reaction. Especially if the guy is relaxed."

"It can," Tabitha agreed. "We even talked about it in class. But three guys? In a row?"

"Oh, c'mon, Steele." Delaney waved a hand. "Don't you think you're being a little *hard* on yourself?"

The women burst into laughter. They'd barely simmered down before Sunny added, "She really is the Woman of Steele," and they all broke into hysterics again.

"Ladies, c'mon," Clementine sputtered, the humor still thick in her voice. "Tabitha needs solutions, not jokes. Can we all please *rise* to the occasion?"

Trying not to laugh was pointless by now. After a while, they all started to talk over each other, each of them offering their own special brand of help. Tabitha heard everything from extra blankets to turning a blind eye.

"Ladies." Red, the only therapist in the car and quiet up until that point, asserted herself with her usual calm, authoritative tone. "This is an easy fix. One Tabitha could've cleared up with a text message." Red gave her a chiding look. "She doesn't need to quit massage school."

"Oh, do tell, Cici." Sunny turned to face her older sister.

"She just needs—" Red covered Tabitha's hand with her own and squeezed "—to use more pressure. If you're giving men erections on a regular basis, then your touch is too light. That's all. It's a rookie mistake, but that's okay. You're in school to learn these things."

"Really?" Tabitha's cheeks burned, but the car was dark, so no one would see it.

"Yep. That's it. You're not the first person to have this problem. There are articles on this topic."

"Where can we find these *articles*?" Delaney quipped. "In the back of the magazine?"

The women laughed while Red smirked and shook her head. Clementine turned the music back up; Tabitha grew quiet and sank deeper into her seat. Of course it was that simple. How could she have been so stupid? Her touch was too light. Just like in every other aspect of her life. "What if it happens at the marathon next weekend?" she pressed.

Red gave her a look. "Trust me, hon. You're not going to give anyone an erection after they've run twenty-six point two miles through Greenview Park. Their legs are going to be Jell-O and the only thing they're going to want from the therapists at the end of the run is a chance to lie flat on their faces and some quick, warm compression. Besides, I'll be there. I'll keep an eye on you."

Again, Red was right. Volunteering to massage runners after the grueling race was optional, but Tabitha definitely needed the extra credit after her last few quiz grades. She'd be there whether the thought of practicing on marathon runners terrified her or not.

"Hey." Red's hand covered her own again. This time, she gave a gentle stroke. "If this isn't really about erections, if it's about something else, you being afraid or anything at all… that's okay. You're still going to be okay. You know that, right?"

Tabitha didn't respond, but she didn't draw her hand away. Instead, she let Red's hand grow heavier over her own, until the pressure felt good. Grounding. Warm. Just like Smoosh Time. She leaned into Trinity, who leaned back. Between the dog's shoulder and Red's hand, Tabitha would at least make it until she reached the party.

She had no idea what she'd be like after that, but hell. It was her birthday. She was at least going to try to let it end better than it had started.

three

The party at Semper Fit was in full swing when they pulled into the parking lot. The bay door was open, despite the light chill, and music and voices flooded out as soon as they hit the sidewalk. The crowd inside was thick, full of people in costumes and kids of all ages streaking around. Rhett Santos, the owner, wearing blue jeans and a T-shirt with the Semper Fit logo, towered over everyone, hands planted on his hips, handsome face tight in irritation, like he was getting ready to kick all the rowdies dancing to the "Monster Mash" out into the street.

"Oh, my God, Rhett's head's going to explode." Sunny elbowed her sister in the ribs and snickered.

Rhett's jaw flexed as someone spilled a drink. The offender rushed for the mop bucket in the corner and Rhett was headed in that direction until he spotted Red in her fortune-teller costume. His face suddenly split into a secret grin and Tabitha could tell that this was the first time he'd seen his girlfriend dressed for the party. The two of them sort of drifted together, wordless, his hand going to her hip, her chin tilting up instinctively. His lips brushed over hers and whatever thoughts he'd been forming about the party seemed to dissolve on the spot.

"Way to show everyone your Achilles' heel, Rhett." Delaney and Clementine laughed together, but the words had only been out of Delaney's mouth two seconds before her smile changed, her sarcastic edge ceding to a rare softness as her gaze connected with Detective Callahan, who stood in the far corner, talking to Pete. Pete looked like he had in a pair of vampire fangs and Callahan held a grim reaper's scythe, which somehow fit with the badge clipped to his belt. They all headed that way, Delaney going for Callahan, Sunny for Pete, and Trinity to her customary spot in the gym, right next to Humphrey, Rhett's old beagle. She settled next to him on his dog bed, off in the corner and away from the crowd. They sniffed each other, Trinity intent on one of Humphrey's ears. Humphrey allowed the nudging, even though he rarely let anyone touch him. Eventually he slumped down and smashed right up against her.

"Well, that was fast," Clementine said. "Two seconds in the door and we lose them all to their men." She nodded toward Sunny, Red, Delaney and Trinity.

"Can't blame them," Tabitha said, eyeing the group. Coach Rhett, who owned the gym, had a rough exterior that shielded a heart of gold. Pete, while a rugged army vet who could hold his own in any situation, wore his heart on his sleeve and always had a smile on his face. And Sean Callahan. Tabitha had a soft spot for the detective who'd found her mid–panic attack in the middle of the produce section at the grocery store last spring and had gone above and beyond his line of duty to help her out, even though she was a total stranger at the time.

"I worry about Trinity and Humphrey, though," Tabitha

said. "That's a spring-winter romance if I ever saw one." Tabitha grinned and turned to Clementine, but she'd already moved off toward the refreshment table and hadn't heard the joke. The table was laden with goodies, including a punch bowl full of red liquid, a Crock-Pot plugged into the wall, cheese and crackers, a veggie tray, popcorn balls and a cooler full of bottled water. Clementine was already filling a plate with meatballs from the Crock-Pot, leading Tabitha to wonder, as she often did, where the petite woman put it all.

A separate, smaller table, off in the corner, hidden in the shadows and away from the kids, had bottles of open wine and liquor and a cooler full of frosty beer bottles. Right next to that cooler was a sandy-blond man of medium height and a thick, muscular build.

Coach Hobbs.

He wore a pair of worn blue jeans, a button-down flannel and rugged boots and carried a plastic axe over his shoulder. He took a pull off his beer and grinned at Serena, a slender woman with marginal athletic ability who loved to take her shirt off midworkout, whether it was hot outside or not. Tonight, she wore a tight black dress and fishnet stockings.

A weird, tingly thing happened to Tabitha's body, leaving her hot and cold all at once, like a fever. She tried to shake it off, like she did every time she saw Coach Hobbs. Leave it to him to be one of the only men who had gone all out to dress up for the party. And unlike Rhett, Sean or Pete, Hobbs was fully a part of the raucous crowd. His boisterous laugh rang out over the booming opening strains of "Thriller." He struck a few dance moves, which looked tight and professional, despite the fact that he was clearly goofing off.

He was nothing like Tabitha. Nothing like anything she liked in a guy. Tabitha had firm rules about that sort of thing. The man she would ultimately give her time and attention to would be a man the exact opposite of Hobbs: he would be quiet and reflective, nerdy, more interested in a woman's brain than her body. He'd never dance to "Thriller" in public or drink to excess, and women like Serena, who thought everyone wanted to see her abs while they were dying during a workout, would only make him roll his eyes. He would be exactly like Thaddeus Winston, the only real boyfriend Tabitha had ever had. They'd met at church her senior year of high school and had been quite serious until Thaddeus got accepted into college out of state. In response, Tabitha enlisted in the navy, trained to be a chaplain's assistant and deployed to Afghanistan. After her time was up, she went into the reserves for a while before getting out completely.

She'd been floundering ever since.

Hobbs's gaze suddenly connected with hers. Tabitha's pulse jumped. She couldn't decide whether to wave or look away, so, like an idiot, she looked away, then waved. Excellent. She'd known Hobbs for months now, been to plenty of his classes, even if she did actively avoid his training most of the time. Not because he wasn't a good coach. Just the opposite, Hobbs was encouraging without being pushy, fun without being a goof-off, knowledgeable but not arrogant. Instead of flat-out telling her she was all knees and elbows or too timid with the barbell, Hobbs liked to say that Tabitha was just a "soft touch."

But Tabitha wasn't a fan of that hot-cold feverish feeling. The way her pulse rose and her skin flushed, especially if she remembered the time he held her hand during her Fourth of July panic attack or was her partner during the Canine Warriors fundraiser workout last summer.

"A little birdie told me it's your birthday."

Tabitha spun to the sound of Hobbs's voice and gave a little gasp when she found him standing only a couple of feet behind her, his smile big, natural, warm. "Which one gave me up?" Only the women knew about her birthday.

"Already told you. A little birdie." He tilted his head toward Clementine, who appeared to be having a meatball-eating contest with a secret-service agent named Duke. He was at least three times her size, but Tabitha's money was on Clementine.

"I'm not doing thirty birthday burpees." Tabitha crossed her arms over her chest. "That's why none of you coaches were informed."

"Who do I look like? Rhett?" Hobbs arched an eyebrow. "I'm not going to make you do burpees. Especially if you just turned thirty. That deserves a drink." Only now did Tabitha notice Hobbs had left his axe somewhere and was holding two shot glasses. He held one out. "Cheers."

Tabitha started to mutter something about abstaining, but Hobbs pressed the glass into her hand. She held it up to her nose, even though she didn't know enough about alcohol to discern what was in the glass. She took a sip.

Hobbs threw his back, then cleared his throat. "It's tequila," he said. "You don't sip it. You shoot it." He smiled beneath the waves of hair that dipped into his eyes. He ran his hand through it, shoving it back while he watched Tabitha with that glint of amusement that he always seemed to regard her with. "C'mon. You can do it."

Tabitha threw back the tequila, just like Hobbs had. It burned her throat. She coughed a little bit.

There went that grin again. It lit up his whole face, which seemed eternally youthful, despite the fact that Tabitha knew Hobbs was in his midthirties. "Let's go get another one."

Tabitha stopped herself from saying, *No, thanks. I don't really drink.* She also stopped herself from thinking about how upset Auntie El would be if she came home smelling like tequila. Who knew if Auntie El would even be awake when she got home?

Clearly, Auntie hadn't been thinking about Tabitha's birthday, so why should Tabitha care about her opinion at all? She followed Hobbs to the drink table and let him pour her another shot.

"This time we do it right." He handed her a lime and a tiny saltshaker. "Lick your hand. Shake the salt. Lick again. Shoot. Then suck the lime." Hobbs demonstrated with his own tequila, plunked his glass upside down on the table with great flourish, then nodded at her.

Tabitha performed the ritual as instructed, feeling like a normal human being doing things that normal human beings did in social situations, not a thirty-year-old recovering from PTSD who normally would've turned around and walked out of this scene as soon as she got here. She had to admit, she liked all these sensations—salt, heat, sour. She smiled, her gaze going to Trinity in the corner, where she lay snuggled with Humphrey. The night suddenly felt warm and good.

"See?" Hobbs said, like he could read her mind. "Feels good to let go a little, doesn't it?"

"Well, I don't know." She really didn't, but found herself thinking about those words as the full force of the shots hit her all at once.

"Come eat something." Clementine was by her side, arm around her shoulders. "Hey, Hobbs." She waved at him and shoved an entire meatball in her mouth. It stuffed her slender cheek so full she looked like a hamster.

As Hobbs waved back, Tabitha felt herself being edged toward the buffet. A minute later she had a plate of veggies and cheese and crackers in her hands.

"Eat that. And be careful how much tequila you shoot with Hobbs."

Tabitha did as she was told, and her brain calmed down. She knew Clementine mothered everyone on autopilot, but she couldn't help but feel a little dejected. Hobbs had melted into the party and now Tabitha was alone again, all tequila-ed up and nowhere to go. Normally she liked being alone, but an odd sort of emptiness hollowed her out, despite the warmth from the liquor.

The games soon started, and Tabitha watched the festivities unfold. There were kids hitting a piñata—like they needed more candy—and musical chairs with medicine balls as seats. Delaney won by sheer force, knocking into Duke and taking him to the ground, one leg outstretched to keep a foot on the med ball like Jean-Claude Van Damme doing the splits between two chairs. Tabitha didn't last the first round, politely giving up her ball to a teenager who got there at the same time. There was a costume parade, with an infant dressed up like Baby Yoda taking the blue ribbon. Tabitha watched it all from the periphery, like a moat around a castle, inactive and gloomy.

Around nine, the crowd began to thin, the food got picked over, grew cold and limp, the kids grew tired. Somebody's date— a muscled guy Tabitha hadn't seen before tonight—lingered near the booze table. Tabitha had watched him throw back shots all evening, sneaking drinks when he thought his girl wasn't looking. Carrie, a regular who brought a new boyfriend to the gym every month, was trying to get the guy to stop drinking while also not making a scene. The guy was getting more and more physical in his attempts to shove Carrie away. Everyone else was involved in their own business—herding their children, talking in groups—but Tabitha's radar was on full alert. She scanned the room until she caught sight of Hobbs. Serena was trying to flirt with him, but he, too, was watching the scene unfold. Their gazes connected. Hobbs nodded, as though he read her mind, then reached over and tapped Rhett on the shoulder. Hobbs pointed in the direction of the couple, just as voices began to rise between the squabbling pair. Rhett immediately jogged over to intervene.

Tabitha swiped at her brow in dramatic relief. Hobbs smiled, but his attention was quickly diverted back to Serena, who would not be ignored.

Tabitha sighed, ready for this night to be over. She collected Trinity and took her outside to do her business before she went to find Clementine for a ride back to her car. The tequila was all the way through her and she'd have no problem driving home. She really didn't know why she'd carpooled in the first place, other than it had made her feel like she was part of everyone else's "normal."

Tabitha crossed the street to where Greenview Park butted up to the road. The park was where they all ran for any distance over eight hundred meters. It was also where a bunch of kids had shot off fireworks last July and sent Tabitha into a panic attack on the gym floor. She had little memory of it, only the weight of Trinity across her chest and the squeeze of Hobbs's hand covering her own when she blinked her eyes open.

A twig crunched behind her and Tabitha spun around, the pulse in her neck going crazy.

"It's okay, Tabby." Hobbs was there, slipping a leash on Humphrey, who had apparently followed Trinity outside. The old beagle tilted his muzzle in the air, sniffing, his cataracts shining in the dim light of a distant streetlamp. "Rhett's so busy cleaning up he didn't even notice his dog left the building." Hobbs rolled his eyes. He'd shed most of his costume, and now just looked like a muscular guy in jeans and a flannel shirt. Though it was cold, he had his sleeves rolled up, neck unbuttoned. He looked thick, warm and inviting. "You okay?"

"Um. Yeah." Tabitha realized she was just stupidly standing there, staring. Trinity had finished her business and now trotted over to Humphrey. She wanted to sniff his ears, but Humphrey had other ideas, trying to get around to her backside.

"Dirty old man," Hobbs said. He turned back to Tabitha, his humor fading a little. "Good catch back there. With Carrie and her shit-faced date. Things were about to get ugly."

Tabitha tried to shrug it off, even though she felt a rush of pleasure at the compliment. "Old habits die hard. I was Religious Affairs in the navy. Hypervigilance was necessary in Afghanistan. Protect the chaplain."

"I knew you were a secret badass."

Tabitha waved that off. "You spotted trouble, too."

"I, uh—" Hobbs smiled uncomfortably "—learned early on in life to read the room or suffer the consequences." Hobbs's eyes narrowed. "You sure you're all right?" He looked toward the woods, like he might be remembering the incident with the fireworks, too.

"Yeah." The word came a little too quick. "I just—" she shrugged "—feel a little…in between." Made no sense, but Tabitha didn't know how to explain it any better. She wasn't a kid anymore. But she wasn't accomplished enough to say she felt mature, either. She had a light service record, no romantic relationship, no kids, not even a job she was good at. She thought about Hobbs's question, after they'd shot the second tequila. "Remember when you asked me if it felt good to let go?"

"Sure."

"I was thinking that letting go implies I've been hanging on," she said. "If I'm hanging on, I'm either trying to stay in place, like clinging to a tree during a hurricane, or trying to go somewhere, like grabbing on to the tail of a kite to hitch a ride. Both are hanging on, but are completely different kinds of hanging on. Letting go in each scenario would mean something different. So I was wondering which way you meant it."

Humor crinkled Hobbs's eyes and a laugh escaped him so quickly it sounded almost like a cough. "Jeez, Tabby," he said. "I was only telling you to have a little fun. There was no deep meaning."

The steady thump of party music that rang out from the gym slowed down, ceding to a warm, sweet '80s tune that was most definitely not the Halloween station on Pandora. Somebody had changed the channel to do a slow dance. Tabitha's money was on Sunny.

"I meant have a little tequila," Hobbs explained. "Or—" he dropped Humphrey's leash and took her by the wrist "—have a slow dance or two." Hobbs gave a little tug and drew her in.

Tabitha swayed on her feet she was so surprised. Hobbs's free arm slid around her waist and steadied her. All the tequila had left her system long ago, but her head was suddenly swimming again. Hobbs's flannel shirt was soft, and up close he smelled like he'd dressed for the party directly after taking a warm, soapy shower.

"When I said let go," Hobbs continued, his voice softer, closer to Tabitha's ear as he pulled her even tighter against him, "I meant enjoy your birthday. Stop worrying so much. Have a drink. Have a dance." After a moment of quiet dancing, Tabitha's heart beating too hard in her ears for her to do anything but follow Hobbs's lead, he added, "Have a kiss."

"A kiss?" That hot-cold sensation raced down her spine. Tabitha turned her face up. Hobbs wasn't supertall like Rhett, but he was just tall *enough*. Hobbs was watching her, a sparkle in his warm eyes. She searched them for a sign that he'd continued to drink tequila long after the last shot they'd shared.

"Sure, everyone should get a kiss on their birthday."

Words started and stopped in Tabitha's throat. Yeah, he'd had a few more tequilas, but he was only happy with the liquor, not swimming in it. She tried to decide if she cared.

She imagined herself saying something witty and sexy, like *Are you volunteering?* But, in typical Tabitha fashion, nothing came out. Her body stiffened against Hobbs's firm chest and quads, which she could feel beneath the flimsy gingham dress.

Hobbs's dancing slowed. "I didn't mean from me, of course."

Was he backpedaling? Or clarifying? "It's either you or my Auntie El," Tabitha blurted.

Sure. As soon as she found her voice, *that* was what popped out. Probably for the best. Every kiss she'd had since her time in Afghanistan had been a disaster in one form or another, anyway. "Auntie El raised me," she continued, unable to stop her babbling. "I'm adopted."

Hobbs's eyes crinkled again. He was probably the only man on the planet that could make eye crinkles look youthful. "Well," he said, brushing his forefinger beneath her chin. The sensation wriggled all the way from her skin to deep inside her body. "I can only speak for me, but I don't want a kiss from my aunt on my birthday."

Tabitha frantically tried to keep her knees from buckling as she thought about how close Hobbs's lips were to hers. Her pulse rose, and she braced herself for that terrible, crushing feeling where she couldn't get air into her lungs.

It didn't come.

"Have you thought about it?" Hobbs said.

"What?"

"Kissing me."

"Yes. No." She'd fantasized about kissing Hobbs more times than she could count, but she wouldn't admit that to anyone, least of all him. "No." Tabitha sort of felt like she already was. Their lips were so close his breath tickled over her skin. Why was she not panicking?

"I have." He seemed to have no embarrassment in the admission. "Can I try? I just want to see. I'm curious."

"Curious about kissing me?"

Hobbs laughed a little bit. "You're funny, Tabby."

"Okay." It might've been a whisper.

Hobbs took that as permission, even though Tabitha still wasn't sure if she meant *Okay, I'm funny,* or *Okay, you can kiss me.* He closed the small amount of space left between them until his lips touched hers. His mouth was soft, warm, a little wet and very sweet. Tabitha's eyes closed and her body leaned in harder. Hobbs's hand went to the small of her back. His other hand slid to the back of her neck and held her still so he could gently kiss her mouth one, two, three times, little teasing kisses that made her go limp in his arms. He suckled against her lower lip, his thumb doing something crazy soft against her jawline. Her body melted into the front of him, her arms going around his waist. He kissed her a little harder, a little deeper. A soft noise of satisfaction escaped Tabitha's throat. Never in her life would she have expected Hobbs to be so gentle. Never in her life had a kiss been this inviting, like Hobbs was a romantic stranger knocking softly on her door to ask permission to court her.

Suddenly, he pulled back. Tabitha's eyes shot open, like someone had turned the water in the shower from hot to cold. Hobbs was looking at her. The smile was still in his eyes, but something had changed in his expression.

"What's wrong?" Tabitha said. When he didn't answer right away she added, "Was it what you thought?"

"No."

"Oh." Great. The best kiss she'd ever had in her life and she'd messed it up somehow.

"Hey!" Rhett's sharp voice barked out from the raised bay door of the gym. "One of you have my dog?" His tall silhouette peered into the night. Tabitha glanced down and saw that Humphrey and Trinity had lain near each other on the grass, patiently waiting for their owners to stop acting like teenagers hiding behind the school gym.

"Got him!" Hobbs called. "Bringing him in now!"

Once Rhett disappeared, Hobbs drew off his flannel and draped it around Tabitha's shoulders. She hadn't realized she was shaking until the warmth enveloped her shoulders, though she didn't have the courage to tell him that it wasn't the cold making her tremble. Hobbs wore a white T-shirt beneath. The short sleeves gripped the biceps and pecs he was so proud of, but at this moment, Tabitha wasn't complaining about his fitness obsession. "Let's get you inside before you freeze, Tabby."

Tabitha parted her lips to ask what he'd meant, about the kiss not being what he'd expected. But that wasn't what came out of her mouth. "The girls made me a cake. I made a really grand wish, like an idiot. Then one of the birthday candles came back to life after I blew it out. The ladies were debating whether or not that counted."

Hobbs offered his easy smile. "Do you ever give your brain a rest?"

Tabitha snuggled deeper into the shirt. It smelled so much like Hobbs she relived the taste of his mouth. Her trembles doubled.

"The ladies are overlooking one simple fact." Hobbs leaned over and collected the dogs' leashes. He handed Trinity's to Tabitha, which she took with cold fingers.

"What's that?" she said as they headed back to the gym.

"You got the kicks." Hobbs pointed at her ruby-red slippers. "You want to make a wish, just click your heels three times and it's all yours, baby."

Tabitha stopped inside the bay door of the gym and looked down at the red glitter on her feet that sparkled in the dark. She couldn't help but smile.

"There you go," Hobbs said. "Smile away all the worry. That's what I do."

Tabitha tried to read his expression. She was pretty good at reading people, but Hobbs was like the birthday clown, covered in face paint and bow ties, ready to pull colored scarves out of his sleeve to distract the crowd.

"I better go help clean up before the boss blows a gasket. Have a good night, Tabby. Thanks for the kiss." Hobbs led Humphrey over to Rhett, who was gathering up trash. Clementine, Delaney, Red, Sunny, Pete and Sean were all helping. There were stragglers still buttoning up coats but most of the crowd had gone, including Carrie and her drunk date. Tabitha joined in, and before she knew it, the gym was clean and she was in the back of Clementine's car with the rest of the bunch. She'd thrown a parting glance at Hobbs as she left, but he'd been too busy chatting with the stragglers to notice.

"You're wearing Hobbs's shirt," Sunny pointed out.

Tabitha had forgotten to give it back. She hoped he had a coat. "We took the dogs out together and I got cold."

"Uh-huh," Delaney said. She had the sort of eyes that could see right through you.

Tabitha closed her own and leaned her head back on the seat. Let the girls think she was tired—then maybe they wouldn't ask questions. It worked too well. By the time they got to Clementine's house, Red had to nudge her awake.

She roused herself enough to drive home, but the smell of chocolate leaking out the front door woke her completely. Tabitha entered a warm house and found Auntie El in the kitchen, wearing her bathrobe and pulling a pan of brownies from the oven.

"I'm sorry, T," Auntie said, without looking up. She settled the pan on the stove and sighed with relief, like the brownies weighed a hundred pounds. "I should've made these earlier." Auntie El swiped some sweat from her forehead with the back of her wrist and fanned herself with the opposite hand.

"Oh, Auntie El." Tabitha turned off the oven and went to the sink to do the dishes. "You shouldn't be baking at ten o'clock at night. I'm a big girl now and don't need special brownies. You feeling okay?" And here she'd been worried about herself and her own problems all day long. Shame seared through her.

"I'm fine." Auntie El batted away the worry. "Just got a little tired today. Was up late, which is why I missed you this morning. Then I was watching a program before dinner and drifted off." She walked over and placed her hands on Tabitha's shoulders, then leaned in and kissed her on the cheek. "Happy birthday." She sniffed deeply. "Is that tequila?"

Seriously?

"A long time ago. And just a little. I didn't drink and drive, Auntie El."

"Mmm-hmm." Auntie El didn't approve of alcohol in any dosage. "I'm going back to bed now. Don't try to cut those for at least an hour." She gestured to the brownies.

"Did you eat dinner, though?" Tabitha turned off the water and faced Auntie El. "You're looking a little thin."

Auntie El snorted. "You don't got to worry about this old lady ever looking skinny." She snorted again and ran her hands over the tattered cloth of the bright pink robe she'd had since Tabitha was little. "I got hips for days. Good night, now. I'll see you in the morning."

Tabitha watched her go. Auntie's steps were definitely slower than usual and a little bit hobbled, like she was in pain. *She's sixty-eight years old*, Tabitha reminded herself. *She's going to start moving slower at some point.*

Tabitha finished cleaning up the kitchen and headed to bed herself. The brownies would have to wait until morning, even though they smelled like heaven. Once she was all tucked in, Trinity by her side, Tabitha was both relaxed and awake enough to relive the kiss she'd shared with Hobbs. His touch had been so gentle, yet so electrifying. At least on her end. Tabitha kicked herself for never asking Hobbs what he meant when he said, *No*, her kiss hadn't been what he'd expected. If her birthday wish really had come true, she'd have had the courage to ask him. All the other ladies in the group tonight would've been bold enough to ask. Not Tabitha. Tabitha with the soft touch hadn't said a word.

Tabitha thought about what Hobbs had said about the ruby-red slippers. She'd ditched them at the foot of her bed and could easily get up, put them on, click her heels three times and redo her birthday wish.

But what would be the point of that? Tabitha wasn't Dorothy. The shoes weren't real. Right now, everything in Tabitha's life was a costume, and wishes were for those strong enough to make them come true. Right now, Tabitha didn't even deserve Dorothy's slippers.

Tabitha closed her eyes and decided, right then and there, if she wanted to be as badass as her friends she was just going to have to make that happen herself.

four

Hobbs wasn't exactly sure how he'd got stuck with making sure the gym was spotless before the doors were locked and he could head home. Everyone had pitched in, but Rhett had assigned him full mop duty before he headed out, citing spilled tequila and sticky messes everywhere.

Sure, Hobbs thought. *Sic mop duty on me and escape into the night with your exotic fortune-teller.* If that wasn't some crap. He didn't really mind, though. Not that he'd ever admit it to anyone, but Hobbs liked the simple joy mundane tasks provided. There was a kind of Zen that came from mopping a floor, getting into a rhythm, cleaning up a space. It freed his mind to wander, to think about things that had happened that day while his body worked on autopilot.

Like the kiss he'd just selfishly stolen from little Tabby Cat. He'd never called her that to her face, but that was how he thought of her. A slinky little striped cat. Not that Tabitha had literal stripes, but when it came to personality, Tabby had more shades than a rack of sunglasses.

And that kiss. Hell.

Hobbs wasn't exactly sure why he'd done it, other than too much tequila and the literal truth that he'd always been curious, but as soon as his lips touched hers he'd felt his mistake. Something deep inside that told him, *No, don't go there.* Hobbs felt bad about leaving Tabitha hanging, but if she brought it up later he'd blame it on the tequila and hope she did, too.

"Hi."

Hobbs jerked his head up, his Mop Zen popped and gone like a bubble in the wind. A girl stood there, just inside the entrance. She was tall, had long hair the color of cinnamon and the kind of face that drew double takes. She wore blue jeans and a dark hoodie. "Hi." Hobbs smiled but reined in his natural urge to flirt. Something told him the girl was even younger than she looked. "Afraid you missed the party. And the gym's closed."

"I'm looking for my mom." She looked around, like her mom might be hiding in one of the corners. "Clementine?"

So her mom really *could* be hiding in one of the corners. "Lily?" Hobbs registered the surprise on the girl's face. "Your mom talks about you all the time." His instincts had been right. He was pretty sure Clementine had said her daughter was sixteen, a junior in high school. "She just left. I'm Hobbs, one of the coaches."

"Nice to meet you." The girl seemed unsettled, hands in her hoodie pockets as her gaze toured the gym.

"Everything okay?"

"Yeah, I just—" Lily pointed toward the entrance "—I've got a couple critters in the car. From the shelter. I was hoping to hit up my mom before she got home."

"That's right. Your mom said you work at the animal shelter. That you're always bringing creatures home." Hobbs had listened to the stories about lame dogs, one-eyed cats, mauled rabbits. Every week Lily brought home an animal slated to die because no one wanted it. Many ended up at Sunny's place, others they kept as fosters until they were given forever homes. None ever stayed, Clementine said, because there was always a new batch to foster every week.

"She's going to freak if I just show up with them." Lily nibbled on her lower lip. "Because we already have Roscoe right now." Lily eyed Hobbs like he was a sounding board, just someone to bounce ideas off of until she hit on a good one. "He's this little terrier that doesn't play well with others. I have somebody interested in him, but they can't come see him until next weekend."

"What you got tonight?" It was against his better judgment to ask, but Hobbs's curiosity was piqued. He pictured a couple of ragtag old mutts.

"I named them George and Gracie." She pushed a tendril of her long hair behind her ear. "See, George is very protective of Gracie. He won't let anyone near her. Everyone who comes to the shelter wants to adopt Gracie but nobody wants George. If you take Gracie away from George, she howls. You see the problem."

"Definitely."

"Well." Lily looked thoughtful for a moment. "Mom will just have to deal with George and Gracie for now. They can stay in my room."

"I think that's fair." Hobbs had no idea what he was talking about, but the girl seemed really rational.

"All right. Thank you." Lily, apparently having figured everything out, turned to go.

"Wait." Hobbs jammed the mop back in the bucket and

surveyed the floor. Good enough. "Let me walk out with you. Make sure you get in your car."

Lily shrugged. "Okay."

Once they were outside, standing right next to each other, Hobbs realized Lily was as tall as he was. Maybe even taller. "Got your height genes from your dad, huh?"

She smiled. "Yeah."

"That your wagon?" Hobbs peered into an old station wagon that Lily was edging toward and spied a large pet carrier in the back seat.

"That's it."

"Can I see them?"

"Who?"

"George and Gracie. I'm curious." Was he? Or did he just not want to go home? Hobbs had been either working or partying all day and evening, and home only meant one thing: no excuses left not to text Victor back. All day he'd told himself he was just too busy to get into it, whatever Victor had to tell him about Pops. But there was putting somebody off and there was rude, and Hobbs was bordering on rude. Or maybe he'd crossed over to rude a long time ago—he wasn't sure. Could you even be rude to your brother, or was that just being normal?

Lily popped open the rear door of her car, like Hobbs's request hadn't been at all weird. She opened the metal cover to the plastic carrier and stepped back. Hobbs poked his head inside the warm interior, where Lily had obviously been running the heater. Only when he was warm did he notice how cold he'd been outside, and only then did he realize Tabitha had worn his shirt home. He kind of liked the idea, even though he shouldn't. What he should've done tonight was respond favorably to all Serena's flirting and they'd probably be together, in somebody's bed right now. Instead, Hobbs had watched Tabitha go outside with Trinity and he'd grabbed up Humphrey as an excuse to follow her. Because, he'd told himself, she shouldn't be outside in the dark, that close to the park, by herself.

Yes. Hobbs had, for inexplicable reasons, used Rhett's crippled old beagle to steal a kiss from Tabitha on her birthday. A kiss that had blown his mind. But Hobbs didn't want kisses that blew his mind. Hobbs wanted kisses that led to instant, quick, temporary satisfaction that went away within a couple of months, tops. Now, instead of being in bed with Serena, getting exactly that, he had half his body inside the interior of Clementine's daughter's car.

What a weird night.

He peeked into the carrier, but the car was pretty dark. No overhead light had come on and Hobbs had to squint to make out the form of a ginger-colored puppy. Looked like a golden Lab mix, an all-over rusty color. Even the eyes were tawny. Huge paws, like she had a lot to grow into, and a sweet face. She looked exactly like Gemma. She crawled forward and nudged her muzzle in Hobbs's direction. His heart felt like it tumbled in his chest.

"That's Gracie." Lily's voice came over his shoulder. "She's a sweetheart. Only six months old but somebody found her in a ditch alongside the road a few weeks ago. She was skinny and so sick she could barely stand."

"Poor thing." Hobbs squeezed his eyes closed, then open again, but Gracie was still there, looking so much like Gemma he wasn't sure he wasn't in a time warp. He leaned farther in but only saw the one pup. "I don't see George anywhere." Hobbs extended his hand. Gracie licked his knuckles just as a sharp hiss came from somewhere inside the carrier. A second later, a pink-faced thing, about the size of a Chihuahua, wrapped its body around Gracie's shoulders. It had huge gray ears like a bat and eyes the color of the moon. Whatever it was, it wore an orange pet sweater with a jack-o'-lantern on the chest. Hobbs jerked his hand back.

"That—" Lily stepped closer, her voice laced with humor "—is George."

Hobbs glanced up and saw the laughter sparkling in Lily's eyes.

"What, exactly, is George?" He peeked back inside and George let out a weird growl. Gracie took it all in stride, whapping her tail and nudging George's body with her muzzle.

"George is a Sphynx cat. They're hairless. Or they seem hairless. He actually does have hair. If you touch him, he feels like velvet. But don't." Lily shook her head, like Hobbs might actually try to pet the thing. "Don't try to touch him right now."

"A hairless cat? No shit." Hobbs glanced up quickly. "Sorry."

"You can say 'shit.'" Lily shrugged. "I'm not five."

Hobbs took another look at George, and now that he knew George was a cat, Hobbs could see it: a pink, hairless cat, with gray bat's ears, wearing a Halloween sweater. Well, sure. If he had no hair, he probably got cold, just like Hobbs was. George had settled into a ball right against Gracie's chest. Gracie laid her head on George's back. George didn't shift, despite probably only weighing about ten pounds. Hobbs watched Gracie a moment longer, feeling like he was fifteen years old again and back in Omaha, then closed the door to the pet carrier, followed by the door to the car. "I take it Sphynx cats aren't friendly."

"On the contrary," Lily said. "They're typically very friendly. In fact, they need a lot of attention and affection. But the night we brought Gracie in, it was late and George was out, hanging around the shelter. We've had him for a while. His family dumped him due to 'allergies.' George hung around us all night while we took care of Gracie and she's been stuck to him ever since. He sort of adopted her and she imprinted on him. Gracie is a dog but thinks she's a cat. She tries to go into the litter with him. She tries to jump up on high things like him. And George allows it. He thinks everyone is going to hurt her. He tolerates me and a couple of the other shelter people, but he acts like this—" she tilted her head toward the car "—to anyone who tries to look at him or Gracie for adoption."

Hobbs wasn't sure if that story was funny or sad. "So you're taking them home? Adopting them?"

"I'm taking them home," Lily agreed. "I don't see Mom letting me adopt them. She'll let them stay while I find someone. I hope."

"Me, too." Hobbs felt the cold air suddenly hit him all at once, like it'd reached his bones. The alcohol had burned off and he was beat.

"You okay?" Lily's tone lowered to a level of concern that didn't typically match someone of her age. But then, she'd named her pets George and Gracie, for God's sake.

"Yeah, sure." Hobbs quickly added, "Gracie reminds me of a dog I had. When I wasn't much younger than you. Kind of a blast from the past, is all." Hobbs wasn't sure he would've admitted that to anyone else, but this kid had some serious nonjudgmental vibes, so his guts just spilled out.

Her eyes brightened. "Really? Cool. Maybe you want to adopt them, then."

"No," Hobbs said quickly. "I mean...no. I don't have pets. But no, I also can't... I can't..." He trailed off, his excuse sounding empty to his own ears. "I'm not a dog person," he finished, knowing he sounded lame. "Not anymore. Hey. You better get home before your mom worries."

"Okay." Lily opened the driver's-side door and ducked inside.

"Nice meeting you, Lily."

"Nice meeting you, too. Good night."

"Night." Hobbs waited until she'd backed out before he got in his truck. Good. She was gone and so was the dog, and Hobbs never had to think about Gemma again. He checked his phone, but there were no new messages from Victor. Double good. Maybe his brother had finally, for once in his life, given up and let Hobbs win.

The drive home was short, and by the time Hobbs pulled into the driveway of his old rambler, his head was thick with fatigue. He was so tired his eyes kept crossing and it took him more than a few seconds to get his keys in the lock. The foyer was dark, the only light coming from the kitchen, where the bulb over the stove popped on automatically once the sun went down. He thought about just going right upstairs to bed, but decided a tall glass of water was in order after all that tequila. He went into the kitchen and had just opened the cupboard and had his hand around a drinking glass when the hairs on the back of his neck rose.

Somebody was there.

Hobbs turned, his gaze searching the living room, a pit of shadows just off the kitchen. A silhouette filled the armchair in front of the TV. With his pulse slamming in his neck, Hobbs had just reached for the drawer where he kept the knives when the lamp on the end table clicked on.

"Hey, little brother." Victor's voice was deep and unhurried, like a hunter who knew he had his prey trapped in his sights. "Long time no see."

Dearest Ty,
Your daughter is something else. You should see the creatures she put in the tree for Halloween. The tree you loved. The one you picked, not the other one. The hornbeam. It's huge and thriving and full of skeletons right now. The golden chain, the one I chose—I don't think that one's doing so

hot, but we'll see come next spring. Anyway, back to Lily.
She's so much like you. Tries to save every blessed thing on
the planet. Tonight she brought home a cat-and-dog pair she
named George and Gracie. Yeah. I knew you'd be proud. I
remember how much you liked that show. You and all your
classic TV. An old soul, just like your daughter. She's like
you in almost every way. Fearless. Compassionate. Stub-
born. And trying to save the world at every turn. The only
way I know she's got some of me in her is the hair color.
It's like God took your black hair and my blond and mixed
it up in a bowl before giving it to Lily.

Anyway, another two sets of paws in the house. At least
temporarily.

Don't worry. I'll keep her safe.

Yours,
Clem

Clementine slid the journal into her nightstand drawer and
clicked off the light. Down the hall, she could hear a hissing
scuffle, followed by the low murmurs of Lily's voice. Then
came Roscoe's yippy bark. George and Gracie were settling in
for the night and Roscoe was disapproving of their presence.
Clementine didn't blame him. Those two were going to be
a challenge. Clementine had taken one look at the energetic
puppy and the hairless cat in the pumpkin sweater and knew
that even Lily, with all her animal magic, had her work cut
out for her. Who wanted to adopt a dog they couldn't get near
because it was being guarded by a hairless pink-and-gray cat
with ears the size of Batman?

"I got this, Mom," Lily had said when she walked in the
door tonight and explained the situation. Clementine had only
been home half an hour and was tired and worn out from the
day and the party. Even though Lily's voice was determined,

Clementine had noted the little tic of worry at the corner of her daughter's mouth, the way she tucked it in ever so slightly when she doubted herself.

"It'll be a new dog or cat or both next week, Lil," Clementine had said. "You know that, right? So we can't keep them."

"I know. I got this."

"Okay. I trust you."

And she did. From the start of their journey together as a mother-and-daughter solo team, Clementine had stressed to Lily the importance of trust. "It's just us," she'd always said. "So we have to be able to trust each other. No matter what."

"No matter what," Lily had agreed, only eight years old at the time. They'd hooked pinkies and Lily's shy smile had that same crook in the corner. Her eyes had been puffy from crying and her hair, less the color of nutmeg and blonder at that age, had stuck to the tears on her cheeks. She'd just been told that her father, aka her hero, aka her best buddy, was never coming home.

Clementine got a lump in her throat. That memory was always fresh. Not so much the memory of the two men in uniform who'd come to the house to inform her that Tyler had been killed in an explosion in Afghanistan—Clementine had figured out how to compartmentalize that one. It was a self-preservation trick. But the memory of her telling Lily had a life of its own, like a wound that wouldn't scab over. They'd layered three-deep in the bed that night—Clementine, Lily and Digger, Tyler's old hound, on his last legs but a devoted companion who watched over them when Tyler was away. Digger had passed away a year later, and the only dogs that'd been allowed in the house after that were Lily's temporary rescues.

Clementine clicked on the TV and felt a wash of safety as the blue artificial light embraced the perimeter of the room. She drew the covers up to her chin and forced herself to think about the night, so that she wouldn't think about Lily, growing up without her dad. Tabitha filled her head, which did little to calm Clementine's mothering instinct but did get her mind off Tyler. She hoped her friend had enjoyed her birthday, despite everything she was dealing with. Thirty could be a big deal. Clementine thought back to her own thirtieth birthday, eight years ago, and remembered only grief. Tyler had just died and the last thing she cared about was her age.

But Clementine and Tabitha had vastly different life experiences. Tabitha at thirty was not Clementine at thirty, and thus Clementine found herself rather useless in helping her friend navigate what she might be feeling right now. Tabitha might be feeling old, with not much to show for it. Clementine, at thirty, had been a widow with a daughter and a flourishing business. Neither was like the other, but the common thread was a woman trying to keep her head above water and just what the hell she was going to do next.

Her eyes growing heavy, Clementine flipped through the channel guide, looking for something to fall asleep to. Ever since Tyler had died, and Lily had grown too old to snuggle in next to her, the TV had been her comforting nighttime companion. The titles were random, none drawing her eye until she saw it. Her chest loosened up and she smiled. "No way." She clicked on the station and *The George Burns and Gracie Allen Show* popped to life in black and white. Clementine couldn't remember the last time she'd found this show, amid the sea of movies and TV programs competing for attention on all the new streaming services.

But there they were, laughing it up in their apartment, with their closet full of hats, Gracie's supposedly crazy mind and straight man George trying to tame her. In real life, Gracie Allen, despite being the younger of the couple, would die first.

George Burns would go on to outlive the love of his life by thirty-two years.

Thirty-two years.

How lonely was George Burns for thirty-two fucking years?

Clementine felt her eyes drooping, and she didn't fight it. "Say good night, Gracie," she whispered to herself.

Good night.

In the year since Hobbs had last seen Victor, he'd grown a light scruff for a beard, but his head full of upswept curls, the color of corn silk and kept on the long side, was exactly the same. He was still tall and big as an ox, longs legs crossed at the ankles on Hobbs's ottoman, the air around him an easy confidence that came from years of being the elder brother, the stronger man. He wore a pair of brown leather boots beneath a raggedy hem of denim. Next to him, on the coffee table, was a glass of water. He'd broken in, helped himself to some water—in Hobbs's favorite glass, the green one that reminded him of old Coke bottles—and plopped down in the living room, like he lived here. "I see you've been pumping a lot of iron." Victor offered a humorless smirk.

Hobbs resisted the urge to rub his hands over his cold arms. A natural-born athlete, Victor's muscles came easily, with a few hours spent lifting weights every week. Nothing like the time and attention Hobbs had to put in to eke out a physique. "What're you doing here, Victor?" He kept the anger out of his voice. Two could play this cool-as-a-cucumber game.

"You had to have known what would happen if you ignored my calls, Chris. You even made me text. That—" Victor lifted his glass and took a gulp of the water "—was uncalled for."

"You breaking into my house and hiding in the dark is uncalled for. I didn't even know you were in town."

"Guess you should've answered your phone."

"You flew?"

"I rode."

"Your Triumph?" If he asked enough questions, he'd never quite make it to the only one that mattered. *Why are you here?* "You rode your Triumph a thousand miles to hide in my living room?" How had he missed a Triumph parked outside? Victor must've tucked it around the corner.

Victor pointed at the motorcycle helmet that Hobbs hadn't seen, tossed on the couch, right where Hobbs liked to sit when he was watching the Huskers on Saturday afternoons. Hobbs resisted the urge to move it, instead went back to the kitchen and got himself that glass of water he'd never poured. He stuck the glass under the faucet, then drank it down in one go. His temples throbbed. Victor didn't budge.

Hobbs caved. "Why are you here?"

"You read my text, Chris." It wasn't a question.

"You said it was about Pops. Me not answering you should've been your first clue that I don't care what you have to say about Pops."

Anyone else would've got up and left. Victor seemed to settle deeper into the armchair. He balanced his glass on his flat stomach and twirled the ice around. "He's dead."

Something funny happened to Hobbs's insides at that moment. Everything dried up, like he'd inhaled the desert.

"Well, almost," Victor amended. "He's real sick. So he's almost dead, not dead-dead."

The dried-up feeling reversed itself, and now Hobbs's lungs felt too full. He exhaled slowly, like he was doing one of the yoga sessions Rhett was trying out on all the coaches before he made them a regular offering at the gym. "You're enjoying yourself, aren't you?"

"I just rode eleven hundred miles on my bike in touch and go weather and my balls are kind of blue. So no, not really."

"And there's the real question." Hobbs was beyond exhausted. Everything good about the evening was gone now, evaporated, wrung out. "Why did you spend a couple days—please tell me you didn't ride it all in one day—to come out here, to my house, where you've never once come, not for any holiday or my birthday or any day at all, to tell me that Pops is dying, when you could have either put that in a letter or, better yet, just kept it to yourself because *I...don't...care.*" Hobbs praised his lungs for holding out through that mouthful. Those stupid deep breaths in yoga had a use after all.

"Well, not to beat a dead horse, but—" Victor drained his glass and plopped it on the end table "—I did try to call."

"I'm done with you." Hobbs turned to go. He headed for the hallway, which would lead to his bedroom. Maybe if he ignored him, Victor would leave.

"It's for Hannah."

Hobbs froze. He turned back around.

"Thought that would get your attention."

Dirty play.

Victor rolled back a shoulder. "She asked me to get you home. Just to see him one more time before he passes. Then you can leave. You don't have to stay until he dies and you don't have to come to the funeral, if there is one. Just come see Hannah. And, while you're there, say goodbye to Pops."

I said goodbye to him a long time ago. "I'm not visiting Pops in prison. I don't care how sick he is."

"They let him out." Victor leaned his head back on the soft leather chair and closed his eyes, as if the full force of his ride out here had just slammed into his body. "Compassionate release. He's had dementia for a long time. Can't remember anything anymore. They say he'll forget how to swallow soon."

"Guess that'll make it hard to drink whiskey." The words escaped Hobbs's mouth before he could stop them.

Victor's expression changed, a tightening around the mouth, though his eyes didn't open. "He hasn't had a drink in decades. Unlike you. I can smell you from here."

"*I'm* not an alcoholic." They'd been over this many times. Hobbs refused to let his father's alcohol habits dictate his own, while Victor went the other direction and didn't touch the stuff. "And I don't beat on people smaller than me."

"So you'll come?"

Hobbs felt trapped. Victor had used their baby sister as his trump card, and now, even though no part of Hobbs whatsoever wanted to say yes, he also couldn't say no. So he said nothing. He went to the hall closet, pulled out a set of mismatched spare sheets and an old blanket his mother had made when he was young. He took them to the living room and dumped them in Victor's lap. "Spare room has a bed, but it's not made. Or the couch is real comfy. I'll see you in the morning."

Victor didn't even open his eyes. "Yep," he said, pulling the blanket and sheets tighter around his chest.

Hobbs showered, brushed his teeth, crawled in the sack and literally buried his head under his pillow. Maybe by morning, with a little luck, Victor would be gone.

five

Tabitha woke to a chilly room, her blankets up to her neck and the smell of bacon thick and rich on the cold air. She lingered, motionless, enjoying the warmth of her bed amid the cold front that had moved in overnight. It was officially November, her birthday was over and the rest of the year lay ahead with possibilities that seemed more promising while tucked safely away from the world.

Life is a balance of holding on and letting go. ~Rumi

Tabitha had peeked at today's Journal of Invincibility quote last night, and the words now rolled around in her sleepy mind. Trinity, sensing Tabitha's wakefulness, started to whap her tail against the comforter from her spot at the foot of the bed. Tabitha stretched, allowing her arms to briefly slide out of the covers before she buried them again. Auntie El set the thermometer low in the winter and high in the summer. You had to be either freezing or dying from heatstroke to get the furnace or the air conditioner to kick on.

"People are spoiled these days," she was fond of saying. "Why, when I was growing up, we didn't even have air-conditioning. And when I was a little girl we had to warm ourselves by the coal stove. Sleep with heated bricks at our feet. Y'all don't even know."

"Okay, Auntie El." Tabitha never argued. Today, she was actually glad for the coolness of the room, which made the warm bed seem that much more decadent. She could use some decadence after yesterday. As she lay there, petting Trinity's head—who'd managed to crawl up next to her and plant her snuggly body right against Tabitha's side—she thought back to the bad run at massage school and the motorcycle shop. The kiss with Hobbs could've been counted as a win if Tabitha hadn't been left wondering how he'd felt about it. His response had been confusing, to say the least.

Rather than dwell, Tabitha reluctantly threw back the covers and stepped onto the cold wood floor. Auntie El polished the floors weekly, so even though they were old, they were beautiful. Typical Auntie El—throw out nothing, but you best keep it shining.

In the kitchen, she sat at the table, dressed in a bright yellow Sunday dress, just finishing up her crossword puzzle. "Somebody's a sleepyhead this morning." Auntie El peered over the top of her glasses, her eyes like a hawk's as she took in Tabitha's pajama bottoms and sleep shirt.

"Long week." Tabitha was glad to see Auntie El up and at it like her normal self. Maybe she'd just been battling a long, silent cold. She searched the cupboard for her favorite coffee mug—'50s sea-glass green, so old it sported veins of coffee stains in the micro-cracks of its interior. She filled it to the brim with the dark, silky brew and buried her nose in the steam.

"I assume you won't be coming to church again." Auntie El

shifted in her seat, pen poised above her newspaper. "Eleven-letter word for *friendship*."

"Not this week." Tabitha had been saying that every week for ages now. Auntie El had let it slide with little comment due to Tabitha's anxiety, the time she spent training Trinity, the general idea of letting her get her life back in order. Lately, though, Auntie El had been pulling out the stern looks. "Maybe next Sunday. I'm going to get in a workout this morning." Tabitha busied herself fixing Trinity's food and eyed the assortment of covered dishes on the countertops. She went straight to the brownies, now cooled, cut and tucked inside Auntie El's Tupperware, and snagged one.

"On a Sunday?"

"It's called Open Hour, Auntie El." Tabitha spoke with a mouthful of brownie. Auntie El's were the best—both cakey *and* gooey. "You can go and do whatever you want, like work on things you're not good at. Since I'm not good at anything, I have lots to work on." Tabitha had never gone to the gym on Sunday, but she was running out of excuses to miss church. Besides, if she really wanted to be as strong as her girlfriends, Open Hour was a good start.

"Well, you're in luck. I'll be having some folks back here for brunch after service, including Reverend Stokes. Maybe a conversation with him will get you motivated. Plus, you can eat something more appropriate for breakfast than chocolate."

Tabitha ignored the comment about the brownie and mentally calculated the time church ran versus the time Open Hour ran at the gym. They were concurrent, but that didn't mean Tabitha couldn't hang out a bit later, if whoever was coaching wasn't eager to get home. The sound of Trinity's dog-door flap and the rush of her paws over the floor signaled she was ready for her breakfast.

"You'll be back from that gym of yours in plenty of time."

Semper Fit was never just *the gym*. It was always *that gym of yours*, like Tabitha harbored a bad vice. She'd never be able to make Auntie El, who considered parking far away from the grocery store a form of exercise, understand that Semper Fit was so much more than a gym. It was a place that, even if she typically did lift the least amount of weight or take the longest to finish the cardio portion, Tabitha could disappear for an hour, not just from the house but from herself. *"Camaraderie,"* she said.

"I'm sorry?"

"Eleven-letter word for *friendship*."

Auntie El immediately filled in the squares. "Mmm-hmm. Fits."

"I'll see you after the gym, then." Tabitha set Trinity's food dish down in front of her and headed for the stairs. If she quickly got ready she'd get to Semper Fit just in time, and she could decide from there whether or not she'd risk Auntie El's wrath by not making it home in time for brunch. No matter how good that bacon smelled, mingling with the church crowd made Tabitha want to crawl back under the covers and stay there.

Open Hour was typically filled with the serious lifters, the people who either hated anything considered "cardio" or the ones who knew that the stronger they got, the easier the "cardio" became. Open Hour used to be Rhett's baby, until Red came along, and now Hobbs always coached Sunday while those two spent the day together. Hobbs didn't mind. He could use the money, and other than being a little hungover sometimes, it was no skin off his nose to come unlock the gym and keep an eye on Tatiana, Duke and Zoe, who were the Sunday regulars. Truth was, those three could probably teach Hobbs a thing or two about lifting, so the hour usually consisted of him holing up in the office on the internet while they snatched and benched to their hearts' content.

This morning, Hobbs was more than happy to have an excuse to leave the house when he found Victor still sacked out in the armchair. He'd opened up the flat sheet and the old blanket and buried himself up to his chin, but otherwise Victor hadn't moved. He still had his boots on. Hobbs thought about shaking him awake, but found himself standing there, studying his brother's face. If he narrowed his eyes, he could still see the teenager hiding beneath the stubble. Victor seemed less intimidating while he was asleep. That jaw that was chronically clenched was relaxed and his lips were parted just slightly, like a baby's. Hobbs sighed and moved off to the kitchen to make coffee. When even that didn't make Victor stir, Hobbs let his brother be and found himself shutting the front door gently behind him.

Now fully awake and jazzed up on caffeine, Hobbs's mind ran amok during the drive to the gym. Pops was dying. And Hannah wanted him to come home. So why hadn't she told him herself? Unlike Victor, Hannah texted regularly. Or she used to. Ever since spring, she'd got quieter and quieter, and it wasn't until this moment that he realized he hadn't heard from Hannah since August. They were close, and they used to text each other at least a couple of times a week. They saw each other at Thanksgiving and Christmas when Hobbs went home to Omaha to visit and they called each other on their birthdays, though Hannah's wouldn't be until January. Hannah was going to be twenty-six and probably didn't even remember. She was a free spirit who cared little about numbers, a sweet girl who liked being home, liked cutting hair for a living, liked rom-coms and putting on pretty dresses in the summer. Her favorite thing growing up had been 4-H club, where she learned to bake brownies and help save the frog population at Lake Manawa. She was a parent's dream come true.

If only she'd had the sort of parents who deserved her.

Hobbs pulled into the parking lot ten minutes late, but Zoe had obviously let everyone in. He paused, hands on the steering wheel, and tried one of those deep yoga breaths again. His nerves settled a little. Then he pulled out the happy face. It was easy. Just paint it on and go. He could wash it off later.

The music was blaring and bars already clanking by the time Hobbs pushed through the front door. Zoe and Duke were spotting each other on bench and Tatiana was setting her phone against her water bottle so she could record herself and post it on Insta later. One story was just like the next, always Tatiana lifting something, her muscles gleaming with sweat, hashtags all over the place: #gainz #getit #swolesistah.

The only surprise in the room was Tabitha. Hobbs was certain he'd never seen her at Open Hour, even though she probably needed it more than most. She was set up in the far corner, away from the beasts, with a training bar, a kettlebell, a wooden box, an assortment of bands, grips and a water bottle. Trinity, the tiniest pit bull in the universe, sat nearby. The idea of Open Hour was to do your own thing. Though a coach was present, coaching did not happen. The coach was there only to open and close and supervise in general. But Tabitha's pile looked, for lack of a plan, like she'd decided to grab one of everything. Even Trinity had her head cocked to the side, the sight of her owner's fitness gear a puzzle. Hobbs knew that after last night he should just say hi, be polite and move on. Tabitha would not fit well into his plan to keep his life perennially superficial.

He ducked into the office, sat down to the computer and mindlessly surfed the internet for a while, his decision to be a fly on the wall going exactly as planned until he heard a crash echoing beneath the strains of gangsta rap.

Hobbs rushed out to the floor and spied Tabitha, one foot hooked in a resistance band looped around the rig bar she clung to. She dangled there, her body swinging as her slender leg did a full split. Nearby was an overturned box, which Tabitha had obviously used to climb into the band because she'd chosen a bar that was too high. Because of her flexibility, she wasn't in danger of anything but humiliation as everyone watched her try to grab the ground with her free foot.

Hobbs walked over and planted his hands on his hips. "Whatcha doin'?"

Tabitha looked up at him, startled. She had these really big dark brown eyes that reminded Hobbs of blackstrap molasses, all shiny and sweet and old-fashioned. His grandma, the only sane person in his family before she died, used to make a mean molasses cookie. "I'm, um, practicing pull-ups," she said.

"Interesting. Would you like some help?"

"Please."

Hobbs set the box upright.

Tabitha planted her foot and untangled the other from the band. "Thanks," she said, once she'd jumped down. She faced her pile of equipment, casting anxious glances at the other members who were turning back to their workouts.

"What're you working on?" Hobbs knew he should walk away. Tabitha was already embarrassed and he'd already decided to sit in the office and ignore everyone—especially her. But something about the image of her hanging there by one foot, doing the splits midair while she twirled in the band, kept him smiling and rooted.

Tabitha twisted her lips. She was the sweet and innocent type, but she wasn't a fool. "I just grabbed some stuff," she admitted. "I don't know what I'm doing. I didn't want to go to church."

"Who does?"

"I'm trying to become stronger." Her smile fell. "Trying to be good at something."

Now they were getting somewhere. "You are. You just have to give it time."

"I'm even messing up massage school." She sighed. "I'm not brains *or* brawn."

"What's giving you trouble in massage school?" Hobbs had a hard time believing it. She seemed like a natural. He watched Tabitha bend in half and wrap her arms around the backs of her knees. If there was one thing Tabitha had on her side in the gym it was flexibility. The fluidity of her joints matched the quiet patience of her personality; only someone good at coaxing, diligence, waiting it out, had that kind of bendiness. Hobbs had seen her do the splits and lay her entire torso down on the floor. She'd called it a pancake, which made him hungry.

Tabitha peeked up from her knees. "Like memorizing all the bones and all their little grooves and divots. Just why? I won't be massaging bones."

"But you need to know where all the muscles connect, right?" Like he knew anything about massage school. But, logically, that made sense.

"Yeah." Tabitha straightened and surveyed her mess of equipment. She had a look in her eyes like she knew she'd overcomplicated things.

"You're just pushing time around." Hobbs leaned one shoulder against the rig and crossed his ankles.

"What?" She arched an eyebrow.

"You don't know what you're doing, you have no clear focus or goal, so you're just pushing time around. Like moving a pile from one room to the other instead of really cleaning up." When she didn't protest, Hobbs added, "You don't need all this stuff."

"Okay." Tabitha clasped her hands behind her back and arched, stretching her chest. She had a ballerina's body, or what Hobbs thought of as a ballerina's body. All legs and arms. "What do I need, then?"

A sudden thought of Victor, asleep at home in his living room, and a possible image of his father, sick in a hospital bed, flashed through Hobbs's mind. He had better things to think about than Tabitha's problems. This was not his business. "You got study materials somewhere? On the bones?"

Tabitha froze for a second. As if she sensed the sudden tension, Trinity, who'd been like a ghost up until now, raised her head, ears perked. Then Tabitha's shoulders relaxed and Trinity laid her head back down. "I have an app on my phone. A quiz that I constantly fail."

"Pull it up."

Tabitha gave her equipment one more glance before she went to the little blue gym bag she had next to Trinity and dug around. It struck Hobbs that Tatiana, struggling beneath a loaded barbell in the corner, never had her phone more than a hand's reach away, including during workouts. The screen even sported a huge crack to prove it, which resulted after a heavy jerk that Tatiana missed and bailed and the bumper plates had landed right on the phone. Tabitha, on the other hand, seemed to not even know where her cell was.

"Got it." Tabitha held up her mobile, triumphant, like she'd found buried treasure. She fiddled around, then handed it over, pointing at the screen. "That's the quiz."

Hobbs hit Start and the first question was a picture of a shoulder blade, with an arrow pointing to a bony prominence and four choices underneath: *A) Coracoid Process; B) Supra-*

spinous fossa; C) Acromion Process; D) Superior Border. He flashed Tabitha the picture on the phone and then read Tabitha the choices in a voice that he hoped sounded like a game-show host.

Tabitha froze, her brows knitting and her teeth worrying her bottom lip. "Can I see the picture again?"

Hobbs held up the photo. "Ten seconds," he said. He started snapping his fingers.

Tabitha briefly covered her mouth with her fingertips, then blurted, "Acromion process!" Despite the loud music, everyone in the gym turned to regard her outburst.

Hobbs suppressed a grin, clicked her choice and watched as the screen turned into a big red *X*, with the correct answer below. "Ohhh noooo, I am sorry." Hobbs did his best Alex Trebek imitation. "The correct answer was the *coracoid* process. Too bad. Ten burpees." He pointed at the floor.

"Darn it! I always mix those two up. It's not fair… Wait." Tabitha's frustration ceded to confusion. "What?"

"I said, ten burpees." Hobbs pointed at the floor again. "Let's go."

Tabitha went to protest, but then maybe remembered that she'd sort of brought this on herself. She dropped down and flattened herself to the floor, then jumped her feet together, rose and extended her arms overhead as she hopped. Hobbs stood over her and counted. Tabitha moved at a moderate pace. She never went full out, but she didn't drag, either. By midway, Hobbs snapped his fingers. "C'mon. Pick it up a little. Show me some aggression."

Tabitha shot him a glare. "I thought you weren't going to act like Rhett and make me do burpees?"

"That was last night. This is now. Go."

Tabitha's glare deepened but she stepped up her pace. When she was done, Hobbs was ready with the next question. The

picture had changed to an arm bone, and the question was
*Name this part of the humerus: A) Medial Epicondyle; B) Lateral
Epicondyle; C) Coronoid Fossa; D) Radial Fossa.* He read the
question and showed Tabitha the picture. Panting, Tabitha
scanned the phone. She reread the choices, mumbling them
under her breath. She cast Hobbs a worried glance, then looked
back to the phone. "I know this," she muttered.

"Prove it. Ten seconds."

After she guessed coronoid fossa, and was wrong, Hobbs
ordered ten kettlebell swings. Tabitha looked like she wanted
to slit his throat in his sleep, but she grabbed the kettlebell
and started swinging.

This went on for another eighteen questions. Tabitha got a
total of five of them right, and by the time she was a wasted
puddle on the floor, she'd done fifty burpees, fifty kettlebell
swings and fifty box jumps. She draped her forearm over her
eyes and lay there, huffing, her knees knocking together and
her skin glistening with sweat. Hobbs loomed over her and
she peeked out from under her arm. "I don't see how this
was helpful at all," she said. "I couldn't think. And now I'm
wrecked."

"Exactly. So now the next time we do this, you'll be better
prepared. You'll know better than to come in here not knowing your bones. Commit them to memory and you won't have
to think. Upside—you got a great workout."

Tabitha moved her arm away and leaned up on her elbows.
"Stop being so impressed with yourself. I hate you."

Hobbs laughed. This was where Rhett would say something like, "Good. Mission accomplished." But Hobbs stuck
out his hand and hauled Tabitha to her feet. She was so light
he overshot and she nearly flew to standing. She stumbled a
little and Hobbs steadied her as she leaned into his shoulder.
She looked up at him with those eyes, sweet as Grandma's

cookies. Last night came back, the kiss he'd practically stolen at the edge of the forest. What a dumb, selfish thing to do. Hobbs lingered for a second, enjoying the scent of her body's natural perfume awakened beneath her sweat, then drew away.

Tabitha cleared her throat and patted her hair down. A few flyaways had escaped her ponytail and were curling against her forehead. "I don't know what you mean about next time," she muttered. "I'm never doing this again."

"Hey, I've been wondering." Hobbs's mind was still on last night. "What'd you wish for?"

Her gaze narrowed into thoughtful slits. "You want to know my wish?"

"Yeah. Last night you said you made a big birthday wish. What was it?"

Tabitha's teeth scraped the bottom of her lip. Then she shrugged. "I wished that I was as badass as all my girlfriends. And my dog." She glanced at Trinity.

Hobbs gave a brief laugh as he watched the pittie study a smear of chalk on the floor like she was judging the person who'd left it there. "You need a list, then," Hobbs suggested. He'd already considered and rejected saying *You're already a badass*. That wasn't what Tabitha wanted or needed to hear. She wanted solutions.

"A list?" Her eyebrows rose.

"A Badass List."

Tabitha mulled this over silently. Then she nodded. "A list," she said. "A list of ways I can make this wish a reality." Her eyes held a determined glint. "I'll do it."

"Good. I'm going to be gone for a bit," Hobbs said, surprised to hear the words, as he hadn't realized he'd made a decision about going home with Victor until that moment. If Tabitha could be strong, so could he. "But when I get back, you better have that list ready. I'm going to hold you account-able."

"Where you going?" Tabitha's sudden cheer seemed damp-ened.

"I have to go home." That was all he'd be saying, to any-one. When he texted Rhett, that would be the extent of the information he'd provide, as well. But Rhett wouldn't pry. Hobbs mentally sorted how many shifts he'd need covered and how many personal training clients he'd have to reschedule.

"Where's home?"

"Omaha."

"Oh. Well. We'll miss you. The gym, I mean. Not that I can speak for the gym, but…me and Trinity, anyway." She shrugged, clasped her fingers together, then quickly strode to the corner and lifted her bag. "Thanks again for the help today."

"Anytime." Hobbs smiled to himself and watched her flus-tered movements as she packed up, even though the thought of actually going home, now that it had been spoken aloud, made him want to do anything but smile. As she headed for the door, Hobbs called after her. "Don't forget about that list!"

Tabitha peeked back over her shoulder and smiled. "I'm on it, Coach."

six

Tabitha had to admit, as she was driving home, that she felt a little stronger. Not physically. Not even mentally. But something was more solid inside of her, like a firming up of her soul.

Tabitha knew she had to be cautious with how she thought about Hobbs. He flirted with every decent-looking woman who walked into the gym and he was nice to everyone. Tabitha wasn't anything special. The fact that he'd spent his Open Hour on Sunday helping her meant nothing. And neither did the kiss. That was just a tequila-induced celebratory moment for her birthday. Tabitha was well aware that she was the type of woman who read too much into things. She refused to do that this time and make a fool out of herself in front of the gym playboy. But still, she felt better than she had this morning.

Tabitha sighed so loud Trinity started whapping her tail in the back seat. She glanced in the rearview. "I'm okay, girl."

The words nearly died on her lips as she pulled up to the house. What did Auntie El do, invite the entire congregation home for brunch? Cars lined the quiet street, spilled out the drive and sat crooked under shade trees planted on the corners. Many of them were the old-fashioned long sedans the seniors preferred. There, right in the driveway, like a blast from the past, was Reverend Stokes's ancient silver El Dorado.

It felt like a wad of cotton filled up Tabitha's throat. Her hands tightened on the steering wheel. She had nothing but good memories of Reverend Stokes, but every time she saw him, he asked when was she coming back to church. Tabitha never quite felt like explaining about Camp Leatherneck, where sexual harassment on a daily basis had been the norm from the very chaplain she'd been sworn to protect.

It took Tabitha an extra few minutes to find a parking space, since her brain froze up. Her usual curbside spot near the mailbox was filled with a classy new Lexus. The only decent place she could find was in front of the Mailers' house, right where Mr. Mailer liked to park his Buick. If he came home early from his own church services, he would not be pleased, even though street parking was fair game.

Tabitha walked slowly toward the house, her grip on Trinity's leash tightening the closer she got. Trinity responded to the tension by pressing her shoulder into Tabitha's thigh, turning her gait into a leaning lope. Tabitha didn't tell the dog she was okay this time.

Voices and laughter filled the cool air as she opened the storm door and stepped inside where it was warm and smelled like fresh bread. Clearly, Auntie El had raised the heat for the church crowd, and for once, Tabitha wished the house was cold. Now it was too warm. Stuffy, in fact. Trinity stuck close to her side, staying calm, composed and in charge as they made their way into the kitchen, which was packed to the gills with women in wool skirts and crisp blouses and men in khakis and button-downs.

"Well, hello, little Tabitha!" Reverend Stokes was by the counter, a plate full of food in his hand. He wore a fine black suit and glasses with thick, dark frames, like he always had. The only real change over the years was he'd gone gray at the temples and apparently let it happen naturally, with no attempt whatsoever to hide it. Something about the gray always made her feel better, like it signaled the safety of maturity.

"Reverend Stokes." The longer Tabitha looked at him, the more the remainder of her tension drained way. Reverend Stokes was the complete opposite of Captain Dorsey, the chaplain who had harassed her. Slender, where the captain had been stocky; smiling, when the captain never did; brown instead of pale. Apparently, all men of the cloth weren't one and the same to her PTSD, which was such a relief she let Trinity's leash go and sensed her hunger rekindling after that brutal workout.

Reverend Stokes shoved his plate to the counter, creating space among all the food, and scooped Tabitha into a warm hug. He rocked her several times, then patted her between the shoulder blades before he pulled back and held her at arm's length. "My girl. We go too long between seeing each other. I think it was last Thanksgiving."

"Yes." It'd been almost a year since Tabitha had been in the arms of the only man she'd felt somewhat like a daughter toward. "Good to see you, too, Reverend." His eyes still held that sparkle, his touch the perfect balance of strength and gentleness.

"Finally back from that gym of yours, I see." Auntie El pushed through the bodies and came up beside them. "She spends a lot of time on her muscles these days, Reverend. Something she learned in the navy, I guess."

"Well, that's good." Reverend Stokes scooped up his plate and took a bite of Auntie El's creamy baked eggs. "She looks healthy and fit." He took another bite. "The food is amazing, as usual, Lavina."

"Oh." Auntie El waved a dismissive hand but grinned.

"Please eat something, dear, especially if you've been working hard at the gym." Reverend Stokes gestured to Auntie El's spread. The crowd had thinned away from the buffet and had dispersed throughout the house, the happy chatter punctuated with laughter. "Later, we can talk and catch up."

"Thank you, Reverend. It's so good seeing you." Tabitha didn't need to be told twice to eat, now that her jitters had died away completely. Trinity followed beside her as she collected a plate and started filling it with eggs and bacon and fresh fruit. She'd just plopped a tall, flaky homemade biscuit atop the pile, then turned and grabbed another at the last second, when she nearly slammed straight into the chest of a tall, slender man.

"Oh!" Tabitha pulled back just in time, rescuing the contents of her plate from spilling in any direction. "I'm sorry."

"Good save," the man said with a smile.

"Thanks." She looked up and had a moment of déjà vu. The man facing her had close-cropped black hair and wore a pair of wire-rimmed glasses. His face was clean-shaven and classically handsome, with strong cheekbones. He looked like…like…

"Tabitha, you remember Thaddeus." Auntie El was right by his side, her hand in the crook of his elbow, as if she'd led him over.

"Oh, my God."

Auntie El brushed aside the exclamation and added, "Thaddeus is a lawyer." Her giant grin faded as her gaze shifted to Tabitha's overflowing plate. "Good gracious. When did we get a horse to feed?"

Tabitha eyed her plate, teetering with food. "I'm hungry, Auntie El. My workout was brutal." She smiled at Thaddeus, even though her cheeks were burning. "Wow. I can't believe I'm seeing you after all these years. You look the same, but… different." Thaddeus, always long and lanky, had filled out. He'd got his crooked bottom teeth fixed at some point and he had an air of confidence that filled the entire kitchen. Back in high school he and Tabitha typically hid out in the library, away from other people.

"You look the same, too," Thaddeus said, eyeing her up and down. "Still light as a feather and cute as a button." His gaze stopped at her plate of food. "That must've been some workout." He offered a polite laugh. "Where do you go?"

"Thaddeus is a marathon runner," Auntie El piped in. "He puts in over forty miles a week."

"That's great," Tabitha said. She set her plate down and quickly made a bacon-and-egg sandwich with one of the biscuits. "I remember you did cross-country in high school."

"It's nothing." Thaddeus waved a hand. "I typically run around the Mall, in the District, before the day gets going. Right before work. Do you run?"

"Not as well as I should." Tabitha took a bite of her biscuit, unable to stave off her hunger any longer. "I go to Semper Fit." She spoke around the food in her mouth, which elicited one last shake of Auntie El's head before she moved out of the room.

"Sounds serious." Thaddeus sipped at a cup of black coffee. It looked silky and smelled creamy and dark.

"It's pretty intense. But I do my best." Tabitha grabbed a clean cup from the array Auntie El had lined up near the thermal carafe and poured herself some of the hot brew. She dumped in some cream and sugar from the pitcher and bowl and took a sip.

Thaddeus snapped his fingers. "Semper Fit. That's one of those extreme fitness places, right? We've done a number of cases against those places."

"Cases? What do you mean?"

"I'm a personal injury lawyer with Sneldon and Schultz. Those types of gyms always have lawsuits. People try to do things they shouldn't, silly things, get hurt and sue." Thaddeus shrugged. "I'm sure you've witnessed it if you've been there for any amount of time."

The cozy warmth of the coffee and bacon turned inside Tabitha's gut. "Semper Fit's not like that. Yes, we do some things traditional gyms don't, but the coaches are excellent and make sure everyone progresses safely."

"That's great to hear." Thaddeus sipped more of his coffee. "Frankly, I'm surprised you go there. You were always so quiet and careful. You never enjoyed sports of any kind. I used to call you my little bookworm, remember that?" He winked, showing off some impressively long eyelashes. They were long back in high school but, if it was possible, they'd grown. "I guess the navy makes you tough." Thaddeus flexed a bicep beneath his dress shirt. "I was shocked as hell when you enlisted, too, to be honest. You never liked to be away from home."

"I'm different now." Tabitha's voice came with an edge she hadn't expected. She quickly took a bite of her egg sandwich to silence herself from saying more, being defensive when she probably had no need to be. He was right, anyway. Tabitha didn't like to be away from home. But she hadn't enlisted in the navy because she was brave. She'd enlisted because she'd hoped it'd make her brave—give her direction, make her stronger, more confident. And everyone knew how that had turned out.

"I can see that." Thaddeus flashed his perfect teeth again. "You look amazing. I can't believe how long it's been."

"Yeah, high school was a long time ago. But also seems like yesterday, am I right?"

"I know what you mean… Oops." Thaddeus had taken a step to his right and bumped into Trinity. Up until now she'd been hidden in the crowded kitchen. "Oh, hi." He reached down to pet her. "Who's this? I remember your auntie would never let you have a dog." Just as his fingers lit on Trinity's head he must've seen the vest because he drew back. "A service dog. Oh, that explains it. She's not yours. Somebody brought their service dog."

"No, she's mine." Tabitha's words came out low, but certain.

"Oh, I…"

"How we doing over here?" Auntie El appeared between the two of them, her big smile still plastered to her face. It looked strained, though, and a sheen of sweat had popped over her forehead. "Catching up on old times?"

"We were just talking about Trinity, Auntie El." Tabitha set the rest of her biscuit on her plate and pushed it away, her appetite shrinking.

"Oh, I see." Auntie El cleared her throat. "Tabitha had some hard times in Afghanistan, but she's all good now. The dog helps." Auntie El gave a nervous laugh. "She's a good dog. All trained up."

Thaddeus peered down at Trinity's upturned little face. "Not much of a guard dog, I'd say. She's so little."

"That's not the type of service she provides," Tabitha said.

"Oh, I see." Thaddeus looked between Trinity and Tabitha and back again, but his expression made it clear that he did *not* see. "Were you wounded over there?" Thaddeus glanced down, maybe checking out Tabitha's legs for an obvious injury. "Your auntie didn't say you'd been hurt."

"Not like that." Tabitha's heart was going harder now—small but determined punches in her chest. "Trinity helps me in other ways." She didn't want to tell him about the IED that had injured Captain Dorsey, because that wouldn't explain anything at all. The chaplain had come away with obvious, physical wounds, but Tabitha's weren't visible at all. And Tabitha's problems hadn't started after the captain's injury, years ago; they'd started after his death, resulting from his injuries, which had taken years and was much more recent. She got the feeling that an explanation for Thaddeus wouldn't come easily, certainly not here and now, during Auntie El's Sunday brunch.

Silence yawned between them.

"Excuse me. It was great catching up with you, Thaddeus. You seem to be doing amazing things. I can't wait one more second to have a shower, though. Come on, Trinity." As soon as Tabitha turned, Trinity followed her out of the kitchen.

"You smell fine to me," Auntie El called. "Tabitha? We have guests!"

Tabitha didn't look back. At the foot of the staircase, she bumped into Reverend Stokes. "Are you all right, my dear? You look a little pale."

"I'm fine, Reverend. I just need a shower. It was so good to see you again." Tabitha resisted the urge to sink against him for another embrace. Just when she'd been thinking about how perfect Thaddeus had been for her back in high school, she'd discovered that he really was perfect. Too perfect. Had he always been that perfect? Or had he changed a lot? Or was it she who had done all the changing—and not for the good?

As Tabitha climbed the stairs, she heard Reverend Stokes say softly to Trinity, "You take care of her now. She's my sweet angel. Found her behind the altar. Quiet as a church mouse."

Trinity, who rarely spoke, gave a little woof in reply.

seven

As soon as Hobbs laid eyes on Tabitha, he no longer regretted Victor's need to stop at the closest motorcycle shop to get a warmer pair of gloves for the ride home. "Triple M Classics is a classic bike shop," Hobbs had said. "Doubt it has what you need." He didn't want any more delays. Once Hobbs had agreed to go to Omaha, Victor had stayed on a few days to rest up before riding back. By midweek, though, they were more than ready to stop bumping into each other in the kitchen. Victor's Triumph was gassed up, tires full, everything checked over and ready to go. All he needed were the gloves.

Let's just get to Omaha and get this over with, Hobbs thought. In truth, Hobbs also didn't want to see Delaney Monroe this early in the morning. Ever since their first meeting at Semper Fit last spring, they'd rubbed each other the wrong way. Hobbs wasn't afraid of tough women, but Delaney didn't give in to his charms easily, which threw him off his game. He always felt a little awkward around her and that was not what he wanted to deal with right before a trip home. Victor had never been one to listen to what anyone else had to say, and he'd insisted they stop at Triple M, anyway.

Behind the counter, inside the inviting shop that smelled of engine oil and pine, was Tabitha. Hobbs had never seen her in anything other than gym clothes or that excellent Dorothy costume that showed off her lean, muscled legs. Today she wore faded blue jeans and an oversized Triple M Classics sweatshirt in a light gray color. Her dark hair was curly and free, like she'd made no attempt to straighten it, and it framed her youthful face. Hobbs knew she had just turned thirty but she looked more like twenty, if he pretended he didn't know her. That was partly due to her slender build but also to her smooth, perfectly clear, warm skin and the innocence in her big, doe-y eyes. She had a customer at the counter, a large dude in a leather vest. Hobbs couldn't hear anything Tabitha said—she had a voice that matched her eyes—but the guy's side of the conversation was loud enough for the entire shop.

"You gotta bone up on your cycle knowledge if you're going to sit behind this counter, little miss." His tone was humorous, ribbing, but Tabitha's face was etched with worry and fatigue, like she'd been through this scenario before. "People come in here and want to talk shop. You gotta know your shop." The guy leaned forward on the counter, apparently attempting to flirt with her by showing her who was boss. Yeah, Hobbs thought. *That* always went over well with women.

Tabitha let out a nervous-sounding laugh. "Let me get Delaney. She's working in the back. She can talk all the shop you want and answer all your questions." She gestured over her shoulder, toward a door that probably led to the back room. Hobbs had never been here. Not only did he not own a motorcycle, he certainly didn't seek out Delaney Monroe outside gym hours.

"No need for that." The guy edged a little closer, practically leaning his torso on the counter now. "I can teach you everything you need to know." He caught her by the wrist as she turned to go.

Tabitha, mouth open, stammered. For the first time, Hobbs became aware that Trinity was in the store, because the dog started barking. Her black head popped up from behind the counter, her muzzle pointed at the man who'd grabbed her human.

Hobbs started toward the counter, a sudden, protective instinct taking over his body. It was a very *dude* reaction, one he didn't normally have, but he wasn't going to stop himself, either.

"Excuse me." Victor stormed over to the pair before Hobbs could even get two steps. "Could you point out the gloves? I need some new gloves." He slapped his old set of leathers down with a *fwap!* This wasn't an unusual sight, unless you knew Victor. Victor was the type of guy who went into a store and found what he needed on his own, avoiding sales help at all costs. A do-it-yourself type, often to a fault.

The big guy in the leather vest released Tabitha, straightened, then sized Victor up, maybe deciding who would come out a winner in a fight. Hobbs had the feeling the guy was rarely intimidated and usually said whatever he wanted. But Victor was tall, had huge quads, even in his blue jeans, and boulders for shoulders, even in his motorcycle jacket. His carriage was one of absolute fearlessness, something he'd cultivated over the years growing up with a violent drunk father, and the do-rag he wore over his ruffled curls made him look thuggish, even though Victor hadn't been in trouble with the law in years.

Tabitha's chest rose and fell rapidly, like she struggled for air. She took stock of Victor, anxiety visibly rising in her face. She pointed to the rows of merchandise off to the right of the store, like she couldn't find her voice. Hobbs had seen her like this before; on the Fourth of July, some teenagers had shot off fireworks at the park near the gym and Tabitha's reaction had been similar, though much more immediate and intense. She'd sunk to the floor and the pit bull had lain over her chest, like a doggy blanket.

"Can you show me where?" Victor spoke to Tabitha but stared straight into the face of the grabby customer. "I get lost easy."

Tabitha was silent, appeared to waver on her feet. Hobbs rushed to her side and slid an arm around her waist. "Hey, Tabby. You okay?" He looked down and saw that Trinity was leaning on the other side of Tabitha's legs. Last time, there'd been a loud noise and a pretty clear connection of what had sent Tabitha into a spiral. This trigger was less obvious, though the guy who'd grabbed her seemed the likely culprit.

Tabitha turned her face toward Hobbs, slowly. She blinked a few times. "Oh," she said. She let out a big sigh. "Hey. It's you."

"Hey. It's me."

She pushed her hip harder against his and leaned in, not like she was flirting but like she was trying to melt into him. "I've never seen you in here. I didn't know you rode a motorcycle."

"Not in a long time." Hobbs used to ride with Victor when they were teens, but they rode for different reasons. Victor had a passion for the things, loved the speed and agility. They were like mechanical cats, he used to say. Hobbs only rode to keep up with Victor. As soon as he was done trying to keep up with him, Hobbs stopped riding. After a long moment, Hobbs shifted away, making sure Tabitha was steady and on her feet. "Tabitha, this is my brother, Victor. He needs some warmer gloves for his ride back to Omaha."

Tabitha looked from one to the other, assessing the familiarity. "I see it." Her stupor was evaporating with the distraction. "You have the same hair color." She touched her own. "The same waves, too."

The grabby guy in the leather vest took this as his cue to get out while he was ahead. He collected his helmet from the countertop, along with a paper bag containing whatever he'd bought, and headed silently for the door.

"Don't let it hit ya," Victor barked. He never could leave well enough alone.

The dude paused in the doorway, but when Victor kept staring him down, he just walked out and didn't look back.

"Thank you," Tabitha said, once he was gone. She encircled her own wrist, like she was trying to wipe the guy off. "Why do men do that?" Her words were quiet, like she spoke to the universe and wasn't really expecting an answer.

"Because they can," Victor said. He never made excuses, for himself or anyone else. "I'm gonna go get those gloves." He headed toward the shelves Tabitha had pointed at, his feet loud as he marched away.

Confusion clouded Tabitha's face. "Should I help him?"

"Definitely not. Once, when we were teenagers, we had a grocery list from my mom. We couldn't find the evaporated milk anywhere. Victor refused to ask, so we just kept wandering the aisles. I finally pretended like I was going to get chips and I asked an employee where it was. Vic was actually mad, when he found out. Said we had to do things on our own, no matter how small a task. That our evaporated milk was nobody's damn business."

Tabitha didn't look nearly as appalled as Hobbs had expected. "That makes sense."

"That makes *sense*?" Hobbs smiled, despite himself. "No, it doesn't, Tabby. It makes no sense at all. Don't make excuses for him." Hobbs watched his brother weave through the shelves, the aisles tiny, his big body knocking into things.

"It makes sense to him," she said. "The important thing isn't that he has to find his own milk. The important thing is *why*." Tabitha studied Victor but didn't move to help him. "Maybe you should ask him sometime."

Hobbs had a funny feeling in his gut as he watched her, head cocked to the side while she puzzled over his brother, bumbling through the gloves. "Maybe," he said. "I'm not sure I want to know. But I appreciate you trying."

Tabitha raised her eyebrows, surprised. "Trying what?"

Hobbs laughed. "Trying to peel back the layers of my annoying brother."

"He's not annoying," Tabitha countered. "He's just, if I had to guess, very private."

Victor, oblivious to their discussion, kept shoving on one glove after the other, all too small. Hobbs smiled at Tabitha. She returned it, bright and pretty.

"I better go help him before he ruins all the gloves," Hobbs told her, and left Tabitha behind to join his brother in the shelves. By the time Victor found what he wanted, in a size big enough for his huge mitts, and they'd headed back toward the counter to pay, Delaney had joined Tabitha.

Victor let out a soft, private whistle. "Who is that?"

"That—" Hobbs lowered his voice as they neared the women "—is taken. By a cop. So just forget it. She owns this shop."

"Hey, I'm just admiring. I don't live here, remember?"

Delaney would be his type. Tough. No-nonsense. She had on jeans, black boots and a plain white T-shirt that showed off a black tattoo etched down the underside of her forearm, up to her wrist. The ink was dark and new, because up until last year she'd been an active-duty marine. No ink below the sleeves. "Hobbs," she said, when she spied him. "I didn't know you rode."

"I don't."

"That makes more sense."

Victor let out a belly laugh. "She hates you, doesn't she?"

"A little bit."

"Who's this?" Delaney tilted her head up at Victor just as Wyatt came streaking out of the back of the shop. He spun once in front of Victor, then sat right down in front of him and said, "Woof." Wyatt's signature greeting was the coolest thing Hobbs had ever heard.

"Woof to you, too." Victor ran a palm over Wyatt's head. "These, please." He dropped the gloves on the counter and Tabitha quickly scooped them up.

"Delaney Monroe, this is my brother, Victor. He's visiting from Omaha. Heading back today. Delaney is originally from Omaha, too."

She looked Victor up and down. "Why's he so much bigger than you?"

Victor laughed again, good and deep. "Pleasure to meet you, Delaney Monroe."

They shook hands. "Likewise."

"This is a great shop you got here."

"Thanks."

"What kind of classic bikes you deal in?"

"All. British. American. Japanese."

"She's got a '33 Indian," Hobbs said. She'd ridden it to the gym once and every guy in the place had rushed out to admire it.

"On the road?" Victor wasn't easily impressed but Hobbs could hear it in his voice.

"Yep." Delaney grinned.

"Cool. Can I see it?"

"Sure, it's in the back. What you riding?" Delaney nodded at the gloves.

"Triumph Tiger."

"Nice. I love British bikes." While Tabitha ran Victor's credit card, Delaney pointed a finger at him. "Good bike to ride all the way down. I can hear Nebraska in your voice, by the way. Heavier than Hobbs here."

Victor stuffed the credit card back in his wallet. "He left too soon."

"Maybe he's smarter than both of us," she quipped.

"I think that's the nicest thing you've ever said about me," Hobbs joined in.

"Probably," Delaney agreed.

Tabitha watched the exchange in silence, but with a little smile on her lips. Her gaze connected with Hobbs as Victor declined a bag and receipt. He slid the gloves right on and flexed his fingers.

"You doing okay?" Hobbs said, while Delaney and Victor headed to the back room to see the '33. Wyatt followed along beside them, with Victor stroking the dog's head and using a thousand more words than he usually did on any given day.

"Yeah." Tabitha smiled a little more. "Thanks."

"That guy was out of line," Hobbs offered. Maybe she didn't want to talk about it, based on her reaction from earlier, but Hobbs thought it important to say out loud. "Nobody has the right to touch you like that. I was planning on punching him in the face, before Victor butted in."

Then her smile fell. She chewed around on something before finally speaking. "My chaplain in Afghanistan used to grab me like that all the time. Always when no one was looking, of course. Sometimes even at night, when I was trying to sleep." Her voice got a little laugh in it that was completely humorless. "I never knew when he was coming. It was—"

Tabitha's voice thickened, like her words got stuck in her throat "—horrible."

Hobbs stayed quiet, because almost anything that crossed his mind seemed violent and not particularly helpful. He knew what it was like to be terrified of someone bigger than you, someone in charge. He knew how useless authority could be, how alone and helpless it made you feel.

"I'm not sure which is worse, though." Tabitha's voice softened. "The grabbing or the attitude. Like we're just supposed to put up with it. Almost like we're supposed to be flattered. Or even grateful." Her tone turned bitter. "And since I was his assistant, I was literally in charge of keeping him safe. Guarding his life."

"And you're all on your own," Hobbs added, without thinking. "Nobody to help you, in no small part because you're ashamed in the first place that you need help. Asking for help is seen as weakness. And nobody wants to be weak."

"Exactly." They stared at each other for a long time. A flicker ran through Tabitha's molasses eyes and her head cocked to the side, just like when she'd been studying Victor earlier.

"Well. That guy was way out of line," Hobbs said. "Nobody's allowed to treat you like that. Not even if you're on the job."

Another long silence passed. Tabitha's fingers were tremulous on Trinity's head. She closed her eyes for a second. When she opened them again, she sniffed deeply, sighed and said, "I didn't know your brother was here. Is that why you're going home? Everything okay?"

Hobbs shrugged. He didn't know how to answer that.

But Tabitha, she didn't react like a lot of people did. Something Hobbs learned more and more every time he was around her. The type of person who didn't think Victor was weird for needing to find the evaporated milk all by himself was the same type of person who seemed to sense that Hobbs didn't want to talk about home right now. And she just let it go. "When will you be back from Omaha?" was all she said.

"Trust me," Hobbs said as he glanced in Victor's direction and saw he was making his manners and heading toward the door. "As quickly as possible. Victor's riding his bike and I'm driving my truck. I can escape whenever I want."

She smiled a little. "See you soon, then."

As they left, Hobbs realized he wasn't really annoyed anymore that Victor had wanted to stop at the bike shop. Despite the heaviness of his conversation with Tabitha, the sun seemed a little brighter. Even though the road was long, and the destination no prize, Hobbs had a tiny spring in his step that hadn't been there this morning.

eight

Clementine swiped the sweat from her forehead and dreamed of a hot bath, even though the Dogwood County Marathon was run at the perfect time of year—first Saturday in November, cool weather, but not cold, and just ahead of all the holidays.

Most people preferred the Marine Corps Marathon, run the previous Sunday, but Clementine liked running through Greenview Park. The Rock Creek Parkway was the only pretty portion of the Marine Corps Marathon, and that came right at the beginning of the race. Running through downtown and seeing all the monuments was great for people not from the area, but Clementine had seen them all a million times and preferred a visit when she wasn't trying not to die. The Dogwood County Marathon had a solid thirty kilometers of the race within the park, which meant trees, shade, rugged terrain and a limited field. The race had become a lottery years ago, but because Clementine had finished it five times, she had an automatic entry each year unless she deferred.

Every year, right about when Clementine reached mile twenty, she rued her decision not to defer. Mile twenty was the moment. The moment where her body was just done, and the only way she was getting through the next six miles was on pure will. The moment where she burst through the trees at the edge of the parkway and had to leave the forest behind, because the remainder of the race was all on the road. Most people liked leaving the hills, dirt and rocks behind and hitting that flat pavement, but not Clementine. For her, it was like being ripped from her cocoon of safety, into the harsh reality of life.

As soon as she left the forest she thought about Tyler, about the day she'd learned he'd died. Something about her fatigue mixed with the sudden, bright light and the hard surface pounding beneath her feet gave her that same sense of helplessness and despair.

Today was no exception, and she had to steel herself to face down that final ten kilometers. She got through the first five by just telling herself the faster she moved, the sooner it would all be over. She got through the second five by turning up the heat, emptying her tank and dreaming about the finish line: the foil blanket, the carbs and the massage.

Postrace massages weren't like the real deal. They lasted only ten minutes, fully clothed, and you were too spent to really enjoy it. But Clementine was hoping to see Tabitha, who'd been worrying as much about her massage school extra credit as Clementine had been about running the race. *I'm finishing this damn thing for Tabitha*, Clementine told herself, with only a quarter mile left that seemed to stretch on forever.

Finally, dragging, she crossed the finish line, smiled for the cameras and accepted her finisher medal from Carole, one of the women in her running group who was volunteering this year instead of running.

"Awesome work, Clementine. How do you feel?"

Clementine forced a smile. "Good. Thanks." She draped the foil blanket Carole handed her around her shoulders. She actually felt more beat up mentally than physically this year. Lily used to wait at the finish line with Mama, years ago, but after Mama passed, Lily refused to stand out alone in the cold or rain or fog or whatever early November usually dished up. Plus, she had a job now, and Saturdays at the animal shelter were busy. Clementine couldn't blame her.

She picked her way over to the commuter lot where they ran the farmers' market every other Saturday. There were medical tents and tables with postrace food like bananas, bagels and even beer. She snagged a minicarton of chocolate milk and drank it down in one go. As she wiped her mouth with the back of her hand and tossed her carton away, she spied the massage tables, set up in the far corner of the lot. Clementine took her time walking over, noting the slight limp in her left leg—that knee always got tweaked when she ran more than a half—and let her body normalize, the muscles and tendons and blood all readjusting and squeezing back in place. As she got closer, Clementine counted about two dozen massage tables set up. She queued up behind a tall guy who smelled like seaweed and peeked at her wrist. She realized that though she'd hit Stop on her GPS watch, she hadn't even checked her time to see if she'd made a personal record. Three hours and twelve minutes. Well, dang. She'd beat herself by about twenty minutes. The only thing she'd done differently this year was she'd joined Semper Fit and had actually decreased her overall training runs. Guess the extra strength building had really paid off.

Why wasn't she more excited? All she felt was tired and

salty. Clementine decided she'd text Lily as soon as she collected her stuff from the storage locker. Lily would get all proud of her and the mood would rub off and Clementine would be happier about how she'd spent her Saturday morning.

Pretty soon, there was only Seaweed Man ahead of her, and Clementine had a better look at the massage operation. Tabitha was only a few yards away. Clementine recognized her dark hair, pulled into space buns, and the fluidity of her movements. She was slender and long-limbed and moved with a certain amount of grace, like a dancer. Clementine figured that between the grace and the quiet, sensitive way in which Tabitha carried herself and dealt with people, she'd be a good massage therapist. There was a calming aura about her that eased your tension when you hadn't even realized you were tense. Right now, though, Tabitha was trying to help a young woman wearing bright pink shorts onto her table. The woman had approached on wobbly legs, but then stopped short. She covered her mouth with her hand and swayed a little. Tabitha had a hand on her shoulder, her lips moving like she was either comforting or coaxing the woman. The runner finally got on the table, facedown. She hung there, like a limp doll.

Trinity, who normally stayed quiet unless Tabitha needed her, rose to her feet and started circling the table. Her muzzle went into the air.

Clementine searched the row of tables for the instructor, who was supposed to be overseeing the students, or for Red, who had also volunteered to be a supervisor, as most of these therapists would be in their first year of school. She spied Red by her strawberry hair and the Semper Fit hoodie she wore, at one end of the long row of tables, busy with a student. The rest of the people were a sea of faces to Clementine. She had no idea who was a teacher and who wasn't, but her runner instincts were kicking in and she couldn't wait it out. "I'm not cutting, I swear." Clementine pushed in front of Seaweed Man and jogged, despite the protest of her muscles, over to Tabitha's table.

"Clementine." Tabitha's eyes widened as she approached. "Hey. I'm not ready for anyone else yet. She just lay down." Tabitha had her hands on the woman's thighs and was massaging upward with short, quick pressure. "But I'm glad you found me. Just wait right there and you can be next."

"Tabitha, I don't think this woman is well. I was watching and she seemed really wobbly. Too wobbly. What did she say to you?"

"Um." Tabitha froze, lifted her hands away, her brow creased. "She was really wobbly," she agreed. "I thought it was just from running all those miles. What she said didn't really make sense. Something about feeling hot and cold and *wavy*. That was kind of weird, wasn't it?"

"Yes." Clementine planted her hand on the woman's back and leaned in close to the face cradle. "Ma'am, are you okay?" When she didn't respond, Clementine gave her a gentle shake. "Ma'am? Can you hear me?"

The woman groaned and made a retching sound. Then puke hit the ground beneath the hole in the face cradle.

"Medic!" Clementine turned and raced for the medical tent. She could no longer feel any pain in her feet or legs; she just flew. With all her yelling, medics met her halfway. "Third table over." Clementine pointed. "She's wobbly, incoherent and vomiting."

The medics rushed over to Tabitha's table and surrounded the runner in pink shorts; she hadn't moved since she'd vomited. Tabitha froze, staring at the medics with her mouth open in shock. "What's happening?" she said. "What did I miss?"

Clementine pulled her away, so the medics could do their job. Two more appeared carrying a stretcher. "Can't say for sure. But it looked like hyponatremia. I've seen it a few times before."

"Is it dangerous?" Tabitha spoke through the fingers that covered her lips.

"Yes. Very. What caught my eyes was her loss of muscle control. That could mean swelling of the brain."

"Oh, my God."

They both watched in silence as the medics assessed the woman's vitals, then shifted her to the stretcher. All the massages either came to a halt or slowed considerably as everyone looked on. A crowd formed around the scene. Both Red and a small woman with short dark hair rushed over to see what was going on. As the medics lifted the stretcher and headed for the medical tent, the woman groaned and shifted. At least she was conscious.

"What happened, Tabitha?" The woman with short dark hair approached, with Red at her heels.

"She came for massage." Tabitha sounded stricken. "I didn't know she was sick. I thought she was just exhausted. I'm sorry, Joy. I know you told all of us to be on the lookout for warning signs of trouble. I don't know how I missed it."

"She's got help now." Joy, who must've been Tabitha's massage instructor, rubbed Tabitha's forearm. "I'm going to start at the head of the line and go down the whole length, checking each runner. You take a break." Joy squeezed Tabitha's hand and walked swiftly to the first table in the row.

Red caught Clementine's eye. "What's going down? Did you see it?"

"Hyponatremia. By the looks of it."

"Oh, wow." Red shielded her eyes from the sun and watched as the medics made it to the medical tent. "They'll probably give her an IV right away and then get her to the hospital."

"What is hyponatremia?" Tabitha reached down and stroked

Trinity's head. The dog had silently followed them and was pressing into Tabitha's legs. "Is she dehydrated?"

"Basically the opposite," Clementine said. "She took in too much fluid. Probably didn't even know she was doing it. She probably drank at each water station, like she's been told or read somewhere. And over time she just took in too much, and her sodium got dangerously low."

Tabitha sank to the grass, rested her elbows on her knees and let her face fall into her palms. Trinity flopped down against her. Clementine exchanged a look with Red. *I got this*, Clementine mouthed.

"I'm going to go start at the opposite end of the tables as the professor and help check on all the runners," Red said. She patted Tabitha's shoulder. "This isn't your fault, Tabitha."

After Red left, Clementine sat down next to Tabitha and leaned in, just enough to brace her from the opposite side. Clementine sat in silence awhile, watching Joy and Red move quickly and professionally from one table to the next, offering suggestions and speaking to each runner before moving on. An ambulance arrived and loaded up the woman in pink shorts from the medical tent.

"Do you think that woman's going to die?" Tabitha picked nervously at the grass.

"If she does, it won't be your fault."

Tabitha flashed a horrified look.

"No, I doubt she'll die." Clementine had no idea, really. "The saline works pretty fast if they do it right."

"You know all this from running for so long?"

"From years of running. Owning a shop. Doing a lot of races. Reading about running. Other than my daughter, my life is running. You get the picture."

"This was something I should've known." Tabitha's voice

was light and a little raspy. "Sensing trouble is kind of my thing. I don't know what happened."

"You know now." Clementine glanced over and saw tears rolling down Tabitha's cheeks. "Hey." She put her hand on Tabitha's knee and shook it a little. "How can you know what you don't know? Until you know that you're supposed to know it?" She tried a smile. "This isn't like being in a combat zone. This is something entirely different. You're learning."

Tabitha sucked in her bottom lip and swiped at her tears with a knuckle. She leaned back in the grass and patted her chest. Trinity climbed on top of her, resting her paws across Tabitha's shoulder. "I suck at everything," she whispered.

Clementine lay back in the grass, too, which had warmed in the sun but was slick. They were going to be muddy when they got up, but what the hell? The first thing Clementine would do when she got home was sink into that hot bubble bath she'd been dreaming about and stay there for a long time. "You've had a rough run lately," she agreed. "But sometimes you gotta hit a few miles of hard pavement before you get back to the forest." She hoped that didn't sound trite. She didn't know Tabitha's whole story. Clementine knew about the IED that exploded in Afghanistan and took out Tabitha's convoy. She knew that the chaplain who Tabitha was protecting had been badly hurt at the time and had died a couple of years ago, which had sent Tabitha into a spiral of PTSD and panic attacks. They'd talked about these things after gym sessions, including Clementine's loss of Tyler in Afghanistan. But Clementine had always thought there was more to Tabitha's story than she let on. There was some serious stuff buried there, ghosts that had invisible, icy fingers keeping her chained to fear.

Tabitha was silent as Clementine stared at the sky, which was bright and blue and beautiful. The air was warm enough at the core to make the chilly edge bearable. It was the kind of weather that made people smile, craving thoughts of spring, even though winter hadn't even technically yet begun. The day she'd learned Tyler was never coming home again was a lot like this day. Clementine preferred the rain.

She wondered what Tabitha saw when she looked at this sky, from beneath the comfort of her dog's weight. Did she like this kind of sky, or did she crave the rain, too?

She didn't ask. She just lay there, next to her friend, and her dog, listened to all her spent muscles throb a sad song and let the world go on around them.

There are two mistakes one can make along the way to truth: not going all the way, and not starting.

~*Buddha*

This morning's quote from her Journal of Invincibility ran through Tabitha's mind on her drive home from the marathon. She'd lain in the grass for a while, eyes closed and Trinity's comforting weight across her chest, Clementine in silence by her side. She hadn't done any more massages, just lay there until she got chilled from the stillness and the damp ground, then got up, went over to her table and packed everything away. She hadn't asked for permission to leave early and she didn't care what anyone thought. She wasn't sure whether or not she'd get the extra credit, in part or in full, for showing up and putting in a solid two hours of postrace massages before the woman who needed medics made Tabitha doubt her entire existence again. And she didn't care.

She just had to get out of there.

Clementine had helped Tabitha pack up without a word, and once they'd loaded her table into the trunk of her car, her friend had smiled at her, given her a hug and said, "I won't be at the gym for a few days. Recovery." She swept an arm over her bedraggled body.

Tabitha had known that there was a lot of invisible pain going on there. Clementine's body had to be seriously beat up from running twenty-six point two miles, but the damage would be invisible to an onlooker who didn't know the story. Tabitha had felt a sort of kinship and comfort in that knowledge.

"But I'll see you there by the end of the week, probably," Clementine added. "Text me if you need to."

Tabitha had nodded, way more appreciative of the only person in her life who didn't have an *opinion* on things than she could express. She wondered if Clementine knew how much of a gift her silence was, neither forcing Tabitha to condemn nor defend herself, and leaving her room to process what had happened without judgment, good or bad.

So far, Tabitha's processing wasn't going well. That quote from this morning kept pushing its way into her thoughts, the ones telling her that massage school was not the place for her. Neither was the motorcycle shop. Neither was the gym. Neither was Auntie El's church. Problem with all that was, Tabitha was left with nowhere to go.

She knew what her therapist would say. At least about today's incident. Much like the session where Tabitha had discussed what went down the day the chaplain got hurt in Afghanistan, and her therapist had asked, "Do you really think you caused the chaplain to get hurt in the explosion, Tabitha? Just because you'd told him that morning that he'd get what was coming to him someday? Do you really think you have that much power?" Tabitha's therapist would apply that same logic to the sick runner. *Do you really think you have that much power, Tabitha? Whatever befalls her, do you really think you made that happen?*

No, she didn't. In fact, Tabitha felt powerless. She knew she didn't cause that woman's hyponatremia today, or any result of it, just like her words to the chaplain in Afghanistan hadn't caused their convoy to hit an IED. But missing the signs of a serious problem, when coupled with all the other issues she'd been having lately, was a lot to swallow. It certainly made her want to quit the process altogether—the process of everything she was bumbling through—no matter what Buddha had to say about it.

But then she'd just be a quitter.

Quitters weren't badasses.

The only thing that made her feel a little better was the memory of Hobbs, coming into Triple M with his brother a few days ago. He, too, had listened to her talk without giving his opinions. He'd inadvertently told her a little bit about himself, about the past he tried to keep hidden behind his clown act, even though he hadn't offered any details. Meeting Victor had only made Tabitha double down on that suspicion. Hobbs's brother hid away just as much as Hobbs did but in a different way, using silence instead of joy, keeping everyone out instead of inviting everyone in. Both had the same effect—the real Hobbs and the real Victor never got seen: one was walled off and the other hidden in plain sight.

Hobbs had made Tabitha feel less alone in the world that day.

She wished he hadn't gone to Omaha. She'd have liked to go to his class tomorrow at the gym, let his happy-go-lucky mood fill her up and ease her worries, even if that was selfish of her. But Tabitha wouldn't see Hobbs for a week, at least. She wouldn't see Clementine, either. That left her with Auntie El, who would have no sympathy for Tabitha missing the signs of illness, nor much for the "crazy person" who'd decided to run twenty-six point two miles and made herself sick. Auntie El would certainly have no sympathy for Tabitha's feelings about quitting everything she was sucking at. And that was if Auntie El was even awake. Her unusual new habit of napping had slowly started to replace the sight of Auntie El in the kitchen or garden.

Tabitha pulled into her spot near the house and killed the engine. She sat there a couple of minutes, gathering herself before she went inside. Maybe she'd take a nap and let her brain work on her problems while her body checked out for a while.

Just after she'd taken off her seat belt, a text message lit up her phone, resting in the console. Her phone had been on silent since this morning and she never played with it while she drove. No name appeared, just a number Tabitha didn't recognize. There was also a missed phone call from the same number. She clicked open the message.

Hi, Tabitha. It's Thaddeus. Your auntie gave me your number. It was great seeing you last weekend. I was wondering if you'd like to get coffee sometime this week? No pressure. I'm pretty busy at work but could squeeze in an hour somewhere, if you let me know when. Take care!

Coffee? Why the heck would Thaddeus want to have coffee, or anything else, with her? She hadn't exactly made the best impression last Sunday, stuffing her face full of food and unfolding her anxiety for all to see. Just the thought of meeting Thaddeus in some café and having to pretend she was as slick and accomplished as he was over cups of cappuccino with designer hearts in the foam made her want to scream.

Tabitha and Trinity went inside and found Auntie El standing over the kitchen sink, eyes closed, breathing in and out, slow and deep. She was still wearing her housecoat and slippers, despite the fact that it was the afternoon.

"You okay, Auntie?" Tabitha rested her hand on Auntie El's shoulder.

She flinched. Her eyes flew open. "I didn't hear you come in." Auntie El's forehead and upper lip were sweaty, like she'd been working out. "I was getting ready to put out the fall decorations." She pointed to the dining table in the next room, where a couple of autumn wreaths, floral arrangement pieces and vases lay.

"I'll take care of that," Tabitha said. "You don't look well. Maybe you should go to the doctor and get a physical. You've been sleeping a lot lately. And not eating well."

Auntie El cleared her throat and blinked rapidly. "I'm fine. I used to be a nurse, didn't I? I would know." Auntie El brushed past her and collected a wreath from the table. It was made up of red, yellow and orange fake flowers inside a wicker circle. "I just haven't been sleeping well at night, so then I get tired during the day. And it couldn't hurt if I lost a few pounds." She rubbed her thick middle. "Are you home early?" Auntie El glanced at the clock over the dining room table.

"No," Tabitha lied. "We finished."

Auntie El nodded. "I'm putting these up, then I'll be making some arrangements for the vases." She nodded at the pile on the table.

"If you're sure you're okay." Tabitha hesitated, waiting. Auntie El had always been strong as an ox. Even when she got sick, it never lasted. After some Vicks VapoRub and a couple of Tylenol she was always back on her feet within a couple of days.

"I'm fine." Auntie El waved her away. "You go shower. You look filthy."

Tabitha watched her walk to the front door, to hang the wreath. Auntie El's steps were slow and calculated. Tabitha closed her eyes. She could sense Auntie El's discomfort, with even the smallest movements. Something was definitely off. But if Auntie El wasn't going to share, there was nothing

Tabitha could do to drag it out of her. She sighed and clicked open a new text message, but not to reply to Thaddeus.

Instead, she wrote to Clementine. If Tabitha wanted to be strong, she needed to do something to salvage this day.

Hey. Still need that massage you never got?

nine

Hobbs had never wanted to leave a motel less in his life. He had a room with a double bed, flat pillows that hurt his neck, a sandpaper comforter, an old television stuck on three local channels and a view of the parking lot. But he'd stay here all day if it meant not having to go visit his father. He woke early and did twenty minutes of squats, push-ups and sit-ups—giving up the idea of pull-ups on the bar in the closet at the last second, certain it would snap in half—and was sweaty from head to toe by the time he realized there was no coffeepot in his room.

When Victor knocked on the door, Hobbs was a grumpy mess. He was also shirtless, in nothing but gym shorts.

"You going like that?"

Victor had on jeans and cowboy boots, so wasn't in much of a position to judge, but Hobbs bit back a sarcastic retort when he saw the two coffee cups in his brother's hands. "Just give me ten minutes."

Victor handed over one of the cups, then sat down on the edge of the bed and stared at the news running on the television.

Hobbs took a quick shower, then faced himself in the steamy mirror. His eyes were bloodshot, because he'd spent half the night thinking about what it was going to be like seeing his father after twenty years and the other half tossing and turning in sheets rougher than canvas. He suddenly had a vision of Tabitha at the gym, revealing her birthday wish and vowing to make a Badass List. Hobbs decided he might actually need a list of his own to get this done.

"You can do this," he told himself. "You have to do this." He'd come all this way. He'd promised Hannah, though not in words. His coming out here, and her knowing about it, counted as a promise, even though he'd rejected her offer to stay at the house like he usually did on the holidays. He didn't want to stay with Mom and listen to her make excuses for his father, as she'd been making excuses for Pops's behavior her entire marriage. Hobbs wasn't down for one single excuse this visit. Not one.

Maybe Victor wasn't, either. By the time Hobbs made it out of the bathroom, Victor had set his coffee down on the end table and leaned back on the bed, eyes closed. He looked huge sprawled there, as big as Pops used to look, in Hobbs's memory. Victor didn't look much like Pops, feature-wise. He had Mom's high cheekbones and thick lips, something Hobbs might not even think about if it weren't for the fact that Pops's thin mouth, pressed into a hard line, was always a clear signal Hobbs better run if he didn't want to feel the business end of a belt, a fist or whatever might be within reach. Victor had Pops's curly blond hair, same as Hobbs, but that didn't register much because Pops had kept his in a buzz cut most of his life.

The size, though. Hobbs remembered Pops being big. So

much bigger than he was, anyway. Bigger than everything. Bigger than life. Bigger than hope.

Victor opened up one eye and sighed. "Ready, princess?"

"I guess."

They drove in silence. Victor, sick of his Triumph after more than two thousand miles in less than a week, had showed up at the motel in his pickup so he and Hobbs could ride together to the hospital. It smelled like mulch and fertilizer. Country music hummed on the radio.

"Is there any chance he died overnight and this will be a quick visit?"

Victor's eyes didn't shift from the road. "That the attitude you're going in with?"

"Seems so."

Victor's jaw flexed but he went quiet. Hobbs settled into his seat and tuned out the music. He suddenly became aware of everything that was the same now as it was in his childhood, even though he never noticed those things when he visited over the holidays. The flatness of the landscape, covered in golden terraces of cornfields. A sky that seemed to go on forever, like the ocean. The smell of manure over the same stretches of highway his school buses used to roll down. Hobbs got so wrapped up in this odd time travel that he barely noticed when they pulled into the driveway of the house he grew up in. The place Victor had left long before he'd actually moved out, often living with friends for weeks or months at a time. The house Mom and Hannah had shared ever since.

"What are we doing here?"

"I lied about the hospital." Victor's voice was flat as he put the truck in Park at the curb. "Well, he *was* at the hospital. When he first got out. But that got too expensive and he's come here to die. I figured you wouldn't come if you knew."

Hobbs took a moment to process that. Pops was right there,

inside their childhood home. Right there, somewhere, inside the prairie-style home, with its geometric, straight lines and big picture windows. Hobbs had got to the point where he could come home for holidays and stay in the house because he'd reclassified it in his brain into an entirely new dwelling, one that Mom and Hannah had made their own over the years, finishing the projects Pops had never finished and eradicating the house of everything that was his. They'd put up the flower boxes that he hated and seeded the lawn he'd never mow. They shared an old Chevy four-door to carpool to the hair salon where Hannah worked and the Stop 'n Shop where Mom had become manager.

The house suddenly looked different, now that Hobbs knew Pops was inside. It looked different because it suddenly looked the same, much like the cornfields and the highways that smelled of manure. All the mental changes Hobbs had managed to make over the years had come unraveled. Seeing Pops in a hospital was one thing—that would be neutral ground. Seeing Pops inside this house was giving the old man home-field advantage. Hobbs was fifteen years old again, his gut was churning, and he did not want to see that man, alive or dead. He broke into a fresh sweat.

"Coming?" Victor had stepped out, slammed the door and was now leaning inside the lowered driver's-side window. The Nebraska air was much colder and drier than Virginia, and Hobbs could feel it in his bones. He was now sweating profusely overtop of cold bones, which gave the illusion of being sick.

Despite that, Hobbs got out of the truck. His feet felt like lead as he followed Victor up the driveway. The water in the birdbaths that flanked either side of the stairs had a thin sheen of ice on top and the welcome mat was muddy and smashed. They stepped inside the living room, which had the same worn beige carpet that had been shampooed over and over for years but never changed. Hobbs had a fleeting thought on how much dirt and blood and dust must be ground into the fibers from all the years. Right this second, Hobbs was walking on dirt from his shoes from twenty years ago. Worse, he was probably walking on top of his own blood, shed at the hands of the man who was now dying inside.

Hobbs stopped short, the door barely shut behind him. He'd expected to have more time to brace himself, but apparently, Pops's sickbed had been set up on the pull-out sofa, because that was where the old man lay, right there in the living room, facing the picture window that overlooked the front yard. Hobbs's first thought was that he was glad Mom hadn't let the old man back into her bedroom, for any reason, after all this time.

His second thought was *Who is that guy?*

If he squinted, Hobbs could see it. The thin, mean lips and the swollen nose with broken capillaries. He had the same buzz cut, but his hair was now snow-white. But Pops was small. A much smaller man than Hobbs remembered. His chest was sunken beneath the open neck of a hospital gown, a patch of wild white hair growing there like a bird's nest. The one exposed hand, at rest near the patch, was lumpy and arthritic.

Hobbs walked right over and stood over his dying father, without even looking for Mom and Hannah, whom he hadn't seen in almost a year. Pops's eyes were closed, his breathing coming in short, ragged gasps. "You look like hell. You sound like hell," Hobbs said, the sweat beneath his armpits drying and his throat loosening as he spoke. "You aren't so big now, are you?" He hadn't meant to say that out loud. He wondered now if Pops had ever been as big as he seemed. Had he ever been as big as Victor, or was that just the illusion of a scared, small fifteen-year-old's mind? "I'd like to see you try to hit me now. But you can't even raise a hand, can you?" It was like he couldn't stop himself.

Pops's eyelids, shot with broken capillaries, fluttered open. Hobbs kept himself from flinching, from moving. Hell, he even kept himself from breathing. He waited. Would Pops recognize his youngest son? Victor had said he was suffering severe dementia, though people with memory loss typically retained many of their oldest memories. Victor had also said that Pops's dementia was so severe he was forgetting how to swallow, so maybe he didn't remember anyone at all. In a hospital, he'd probably be hooked up to all sorts of crap to keep him going, but here in the living room, in the very spot he used to sit and stare at TV, his feet surrounded by a shameless array of empty beer and liquor bottles, there was nothing to help him. He was alive on sheer will at this point.

"Do you feel helpless and scared?" Hobbs said, once Pops's eyes were clearly locked in his. "Lying there like that? Sick and dying?" At sixty-five years old, Pops looked ancient, an object of his own self-destruction. Hobbs leaned in a little closer, searching the old man's eyes. He smelled like rot, but Hobbs stayed put. He wanted to see it, if it was still there. That glimmer in Pops's eye. The one he'd get just before he struck: a glimmer of sentience.

Hobbs probably couldn't describe it well if someone asked, but it was a moment when, based on gut instinct alone, Hobbs *knew* that Pops knew what he was doing. He might be drunk, as people liked to say, because it made them feel better to give Pops an excuse. People liked excuses for cruelty because then they felt better, safer, more in control. Cruelty was more explainable if liquor was involved, if liquor was the *reason*.

People wanted a reason.

Hobbs knew the truth, even if nobody else did, because Hobbs was the one Pops liked to come after the most. Victor got too big, stayed too quiet, wasn't enough fun. Pops had never laid a hand on Hannah because apparently hitting girls under the age of twenty was outside his accepted form of sadism. But Hobbs—nothing but a skinny kid waiting for a face full of sand—was not only fair game, he was the favorite game.

Hobbs wasn't that weak kid anymore. Despite having grown a little taller, a lot buffer, served in the USMC and done a tour in Iraq, Hobbs hadn't really been sure of that fact until right this moment. He didn't want to hide. Didn't want to run away. He wanted the old man to get healthy, stand up and try to come after him now. Hobbs wanted to win a fair fight. Clearly, that wasn't going to happen. Hobbs wasn't going to get the fist today, so he wanted the look. *At least give me that, old man. Give me that.* Hobbs leaned in so close he could feel Pops's breath on his face. He waited as the look in the old man's blue eyes, paler with age, changed. Cleared.

Yes. Hobbs saw it now. The look. The sentience.

The old man saw him. He *saw* him.

And right after Pops saw him, he said it. The same words he'd said twenty years ago.

"Christopher." His voice was rough, like the turn of a rusty, outdoor faucet. "You don't want to shoot your old man, do you?"

Hobbs's eyes narrowed. His fingers twitched, like he still held the rifle. In his mind, he heard the ghost of fireworks, exploding in the sky. The dark night split with a fountain of reds, greens, blues and golds. "Bang," Hobbs whispered.

Pops's eyes grew bigger. "Christo…" His voice garbled over Hobbs's name until it morphed into a gurgling sound, like a partial choke.

"What's the matter, old man?" Hobbs waited, ready. Ready for the old man to apologize (that would never happen), tell him to go to hell (very likely) or gurgle his way back to a semiconscious demented state (most probable). Hobbs was ready for anything.

Except for what came next.

Pops gave a great gasp, tipped his head back deeper into the pillow, then went completely still.

Like he'd been waiting for Hobbs to come home just so he could die.

ten

Clementine's pen moved over the page of a black-and-white composition book while Tabitha applied pressure along the soles of her feet. She wrote with the fluid, determined strokes of someone who'd done a lot of writing by hand. She paused and peeked over the top of the journal. "That's perfect, what you're doing right there. Give more pressure than you think. You aren't going to hurt me. And trust me, my feet are sore."

"No erection, then?" Tabitha couldn't resist a joke at her own expense. Her mood had lightened considerably since coming here. Unlike her house, where Auntie El kept the wood polished and the heat low, Clementine's floors were scattered with bright rugs, her gas fireplace crackled with warmth and there were piles of books everywhere. It was a lived-in home that invited comfort.

Clementine scratched away with her pen for a second. "One can always hope," she said with a grin.

Tabitha smiled back and squeezed a little more lavender foot lotion into her palm. Just a little. Joy was always warning the students about not using too much lotion. The result would be a slick mess that gained no traction and made it more difficult to get deep into the muscles. Despite all her running, Clementine didn't have rough feet. She had tiny, smooth feet with nails painted to match her fingers, which right now were bright pink. The only places she had calluses were on the outer edges of her big toes and around the edges of her heels. Tabitha focused her attention there with the extra squeeze of lotion.

"Thanks for coming over to give me the massage I missed." Clementine set her notebook down on the coffee table next to her. She was stretched out on her back on the sofa, her feet propped on pillows in Tabitha's lap. "It wasn't necessary but it sure is nice. I can't remember the last time I had a foot rub."

Tabitha didn't admit she'd come over as much, or more, for herself as she had for Clementine. Despite not being able to stay one more second at the race, she also hadn't wanted to hang around the house and watch Auntie El fumble through her fatigue and odd brain fog, either. "I keep a journal, too," she said, while she pressed her thumbs down to the center of Clementine's foot. "It's called a Journal of Invincibility. My therapist recommended it." She gave a wry smile. "I don't think it's working."

Clementine glanced at the book on the table and shook her head. "I write to my dead husband in that."

She said it so bluntly Tabitha suppressed an inappropriate chuckle. "That's sweet."

"Is it? He's been gone for eight years. I got three more of those, full, upstairs." Clementine pointed at the ceiling. "I wonder what your therapist would make of that."

"Eight years is a long time," Tabitha admitted. "Have you ever dated?"

"It's never been a priority. Lily's always been the priority, and bringing strange men around just wasn't something I wanted to do."

"Does Lily remember much about him?"

"She has very specific memories," Clementine said as Tabitha pressed her thumbs up the "lines" of the foot. "Tyler was gone a lot. Served two tours in Afghanistan while she was young and a lot of TDYs in between. A lot of Lily's memories are of Ty coming and going. But—" Clementine shrugged "—she's got some happy ones from when he was around."

"That's good."

"You know what's good?" Clementine's voice brightened, and Tabitha knew a topic change was imminent. "Your foot massage. I don't know what you're worried about, girl. You've got some talent."

"You think so?"

"I mean it. This is a good foot massage."

"Thanks." Tabitha's mood felt a little bolstered. "Joy taught us a Thai foot massage routine early in school. She wanted us to have something in our bag of tricks that we could do with confidence, so that we'd be ready for all the other body parts."

"None of us pay enough attention to our feet. We're on them all day, but we never give them any love."

Just as Tabitha finished with the last toe, Trinity rose, walked over to the dog bed by the fireplace and sat facing it, ears perked.

"The monsters must be stirring." Clementine swung her legs around to face the brood as soon as Tabitha released her foot. There was a cat-and-dog pair named George and Gracie, both sacked out on the animal bed in front of the fireplace. They were an inseparable pair, according to Clementine. Since Tabitha had been here they'd been asleep, curled together in what looked like a golden ball of fur.

Now that they were waking up, unwinding from each other, Tabitha saw that indeed there was a hairless cat in the mix. George had been balled up against the puppy's abdomen like a snake coiled in a basket. He sat up, wobbly with sleep. His pink skin, yellow eyes and huge ears made him look like a grumpy alien. To top it off, he wore an orange sweater with a smiling jack-o'-lantern on it.

Trinity was fascinated. Her tail whapped against the carpet as she watched them, otherwise not moving a muscle. George hissed at her. Trinity cocked her head to the side. Gracie, who had clown shoes for paws, clambered to her feet and leaned back into a stretch, straightening her front legs. George circled around Gracie, like she was a maypole, paused to glare at Trinity, then circled her again.

"You see why nobody wants to adopt them." Clementine slid her feet into a pair of ratty pink slippers and rose. "C'mon, Gracie. Let's go outside."

Gracie bounced with excitement and raced to the back door. The cat followed.

"Wow, they've made themselves at home." Tabitha grabbed her coat from the arm of the sofa and slid her arms inside. Clementine was already pulling open the sliding glass door that led to a fenced-in yard. Gracie bolted out and George scurried after her.

"Yeah, they're home for now. Until someone takes them." Clementine had on a gray sweatshirt with white paint stains down the front. She crossed her arms over her chest against the cold air that blew in the open door.

"Nobody's shown any interest at all? I mean, yeah, they're odd. But that's part of their charm." Tabitha smiled as she watched the cat follow the puppy all over the yard. When Gracie squatted to do her business, George politely turned his back to her, sat in the grass and waited.

"Not at the shelter. Lily hasn't had anyone by yet. She was focused on finally getting Roscoe into his forever home this week. But hey. You know who met them?" Clementine's eyes widened. "Hobbs. Lily said she ran into him at the gym on Halloween and he insisted on seeing what they looked like. She said he had a funny reaction to Gracie. That she reminded him of a dog he had when he was a kid. I don't know." Clementine shrugged. "Lily has good instincts for stuff like that."

Tabitha smiled. "I'm having a hard time picturing Hobbs with a pet." Well. She had a hard time picturing the Hobbs who showed up at the gym with a pet. The Hobbs who'd kissed her behind the gym and the Hobbs who had visited the motorcycle shop—that Hobbs she could 100 percent picture with a sweet, goofy golden dog like Gracie.

"I know, right? I can't imagine him with any kind of baby, furry or otherwise. He seems like he'd have a hard enough time taking care of himself."

"Well, I don't know about that." Tabitha spoke too quickly. "I mean, I think he puts on a good cover. I think there's more there than meets the eye."

"Oh, really?" Clementine clapped her hands together and Gracie came barreling inside. She waggled all around Clementine's legs, then did the same to Tabitha's. George strutted in last, sat nearby and waited for the raucous behavior to settle. Trinity, who'd taken over their spot on the dog bed by the fire, watched like a patient nana. Clementine glanced up from a wave of blond hair that had fallen over her eye as she bent to pet the puppy. "You like him, don't you? Just a little?"

Tabitha, who'd leaned over to try to pet George, rose back up as he flinched away from her. "He's cute in a grumpy way. I'm sure he'd grow on you. And probably ease up on his attachment to Gracie after he was in a secure environment."

"I meant Hobbs."

Tabitha's coat suddenly felt too warm. "Oh, sure. I mean, he's a little too rowdy for my tastes, but…" Tabitha trailed off into a shrug. "I got to know him a little better before he went out of town last week. He came into the bike shop on his way out. He's got an older brother who's like…" Tabitha stood on her tiptoes and reached a hand high over her head. "He's as reserved as Hobbs is rowdy. You'd never know they were related but for the hair." Tabitha twirled a lock of her own. "But I got the gist there's a lot going on there—with Hobbs's family and his past."

"Oh, I see." Clementine straightened up and pushed the sliding door closed. "You like him more than I thought."

"No, I don't."

"Hmm. Okay."

Gracie ran over to the pet bed and got into down dog in front of Trinity, her butt in the air as she leaned into her front paws. She gave a playful woof. George circled around behind her and settled by her left side.

"I kissed him," Tabitha admitted. Something about Trinity, her calmness in the face of the puppy's boisterous moves, gave Tabitha courage. "Well, he kissed me. On my birthday. It didn't mean anything, though. It was just a birthday moment."

Clementine kept her face straight. It was probably a mom thing she'd learned over the years—how to not react. Tabitha figured moms had to learn how to read the room really well in order to be good at their jobs. "Was it good?"

Tabitha wasn't expecting that question. "I haven't kissed a lot of guys. There's Thaddeus, my high school boyfriend, who I saw the other day, actually. He wants to have coffee. He always kissed the same way." Almost like a routine, Tabitha didn't add as the thought struck her. Lots of tongue shoved in her mouth with little buildup. Too much spit. "And then there are a couple of guys when I was in the navy." She didn't add what their kisses were like because she didn't remember enough about them to care.

"Which doesn't answer my question."

Gracie had a ratty stuffed mallard that she was shaking in front of Trinity, trying to get her to play. "Trinity, break," Tabitha said, glad for the interruption. Trinity grabbed the other end of the mallard and shook it back and forth, just hard enough to give Gracie a challenge but not enough to steal the toy. Gracie growled good-naturedly. George reached up one long, pink leg and batted at the mallard, hooking it with his nails and pulling it in a third direction, which made the toy's neck bend.

"Typically, guys like Hobbs, who put up a lot of talk, don't have so much walk." Clementine shrugged. "So I was just curious if..."

"Kissing him was like finding another person buried inside. I still knew it was Hobbs, but I completely forgot what he typically acts like while I was kissing him. In fact, I couldn't think at all." Tabitha had never been kissed like that. With such care and sweetness. Tabitha had felt like she was something special, something worth savoring.

"Oh, wow. He made you forget how to think?" Clementine smiled so big she got a couple of laugh lines around her eyes. "That good, huh?" She tucked in her bottom lip, thoughtful. "Interesting."

"I should get going." Tabitha's cheeks were hot, not because she'd told Clementine about the kiss but because she was now reliving it in her mind, which made her feel like she was naked in front of her friend. "Come, Trinity."

Trinity released the mallard and Gracie fell backward on her butt.

"So this Thaddeus." Clementine followed behind as they headed for the front door. She seemed to have picked up on the fact that Tabitha needed to stop talking about kissing Hobbs. "What's he like? Are you going to have coffee with him?"

Tabitha slipped the foot lotion into her coat pocket. "Thaddeus was a geeky jock in high school. Really smart but also on the track team. He had brains and brawn. We dated for a year. Then he went to school and I enlisted in the navy. I hadn't seen him in years. He came over to Auntie's brunch last weekend, which I know she planned. He's a lawyer now."

"Wow. Sounds perfect for you."

Tabitha shrugged. Clementine was right. He did sound perfect for her.

Clementine studied her face in silence for a moment. "It's just coffee," she finally said. There went that mom magic again.

"Good point."

"Thanks for coming. My feet are very appreciative. Once Lily's home from dinner with her friends, I'm hitting the sack."

"Great idea."

The sound of something plastic hitting the floor rang out from the kitchen. It sounded suspiciously like a dog bowl.

"That's Gracie, asking for dinner. I better go feed the weirdos."

"Night, Clementine."

"Night."

Once she and Trinity were loaded up in the car, Tabitha leaned into her seat and sighed deeply. She was exhausted, but relaxed. She could feel the day deep in her bones and in all of her senses. She could feel every person she'd touched, smell the scents of the woods and open sky in the back of her throat, hear the sounds of the crowd and taste the acridity of witnessing that woman pass out on her table. Surrounding all that, like a membrane, was the itchy, all-over vibe that something was wrong with Auntie El.

But Tabitha also felt the warmth of a good friend and the memory of Hobbs's kiss, now that she'd actually discussed it with someone. It had been a really good kiss. Though she probably wasn't being fair to her memory of Thaddeus. Their relationship had been a long time ago and Thaddeus had been a kid then. Tabitha remembered Clementine's words—*it's just coffee*—and also the sadness in her voice when she talked about her lonely eight years without her husband.

Tabitha opened up her phone and faced the text message she'd never replied to. She took a deep breath and tapped out a reply.

Sure. Coffee sounds great. How about Friday?

eleven

"Chris? Did you kill him?"

It was the first time Hobbs had laid eyes on his little sister since last Christmas. At first, he didn't know what to say, even though she was the same old Hannah: small, feminine, wearing a flowy shirt with bright pink flowers, her honey-colored hair pulled back with a barrette, her voice gentle.

Victor stood behind her, towering over their baby sister, leaning in the entryway. He seemed far less concerned than Hannah that Pops might've just died.

"Is he dead?" Hannah stepped into the room and cautiously approached the sofa bed, as if Pops might shoot straight up like Nosferatu.

"Um." Hobbs didn't have words. For any of it. Had his father just died? He definitely looked dead. Hobbs didn't know whether to feel vindicated or cheated.

Hannah held Pops's wrist in her hand. Her fingers were pale and smooth against his ruddy, wrinkled, hairy skin. "He really is dead." She turned to her brothers, fingertips covering her mouth, chin dropped. "Did he say anything?"

Hobbs cleared his throat. "No. He just…gasped." He wasn't about to tell Hannah Pops's last words. No point in making her relive the past, too.

"That's it?" Hannah turned back to Pops and stared down at him. "That's it?" she repeated, her voice softer.

Hobbs couldn't agree more. If the son of a bitch really had up and died, Hobbs had a thing or two to say about that. He'd wanted more, he realized, now that he was here and had looked the old man in the eyes. He'd been secretly hoping that Pops wasn't that far gone, would remember everything and would have the chance to either show some remorse or prove what a horrible human being he was by not being sorry at all. *Something*, Hobbs thought. *You don't get to just up and die.*

"He's gone?"

Everyone spun toward Mom's voice, coming from the entry-way. She stood inside the door, her words punctuated by a gust of cold wind that swept in after her. She wore a pair of black slacks and a white blouse with a navy windbreaker over top. Her name tag, peeking out of the open jacket, was pinned above the pocket of her shirt: *Stop 'n Shop. Tanya. Manager.* She had a plastic sack in each hand, her fingers looped through the handles. Poking out the tops were a bag of chips, the leafy end of a bunch of celery and a cellophane baggie full of bakery rolls.

Victor strode over to the bedside and checked Pops's neck with his fingertips, then held his hand about an inch over Pops's mouth. "Yep," he finally reported. "He's gone." There was about as much emotion in Victor's voice as though he were reporting on the weather.

Mom stood there, frozen, the wind rolling inside like a welcome, cleansing gust that gave Hobbs a shiver. She finally pushed the door closed with her foot, but it was with slow reluctance. "Well, that's it, then." She leaned against it with her backside and set the bags on the floor.

Only Hannah looked sad. The corners of her mouth turned down and she worried her hands together.

Hobbs at least had the consolation prize that Pops's last words had been for him. Whether Pops was remembering their last moment together with eerie detail or was reliving it didn't really matter. Either way, that moment had stuck with the old man as much as it had Hobbs. Good. Now he could take that shit straight to hell.

Hannah's hands fluttered to her cheeks. She glanced over at Pops's lifeless form. "Oh, wow." She sank down on the edge of the sofa bed, next to him. "He's gone."

Victor went to Mom, collected the bags from the floor and gestured at Hobbs with a tilt of his head toward the kitchen.

"Hey, Mom." Hobbs opened his arms and headed her way.

She looked over, her eyes big, her gray-streaked hair curving near her chin in a smart new cut Hobbs had never seen so short. She shook herself, like breaking a spell, and closed the distance between them. "Welcome home, Chris," she said. "I'm so glad you're here." Hobbs knew Victor was waiting for him in the kitchen, but Mom's embrace was like a vise. "I'm so glad you're here," she repeated.

"Me, too." He wasn't. And he kind of resented that his mother clearly needed him right now, when she'd never been there for him. But that was no way to be. The past was the past, and one big chapter of it was finally over. Once Hobbs was able to step back, he assessed Mom's expression. He knew how to check his mother's face and read exactly how she felt. Right now, she was lost. Relieved, yeah. But maybe not as happy as she thought she might be in this moment.

"How long are you staying?"

"I only came because Victor drove his stupid bike a thousand miles to get me. And now the old man went and died, so this was all kind of fruitless." Even as he spoke, Hobbs thought about that look in Pops's eyes. Then those words. *Christopher. You don't want to shoot your old man, do you?*

"Go talk to your brother." Mom nodded toward the kitchen. "I'll go sit with Hannah. Figure out who to call."

Hobbs watched her walk over and settle on Hannah's other side, both of them now sitting on the sofa bed next to the dead man Hobbs hadn't seen in twenty years and had never wanted to see again. He felt a mixture of unpleasant emotions roll around in his gut—resentment, sadness, envy. He left them there and found Victor in the kitchen, leaning against the counter, drinking a glass of water. The green-and-white linoleum was caving in the center and the oak cupboard doors needed replacing, the edges worn and some of the hinges loose. The grocery sacks Mom had been carrying sat on the gray countertops, stained, with permanent knife marks from years of use.

"How'd that happen?" Hobbs tilted his head toward the living room. "I know you said he was dying, but..."

"If looks could kill, little brother. Guess yours did."

"Funny."

"You don't see me laughing."

"All this way." Hobbs wanted to kick something. "For nothing."

"You're here for a bigger reason, actually."

Hobbs wasn't sure he wanted to know what that meant, so he started to unload the grocery sacks. He spied a six-pack of chocolate pudding cups, the kind of stuff Mom used to buy when they were kids, and realized he was starving. She always did that when he and Victor came for the holidays, bought pudding and Twinkies and potato chips, all the junk food they medicated themselves with as children. They ate it, too, even though it tasted cheap and no longer fit their lifestyles. Craving food made no sense right now, but Hobbs didn't care. He dug out a spoon, the one with flowers down the middle that Hannah had insisted on using for every meal when she was a little girl, and ripped the top off one of the puddings.

"Hannah started seeing this guy not long after Christmas last year," Victor said, when he recognized Hobbs had chosen to eat instead of respond. "Right after you left. She met him at work, gave him a haircut. James Timbley." Victor dragged his voice over the guy's name. "She was head over heels for this fool. He acted real good, I'll give him that. Came off real smooth and romantic. Did things Hannah wasn't used to, like buy her flowers and take her nice places. But I knew something was off the moment I met him. He was too attentive. Too much in her space. Too much *too much*. You know?"

"I'm getting the idea." Hobbs ate the pudding cup in two bites and still felt hungry, though his stomach was starting to harden like a fist at Victor's words.

"Even Mom didn't like him. She thought he was too much of a kiss ass, all fake. But this was the first guy Hannah was serious about since Ryan, so we tried not to get in her face with our opinions. The longer she dated this guy, the more controlling he got. Hannah started missing stuff she'd never miss, like Mom's birthday dinner. She got real quiet, didn't smile much anymore. She had plans to move in with him. Then one morning she shows up with bruises, a black eye and a split lip."

Hobbs had been sucking the rest of the pudding off his spoon. He dragged the utensil slowly from his mouth. This explained a lot of things, namely the mystery of why Hannah had gone radio silent on him. "And this guy, this James Timbley, is still alive?" He glanced briefly at Victor's scarred fists. He had pale, silver skin on his knuckles and knotted ridges that ran up his wrists and forearms. Old wounds that had healed reluctantly.

"Trust me. I went over there. James and I had a…conversation." Victor leveled his gaze into Hobbs's. Hobbs had seen that look in his brother's eyes only a few times before. That look, in the past, had been reserved for Pops. "Hannah freaked out and put a stop to my *conversation* with James, but she listened to me and quit seeing him after that. We went to the police and there was a whole mess of 'he said, she said,' because apparently she hit him, too, even though it was in self-defense. Plus, she waited to go to the police, so there was that. But we eventually got a restraining order."

Hobbs shook his head. "How? Just how does someone who grew up with an abusive father end up with a guy who hits her?" He shook his head again. "Don't answer that."

"Haven't seen hide nor hair of him for a month, but we all want it to stay that way."

"Smart," Hobbs agreed. "But you're playing Russian roulette. You know what abusers are like. He's not going to stay away just because there's a restraining order or because you can kick his ass. He'll find a way. He'll find a way to hurt her." Hobbs's words rushed out as he crushed the plastic pudding container in his fist. The sharp edges cut into his palm and the chocolate was sticky. "Dammit, Hannah." He lowered his voice now, too. "She's so trusting. So sweet by nature. You should have told me about this sooner."

"I'm telling you now. This is when I need you." Victor pushed off the counter and started putting the stuff that Hobbs had unloaded into the fridge.

"I'll gladly kill the guy." Hobbs deposited his broken cup into the trash and flipped on the faucet to wash his hands. "But you already tried that."

"I don't want you to go anywhere near James Timbley."

Hobbs turned off the water and snagged the dish towel Mom had hanging on the door under the sink. It was covered in bluebirds. "What do you want me to do, then?"

Victor closed the fridge, then balled up the plastic bags. "Well, I sure as hell didn't ask you out here to see that old fool die." Victor tilted his head toward the living room. In the silence, Hobbs could hear Mom on the phone, telling whomever was on the other end of the line that her husband had passed away.

"You want me to talk to Hannah? She listens to me more than you. I'll make sure she stays away from that guy. She'll need to switch jobs. She knows that, right? She can't go to familiar places."

"I agree. Which is why I want you to take her back to Virginia."

"You want me to what?" It felt like it came out of nowhere, when, really, Hobbs should've seen that coming.

"She's not safe here." Victor turned to face him. "There have already been signs he's sniffing around. Hannah's pretty sure she's seen him following her in more than one place. You need to take her home, Chris. At least for the holidays. Maybe longer. Long enough to let Timbley know Hannah is out of his reach. You need to get her out of here."

"Well, shit," Hobbs said. "Why didn't you just bring her out when you came?"

"She wouldn't go. Only you can convince her. You know that."

Yeah, he knew. So now Hobbs had traveled a thousand miles to watch his father die in a really eerie way and to learn that his baby sister was being stalked by an abusive ex.

Welcome home.

twelve

A full week had come and gone without Hobbs's return to the gym. Tabitha hoped he was okay, despite the fact that her intuition was telling her otherwise. She settled at the kitchen table alone on Sunday morning and realized she hadn't started her Badass List. She briefly wondered if it was worth it. Surely Hobbs had better things to worry over and wouldn't give this list they'd discussed a second thought. By the time he returned from Omaha, he would've forgotten all about it.

Still, Tabitha opened her Journal of Invincibility to the back, where there were a lot of clean, blank pages, and wrote the title out in bold block letters: THE BADASS LIST.

Then, while sipping a cup of coffee, she gave it a go.

Don't act like a freak when you have coffee with Thaddeus on Friday.
Learn about motorcycles.
Possibly ride one.

Ace massage quizzes.
Excel at massage.
Run a race with Clementine???

Tabitha stared at the list and wondered how she could achieve any of this. She could study up on motorcycles during her downtime at the shop, and probably even get Delaney to take her on a ride sometime soon. She could double down on her study time for massage, too. As far as running with Clementine, Tabitha wasn't sure that was even a goal, but if she actually went through with her coffee date with Thaddeus this week, she could get running tips from him, which would also serve to make him feel big and important. The less they focused on her, the better.

As far as becoming better at massage itself, Tabitha was trying hard to push memories of her post-marathon-massage fail from her mind. She hoped the woman who had been carried off on a stretcher had recovered. Tabitha was pinning her hopes on the text she'd received from Red this morning, suggesting Tabitha come out next Saturday to Pittie Place. Red needed her help with something that would benefit her work in massage school.

Of course Tabitha had agreed.

But now she sat, alone with her thoughts, glancing back and forth between her list and Auntie El's crossword puzzle. Auntie had filled in about a third of it, but was nowhere in sight. The kitchen was quiet and the coffee tepid. She must've been up with the dawn, then returned to bed.

Or, a voice in Tabitha's head suggested, *she never went to sleep and only just crashed recently*. Tabitha's eyes closed and that worried feeling gnawed at her gut again. Something was definitely wrong. Auntie El was a notorious early bird. An emergency room nurse in her early days, she'd switched to becoming a foster mother. There were always other kids around the house, ranging in age from toddlers to teens. Auntie El was a solid, safe haven who ran her household with rules, boundaries and a lot of love. At Auntie El's house, you couldn't get away with anything, but you always knew someone had your back. Her energy seemed limitless in those days, and only as she grew older and retired did she slow down even a little. Sleeping in the middle of the day and limping around the house was not Auntie El.

Tabitha wondered, as she often did, where she would be without Auntie. Would anyone else have adopted her? She knew full well that Auntie El was one of the rare good ones in this world and that, though she'd been abandoned at a church, Tabitha was one of the lucky ones. Here she'd been so caught up in her own life and her own problems for so long she hadn't even noticed what was going on with the woman who'd raised her.

She lifted Auntie's crossword pen from atop the paper and added another task to her Badass List. This one went at the top, above all the others.

Help Auntie El.

Hobbs took more time getting home than he had getting to Omaha. He let Hannah's moods dictate how much he drove in one spell and texted Rhett when he realized he'd need more coverage for his clients and classes than he'd planned. By the time they made it to Virginia, it was late Thursday night, he'd been gone a week and a half and Hannah was exhausted.

She stood inside the entryway to his rambler and froze there, arms limp at her sides while Hobbs brought in her suitcases. "Hey." He put a hand on her shoulder as he pushed the door closed. "You all right?"

"Yeah."

It was a throwaway answer. It meant nothing. It had been a throwaway question, too. Hannah had been far more compliant than Hobbs had expected about giving up the only life she'd ever known to come out here, even if she had been told it was only temporary. But then again, Hannah had always done anything Hobbs told her to do. Victor, twelve years older than Hannah—as opposed to Hobbs's nine—hadn't been as involved in her upbringing, and Pops, who'd been out of her life since she was young, seemed to have been viewed as some kind of uncle or grandfather, misunderstood and feared. Other than her initial reaction of shock, Hannah hadn't seemed to grieve Pops's death any more than either of her brothers.

"Come home with me for the holidays. We'll figure things out after that," Hobbs had told her. It was just after Pops's body had been collected and the living room scoured by Mom, wielding bleach and a bucket and a huge sponge the likes you'd use to wash a car. There was no memorial service or funeral planned. Mom had donated his body to science. Hobbs had given little thought to how Pops would've felt about becoming a cadaver for students to cut up and learn on, and it had been worth the small space in his brain in exchange for the morbid shot of jaded satisfaction he got picturing it.

"How long after that?" Hannah had said, not even arguing, though she kept glancing in Mom's direction to see if she'd object.

"Just a little while. You come with me, and Victor will watch over Mom."

Translation: until Victor could ascertain that James Timbley was gone from the picture for good, that he'd forgotten about Hannah and had moved on, hopefully from the area, definitely from her life.

"Vic. You'll take care of Mom?" Hannah had lowered her

voice and peeked in Mom's direction; she was on her knees, scrubbing stains in the carpet that had been there for decades. The suds under the scrub brush had turned black, matching the circles on the knees of Mom's gray pants.

"Mom, leave it," Victor had said, as though to prove his point. "I'll buy you a new carpet, okay? Trust me. The stains in this house are never coming out."

Mom had sat back on her heels and just stared at the wet mess in despair.

"Come on in and get a load off," Hobbs said, once Hannah had stood in the foyer too long, looking sad and lost and ready to cry. She'd feel better once he got her feet up and made her a cup of hot tea, her favorite.

"I've been sitting all day, remember?" Hannah's hand went to her legs, rubbing down her quads. "I need to move a little."

"Right," Hobbs agreed. "Let's go for a walk. It's warmer here than it is at home. A light jacket will be fine. November is fickle, though. Can't make up its mind, goes back and forth between cold and warm. A lot more humidity here, though, so it'll feel warmer than it is."

"Okay." Hannah sucked in a deep breath, but didn't move.

Hobbs reached out and grabbed her by the fingertips, then pulled her in. She didn't resist. Hannah laid her head on his shoulder and slid her arms around his waist.

"I'm scared, Chris. And I'm mad. And sad."

"I know." Hobbs rubbed her back. "It's gonna be okay. You're safe now." Even as he said it, he wondered if that were true. Hobbs just didn't trust abusers. They always found a way to hurt you. Even now, he wondered if Pops would find some way to haunt him from the grave.

thirteen

Guess what I got your daughter to agree to? She's coming to the gym with me today! See, we made a deal. She wanted to bring home another dog from the shelter—this time an old wiener dog that's lived in a cage all his life. She's named him Benedict and he's the sweetest thing you've ever seen. You'd never guess someone's had him locked up for two years, other than he's very shy and justifiably not very trusting. Problem is, we still have George and Gracie. The deal Lily and I have always had is she can bring anybody home that needs saving but one has to be adopted out before the next one comes in the house. Since she's breaking that rule she has to do something I've been nagging her to do since last spring, and that's try Semper Fit. This means I might actually get your yoga-loving ballerina to sling some weights around today! I can't wait. I'll keep you posted.

Yours forever,

Clem

Lily had dressed in yoga pants and a crop top that said Hit the Barre across the front. The fluttery, short sleeves high-lighted her long, slender arms and the short length gave an oc-casional peek at her defined midsection when she stretched at certain angles. She'd put her hair in a French braid and wore the only pair of sneakers she owned, which she typically wore to and from the dance studio. She'd been silent on the ride to the gym, not complaining, but not engaging in Clementine's chatter, either. Lily was holding up her end of the bargain with neither attitude nor excitement. Her expression read: *I'm doing this for the dogs.* Typical Lily.

The gym was busy for a Friday evening. There were peo-ple near the cubbies and on the floor warming up; both bath-rooms had "occupied" notices on the handles and the coach was already engaged in conversation with one of the regulars, Hank, who was clearly describing his latest muscle tweak by the way he was working his shoulder. Clementine was sur-prised to see Hobbs, as he'd been gone for a couple of weeks now. In hindsight, she probably should've brought Lily to a quieter class, maybe one coached by Zoe, who had a bright, confident personality that Lily would appreciate. Clemen-tine's jaw about hit the floor when Lily caught Hobbs's eye and, prompted by his big smile, gave him one in return, along with a wave.

A zip of panic ran through her before Clementine remem-bered that Lily and Hobbs had met on Halloween night. She reminded herself that though Hobbs was a player, he wasn't a sleaze. She doubted he'd hit on a teenager.

Lily had no bag, only her water bottle emblazoned with an *en pointe* sticker, so she skipped the reception area with the cubbies and went straight to the floor where everyone was warming up. She melted into the crowd, unafraid and oblivi-ous to the looks she was already getting, from both men and women alike. Clementine knew that her daughter was a head-turner—the combination of height, striking looks and poise was hard to miss—but she never got used to the instant attention Lily got in public. Lily, on the other hand, was oblivious, or at least acted like it. So much like Tyler, with that cool confidence and irreverent beauty. When Clementine had first met him during the Marine Corps Marathon, both of them only nineteen years old, one of the thoughts that had run through her mind was how beautiful he was, even with sweat all over his face and a good twenty miles behind him.

Hobbs ditched Hank and made his way over to Lily, who greeted him with a grin of familiarity. Hobbs said something and Lily started laughing. As soon as her face broke into that dimpled smile, a few more people sneaked glances in her direction. Clementine rushed to dig her lifting shoes from her bag, eager to get on the floor and hear what they were talking about, but she reminded herself that Lily was old enough to hold a conversation and wouldn't appreciate her mom butting in. By the time Clementine headed in their direction, she saw that another woman had joined their huddle. The woman was of medium height, had blond hair that leaned in the direction of golden and had an aura of worry that weighed down her soft, rounded features. She wore a large T-shirt over a pair of black yoga pants.

"Clem!" Hobbs's jovial voice rose a notch as she approached. "You brought your girl to work out. This is awesome."

Clementine had never told Hobbs that nobody called her Clem except Tyler, because Hobbs meant nothing by it. Giving people nicknames that stuck was kind of his thing. Tabitha had once told her, "Yeah, nobody calls me Tabby, either, but I don't mind when Hobbs does it." He just had that way about him, a congenial sort of openness that welcomed everyone, made them all feel safe and a part of the tribe.

"It's payback," Clementine said as she joined the trio. "Lil broke the rules on the number of pets in the house, so she has to work off their room and board by giving in to one of my whims." She opened her arms to indicate the gym.

"Well, that's not really punishment," Hobbs said. "Lily's getting the better end of this deal. Speaking of…how are George and Gracie?"

"They're actually in the car," Lily said. "Gracie is asleep in a big blanket in the back seat and George is curled up against her. They didn't even budge when we got here."

"They wore themselves out this morning," Clementine added. "Gracie wants to play with Benedict, the new dog Lily brought home. Benedict wants nothing to do with Gracie. George wants nothing to do with Benedict. Much chaos has ensued. Our only choices were to lock up Benedict, which we didn't want to do because he's lived in a cage all his life, or lock up George and Gracie, which would result in a huge mess, so…we just brought George and Gracie along. They at least have each other and we're not sure how Benedict would react to being left in the car."

Hobbs's eyes had glazed over a little, like that was way too much responsibility for him to deal with, but forever laid-back about everything, he laughed. "Gracie is the one I told you about," he said to the woman in black yoga pants. "She looks just like Gemma."

"Aww." The woman's face finally shed the worry and fear that had been clouding it and turned to a warm, misty reminiscence. "Can I see her?"

"Sure," Clementine and Lily both said.

"Oh, sorry." Hobbs shook his head. "Clementine, this is my sister, Hannah. Hannah, this is Clementine, Lily's mom. Don't let her miniature size fool you. Clem's a beast."

"Hi," Hannah said, turning to Clementine with a soft smile.

"Your sister." Clementine clapped her forehead with the heel of her hand. "I see it now." Hannah and Hobbs had the same color eyes—a pale, liquid blue rimmed by a shade of indigo. Hannah's hair had a red color mixed in that Hobbs's lacked, but if Clementine looked closely she could see that same red poking through the three days' growth of beard Hobbs had failed to shave. "Nice to meet you, Hannah. Sure, you can see Gracie. And George. No way you're seeing Gracie without seeing George, am I right?" Clementine bumped Lily with her hip.

"This is true," Lily agreed, though her smile was tight.

"How about after the workout? Is Hobbs just now getting you to join the gym?"

Hannah's smile, rather than brightening her face, softened it, making her seem even more affable and gentle. "I'm here to try it out. Get my blood flowing. After the workout sounds great. I love dogs."

"She just got here," Hobbs added. "From Omaha. Trust me, if she lived here I'd have had her in years ago."

She gave him a shove. "You could try."

Clementine could definitely see the familial likeness now. She tried to picture them as kids, playing together, getting in fights, ruining each other's things, keeping secrets—all the things Clementine did with her brother growing up—but there was definitely something parental about the way Hobbs treated her, which hinted at a large age gap.

"Ballerina, right?" Hobbs turned to Lily. "So, you're already superstrong."

"The legs, definitely," Clementine chimed in.

"The core," Hobbs said, rubbing his middle. "That's the important part. Her core is probably crazy strong. And her flexibility won't hurt none, either."

Lily smiled, looking less like she was here under silent protest and more interested in what might be in store for the next hour.

Clementine had to admit, when it was all over, she hadn't been prepared for what was in store herself. The workout consisted of rowing, sit-ups on the Glute-Ham Developer, or GHD, and front squats, all of which Lily picked up with ease. The rowing didn't surprise her—Lily was tall and rowing was all about the legs. Neither did the front squats, now that she thought about it, which were all core strength and mobility in the hips and ankles. The GHD sit-ups were something that were almost never encouraged for newbies, but Hobbs had allowed Lily to try, and once she'd got the hang of using her legs to shoot herself up, she'd been good to go for half the scheduled reps.

"What'd I tell you?" Hobbs's face spread into his typical big, infectious grin. "Strong core wins the day. Great job, Lil." He gave her a high five. They were about the same height, so they nailed it, their palms loud enough to make a smacking sound.

A lot of people gave Lily high fives, many of them shaking their heads, saying things like, "I still can't do GHD sit-ups," and, "Wow, your flexibility is amazing."

"See?" Clementine wiped the sweat from her brow with the back of her wrist. "I knew you'd crush it. With just a little bit of time you'll be nailing everything in here."

"Mom." Lily rolled her eyes. "Calm down. I came this once because you made me. That doesn't mean I'm going to join."

"I know." Clementine tried to mask her disappointment. She'd tried hard to never make her passions her daughter's, to force her to do things she hated or, God forbid, make her hate exercise. She'd learned long ago that Lily loved ballet and yoga—things Clementine was marginal at, at best—and wasn't partial to running, the one thing Clementine loved above all others. As long as they were both moving on a regular basis, she figured she was being a good mom.

Hannah, who'd scaled everything and moved pretty slowly, still had popped a sweat and her skin had gone pale, with rosy splotches at the outer edges of her cheekbones. "I am so out of shape," she moaned. The aura of sadness was still there, had never once left her during the workout, her body like it moved through mud.

"Hey, give yourself a chance." Clementine tried a smile. "This was only one workout."

"Plus, you just traveled over a thousand miles," Hobbs added.

Hannah sank down on one of the wooden boxes and sighed. "Yeah," she agreed. "But I'm still way out of shape. I can't remember the last time I exercised, other than going for a walk."

The woman seemed truly beat. Clementine wondered how old she was—she looked about Tabitha's age, maybe a little younger. She also wondered why Hannah had just traveled over a thousand miles to visit her brother. It seemed kind of sudden, but then again, what did Clementine know? Whatever the case, Clementine certainly wasn't going to pry, so tried the one thing that had made Hannah perk up earlier. "I'm going to go get George and Gracie, now that everyone is leaving. That was the last class for the night, right?"

"Yep. Good idea." Hobbs gave her a grateful smile. "I'll lock up after you bring them in."

Lily came out to the car to help, silent but willing, and decided to carry George while Clementine leashed up Gracie. Once they were back inside, and saw the gym was closed up and empty of everyone but Hannah and Hobbs, Clementine let Gracie loose.

"Oh my goodness!" A huge smile split Hannah's face, but it was all for the puppy that went barreling toward her like they'd known each other all their lives. Hannah dropped to her knees and opened her arms and Gracie tore into them. Her big paws landed on Hannah's chest and nearly tipped her over backward. "Look at you, you big, sweet thing!" Gracie licked all over Hannah's face. She laughed and rubbed her ears. "She does look just like Gemma." Hannah turned to Hobbs, who was watching the pair with a quiet intensity that Clementine had never seen on the boisterous coach.

Lily knew better than to hang on to a wiggling cat, so she set George down, and he came flying over to Gracie. He did circles around the Lab mix puppy, who was plopped down a foot away from Hannah, joy all over her canine face. "That's George," Lily said. "He thinks he's Gracie's bodyguard. If you get too close, he might slap you. He keeps his claws in, most of the time, but his behavior unnerves people." Lily offered her wrists and forearms as proof, showing off the handful of tiny scratches there.

Hannah, still on her knees, burst into laughter. "George is a cat?"

"Yep."

"A hairless cat?"

"Yep."

"That's just—" Hannah's body shook with her mirth "—the funniest thing I have ever seen. Oh my gosh."

"I wish more people reacted like you," Lily said. "This is why nobody will take Gracie. They're a bonded pair and nobody wants George."

"Nonsense." Hannah shifted and settled on the floor with her legs crossed. "He just needs a little patience."

"Exactly." Lily's eyes lit up in that way that happened only when she was talking about animals. "He's learned to tolerate me and we make a little progress every day. George just needs someone who will understand him. His previous owners abandoned him and now he's lost and insecure. Gracie makes him feel needed."

"Everybody should feel needed." Hannah's voice softened.

Gracie gave a little woof, tossed her head and then jumped into Hannah's lap. Lily pulled a rope bone she'd stuffed in the side pocket of her leggings and tossed it to Hannah, who caught it with one hand. George trotted over and slunk around Hannah, circumambulating and rubbing his body against Gracie's head.

"You don't know how glad I am you brought them tonight," Hobbs said as he and Clementine watched Lily and Hannah navigate the animals and the oddities of everyone's personalities.

"The dog really seemed to perk your sister up." The weird animals and her daughter's offbeat patience with them were not a new sight to Clementine, but she knew how all this must look to the likes of Hobbs. "Who was Gemma?"

Hobbs cleared his throat, maybe caught off guard. "Dog from when we were kids. Hannah is quite a bit younger than I am. I was a teenager when Gemma came around, but Hannah was only seven or so. Man, she loved that dog." He looked like he was going to say more, but stopped.

"Look—George is actually settling down next to her," Clementine mused, noting how sweet the puppy looked curled around Hannah's abdomen. George didn't actually touch Hannah, but he did sit near her feet and offer a glare. And, at least for now, he kept his paws to himself.

Hannah peeked over her shoulder and smiled at her brother.

"Our dad just died," Hobbs said, like he'd made a decision to speak about something he didn't really want to bring up. "And things aren't great with my sister's ex-boyfriend. So my sister's not in a great place, emotionally. This is the first time I've seen her happy all week."

"Oh, I'm sorry to hear that. About the boyfriend and about your father, too."

Hobbs shook his head, parted his lips to speak, but was drowned out by Hannah's shriek of laughter when George started batting her sneaker with both of his paws, like he was boxing. Unlike most cats, who would flee from such an abrupt noise, George doubled down. His little paws flew, Hannah's shoelace got caught in his nails and came undone, and her laughter made her whole body shake.

"You know what." Clementine nudged Hobbs with an elbow. "This would be a great opportunity for your sister to take her mind off her troubles. She could foster them."

Both Hannah and Lily snapped their heads in Clementine's direction. "Oh, Chris, could we?" Hannah glanced up at Lily. "They're for adoption, right?"

"Yeah." Lily's voice was quick and bright. Almost too quick and bright. "Definitely. Like I said, nobody wants George."

"Right," Hobbs agreed. "Including me." His jovial personality had returned, the laid-back grin and boyish playfulness taking over whatever somberness from deep inside had tried to claw its way out. "I am a bachelor for a reason, Hannah. I'm enough to look after all by myself."

"I'll look after them," Hannah said, stroking Gracie's head. The puppy was happily tearing up her rope bone in the middle of Hannah's lap. "I've got nothing else to do, Chris. I don't have a job here. I could help George get over his fear of losing Gracie...without actually taking away Gracie."

Lily's face relaxed. A rose color had tinged her cheeks, like when she got upset. "That's awesome, the way you put that. Yeah. I think you'd be perfect for them. And I trust Coach Hobbs, which means you must be okay, too."

You trust Coach Hobbs? Clementine bit back the words. Lily had never seen Hobbs hit on every pretty woman in this place, or strip his shirt at every possible opportunity, or come in hungover, sunglasses hiding his bloodshot eyes, even though his humor was never any worse for the wear. And there was no need to tell her about those things because Lily would just shrug and say, "You don't know what his life is like. And I'll make my own opinions about him, thank you."

"Can we talk about it at least?" Hobbs sighed, but sounded like he'd already accepted defeat. "I'm not ready for George and Gracie tonight. At least let me go home and prepare."

"Deal." Hannah extended her arms. "Now help me up. My butt is getting sore."

Hobbs grabbed her fingertips and hauled her up.

As Hannah's weight shifted, Gracie crawled from her lap in the direction of George. She nudged him with her muzzle and he tipped over. Everyone laughed, but George just rested on his side and let Gracie give his face a big, sloppy grooming with her pink tongue. When George got sick of it, he batted her away and started grooming Gracie's ear in return.

"What a pair," Hannah said.

"Give me a text tomorrow, Hobbs." Clementine leashed up Gracie while Lily collected George. "We can figure out when to bring them over to visit your place." Clementine didn't add that she was kind of interested in seeing where the infamous Hobbs lived. She envisioned a messy, small apartment or condo.

"All right. And hey." Hobbs shouted after them as they headed for the exit. "Where's your buddy? It's not like Tabby to miss a Friday workout."

"I'm pretty sure she had a date tonight. Something about a coffee date that turned into a drinks date."

"A date, huh?" Hobbs's smile fell. "That's no excuse to skate on her fitness."

If Clementine didn't know better, she'd think Hobbs sounded

jealous. She remembered what Tabitha had said about kissing him on her birthday. "I don't think one date counts as skating on her fitness."

Hobbs grunted something, but Lily was already out the door, so Clementine waved goodbye and went after her. After they got the pets loaded up and were buckled into their seats, Clementine said, "Spill it. What are you mad about?"

"Nothing."

"Lil."

"The pets are my job, Mom." Lily faced her with those intelligent, fearless eyes of Tyler's. "Would you like it if I came into your running store and told you how to sell your shoes? Or gave people marathon advice?"

Clementine's knee-jerk reaction was to be defensive, to say that she was only trying to help, but she drew a deep breath and simply answered Lily's question. "No. I wouldn't like that. I'd think it was out of place and I'd wonder why you were doing it."

Lily raised her eyebrows, tilted her head to the side, then looked away.

Point made. Clementine thought back to how it'd all gone down and felt a stab of shame. "I'm sorry. I should've let you handle George and Gracie. And yourself. I kind of butted in about your fitness, too. I did that thing where I take over, didn't I? I over-mommed."

Lily sighed, then shrugged. "I know you were just trying to help." She had confidence and independence in spades. Grudge holder and drama queen she was not. "But I know how to handle the pets. It's what I do. And I can handle myself, too. I'm not a baby."

Clementine reached over and squeezed her shoulder. "I'll let you handle the rest of it. I'll even give you Hobbs's number and you can arrange the visit."

Lily faced her again, her eyes softer now. "Thank you."

Sometimes, her daughter was so much like Tyler it made Clementine want to cry. "That situation with the sister is kind of different, isn't it?" She changed the subject and started the engine.

"Hannah's definitely got something going on," Lily agreed. "Something weighing her down, big-time. She reminds me of a lot of the dogs who come into the shelter. Scared and lost. I get the feeling somebody hasn't been very nice to her."

Clementine peeked in the rearview and caught a glimpse of George and Gracie, curled together in their blanket. Scared and lost, indeed. "I think you may be right."

"I know I am."

fourteen

Be yourself; everyone else is already taken.

~*Oscar Wilde*

Tabitha didn't think being herself was all that great, but the quote from her Journal of Invincibility kept running through her mind Saturday morning as she drove through the back roads that led to Pittie Place. Focusing on the quote was better than reliving what an abject failure her date with Thaddeus had been. When he'd been too busy for coffee yesterday morning he'd suggested evening drinks instead. Tabitha had tried her best—dressing up a little and hitting a bar midtown, which she hadn't done in ages—but the noise had been too much and she'd been too nervous to drink or even focus on their conversation. The way Thaddeus had kept looking down at Trinity, with what seemed like a resentful expression, had made Tabitha squirm and she'd called it a night early. Thaddeus hadn't texted since and she didn't really expect him to.

The drive out was soothing to her frayed nerves. The old trees that flanked her on either side were ablaze with the colors of autumn and shot up to the sky. The sign for Pittie Place and Canine Warriors, where Trinity was from, popped up as Tabitha neared the turn that led into Sunny's driveway. Sunny had been running Pittie Place, her dog rescue, for years, and her boyfriend, Pete, trained some of these rescues to become service dogs for wounded military veterans. Sunny had paved over some ground to create parking spaces for the people who rented out the cabins that surrounded the rescue, and Tabitha took one near the rear of the lot, preferring not to have anyone around her. It wasn't that she was protective of her dumpy old car; she just liked a safety net of space, at all times.

Red's last text had instructed Tabitha to meet her out back, which meant Tabitha had no excuse to knock on the front door of the beautiful Queen Anne that Sunny called home. Tabitha had always loved that house, with its turrets and fish-scale siding. She imagined Rapunzel living inside one of those towers, throwing out her long hair to be climbed by the intrepid prince.

Trinity wagged her tail and quickened her pace as she caught the scent of Pittie Place. "You remember, don't you?" Tabitha stroked along her back and felt a sense of calm that she rarely got anywhere else on earth. Something about Pittie Place made both canine and human feel instantly at home.

She went around back, as Red had instructed, and picked her way along the path until she got to the gate. Trinity sat and waited patiently, but her ears were perked and a smile was plastered all over her face, if that was possible. Tabitha undid the latch and pressed inside. Roger, who had been the caretaker here as long as Tabitha could remember, had his own cabin, which sat in the center of the grounds, rebuilt and looking sturdy and fresh after the treacherous fire that had almost taken it out a year and a half ago.

"Hey, Tabs!" Sunny waved from afar, over near the Puppy Pit, which was what she'd recently dubbed her playground for the youngest rescues. The pit, a large fenced-in area to play, reminded Tabitha of a gymnastics room, with all its various delights, such as a plastic tunnel, toys hanging from beams for the puppies to try to catch and, in warmer weather, a kiddie pool full of water.

Sunny wore a pair of blue jeans and a light windbreaker and was watching a brood of about a dozen puppies run, roll and leap at the toys and each other. Red was next to her, the two of them laughing and talking over cups of take-out coffee. "Hey there," Red greeted her, and snuggled deeper into her Semper Fit hoodie. Tabitha guessed it might've even been Rhett's hoodie because Red was drowning in it, the hem going all the way to her knees.

"What do we have here?" Tabitha peeked in at the puppies. They were small but had big paws, like they had a lot of growing to do. Their fur was short and straight, some brown, some black and brown mixed. Trinity sat next to the chain-link fence and watched, her front feet shifting and tapping like she wanted to play, too.

"This is the *Star Trek* litter," Sunny said with a grin. "Probably Lab with shepherd mixed in. There's Kirk, Spock, Uhura, Crusher, Sulu and Cumby. Lily named them. She comes here about once a week. She's my official shelter liaison. You'd never know that kid is only sixteen."

"Right?" Red added. "Sixteen going on thirty, more like."

Tabitha watched the pups a moment, wild and free and rolling with abandon. "Wait a minute," she said. "Cumby? I don't recall a Cumby in *Star Trek*."

"Benedict Cumberbatch," Sunny said. "Took us a minute,

too. He starred in one of the *Star Trek* movies. Lily insisted, because Cumby is smart, independent and handsome." Sunny pointed out the puppy, who was up on his hind legs, using his front paws to grasp one of the dangling bones. A second later the whole contraption, made of interconnected PVC pipes, came toppling down. The puppies squeaked and ran, and Cumby did a somersault and ended up on his furry butt. Despite all the laughter, the puppy stood, shook himself and dived after the bone he'd worked so hard to get. It was still connected to the toppled contraption by a piece of leather, but now that it was on the ground, Cumby settled down, collected the bone in his paws and started gnawing on it.

"Clearly Lily was right," Tabitha said.

"Let's go in the house," Red said as Sunny went inside the fence to fix the wrecked toy.

Tabitha followed her toward the Queen Anne, excited to be able to go in the beautiful house that Sunny had said her father helped her restore before his passing.

"A mother dog came in yesterday." Red spoke as they walked. "Along with those pups. Those aren't her pups, though. Hers are still…" Constance rubbed her midsection. "We don't have a lot of backstory, but we both agree that this poor mother has been bred over and over. She's exhausted."

They entered the house through the lower level, which was a large, open area that had a bar and what could be a dance floor. Tabitha had heard Sunny threw a mean Christmas party for donors to the rescue and she had a feeling this might be where they celebrated. Red led her upstairs, through a grand kitchen with stainless-steel appliances and a large, granite-topped island and into a more casual, relaxed family room. There was a leather chair with ottoman and a matching sofa, both tossed with clean, well-loved quilts, and a television mounted on the wall. Tabitha could easily picture Sunny here, unwinding after a long day, probably with Pete by her side.

"There she is." Red approached the corner on the other side of the leather chair and that was when Tabitha saw the mother dog. Curled on a dog bed in the peace and quiet of the house was what looked like a pit bull with a copper-colored coat, red nose, eyes and nails. Her midsection was heavy with pups, but her ribs were still more visible than they should have been. She only blinked at them as they approached. "This is Candy," Red said. "She kind of looks like a candy apple, don't you think?"

"She is all red," Tabitha agreed. "And seems very sweet."

"The vet says she's healthy, though underfed. We're trying to rectify that before the pups come." Red sank down next to the dog and raised a palm over her back. She paused, without touching her. "As you know, I massage a lot of the dogs. But most of my massages start this way." Red's voice was low and careful.

"You get her used to you being nearby first," Tabitha acknowledged. "Just being in her space will be cause for anxiety. You can't just plop your hands down on her and start rubbing." Tabitha noted that the dog's rib cage expanded and collapsed at a quicker pace now that they were so close.

"Exactly." Red smiled softly. "Here." She scooted away. "You do it."

"What? Me?" Tabitha noted that Trinity had stayed at the opposite end of the room, flopped on the floor near the entryway. Even she sensed that Candy wouldn't appreciate a crowd.

"Of course you." Red smiled and scooted back on her bottom until her spot near Candy had been freed up for Tabitha. "Why do you think I wanted you to come over?"

Any anxiety that Tabitha would've normally felt by having a surprise massage lesson sprung on her was completely absent in the face of the client being a dog. It wasn't that she thought dogs would be easier—quite the contrary, as dogs couldn't communicate in the same way as humans. She just felt more comfortable around them, more in her element, more needed. Because of her relationship with Trinity, and the long months of training, Tabitha felt like she understood dogs. She couldn't say the same about humans.

Tabitha settled next to Candy and closed her eyes. The air was heavy, ragged, worn. Tabitha found it harder to breathe, but then used a trick that often worked for panic attacks: she focused on expanding her rib cage from the bottom up and slowing her inhalations. She waited until the air had lightened and her throat had loosened before she opened her eyes again. Her hand was resting on the dog's back, but she didn't remember putting it there.

Candy hadn't flinched. She'd laid her head back down and closed her eyes. The rapid breathing from when Red was near had calmed. Tabitha tested running her palm down Candy's spine, to her haunches. The dog's muscles jumped under Tabitha's hand, but it was involuntary twitching, not flinching.

"What do you feel?" Red sat a few feet away, her arms wrapped around her shins as she watched quietly, from afar.

"Trauma." The word popped out of its own will. Tabitha had actually been formulating how to reply, what Red might want to hear, how she could sound smart and clever, but her brain obviously had other ideas. "I'm sorry," she said. "I mean—"

"Don't apologize," Red cut in. "You're right. Candy has suffered quite a bit of trauma over the course of her life."

Tabitha ran her hand along the dog's haunches, then back up to her spine and over her rib cage. For now, she kept away from the swollen belly. "It wasn't really a good guess on my part. Most of the dogs here have suffered trauma."

"You didn't guess, though," Red protested. "Your response

was reflexive, based on what went through her body and into yours. You felt her trauma. The body talks to you, Tabitha. Anybody can teach you the bony prominences and the muscular attachments and the neurology—and all of that is important. But no less important, and much harder to teach, is what you're good at naturally. Sensing. Empathizing. Helping others release their trauma. I brought you here to prove it."

Tabitha went to protest, but the truth was, she did feel Candy's trauma. The rippling of the dog's muscles, beneath her hand, was barely discernible. The trauma came up out of the dog in micro-tremors that made Tabitha's palm vibrate just slightly. If she weren't paying attention, or if she were touching the dog too deeply or in a hurry, she would miss it entirely.

"The good thing about dogs is that they don't typically hang on to their trauma as hard as humans do. They're quite happy to let you help them ease their pain. Humans fight it, tooth and nail. If you want to visit Candy a couple times a week until she gives birth, I'll sign off on your massage form," Red said.

"Wow, really?" Tabitha knew that Constance was referring to the sheet where she had to list all her outside massages and collect signatures from the recipients as proof of her practical work.

Red cocked her head to the side and smiled. "Really." She rose, slowly and carefully, but Candy didn't move. "I'm going to go back out and help Sunny. You just hang here with Candy and follow your instincts."

Red disappeared and Tabitha spent the next half hour quietly easing into some kind of massage for the pregnant mama dog. As she just barely palpated some of her muscles, Tabitha recalled the illustrations in one of her textbooks that outlined the differences of the location of dog muscles versus humans. She could picture the little beagle in the book and the arrows pointing to his serratus anterior. Tabitha wasn't going to massage those today, but maybe next time. By the time Sunny popped in, smelling woodsy and smoky, like the outdoors in autumn, Tabitha had been able to work her way to Candy's foot pads and give them all little depressions with her thumb.

"Wow," Sunny said, her cheeks pink and eyes bright with the cold. "I don't know if I'm more impressed that Candy is letting you massage her or that my sister is letting you massage Candy." Sunny put the back of her hand next to her mouth, even though Red was nowhere within earshot, and hissed, "Cici is pretty possessive of her dog massages."

"I'm not surprised. This is very rewarding." Tabitha was pleased at how much Candy had calmed down with thirty minutes of selective, gentle massage. What she hadn't expected was how relaxed her own body felt. *Massage is a two-way street,* Red was fond of saying. *It's not fifty-fifty, but energy is shared. Good or bad, you'll share whatever you bring to the table. On the flip side, you also have to be careful what you take in from your clients.*

Today, at least, Tabitha had managed to ease Candy's trauma and not share any of her own. She'd come in here feeling peaceful and relaxed, and that had transferred to Candy with slow persuasion.

"I knew it," Red said, when she appeared a moment later. Fezziwig, her three-legged pit bull, was hopping by her side. Her face spread into a slow smile. "You're a natural with those who've suffered from trauma."

"Maybe." Tabitha finished her gentle rocking of Candy and rose slowly to her feet. "It's only one dog. Maybe I got lucky."

"I don't believe in luck."

"I do," Sunny countered. "But not this time. Cici's right. You've got the magic touch."

By the time she collected Trinity and headed for the gym, Tabitha felt better about herself than she had in a long time.

Maybe she could do this massage thing after all. At least with animals.

Only time would tell with humans.

fifteen

By Monday morning, Hobbs was starting to normalize again, shaking off the time on the road and the bad juju he'd collected seeing Pops die in his childhood house of horrors. He'd thought about that moment a lot since it'd happened, but he'd come no closer to deciding if witnessing Pops's death, and those final words, had been exactly what he wanted or the farthest thing from it.

The morning was quiet. Hobbs peeked into the spare bedroom and found Hannah curled in the fetal position on the twin bed Hobbs had bought at the Swedish do-it-yourself superstore, hands tucked under her pillow. Her lips were slightly parted and her hair messed and hiding most of her face. Her shoulder rose and fell in silent sleep, the curtains drawn and blocking out most of the morning sunlight. If it weren't for her size, she could be a kid again, sacked out after school. She had such a quiet nature that large, busy places always exhausted her, and school had certainly been no exception. Hobbs, who was often her primary caregiver, remembered spending a lot of time getting her out of her funk and into her homework or to the dinner table or whatever had to be done. Red licorice whips worked, as well as the marshmallows from the cereal boxes. Nothing like a jolt of sugar and red dye number five to get a kid going again.

Hobbs decided not to wake her to see if she wanted to go to the gym. She'd been so worn out and had spent much of the weekend lying on the couch, texting Mom and being generally sad, mopey and lost. Any attempts Hobbs had made to get her to open up had been rebuffed, so he'd given up and they'd just watched television until Hannah had fallen asleep. He'd go coach his ten o'clock class and be back in a couple of hours. By then she'd be awake and hopefully in a better mood.

Hobbs slipped into coach mode easily, and though he was relieved that there was no sign of Clementine—he wasn't exactly eager to have a wild puppy and her crazy cat bodyguard move into his house—spotting Tabitha lifted his spirits. Her eyes popped with surprise when she saw him and she offered him a welcoming smile. Once class started he forgot all about Hannah, Mom, Pops and Victor, all of whom were taking up way too much space in his head, and just lost himself in his work.

By the time they were done, Tabitha lay on her back on the floor, a sweaty mess, the giant gym ceiling fan going around and around. It had been a typical day at the gym for her, performance-wise. She worked harder than everyone else but still struggled and took longer to finish than most people. Hobbs had watched her time and again, whether it was weight lifting, gymnastics, plyometrics, and despite her effort, nothing came easily to her. Though there was nothing wrong with that type of learning—which often led to more solid results down the line—Hobbs could tell Tabitha got frustrated when people with more natural ability made everything look so easy.

With power cleans on the menu today, Hobbs had visited her multiple times during the workout to suggest the same thing with various cues: more aggression. "You've got the strength to lift that weight," he'd told her. "You're just not opening the hips and dropping under with enough speed. Get angry, Tabby."

She looked angry now, lying there in a mess of sweat, gasping for air.

Hobbs stood over her, fists on his hips. "How was your date the other night?"

It took a moment for her eyes to blink open. "Hello to you, too. Haven't seen you in two weeks and you open with that?" She pushed up onto her elbows. "How did you know I had a date?"

"Omniscience. I'm all-seeing and all-knowing."

Tabitha regarded his lie with a long stare, like she was trying to figure out how he really knew. She either decided it was Clementine or didn't care, because she finally just said, "Thaddeus asked me for coffee last Friday. Then he couldn't make that, so we rescheduled for later in the evening and went for drinks instead. I only had water. I left early. It was a total bomb."

"Thaddeus?" Hobbs suppressed a grin. "His name is Thaddeus?"

"Yes."

"Did you have a smashing good time, then, lovey?" Hobbs tried an accent, which failed so miserably it made Tabitha arch an eyebrow.

She stood up and stretched her arms overhead. "I don't know what you're going for. I don't know what this is." She gestured to Hobbs's puffed-up chest.

"I'm acting like a snobby rich kid who went to an Ivy League school and became a lawyer." Hobbs shrugged.

"Well, it's bad." Tabitha shook her head. "And how did you know Thaddeus was a lawyer?"

"See?" Hobbs pointed at her. "Not *that* bad."

Tabitha shook her head. "I see you're back from Omaha finally."

"That's what I like about you, Tabby. You're observant."

"Did it go okay?" Tabitha started cleaning up her equipment, ripping the collars and plates off the barbell with more force than was necessary.

"It went." Hobbs had long ago learned what face to wear in the gym. Keep your troubles to yourself, put on a smile, give good feedback and don't get too personal. Even his flirting and dating were casual, which meant there was never any cause for anyone to have expectations and then get mad when they weren't met. Which meant nobody ever quit the gym over bad feelings concerning him. But it was harder, for a reason he hadn't yet put his finger on, to keep behind the gym facade with Tabitha.

"Still being secretive, huh?" She tossed her bumper plates in the pile with a flourish.

"See, now that's the kind of aggression I needed from you during the workout. Not now, when it's all over."

Tabitha finally let a smile play around her lips.

"How's school?" Hobbs grabbed a lacrosse ball from the box resting in the windowsill and tossed it from palm to palm. Distraction in layers was best. Merely deflecting might not get the job done with Tabitha, but if Hobbs distracted her with a question about herself as well as the tossing of the ball, she might not even notice he was avoiding her questions about Omaha.

"School. Let's see. Do you want the story about how I missed the woman with hyponatremia at the Dogwood County Marathon or the story about how I failed my bone markings quiz?"

Hobbs stopped tossing the ball. "What? I can't even be gone a couple weeks without all my hard work going in the crapper? I quizzed you mercilessly for that exam."

"Oh, I remember." Tabitha hefted her box with a grunt. Hobbs followed behind her as she carried it over to the stack. "No, apparently you can't be gone that long. So how was it? Tell me it was worth it, considering you slacked and now my grades are suffering."

Even the Distraction of Multiple Senses didn't work on Tabitha. So be it. "My dad died." Hobbs gave the box that was teetering in Tabitha's grip a shove, aligning it on top of the others. Then he went back to tossing the ball.

"Oh." Tabitha's joking humor faded. "I'm sorry to hear that. Is there anything I can do?"

"I'm fine. We didn't get along." Hobbs tossed the ball on the ground, where it bounced, struck the wall and bounced back in his direction. He caught it and repeated the action a couple more times. "There's got to be something good that happened in school. Lay it on me."

Tabitha watched his ball slinging in silence for a moment before she faced him with pursed lips, like she had resigned herself to his deflective ways. "I went out to Pittie Place on Saturday. Red had me try massaging one of the dogs. A pregnant dog, in fact. A pregnant dog who's been mistreated and overbred and is in a bad way. And, shockingly, it went really well."

"You massaged a pregnant dog," Hobbs repeated. He'd got into a rhythm with the lacrosse ball. *Bounce-ping!-bounce-catch.* "And you were good at it."

"Yep."

Bounce-ping!-bounce-catch.

"Why do you think that is?"

"I don't know." Tabitha watched the ritual with the lacrosse ball. "Red says it's because I'm calming. Sensitive." She shrugged. "The dog relaxed. Her muscles were shaking really bad. Not like shivering, but like… I don't know. It was like her body was shedding the stress with vibration." Tabitha shrugged again. "I probably just got lucky."

Bounce-ping!-bounce-catch. Hobbs's wheels were turning, though he couldn't really settle on a solid thought, caught up in his own rhythm. Next thing he knew, Tabitha was in front of him, the lacrosse ball was in her hands and a no-nonsense look was on her face. "What do you mean you didn't really get along? That's not something people usually say when their dads die."

"No?" Hobbs clapped his palms together, feeling suddenly lost without the ball. "What do they say?"

Tabitha cocked her head sideways and narrowed her eyes. "Well, I don't know, from experience. But usually people are sad. Or upset. Or even relieved. They're usually something, though. Not all this nothing you got going on." She planted a hand on her hip. The other one still gripped Hobbs's ball.

"I haven't figured out how I feel about it yet." Hobbs hadn't planned to be honest, but Tabitha was finally, for once, being relentless and he didn't want to discourage that. "That okay with you?" Hobbs tried to attach a smile, because Coach Hobbs always smiled.

He must've failed, though, because Tabitha's expression changed. "Yeah." She stretched her arm out and offered him the ball. "That's okay."

"Thanks." Hobbs took the ball, but he no longer felt like bouncing it. "Hey. Whatever happened with your—" he snapped his fingers until it came to him "—badass list? Did you make it?"

"I did. I don't know if it's any good, though."

"Do you have it on you?"

"I have it in the car."

"Let's see it."

Tabitha paused, maybe to assess his seriousness or maybe to decide. "All right," she said. "Trinity, stay. I'll be right back." Tabitha was gone a few minutes and returned carrying a notebook. Up close, the cover read Journal of Invincibility. She must've caught him looking, because she explained, "It's got daily quotes and space to journal and organize your day." She flipped to the back, then handed over the journal.

THE BADASS LIST

Help Auntie El.

~~Don't act like a freak when you have coffee with Thaddeus on Friday.~~

Learn about motorcycles.

Possibly ride one.

Ace massage quizzes.

Excel at massage.

Run a race with Clementine???

The one about Thaddeus had a thick pencil line slashed through it. Tabitha was quiet, watching him read. Her eyes were bright and curious when he looked up. "Well?" she said. "What do you think?" Then her brows knitted. "Oh. Except that one." She attempted to cover the line about Thaddeus, must've realized that was dumb, Hobbs had already seen it, and retreated. "Ignore that one."

"Oh, I'll definitely ignore that one." Hobbs wished he had a pencil handy so he could erase it entirely. "This list is a good effort." Hobbs had learned over years of coaching to always start with something positive. "You covered a lot of topics."

If her expression was any indication, Tabitha wasn't fooled by the whole positivity thing. "But?"

"But I think you'd find this list more helpful if you had specific, achievable goals. Preferably with a time frame." When Tabitha's face didn't change, Hobbs pressed on. "For example, this one here. *Excel at massage.* How are you going to do that? Are you going to study your bones for a half hour a day every day until the quiz? Are you going to practice massaging more? If so, how many and when? Be specific. And make the results measurable and achievable."

Tabitha extended her hand and took back her journal. Then her face finally relaxed and she offered a small smile. "You're right. That makes a lot of sense. Thanks, Coach."

"I can help you, too," Hobbs pressed. Anything to keep that smile on her face, or even make it bigger. "With massage, maybe. Are you good at massaging sad humans, too?" It occurred to him that this was not a good idea, but he couldn't stop himself. If Tabitha had made the abused dog feel better, maybe she could make Hannah feel better, too.

"I'm not good with humans at all. Why?" Tabitha got a sneaky look in her eyes. "You sad?"

"Maybe." Hobbs felt bad for lying. If there was one thing he was *not* over his father's death it was sad, but Tabitha got anxious quickly and might not go for massaging a stranger. At least if she thought she was massaging him, there was a chance she'd say yes. "I was just thinking I could help out," Hobbs said quickly. "I could be one of your guinea pigs and give you feedback."

Tabitha lowered her gym bag from her shoulder to the floor, like it suddenly got too heavy.

"One of your very unspecific goals is to excel at massage, Tabby. You're never going to get good unless you practice.

And you can't just keep massaging Red. You have to branch out."

Tabitha stood there, frozen, saying nothing, until she finally drew a deep breath and said, "Yeah, okay."

"Yeah?"

"Yeah, you're right. But I don't have a lot in my repertoire yet. I'm still first semester. I'm good at feet and necks and shoulders."

"I'll take it." Anything to get her to come over. From there, maybe he could somehow work Hannah into the picture. Hobbs didn't know much about massage, but he did know that Red was right—Tabitha had a gift for getting inside you and making you think and feel things you needed to think and feel, even if you didn't want to. He didn't like it one bit, but her superpower might prove useful with Hannah.

"You can be one of my people this week." Tabitha collected her bag and slung it back on her shoulder. "But no jokes." She pointed a finger at him.

"Never."

There went that smile again—bright, genuine, lit up her eyes.

"Oh, and the part about the motorcycle." Hobbs nodded at the journal. "I can help you with that, too. I haven't ridden in ages, but I wouldn't mind getting back on a bike soon if it meant giving you your first ride."

Tabitha cocked her head to the side. "Oh, yeah? You'd do that for me?"

"I'd definitely make the sacrifice. I don't have a bike but…"

"Delaney would let us borrow one, I'm sure. She's always got bikes in the shop that need testing."

"Awesome. We'll just wait for a warm day. Virginia gives us plenty of those before January, but if not, we can wait until spring. Either way, it'll happen."

Tabitha's smile infused her whole body now, her shoulders straightening and chin tilting up. She looked filled with sunshine. "Deal," she said. "I can't wait."

"Deal." They shook on it. "Now, go home and make that list more specific. Remember, short, specific, achievable goals with a time frame."

"Oh, I'm going to." Tabitha had a little swagger to her walk now as she headed out, Trinity trotting by her side. "You can count on it."

sixteen

"Thaddeus can't come to Thanksgiving, Auntie El. He's got plans with his own family." Tabitha slid her massage lotion into her bag and thought about what else she might need. Maybe her paperwork, with the neck routine written out on it, or the sheet where she'd jotted down her teacher's notes on how to do the Jelly Jar on the arm and shoulder. She put those notes in her bag, then took them back out again. What was her problem? Never once had Tabitha packed and repacked when she'd been heading out to do a massage. Now that it was Hobbs, her anxiety was through the roof, despite having just spent half an hour on her meditation app. The session had been half an hour of focused positivity while the sounds of water pouring over rocks and trickling into a stream had punctuated the gaps of silence. Ten minutes of that and Tabitha had got sick of the woman's voice and the water made her have to pee and now she was less relaxed than when she'd started.

"Have you seen him again?" Auntie El hovered her pen

over the crossword and peered at Tabitha over the top of her glasses. She'd slept in again this morning and was now trying to finish her puzzle with a groggy, after-dinner attitude. "All I hear about is your drinks last week and then nothing."

Tabitha sighed and glanced down at Trinity, an apologetic look on her face as she waited patiently to leave. The pittie knew the bag meant business and she also knew that Auntie El's questions often made Tabitha tense, so Trinity was ready to offer support and also eager to get in the car. "I don't know what to tell you. We just had drinks and talked. But it was so loud and I was uncomfortable." She shrugged. "At least I didn't have a panic attack. I haven't really had one of those since my first day at massage school."

That had happened right after Joy had explained that a large part of their grade was devoted to doing student massage exchanges on a weekly basis. First, Tabitha had felt the trembling start. The sweat came next, followed by the pounding of her heart. Luckily, Joy had noticed something amiss and had called for a lunch break. As everyone left, she approached Tabitha, tucked away in the back corner of the room, moved a few desks out of the way and helped Tabitha onto the floor where Trinity could climb on her chest. Then she'd left her alone and the attack had passed before any of the other students returned. Joy had never mentioned it again, though she did often look Tabitha's way with prolonged pauses, as though watching out for her. That was the day Tabitha had known that Joy was a superhero.

"Are you going to see Thaddeus again, or not?" Auntie El slugged down the rest of her tea, which she had every afternoon with two Biscoff cookies, set on a matching saucer. "Six-letter word for *heavenly*." She counted the squares with the tip of her pen.

"He's awfully busy," Tabitha said. "And his schedule is unpredictable. Lawyers put in a lot of hours. You remember how he couldn't make coffee and we had to force in drinks. He hasn't been available since, but we've been talking." Not that Tabitha cared, really. Thaddeus had waited three full days after their date to text again. She only texted Thaddeus back because she wanted to be polite and they'd known each other a long time. It'd felt like catching up with an old buddy from high school who you realized you no longer had much in common with. Right now, all Tabitha cared about was not messing up this massage with Hobbs. Just the thought of putting her hands on his bare skin and rubbing his muscles was making her stomach do flips. *Oh, Lord, give me strength.*

"Talking?" Auntie El wrinkled her nose.

Tabitha held up her phone. "Texting."

Auntie El pulled a face. "That's not talking. You kids with your gadgets. In my day, if a man was courting, he had the decency to ask you out proper. There wasn't any of this tap-tap-tapping on cell phones, with all kinds of ignorant shorthand and little pictures in place of words. In my day, men used real words, Tabitha Jo." Auntie El shook a forefinger.

They didn't have cell phones in your day, Auntie El. They're called emojis, Auntie El. And also: *Who are all these men you speak of, Auntie El? You're almost seventy and you've never been married.* But that wouldn't be fair. Tabitha knew that Auntie El had put everything aside to host dozens of foster kids, including her relationship with a guy named Henry, who Tabitha remembered vaguely as a nice, skinny man who wore church clothes all the time, even to picnics, and who called Tabitha Little Miss T. His disappearance, sometime around when Tabitha was eight years old, was explained away as "he moved for work." Tabitha suddenly wanted to ask Auntie El about Henry, about what really happened. Just maybe they could reconnect over modern-day technology and discover the joys of emoji hearts and kissy-faces.

Tabitha made a joke instead. "I'm sure when your suitors collected you in a horse and buggy for the barn dance, it was simply swoon-worthy."

Auntie El peered over her glasses again. "You watch, now."

Tabitha suppressed a laugh. "I have to go, Auntie El. I have a client. For school."

"Mmm-hmm." Auntie El barely looked up from her puzzle. "Invite whoever you want, then, for Thanksgiving. It's next week and I need people to cook for. Most of the church folk got plans this year. I got the reverend coming but that's all. You can ask your gym friends, if any of them need real food this Thanksgiving. None of this going out for Chinese or heating up microwave trays, or whatever it is these fools do. I don't know what's with you young people these days. Maybe you can send each other pictures of dinner instead of eating it."

"Okay, Auntie El." Tabitha wasn't as irritated by Auntie's crankiness as usual. If she was cranky it meant she was feeling a little better. Still, Tabitha had no intention of inviting anyone here for Thanksgiving. Auntie El's food was divine but her moods had been so unpredictable lately. "*Divine*, by the way. Try *divine*." She nodded at the puzzle. "Six-letter word for *heavenly*."

"Yep. That's it." Auntie El wrote in the word. "Send Thaddeus one of those faces, then. Not the one with the hearts for eyes that Geneva uses for every blessed thing. 'Let's play bridge.' Then a heart face. 'I just got my nails done.' Heart face. 'I done mopped my floor.' Heart face." Auntie El shook her head. "Who makes heart eyes over mopping their floor? Send Thaddeus something more modest. Do they have a face in a nice sweater and maybe a flower in its hair? That'd be nice. Don't let him slip away."

"Sure, Auntie. I'll be sure to send Thaddeus the smiley face with the flower in its hair."

★ ★ ★

"Where are you going?"

Hannah halted in the doorway, like a child caught sneaking out of the house in the middle of the night. She wore her jacket and clutched a set of keys. She turned to face Hobbs, who'd just come out of the shower, and sighed. "I'm borrowing your truck and going for a ride." She nodded toward the kitchen counter. "I left you a note."

Hobbs scanned the elegant writing on today's sheet from his Get Shit Done page-a-day calendar. Underneath the heading *Shit to Do*, where Hobbs had written in his personal training appointments, Hannah had written: *Going for a drive. Back soon.*

"How long will you be gone?" Because he couldn't say, *You can't leave. I've got someone coming over that I'm tricking into giving you a massage. She'll be here any minute.*

Hannah shrugged. "I don't know. I'm going a little stir-crazy, Chris. Remember, I'm used to working every day. Doing most of the shopping for Mom. I've been here a week and I'm doing nothing but walk the park and cook your meals. I need to get out. Think. Clear my head."

"I told you that you didn't have to cook for me. I'm used to feeding myself."

"That's not the point." Hannah's hand tightened on her purse strap. "I want to cook. I like to cook. It keeps me busy. But I feel trapped. I need to just…go. Without you." She held up a hand, like Hobbs might approach and offer to drive her around. Which he would do if Tabitha weren't on the way.

There really wasn't much more Hobbs could say, without admitting the trick he'd planned. He probably should've just asked, but he knew Hannah would've got all flustered about him making a fuss and she would've said no to the massage. "Okay, just…don't be long. The sun's already setting. Text me if you get lost." He nodded at the keys. "It slips a little in third gear."

Hannah smiled and turned for the door. "I'll be fine. I'm going to hit the back roads, so there won't be a lot of starting and stopping."

Hobbs went to the window and watched her pull away, then texted Victor to let him know that Hannah was "exploring." He wasn't sure if this was good or bad news—did it mean she was feeling more or less homesick?—but one thing he did know was he'd never texted his brother this much in his life. It'd been daily since he left Omaha, and even though Hobbs guessed the texting was done grudgingly, there was no way Victor would let Hannah go without a daily check-in.

Victor texted back. Good she gets out. All fine here. Mom still out of it. Depressed without Hannah. No sign of trouble.

Victor texted like a caveman. Me text. Mom good. No trouble.

Although no sign of trouble was the most important part. If the guy who'd been smacking Hannah around had stayed away, then odds were he was gone from her life. He'd taken Victor's threats seriously and would disappear and, in time, Hannah could go home, and everyone's life could get back to normal.

Hobbs gave Victor's text a thumbs-up just as Tabitha pulled up to the house in her old sedan. Of course she'd just missed Hannah. Now Hobbs had no choice but to get a massage, because what else could he say? Not that he was complaining. Not at all. It was just that getting a massage from Tabby might not exactly be the best idea given the fact he'd kissed her on her birthday and had kind of imagined doing all sorts of other things with her ever since. During quiet moments, of course. Which had been few and far between since the moment his brother had shown up in his living room.

"Hi." Tabitha stood on the front stoop, her slender hand white-knuckling the strap of the giant bag slung over her shoulder. The sunset behind was a wash of pinks and oranges, lighting up her dark hair and eyes. Her smile seemed a little too big, like it was forced. Trinity stood by her side, wearing her service vest, alert, happy, confident.

"C'mon in, Tabby. Trinity." Hobbs grabbed the bag from her without asking, figuring it was some kind of massage chair. It was surprisingly light, just bulky. He stepped aside, hoping he'd be able to help her relax. No use having a massage from someone so nervous they couldn't get their hands straight.

Tabitha walked in, followed by her dog. She popped off her sneakers in the entryway and followed Hobbs into the kitchen. She looked around, her face like she'd just entered an alien spaceship. Hannah had worn a similar expression the morning of her first full day here. Then she'd asked, "Is this all you have for cookware?" and poked Hobbs's Everything Pot, which rested on the stovetop. Things had only got worse from there once Hannah opened a drawer and eyed the pile of plastic forks and knives that constituted most of his flatware. Luckily, Tabitha shouldn't need a fork today.

"Do you want anything?" Hobbs set the bag on the floor. "Water?"

"No, thanks." Her brown eyes looked especially pretty when she was nervous, because they were so big and bright.

"Tequila?"

Her eyes got even bigger.

"I'm kidding, Tabby. I can see you're not in a joking mood. All business. That's great." He clapped his hands together. "Where do you want me?"

"Um." Tabitha grabbed up the bag and scanned the living room, just off the kitchen. It was already dim, lit only by one lamp with a multicolored shade that cast the room in quiet ambience. "Anywhere is fine." She pointed at the space between the couch and the chair where Victor had fallen asleep. "There?"

"Anywhere you want."

Hobbs snapped off the kitchen lights and watched for the next five minutes as she carried the bag into the living room, opened it, withdrew a long piece of metal and began unfolding it, sliding in a headrest and adjusting knobs. She messed with everything, her movements flustered and quick, her hands going like little birds. Once she seemed to have everything in place, and was again playing with all the knobs, Hobbs walked over and stilled her movements with a hand to her shoulder. "It looks great. Should I climb on?"

Tabitha glanced at his hand, then up into his eyes, and cleared her throat. "Yes," she said. "Get in the chair. I'll turn on the music and go wash."

Though most chair massage was done clothed, Tabitha asked Hobbs to take off his shirt so she could practice her routine on his back. He peeled his sweatshirt over his head without question and tossed it on the couch, leaving behind the warm, soapy smell of a recent shower. Nobody ever needed to tell Hobbs twice to take off his shirt, and though it was a running joke in the gym, he certainly had nothing to be ashamed of. He had a solid, muscular build with body fat so low Tabitha could see every delineation, which, despite being nice to look at, was an unexpectedly helpful study of the muscles.

"You can see your serratus anterior," Tabitha mused. "I never noticed before." Twice now those muscles had popped into her work, once with Candy and now with Hobbs. Names that had seemed impossible to remember were now coming to her in practical situations. Maybe she wasn't going to fail all her quizzes after all.

"My serratus anterior?" Hobbs glanced at his midsection.

"Your boxer's muscles." Tabitha pointed near his ribs. "Your body makes everything really easy to see. Not just on paper or some mannequin. I've never seen them pop out as much as yours."

Hobbs smiled. "Glad to be of help."

Tabitha motioned to the chair and Hobbs climbed on, face in the cradle, his arms at rest on the padded shelf. His back was another wonderful story. As he shifted around, Tabitha could see the outline of his traps and lats, as well as the deep well of his spine thanks to the bulkiness of his spinal erectors.

"Everything okay?" Hobbs's voice came muffled from the cradle after some time had gone by and Tabitha had yet to lay hands on him.

"Um. Yeah. Sorry." Tabitha snapped to and dug out her lotion. *Don't use too much*, she told herself. She squeezed a dime-sized amount in her palm, then rubbed her hands together, which were cold, despite the hot water she'd used to wash up. "My fingers are kind of chilly," she warned. She hovered just over Hobbs's skin, like she had with Candy, and could feel the heat radiating from him. When she finally made contact, he gave a little jump. "Sorry," she said. "They'll warm up."

"It's okay."

Tabitha practiced her effleurage by gliding her hands all over his back and shoulders, hoping to warm up both her hands and his skin. As she worked her way around, the smell of his soap rose up and filled her; it was some kind of flowery scent that surprised her. "What is your soap?" she mused aloud. "Lilacs?"

"Not sure. It's a bodywash with white flowers on the bottle."

"Really?" Tabitha chuckled to herself, then realized she'd already made several errors. One, don't ask your clients about their soap or comment on their bodies in any way, unless you were pointing out a bruise, rash or suspicious mole. Two, never laugh at your client. Three, keep quiet and let your client relax.

"What? It was the cheapest one," Hobbs said. "It was buy one, get one free."

Tabitha laughed out loud now. She'd already racked up the errors—might as well keep going.

"So I'm supposed to use a manly bodywash, is that it? Something like 'Sand and Grit for Men'?"

"Ouch." Tabitha's laughter doubled. "That sounds painful. Perhaps 'A Walk in the Woods at Midnight'?"

"I'd definitely use that. That sounds manly. But also a little magical. What do you think it would smell like?"

"The moon, of course. And trees. Definitely trees."

"Trees are manly," Hobbs agreed. "The moon is female, though. A celestial, sensual orb that controls the tides."

"Wow. I didn't know you were so poetic."

"It'll be our little secret."

Tabitha's laughter died down as she reached Hobbs's shoulders, where she could actually see the separation of anterior, middle and posterior delts, like he'd just pumped some iron. She knew by his damp hair, though, that he really had just got out of the shower. She glided over the delts, trying out the Jelly Jar technique Joy had taught them, which involved rolling up the triceps, over the delts, around the scapula and over the upper traps while using both hands. The first time Tabitha had seen Joy do it she'd been fascinated; the Jelly Jar was a magic trick, sleight of hand and twist of fate, and she'd soaked it up like a child watching a magician lose a quarter behind someone's ear.

"It feels like you have a hundred hands," Hobbs said, which made Tabitha forget herself in a rush of adrenaline. The Jelly Jar worked!

She moved to his upper traps, which were easy to grip and roll through her fingers and thumbs. "How's this pressure?"

"It's all great, Tabby. You've got good hands."

They both went quiet after that. There was nobody else in the house, as far as Tabitha knew, and Hobbs didn't appear to have any pets, so the only sound came from the little speaker hooked up to her phone, which was playing spa music, something ethereal and flute heavy that transported her to another time. Talk about A Walk in the Woods at Midnight—she could be massaging Hobbs in a wooded glen in the fourteenth century and this would seem normal. She got into a flow with her movements, no longer worrying about executing the perfect Jelly Jar or neck routine, and simply listened to what Hobbs's body was telling her through her own touch and his reactions to it. Tabitha knew when she found a sore muscle fiber based on the slight flinch to Hobbs's back. She knew when a stroke was working by the way he sank deeper into the massage chair and loosed a contented sigh. She knew when the medial side of his scapula needed a little more attention because her elbow wanted to linger there, to keep stroking until the tissue relaxed, flattened and opened up.

This was all new for Tabitha. Usually, she was either just trying to get through her student exchanges or she was trying hard to impress Red. With Hobbs, she'd let her guard down, had merely laid her hands on him and let her touch and instincts be her guide, had melted into the experience as much as her client had, marking this as the first time anything had actually clicked for her with a human subject.

Hobbs's forearm glided down through her palms, where Tabitha started to work on his right hand, the skin near the base of his fingers rough with calluses, a contrast to the smoothness of the center of his palm, almost delicate. Tabitha worked her thumb over the calluses and her fingertips over the palm and slowly the atmosphere changed. It seemed like the room grew quieter, even though nobody touched the volume of the music, and the air thicker, though the vents kept blowing heat at the same rate. If Tabitha had ever doubted that Hobbs carried a lot of hidden stress, buried deep from his past, covered up with his antics at the gym and constant smile, it now vanished. So much for the eyes being the mirror to the soul. Right now, Hobbs's soul lived in his hands.

His muscles twitched the tiniest bit. She went a little deeper with the pressure, then stroked each finger and worked his wrists in circles in each direction. Hobbs's words about his father's death came to her in that moment. *We didn't get along.* The words were nothing. Fluff. A magic trick, like the Jelly Jar. It felt like a hundred hands, when there were only two, and Hobbs's father's death was a lot more than *not getting along.* There was so much pain there Tabitha sensed that Hobbs's hand ached to grab on to something, to secure himself, to anchor somewhere, maybe to feel safe for once in his life.

His fingers closed just the tiniest bit over hers. Then, suddenly, Hobbs was sitting up straight.

"Did I hurt you?"

"No. I'm just..." Hobbs trailed off, still straddling the chair as he faced her. She needed to say something but words wouldn't come. Hobbs slid off the chair and squeezed his hands in and out of fists. Tabitha expected him to tell her the massage had been horrible, but he looked down at her and said, "Sorry, Tabby. I think that's enough massage for tonight."

"Sure. No problem. But...just for my notes. What did I do wrong? I want to get better."

"You didn't do anything wrong. I promise."

"Are you sure? Is it...was it...when everything changed?" She lowered her voice and went for it. "Did you feel that, too?"

Hobbs said nothing. Just when Tabitha started to feel foolish, started to think she had imagined everything, he nodded.

"You have a lot going on inside you," Tabitha said, relieved she wasn't going crazy and a little freaked that she'd sensed all that. She looked down at Hobbs's hands and the warmth that had washed over her body came back for another slam. She realized now she probably should've backed off as soon as she felt all those things being unearthed. "I'm sorry," she said. "Things were going so well. We can try again if you want." Tabitha motioned toward the chair. "Not go so deep."

"I can't." Hobbs made no move toward the chair. "You didn't do anything wrong. But I can't do more tonight." The room filled with the sounds of pan flutes moaning in the background, the smell of buy-one-get-one-free lilac body-wash and Hobbs's steady gaze. Well. She'd already made half a dozen errors with this massage. Might as well add one more.

"When you said you didn't get along with your dad—" Tabitha's voice cut through the music "—that wasn't really even close to the truth, was it?"

To his credit, Hobbs didn't look away. "No," he said.

"Is that why you're always goofing off? Making a joke out of everything?" Tabitha felt emboldened by the atmosphere, the music, the force of whatever had rooted itself deep inside of Hobbs that had loosened and leached into her own body during their exchange. His memories, and all the feelings attached to them, had fed into her veins like osmosis. "Pretending life is one big party?"

Hobbs took a step closer to her, closing off any safe space that Tabitha might've kept around her perimeter. Trinity, asleep on Hobbs's couch, didn't even stir. "You're so full of questions," he said, with no trace of irritation in his voice. "Maybe I'll answer. If you answer one of mine."

Tabitha uncrossed her arms. "What do you want to know?" She braced herself, ready for him to ask about Afghanistan, the IED, the explosion, the moment in her life everyone wanted to pinpoint as the root of her *problems*, like they could reduce everything she was now into that one incident.

"Why do you always doubt yourself?"

Tabitha stammered for a moment. Finally she said, "I don't *always* doubt myself."

"You're doing it now. I said this wasn't your fault, that your massage was great, and I meant it. This was all me. But you doubt yourself. You do the same thing at the gym."

Tabitha stuck her chin in the air, wanting to argue but with really no case to make. "Well, that's why I have the Badass List. I'm working on it. Which brings us back to my question. I answered yours. Now you have to answer mine. About your dad. About the things you hide. Which you deflected again. You really are a master of the colored scarves."

"You should see me with a set of rings."

"Do you ever stop joking around?"

"Trust me. I give you guys the best version of me." Then, without warning, he reached out and tucked a stray piece of hair behind her ear.

A shiver ran over Tabitha's spine. It occurred to her that this had been a two-way street. She had got a little peek at the depths of Hobbs. Might he have got the same from her?

"You'd better start figuring out how awesome you are before things get too far with Thaddeus, you know." Hobbs's tone was light, amused. "So he doesn't take you for granted."

"I'm not sure I want things to get far with Thaddeus."

"Why not?" Hobbs's voice softened. "Have you even kissed him yet?"

"I'm dreading kissing Thaddeus, if it ever comes to that." There was no point in lying. "He'll lean in, I'll step on his feet or something, Trinity will bark, our lips will miss, like a bad high five…"

Hobbs's smile spread slowly over his face, but it was different from his usual offering, the happy persona he gave to everyone in the room. This had a tinge of affection to it, a new sight, like seeing artwork from an entirely different angle. "Were you dreading kissing me, too? On your birthday? It didn't seem like you were dreading it. If I thought that, I would've stopped."

Tabitha stammered something that couldn't count as yes or no. "I didn't have time to dread it. It was so unexpected."

"Another ringing endorsement," Hobbs said. "If only I'd had time to dread it."

"You've never said anything about that kiss, either."

"What do you mean?" Hobbs was really close now, the personal space gone, his warmth reaching out and drawing her in like a gravitational pull.

"You said it wasn't what you were expecting. You didn't say why."

His smile softened. "No. I didn't."

The room was so warm now. Tabitha imagined her body felt like the core of the earth. She hated that all Hobbs had to do was smile to get her to feel this way.

There was something about him, starting way back on the Fourth of July, when she'd pulled out of her panic attack and found his warm, strong hand gripping hers. He helped free something inside of her, with his cavalier attitude and bullish optimism, his strength and easy charm. It was like finding a companion on a dark, gloomy trail. You were still in the fog but you were no longer alone.

"Hey, if you're really worried about kissing Thaddeus, I'm willing to help you out," Hobbs said.

Tabitha felt sizzly all over. Was he serious? Or just trying to change the subject?

"Go ahead," Hobbs continued. "Practice makes perfect. What was first? Oh, right. I lean in." Hobbs reached out, slid an arm around her waist—a light, sensual touch—then bent his head down, closer to hers. "Now you're supposed to step on my feet, according to your order of operations."

Despite how ridiculous she felt, Tabitha's body had its own ideas. The arm around her waist felt like it was burning straight through her, heating up her whole body. She slid one of her feet between his. The other went just outside of his left foot. She had socks on and Hobbs's feet were bare. His toes felt cold against her sock.

"Wow. Not one stomp," Hobbs said, his voice light, playful. "Now the dog is supposed to bark." He glanced at the couch, where Trinity lay. Tabitha followed his gaze and saw that the pittie was fast asleep. Hobbs pressed his lips together and raised his eyebrows like *Guess not?*

Tabitha whispered a laugh and forced herself not to look away, to hold Hobbs's gaze.

His smile fell. "Only one step left." His voice dropped in timbre. "You gonna miss like a bad high five? Let's see what ya got, Tabby."

Tabitha hesitated, a lump forming in her throat. She wasn't afraid she'd miss. She was afraid she wouldn't.

"Try putting your hands somewhere," Hobbs suggested. "Stir things up. Make your intentions known. Let me get excited about what's coming next."

Tabitha's arms were currently hanging at her sides, limp and awkward. She reached out and rested her hands on either side of Hobbs's bare waist. She lightly stroked his skin, still warm. Despite having just been massaging that same body, the contact felt different. The *intention* was different, just as Hobbs had said.

"That's it," Hobbs whispered. He was so close now the waves of hair on his forehead brushed over hers. "I feel it now. What you want. Where you want things to go. Are you getting the same?"

Tabitha nodded, her ability to speak gone. The world was so thick and hot now. Every movement felt like slow motion. She tilted her head up and leaned in until the softness of Hobbs's lips met hers. The contact stole one of her heartbeats, her chest a thudding mess. The arm around her waist drew her in, tight against Hobbs's body, forcing their kiss to deepen. Tabitha slid her hands up his chest and around his neck, her lips parting to accept more of him, the desire to get deeper, tighter, hotter, compounding with every breath.

The smell of free lilacs had changed to something warmer, more layered, earthy, like lilacs in fresh soil. *Lilacs in the moonlight.* Hobbs's hands trailed over Tabitha's backside, smooth, testing, and rather than recoil she leaned into it, pressing harder against his body, enjoying the rigid feeling of his arousal. A rushed sigh of pleasure escaped Hobbs's lips and the pressure of his hands increased, softly grinding her against him. Tabitha's body no longer felt like hers. The tight, awkward uncertainty of her was gone and somebody new was blooming and melting against Hobbs, like a watercolor.

Hobbs pulled back slowly, withdrawing with obvious reluctance from their kiss. "Dang, Tabby," he said. "Thaddeus is in trouble."

Tabitha's words came with short breath, beneath the thudding of her heart. "I don't want to talk about Thaddeus. I don't want to talk at all."

Just as Hobbs's lips parted, a question in his eyes, a woman's voice rang out from the hallway.

"Chris? Is somebody here?"

seventeen

Aw, damn it to hell.

Hobbs dropped his hand away and grabbed his shirt from where he'd tossed it on the couch. He slipped it over his head and willed his body to relax, blood to go back to all the places it belonged. He glanced at Tabitha, whose eyes were large and questioning, but the sight of her freshly kissed lips and hot cheeks wasn't helping, so he cleared his throat and reminded himself his sister was approaching—that did the trick—just as the kitchen light snapped on.

"Hey."

Hobbs hadn't wanted Hannah to go, and now that she was back he wished she'd taken a little longer to drive around those back roads. He eyed her curious, lost expression, the same look she'd had on her face the time he'd brought Kitty Banes home after a date at the movies. They'd seen a Stephen King flick, so Kitty was already scared and in need of comforting, and it being Friday night meant Pops would've started drinking extra early and probably been passed out by then. Mom would be out, at book club or bridge club or one of the many clubs where she escaped from her family, and Victor had already moved out. Hobbs would have the place to himself and finally score some alone time with Kitty. Which was working great until Hannah padded into the living room, wearing her Snoopy jammies and carrying that ratty old quilt Gran Gran had made her when she was born. The colors were faded to pastels and the edges ratty, but Hannah carried it at night, sometimes during the day, too, and that night was no exception. Hobbs had looked up from kissing Kitty and saw Hannah there, peeking out from behind that quilt, her confusion ceding to fear, which wouldn't make sense in a normal house. But they didn't live in a normal house, and anything that stole Hobbs's attention shook Hannah's sense of stability, so he'd taken Kitty home and that'd been the last date they'd ever had.

"Tabitha, this is Hannah." Hobbs gave his throat another big clear as he ran his hands through his hair, hoping to brush off the tension that hung thick in the air. Hannah stared and Tabitha's jaw looked like it was working not to drop. "My baby sister," he added.

Tabitha mouthed, *Oh.* Then she said it aloud. "*Oh.* Oh, hi." She straightened her shirt, ironing over the front of it. "Nice to meet you, Hannah."

"Hi." Hannah waved.

"I didn't even know you had a sister." Tabitha tried a smile. "I can see the resemblance." She touched her hair.

"Hannah came home with me." Hobbs felt the rest of his arousal wash away. "She's from Omaha. Never been outside the Midwest."

"Until now," Hannah said, irritation gritty in her voice. Brother of the Year Award was definitely in his future. Followed closely by Coach of the Year. In the span of a few weeks he'd gone from living alone in his bachelor pad to putting up his depressed sister and kissing the one woman from his gym he'd told himself was off-limits. Both women looked like they didn't quite know where to be or what to say.

"Oh my gosh, what a sweetie!" Hannah's mood changed so fast it made Hobbs feel light-headed. She headed for the couch, crouching down to put herself at eye level with Trinity. "Oh, she's a service dog." Hannah stopped just short of petting her as she spied the vest. "Is she yours?" She turned to Tabitha.

"Yes." Tabitha's smile was full and genuine now. "We were just… I was just…" She motioned toward the massage chair, forgotten in the middle of the living room. "I'm in school to become a massage therapist. Hobbs agreed to be one of my guinea pigs. Trinity is my service dog. You can pet her, though. She's not working right now." Those last words came out of Tabitha's mouth long and slow, like they'd given her pause or food for thought.

That was all Hannah needed. She was all up in Trinity's face, petting her ears, her shoulders, almost nuzzling her nose. Trinity looked both confused and conciliatory: *Is this human losing her mind? Okay, then, I got this.*

"You lucky duck." Hannah glanced over her shoulder and gave Hobbs a look that could only be described as accusatory. "You know a massage therapist? I'd give my right arm for one of those right now." She arched her back and planted a hand there, keeping her other one on Trinity while she stroked her fur.

Hobbs didn't have time to say anything before Tabitha piped in with, "I'd be happy to massage you," like she'd known Hobbs's master plan all along. "I'm not licensed yet, so I can't guarantee how good it will be, but I could do your feet. Your neck. Anything, really."

"Are you kidding?" Hannah gave Trinity a kiss on the top of her head and stood up to face her. "I'd love you forever."

"Anything for Hobbs's sister." Tabitha glanced in his direction. She smoothed out her sweatshirt again.

Hannah gave him a withering look. "You make people call you by your last name, Chris? How douchey."

Hobbs shrugged. "It started in the corps. Almost everyone calls me Hobbs." Hobbs nodded at Tabitha. "Tabitha calls me Chris sometimes." Though she hadn't, not since that one time. She'd asked for his first name last spring, when they'd partnered for the charity workout at Canine Warriors.

Tabitha glanced over and smiled. "I'd better pack up."

Hobbs helped her gather her things while she and Hannah discussed a day and time to do a massage. Hannah stayed glued to Trinity's side, her hand never once leaving the dog's vest, where it rested like she was drawing in strength from the little pit bull.

"So you don't know how long you're here," Tabitha said, zipping up the black canvas bag around her folded chair. She murmured over the words, like she was trying to figure out the whole story of Hannah's sudden appearance, Hobbs's silence about it all, without actually asking direct questions. "Which means you don't have Thanksgiving plans, either. Would you like to come over? My Auntie El makes the best food on the planet."

Hobbs almost said no on reflex. The last thing he needed was a family holiday with Tabitha. But Hannah's face brightened for the second time in less than half an hour, a look Hobbs had not seen since she'd met George and Gracie. Hannah turned to Hobbs, eyes big and questioning. It didn't take a rocket scientist to figure out what she wanted him to say. One of her major sads about coming out here, despite the obvious, was that the holidays wouldn't be the same without Mom and

Victor. Hannah hadn't even wanted to talk about it, maybe was pretending the holidays weren't happening, that none of this was happening.

"Great," Hobbs said, forcing the word out. "We'd love to. Thanks."

Hannah's face broke into a smile. She ran her hand down Trinity's back.

Hobbs carried Tabitha's chair out to her car, even though Tabitha insisted she could get everything herself. After he slid it into the trunk, he found her facing him, worry in her eyes. "I don't think I can massage you again."

"I totally agree." Only now, with the cool air clearing his head, did Hobbs realize just how fortuitous it was that Hannah had come home when she did. How far would things have gone? Too far, probably. "I'm going to be honest. I asked you out here to massage Hannah. She threw a kink in my plans by deciding to go for a drive right before you got here. It just seemed easier, after that, to let you keep on thinking you were here for me."

Tabitha started to say something and stopped. Her breath turned to steam in the cold air, the streetlights casting her skin in a light that made her look sleepy and warm. "I don't know if I should be mad about that or not." She shrugged. "But I'm not. I'll definitely come back to massage her, like I promised." Tabitha looked like she wanted to say more, maybe ask some questions, but she didn't.

"Listen. Tabby."

She put up a hand. "Don't do it."

"Don't do what?"

"Say whatever you're going to say, and ruin what happened between us in there."

Damn. She was too good at sensing things. It was like Hobbs had nowhere to hide.

Tabitha glanced down at Trinity, who'd just finished peeing in Hobbs's yard. "I better go."

Hobbs reached out and ran a finger under her chin. Tabitha looked up at him with a mixed expression, something hard over a soft center, like a wintry mix, when sleet fell after snow. "I'm sorry about ending the massage. You just got to me, is all. With your magic hands and all that." She was quiet, her eyes cautious. "I went somewhere I wasn't ready to go." Hobbs shrugged, then gestured toward the house. "Then after that, I was—"

Tabitha held up a finger to silence him. "You're going to ruin it. Don't."

Hobbs sighed. After a second of silence, he tried again. "The stuff with my sister was sudden. I didn't know until I got to Omaha. I certainly didn't know she'd be coming back here with me. The guy she was seeing turned out to be abusive and we all agreed she needed to get away for a while."

Tabitha's whole body changed. Her expression slackened but her body tensed, which was an odd thing to watch, like plastic wrap grabbing on to itself. "That's horrible," she said, her voice almost a whisper. "I thought Hannah seemed sad. I'm sorry, Chris. I'll definitely massage her as much as she needs."

Chris.

"Thanks, Tabby." Despite the fact that he'd told himself Tabitha was definitely off-limits, he had a strong urge to hug her goodbye. Just draw her in and feel those hands on his back while he held her body close to his. But that would be even more selfish than he'd already been. "You definitely made progress tonight on your goal. The one about excelling at massage. No jokes, you did great."

Tabitha's mouth relaxed into a resigned smile. "Thanks. I still need to fix my Badass List. It's still unspecific as hell."

"And the motorcycle ride." Hobbs pointed at her. "That's

still ours, right? No matter what else happens, I'm taking you on that ride. Promise?" He offered his pinkie, like he was a teenage girl.

Tabitha's smile proved up. She hooked his pinkie with her own. "Promise."

"Good night, then." Hobbs took a second too long to pull his finger away. He cleared his throat. "See you soon."

"Night," Tabitha said, turning away. "See you soon."

Hobbs watched her drive away. She flashed her head beams at him and disappeared. He stood there a little while longer, alone in the cold dark, wondering again what the fuck he was doing. His relationships with women were always so cut-and-dried. Easy. No strings and no misunderstandings. Now Hobbs felt like his head was spinning.

When he got back inside, Hannah was waiting for him in the kitchen, a cat-ate-the-canary smile on her face. "Is she your girlfriend? That would be a first."

"She's not." Hobbs grabbed his favorite glass and filled it under the tap. The water was that unpleasant, sat-in-the-pipes room temperature but he glugged it down, not realizing how parched he was until the liquid hit his tongue.

"She's not what I'd expect." Hannah went to the stove and lit a flame under the teapot.

"What do you mean?"

Hannah rooted a mug from the cupboard and opened the box of tea bags she'd bought their first visit to the grocery store. There was a cartoon bear in a nightcap on the front and the inside smelled of cinnamon. "You usually go around with faster girls," she said. "Based on what I remember. And things you've told me."

"We're not a thing."

Hannah plopped a tea bag in her mug and looked up from her task. "Okay" was all she said. As the silence crawled to uncomfortable, she added, "Well, she seems great. Smart. Pretty. Young?"

Hobbs refilled his glass and slugged that down, too. This one was colder. "In between our ages. She just turned thirty."

"Nice. Just—" Hannah shrugged lightly. "Be careful with this one."

Hobbs considered a third protest, but Hannah had always been able to see right through him. "I'm not sure you should be giving me advice."

Hannah's face fell. The teapot started humming on the stove.

"Don't give me that look." Hobbs didn't care if he sounded harsh. "Are we ever going to talk about this guy who was hurting you?"

"Not right now." Hannah snapped off the burner before the teapot started a full whistle. She poured steamy water in her mug, the tea bag making pleasant crinkling sounds as it opened up and the leaves plumped. "I can't." She dug a teaspoon out of the one drawer she'd tidied up her second day here. "I just can't right now."

Hobbs didn't argue. "Do you really want to go over at Thanksgiving? Or were you being nice? Because I can whip up a mean protein shake. Some eggs and bacon, maybe. Big bowl of broccoli."

Hannah's head snapped up. "I want to go over. I can't just hide in your house until spring, Chris. And what about the lady with the dog who looks like Gemma and the bodyguard cat? You promised you'd text her."

Hobbs had been hoping that if enough time passed, both Hannah and Clementine would forget about George and Gracie coming over to try things out. "I will tomorrow." At the look on Hannah's face, Hobbs spread open his palms. "Promise."

★ ★ ★

Hobbs had never been to the Dogwood County Animal Shelter, which was a large, rectangular building off the highway, right near the dump. Hobbs had been to the landfill plenty of times, usually to help friends toss out old furniture because Hobbs was typically the go-to guy to help friends move furniture. He'd never even considered fostering a pet, not because he wouldn't foster but because he didn't want pets. Especially not a dog. Especially not a cute Lab mix puppy that looked like Gemma.

But here he was, walking into the shelter where Lily worked, because that was where Clementine had told him to go when he texted this morning.

This is Lily's bag. I got in trouble for taking over, so you're going to have to deal with her directly. She'd shared Lily's contact information, and when Hobbs had texted, Lily had written back within the hour.

I'm at work this morning. George and Gracie are with me. Feel free to stop by.

Hobbs could hear barking dogs as soon as he neared the heavy metal door at the end of a crumbling sidewalk. He could see a large dumpster out back, as well as a fenced-in, covered range of land about the size of half a football field, presumably for giving dogs exercise. The sign over the door read Dogwood County Animal Shelter in black print so old the letters were scratched up but readable. Hobbs stepped inside and was immediately greeted by half a dozen dogs in various sizes. They approached him in different speeds, some racing up to his legs, others coming in sideways and a couple that both hung back and moved forward, like an uncertain dance. There was a golden chow with the hair around its face shaved down, a red dachshund who spun in circles, a thick golden retriever with a noticeable gimp, a little white terrier of some kind with stand-up ears like a Scottie, a skinny beagle with more white than black coloring and a pit bull of some kind, all black, a lot like Trinity but much larger in size.

"Hi." An older woman with long, straight blond hair pulled back in a ponytail waved at him from behind a desk. She wore glasses with thick black rims and had a patient smile on her face, like everyone's favorite librarian in school. "They're all out to play, but they're all friendly." She came around the desk, to the large, open area of cheap carpet and assorted dog toys where Hobbs stood.

Hobbs knelt down and the terrier immediately climbed up his leg and got in his lap. The pit bull clearly thought that was a good idea because he shoved his rear end against Hobbs's knee, trying to wedge in on the other side. Hobbs lost his balance but caught himself, one hand planting on the rug and the other gripping the terrier, who didn't budge.

"That's Mel," the woman said, her voice indulgent. "He thinks he's as small as Mabel."

Hobbs gave in and sat on the floor. Mel fell against him, his front legs dangling over Hobbs's knee, while Mabel lay curled on the other side. The other four dogs either got in Hobbs's face or went around him in circles, sniffing. "Where'd they all come from?" His mood had shifted from duty-bound to a little sad, seeing all these creatures so ready to give and get some love, when they obviously had nobody.

"They all have different stories." The woman pushed her glasses up the bridge of her nose. "Mel was brought in by a guy who said he wanted to get his newborn son a puppy instead. Mabel belonged to an elderly woman who passed away. The stories are as varied as the animals who come in here."

"Look at you."

Hobbs glanced over his shoulder at Lily, who'd appeared from somewhere in the back. She wore a pair of blue jeans and a camouflage-patterned sweatshirt, her hair up in a messy bun. The dogs rushed to her, pressing around her body like Siamese cats. Only Mabel stayed put. Mel barreled into Lily so hard she stumbled, but she must've been used to his behavior because she'd braced herself and didn't go down.

"Hey, Lily."

"Hey, Hobbs." She grinned. "You're not used to animals, are you?"

"Why do you say that?" Even though it was true. At least, not in a long, long time.

"You look awkward. Like you don't quite know who to pet or what to do. Am I right, Sally?"

Sally offered a soft laugh. Hobbs stood up and set the little terrier down. She swayed for a second, wobbly, then marched over to Lily and stared at her expectantly.

"I can't hold you right now, Mabel." Lily fisted her hips, peered down at the little terrier and used a toddler voice to speak to her. "She'd sit in our laps all day if she could. Sometimes she does." Then Lily turned to Sally. "He's come for George and Gracie."

"Oh." Sally's mouth made a circle of surprise. She glanced in the corner, and only then did Hobbs see them. In all the commotion, he hadn't noticed the dog-and-cat pair in the far corner, atop a dog bed. Gracie was lying down, but alert, like she wanted to come play, and George sat nearby, watching with intent. He wore a steel-gray sweater today, like the color of storm clouds, which Hobbs figured suited the hairless cat to a tee.

"Gracie wants to play," Lily explained. "But she knows that if she does, George will get in the mix and behave badly.

Like that kid in the schoolyard who doesn't know how to get along? So he ruins the game for everyone else."

"Yeah." Hobbs knew exactly what she meant. There was a kid named Todd Wells back in grade school who was awkward and angry most of the time. Nobody wanted to play with him because he cheated at games or said random, rude things out of the blue. Whenever he was invited in he'd steal the dodge ball and go hide with it, run in the middle of the girls' jump ropes or smear mud all over the monkey bars. Everyone called him Odd Todd. Victor had told Hobbs years later that Odd Todd came from a house where nobody paid attention to him; the parents were always gone and Todd and his older brother were left to fend for themselves.

"If you want to leash up Gracie, I'll get George." Lily grabbed a leash from a group of them that hung from pegs on the wall. "We can take them to your house, see how things go."

Hobbs liked the young lady's in-charge, no-nonsense attitude. Reminded him a little of Rhett, even though Rhett got on his nerves a good part of the time. But Rhett got things done, and the sort of trust he imparted to his athletes was hard-won and came from the sort of confidence Lily had already cultivated.

"What about all these guys?" Hobbs felt sad to leave them. They'd been so excited to see him, rushing over like eager children when the uncle from out of town came to visit with bags of goodies.

Lily spread her hands out and managed to make contact with every one of them, even the ones settling down with toys. "I'll be back, my babies," she said. She turned to Hobbs. "They'll be okay. We'll take care of them until they get homed. It's the ones still out there that I worry about."

Hobbs took the leash Lily offered and slipped it on Gracie's collar. She sat up and wagged her tail, looking up at him with her tawny eyes. A wave of sadness rolled through him so hard he felt unsteady on his feet. He hadn't realized it'd happened until Lily waved a hand in front of his face. "Hey," she said. "You got this?"

Hobbs blinked, and the moment passed. "Yeah. I got this. Let's go."

"You made Nana's pierogi." Lily eyed the steaming bowl of potato-and-cheese dumplings suspiciously. "You only ever make them for my birthday."

Clementine finished panfrying the last round of half-moons and dumped them in the bowl with the rest of the batch. "I had the day off. Brittany covered the store." The pile of blistered dough hiding a creamy center of mashed potatoes and sharp cheddar looked like a lot for two people, but Lily would eat them for days until they were gone. Clementine scraped the last of the butter and shallots from the pan into the dish, the pink bits of onion looking like candy sprinkles atop a dessert.

Lily's brows knitted at the center, Tyler's sharp gaze hiding inside her hazel eyes. "That still doesn't sound like you. You usually use your day off to hit the gym early, then lie on the couch with a book. And then we order pizza."

Clementine shrugged and tossed a piece of trout into the empty skillet. There was enough residual butter in the non-stick pan to get the job done. "I thought you might like them tonight. I had a craving." This wasn't a lie—Clementine always had a craving for Mama's pierogi, handed down for generations and an instant comfort with their buttery taste and contrasting textures. One bite and she was transported to childhood visits to her grandma's house, where pierogi were frequent on Fish Fridays, you had to wash and dry the dishes by hand and everyone said grace before anyone could touch a bite to eat.

Lily set the table with two plates, a small one for her—being a vegetarian, she would only eat the pierogi—and a larger one for Clementine. "I took George and Gracie to Hobbs's house today." Her voice was quiet, not full of the usual joy she typically had when somebody she'd been fostering got placed. Lily had nearly thrown a party when Roscoe went to a retired couple who lived in a small cottage near a lake, and when Benedict had been adopted by a family with a five-year-old boy whose personality matched the dog's. Ever since she'd come home from work today, she'd been holed up in her room, her answers to Clementine's questions brief and flat.

"Oh, right." Clementine pretended like she'd forgotten about that as she squeezed some lemon over her trout. "How'd that go?"

"Good." Lily set out napkins and forks. "They're going to foster them for now. Hannah is definitely a good choice. She already has plans to take them both on daily walks. When I got there she was really excited to show me the matching pink harnesses. Nobody's sure George will actually walk in it, but if Gracie goes, he probably will."

Clementine smiled to herself, picturing little George, all dolled up in one of his sweaters, pink harness showing off his moon-colored eyes. Gracie would probably strain against the leash until she was trained and George would keep her in check, his little legs going fast to keep up.

"Are you picturing it?" Lily got a half smirk on her face.

"Totally." Clementine dumped her fish onto her plate and settled into her chair.

Lily brought the big bowl of pierogi and began sliding them onto her plate, one at a time, like they were precious treasure.

"How did Hobbs feel about it? Could you tell?"

"He's definitely hesitant."

"Doesn't surprise me." Clementine accepted the spoon from

Lily when she was done and scooped up a few pierogi. "Hobbs clearly likes being single and the party life, from what I've seen."

Lily shrugged. "I don't know anything about that. I meant there's something about Gracie that gets to him." She rubbed her hand over her chest. "I don't know how to explain it. I just know it's there."

"Oh, okay." Clementine almost suggested that Lily didn't know Hobbs like the rest of them, but then she thought about how it might be easier for Lily to see a different version of Hobbs for that very reason. Lily had no biases.

Lily stabbed a pierogi with her fork tines and bit into it. "It's fine, though. Hannah will take care of them, no matter what."

Clementine sliced off a piece of her own pierogi and felt guilty as she bit into it. She realized she'd been trying to soothe herself with her grandma's food as much as she'd been trying to soothe Lily. "You really liked George and Gracie, didn't you?"

Lily chewed, her cheek full of pierogi. She didn't answer until she'd swallowed it down. "I like all the animals. In one way or another."

"Yes, I know, but..." Clementine poked her fish around her plate. "You liked them a little more. You didn't exactly rush to get them over to Hobbs's house. He had to contact you, rather than the other way around."

Lily stuffed another potato dumpling into her mouth. "I did that on purpose." This time, she spoke with her mouth full. "That's when I knew they were serious."

"Oh." Clementine felt the tension that had taken up residence in her shoulders for the larger part of the day start to melt like the butter in the dinner skillet. "That's really smart."

"But you're right." Lily gave her an unflinching gaze. "I did have a soft spot for George and Gracie. I kind of wanted to keep them. But I know you have your rule." Her voice hardened at the end, just a touch, like the stale edges of a marshmallow.

The tension came rushing back. "We agreed on that rule." This was one of those times Clementine hated parenting alone. It was bad enough that being a parent meant questioning everything that you did; when you were the only parent, you had no one to support you, keep you in check, give another point of view or just reassure you that you weren't going insane. It was like being stuck out in the middle of the ocean with only one oar. "If you want to be able to foster any animal who needs saving, we can't have a bunch of permanent pets."

"I know, Mom." Lily's usual enjoyment over pierogi was absent tonight. She'd been right; they were mostly reserved for her birthday or Christmas because they were such a pain in the butt. Clementine had spent a good part of the day making the dough and the mashed potatoes, as well as doing the assembly and cooking, which was twofold because they both enjoyed them fried after they'd been boiled. Usually they talked about Nana, who'd passed away a couple of years ago, while they ate way more than they should. But tonight the mood was definitely muted.

In fact, the whole house was pretty quiet.

"Do we have any rescues in the house right now?" Clementine laid her fork against her plate and looked around the room, like a dog, cat or rabbit might pop out of the shadows and start barking, mewing or running in circles.

"Nope." Lily polished off her last pierogi, scraping it around her plate to get the last of the sour cream before she shoved it in her mouth. "It's all peaceful for once. You should be happy."

"I've never complained about the rescues, Lil." Clementine thought about it. "Well, not much. I don't complain much."

Lily rose, plate in hands. "It's okay, Mom. You've let me

have loads more pets than most mothers do. Thanks for the pierogi. I'm going to bed to read. It's been a long day. G'night."

Clementine stayed silent as Lily loaded her dish and fork into the dishwasher and disappeared upstairs. She left the rest of her fish untouched, wondering why she felt so bad inside, when Lily seemed mostly okay about giving up George and Gracie. Lily wasn't the type for drama, though. She didn't throw fits or cry or demand attention. Clementine remembered back to when Lily was three years old, racing around the living room with Digger, who was a basset hound with big feet, so when he'd jumped on Lily's back she'd gone flying into the coffee table face-first, banging her head as she went down. When Clementine rushed over, Lily just stood up, blood streaming down her forehead, and giggled as Digger had gone for the blood, trying to lick her face. Lily had ended up needing five stitches, which she patiently sat through, her little hands clenched into fists as the doctor gave her a shot to numb her. She still had a faint, pale scar at her hairline.

"I can't believe that didn't hurt," Clementine had said, giving her a kiss.

"It did hurt." Lily's voice had sounded tiny and sure.

That was the moment Clementine had learned that Lily felt the same pain as everyone else—she just kept it to herself.

After Clementine cleaned up the dinner dishes, she went upstairs and walked past Lily's door, where she could see the faint yellow glow of her reading lamp from the gap. She paused, ready to knock, but then changed her mind. The house was so quiet it seemed almost obscene to make a knocking sound.

The house was just so damn quiet.

Clementine took a shower, and something about all that warm water got to her, and the tears started. Before she knew it, Clementine was full-blown crying in the shower, all the while chastising herself for not even being as brave as a three-year-old getting stitches. Once all the tears and snot were washed away, Clementine dried off, brushed her teeth and got in her jammies. The bed felt colder than usual as she crawled in, so she put on the TV and hunted around for George Burns and Gracie Allen. It wasn't on, just some reruns of *The Andy Griffith Show*, so Clementine pulled out her journal.

Dear Ty,
I'm mad at you for dying.
  That is all.
Love,
Clem

eighteen

As long as you live keep learning how to live.

~*Seneca*

There were a few stark moments in Tabitha's life where this mindset had saved her life. Waking on Thanksgiving Day to a cold, empty kitchen might not be one of them, but it sure felt like it. Normally Auntie El spent the entire morning spinning like a tornado from counter to counter, stove to sink to microwave. By noon, the table would be set with her old bone-white china and the food spread buffet style on the island. There would be turkey and ham sliced in mounds on platters; a pile of collard greens, braised for hours and shining in the pot liquor inside the peach-colored Dutch oven; fluffy mashed potatoes, like pillowy clouds fallen from the sky; poor man's brioche, warm and sliced thick as Texas toast; boats of gravy on either end of the table; and roasted, charred sweet potatoes, earthy chunks seasoned with turmeric and garlic—a far cry from that horrid mess of orange slop coated in melted marshmallows.

There was none of that. No food. No heavenly aromas. No Auntie El.

"Oh, no." Tabitha froze. Guests were coming at noon.

Auntie El would never let this happen.

Unless…

Tabitha rushed to Auntie El's bedroom, Trinity at her heels. She pushed open the door, allowing the morning sunlight to spill over the bed. Auntie El was a motionless mound beneath the covers. Tabitha crossed the room and laid her hand on Auntie El's shoulder. A tightly held breath escaped Tabitha's lungs. Auntie El was still warm and her shoulder rose and fell gently beneath Tabitha's touch. She mumbled something in her sleep.

Tabitha leaned in closer and closed her eyes. It sounded like she whispered, *Casey*, but Tabitha couldn't be sure. With her eyes shut and her hand still on Auntie El's shoulder, she could feel Auntie's fatigue like a thick wave. This was a paralyzing, desperate sleep. Auntie El's body wanted to heal, to snatch whatever time it could under precious, stolen slumber.

Thanksgiving dinner wasn't going to be cooked on time whether Tabitha woke Auntie El or not. Guests would be here in two hours and nothing cooked that fast. Tabitha drew the covers over Auntie El's shoulder and backed out of the room. She closed the door as quietly as she could, even though it didn't seem likely that anything would wake Auntie El right now.

She went back to the kitchen and went about various tasks, such as feeding Trinity, starting the coffee and going to the end of the driveway to grab the paper. Back inside, she laid out Auntie El's crossword puzzle so she'd have it when she woke. Then she faced the empty kitchen again and tried to decide what to do.

How selfish she'd been, sleeping in and thinking she would only offer the same contribution she made every Thanksgiving: wake on her own time, stir the gravy and wash the dishes. Tabitha had known Auntie El wasn't her old self and yet she'd still been sunk neck-deep into her own problems. She'd spent the week studying for finals, finishing up her massage exchange records and working at the bike shop, not once spending any time on what she'd put at the top of her Badass List: *Help Auntie El.*

And now it was too late. At least there wasn't a big crowd coming.

But people *were* coming, and the best way Tabitha could help Auntie El right now was by making sure they ate something.

"One badass dinner, coming up," Tabitha muttered. The next hour was a hot blur as Tabitha cranked up the dual ovens and pored over recipes online. She could still cook the turkey and heat the ham—they just wouldn't be done at noon. When people came at twelve, they'd just have to eat something else. Tabitha pulled cheese and butter from the fridge and grabbed a loaf of Auntie El's brioche. Thank God Auntie El always made the bread and pies the day before. Tabitha sliced up the loaf, softened butter in the microwave and layered squares of Havarti and provolone on the bread.

Thanksgiving grilled cheese was a thing, right?

Nobody would care as long as there was pie, right?

Just as Tabitha finished layering the last sandwich, the doorbell rang.

"There's my angel," Reverend Stokes said after Tabitha had whipped open the door, smoothed out her clothing and tried not to look frantic. "Happy Thanksgiving." He collected her in a hug, just inside the foyer. As he pulled back, his eyes narrowed in concern. "What's wrong?"

Tabitha invited him inside, settled him at the table with a glass of white wine and spilled her guts about her concerns over Auntie El. Reverend Stokes listened in silence as Tabitha finished tidying up the kitchen.

"She asked me not to say anything," Reverend Stokes said after Tabitha went quiet. "But Lavina did go to the doctor."

"And?" Tabitha removed her dirty apron and hung it inside the pantry door. "What'd they say?"

"They just don't know." Reverend Stokes shrugged. "She's fatigued. Sore all over. Moving slowly. They ran a blood panel, and other than slightly high sugar, there's nothing they can see that's wrong."

"High sugar?"

"They gave her meds and a diet to follow. I think they gave her some sleep meds, too. Maybe she took one last night."

"But they don't know what's wrong?" Tabitha pressed. "Are you sure Auntie El is telling you everything? Why didn't she tell me?"

Reverend Stokes laughed a little. "She's a private woman for sure. But she seemed sincere. And she doesn't want you worrying. Said you have enough to worry about in your own life."

"She's part of my life. A big part."

"She's your mother. Mothers don't want their kids worrying about them."

A lump formed in Tabitha's throat. "Casey." The word slipped out. Reverend Stokes's eyes widened, so she pressed further. "Does that name mean anything to you?"

The reverend's lips tightened into a thin line. "Where did you hear it?"

Tabitha pointed over her shoulder. "From Auntie El. She was talking in her sleep."

Reverend Stokes drummed his fingers over the table a moment, then took a large drink of wine. "He was one of Auntie El's fosters. About twelve years old. Do you remember him at all? You might not. You were quite young when Auntie El had him here and he only stayed a year."

Tabitha thought hard, but nobody was coming to mind. There were so many kids who came and went. She'd never formed any lasting attachments.

"He went back with his mother after she did some time," Reverend Stokes continued, not waiting for Tabitha's answer. "His household was always precarious, at best. Casey grew up and went through a few jobs. Was in and out of the system himself a few times. Auntie El heard recently he committed suicide. She took it real hard."

"Oh." Tabitha covered her heart with her hands. That explained a lot. Auntie El had always thought of all her fosters as her own, at least in some way. Some of them even kept in touch with Christmas cards or the occasional visit. Tabitha's memories of most were fleeting; by the time she was ten, Auntie El stopped fostering. She'd always said she wanted to focus on Tabitha, but Tabitha had always suspected it just got too heartbreaking. "I'm really sorry to hear that."

"Casey was one she fought for," Reverend Stokes added. "He didn't want to go home to his mother, but the way the law works in Virginia, it's almost impossible to keep a mother from her kids. Auntie El stood no chance. She was devastated at the time. Casey dying just brought all that back."

Tabitha slumped into a chair next to Reverend Stokes and thought again how lucky she was to have had Auntie El from the start. The death of Casey would explain a lot, though Tabitha wasn't sure it explained everything. At least it was a clue.

The doorbell rang, leaving her no time to think more on

it. "That'd be my guests," she said. "I hope they like grilled cheese, Reverend."

Reverend Stokes grinned. "Who doesn't?"

Delaney, Sean and Nora came first. Tabitha had mentioned during work this week that Hobbs and Hannah were coming to Thanksgiving dinner and that she was nervous about it. Nora had inserted herself in classic Nora Style. "Can we come, too?" she'd said. "I'll keep you from being nervous. Anything so I don't have to eat any more of her vegetarian food." She'd hooked a thumb over her shoulder at Delaney.

"You're free to go back home to Williamsburg and eat all the meat you want," Delaney had replied, not even looking up from the bike she was working on. Despite Delaney's frequent threats to kick Nora out, Tabitha had the feeling that Delaney was getting used to having her estranged mother around. They'd only just started to get to know one another again over the past few months. Then she'd added, "We'll come if you want, Steele. Since you said your auntie likes a crowd."

The first thing Tabitha saw when she opened the door was Delaney's dog, Wyatt, waiting with an eager smile on his face to get inside and see Trinity. He tugged so hard Delaney went flying over the threshold. "Slow down, boy," she scolded, then finally undid the leash and let him run. He and Trinity leaped into each other, bumping chests, like some kind of Dude High Five after winning a sporting event.

Tabitha led them inside and made introductions with Reverend Stokes. Delaney wore a formfitting gray sweaterdress and a pair of fashionable leather boots. It was hard not to stare, as Tabitha had never seen Delaney in anything but jeans and motorcycle boots or workout clothes.

"Pick your jaw up, Steele," Delaney muttered. "I can look pretty."

"You look amazing," Tabitha countered.

"Sorry we're a little late," Nora said. She wore blue jeans, a sweater and her typical cigarette behind her ear. "A group of people showed up at the shop as we were leaving, thinking we'd be open today. Can you believe that sh…" Her curse trailed off under Delaney's withering glare.

"Here you go." Sean handed over a bottle of red. "Thanks for having us." Detective Callahan wore a pair of dress slacks and a button-down, but today he was missing the badge that he typically wore on his belt or around his neck.

Reverend Stokes smiled and shook everyone's hands.

The doorbell rang again. Tabitha drew in a deep breath and braced herself. She opened the door to Hobbs's big smile and her nerves softened even more, but in a different way. This wasn't necessarily a relaxing feeling, due to the instant attraction that robbed her lungs of breath, but the anxiety that had come and gone in waves since this morning dissipated. Hobbs was also wearing dress slacks and a button-down shirt. Tabitha had never seen him cleaned up that way and it made her knees go oddly weak. Then she glanced down at the hairless cat in his arms and burst into laughter. "Is that George? Did you adopt George?"

The cat wore a brown sweater today, his pink face and big moony eyes indignant, like he resented being carried around like a doll.

"I'm fostering George. And Gracie." Hobbs pointed over his shoulder, to where Hannah stood behind him, hiding behind his big shoulders. Gracie peeked around, her golden face eager and happy, her tail wagging.

"Well, of course. You can't have George without Gracie."

"Literally."

Tabitha stifled a laugh as she pictured Auntie El's face if she woke up in time to witness this circus of animals.

"I should've asked. I'm sorry." Hobbs scratched the back

of his head. "It was really a last-minute thing. They've been settling in and we didn't think leaving them alone was a good idea. Gracie started whining when we went to leave, which made George howl like an alley cat. They're a little bit—" Hobbs watched as Gracie yanked away from Hannah's grip and ran headfirst into Wyatt and Trinity's game "—wild."

Gracie latched on to the middle of a stuffed raccoon that Wyatt and Trinity were tugging over. The toy barely had any stuffing left as it was and gave off a ripping sound.

"It'll be fine." Tabitha turned to Hannah, who was quiet as a mouse, looking like she wanted to disappear inside herself. "Come on in, Hannah. I'll introduce you." She put her arm around Hannah's shoulders and guided her to the dining room, where the others were all chatting and laughing.

Hannah smiled and leaned into her a little bit, leaving Tabitha feeling a little jolt of surprise. When was the last time someone leaned on her? Lately, Tabitha was the one doing all the leaning.

Hobbs followed along on Tabitha's other side, George still against his chest. "How's your week been? I haven't seen you at the gym."

"I've been too busy finishing up school for the semester."

"How's that going?"

"Well, let's see," Tabitha said. "For midterm practicals we had to pick a body part at random from a bag to massage on the instructor. I drew the hip and accidentally exposed Joy's gluteal cleft."

"Are those fancy words for *butt crack*?"

"You got it."

They laughed together. "And how has your week been?" Tabitha squeezed Hannah's shoulder to include her.

"It's been a wild week," Hobbs said, glancing over at his sister. "But they're coming along. Gracie is learning to walk on a leash and George is…" Hobbs paused to sigh. "Learning to walk on a leash."

"Really? That's amazing."

"Yeah. He's quite the character. Unfortunately, Gracie likes my bed. So I wake up to her licking my face most mornings. And where Gracie goes, George goes. So I wake up to puppy breath and the first thing I see when I open my eyes is this hairless cat, in one of his various sweaters, staring at me like something out of a horror movie."

Tabitha burst into laughter just as they hit the kitchen. Now she faced a hungry crowd, waiting for the famous spread Tabitha had talked up all week. "I hate to break this to you guys," she said, once everyone had gone quiet. "But my aunt isn't feeling that great, and the food didn't get made."

"Nonsense," Reverend Stokes piped in. He went to the stove and lit the flame beneath the cast-iron pan. "Grilled cheese is food. And Tabitha has been working on these grilled cheese sandwiches all morning."

"Grilled cheese?" Nora took the cigarette from behind her ear and stuck it between her lips. "I came for meat. I came to get away from grilled cheese." She gave a pointed look in her daughter's direction.

"I could throw some lunch meat on yours," Tabitha suggested.

Delaney glared at her mother, then rubbed her hands together and grinned. "Grilled cheese? Now you're speaking my language. Thank you, Steele. I couldn't ask for more."

"Grilled cheese is great," Sean added. "I eat it all the time at her house." He pointed at Delaney, who gave him a smack on the arm.

"Sounds great, Tabby," Hobbs said. "Sorry to hear about your auntie. Can I help?"

Tabitha gave him a grateful smile. Hobbs sidled up next to

her at the stove and started handing over the buttered sand-wiches, which Tabitha transferred to the skillet. The butter soon sizzled and gave off a rich, toasty smell. As delicious as it was, Tabitha couldn't help but prefer the warm scent of buy-one-get-one-free lilac bodywash coming from Hobbs's direction.

"What's wrong with your auntie?" Hobbs said as the cheese oozed out the thick-cut brioche and started to caramelize in-side the melting butter.

"I'm not sure yet." Tabitha's stomach got a little knotted as she was reminded of Auntie El. "But I'm going to find out." She scooped up a sandwich with her spatula and transferred it to a plate. Two more followed.

"I'm sure you will." Hobbs lifted the plate and carried it to the buffet table, where Reverend Stokes was opening a bag of chips he'd taken from the pantry and Delaney was pour-ing glasses of wine.

Grilled cheese, potato chips and wine. Tabitha shook her head. If Auntie El were here to witness this, she'd have a coronary.

Once everyone had food, Tabitha got Trinity settled in her dog bed. Wyatt sat nearby, not actually relaxing but not running all over the house with a toy, either. Gracie, much younger than either of the other two dogs, was more insistent. She brought the shattered raccoon to Trinity and dropped it by her paws, begging for her to take the bait. Trinity reacted like one of the royal palace guards—stiffly on duty, now that Tabitha had made her settle. She could see you, but there was no way you could make her flinch. Gracie turned to Wyatt, desperate. Wyatt started to lean into his front legs, rump in the air, tail wagging, but Delaney snapped her fingers and said, "Wyatt, come," in a voice that made everyone in the room sit straighter. Wyatt obeyed, went to Delaney's side and settled on the floor near Delaney's chair. Gracie was left alone, one ear flipped back and the shredded toy hanging from her mouth like roadkill.

Hannah turned to Delaney. "Will you teach me that?" She nodded at Wyatt.

"Sure, hon." Delaney patted her hand.

Gracie trotted over to Hobbs, who once again held George in his lap, and slumped near his chair. George immediately slunk from Hobbs's lap and curled into Gracie's middle.

"Well, I never," Nora said. "The hairless dude thinks he's a dog."

"Actually, it's the dog who thinks she's a cat," Hobbs said. "She keeps trying to get into the covered litter box and she grooms George just like he grooms her."

"Well, I never," Nora repeated. She took a bite of her sandwich, then chased it with a slug of water, the only person not drinking wine.

Tabitha shifted her attention to Hannah, who sat on her other side, quietly pecking at her food while everyone else chatted. "How are you settling in?"

"Good, thanks." Hannah offered a smile, though Tabitha sensed that same sadness deep inside her that she'd felt while massaging Candy. On the upside, Candy had opened up more when Tabitha had given her a second session yesterday, the mama dog's body relaxing so much she'd even fallen asleep.

"I can't believe you convinced your brother to foster George and Gracie. They're definitely quite the pair."

"They like him better than me," Hannah admitted with a rueful smile. "Gracie seeks him out, which is funny because he really wants nothing to do with her." Hannah shook her head quickly. "He's not unkind. He just…" She trailed off. "Isn't a dog person. But Gracie adores him. We can't figure out why."

Tabitha glanced at the golden puppy by Hobbs's side. She'd

nodded off, her hairless cat tight in a ball against her belly. Hobbs was deep in conversation with Sean, the two men talking story about some kind of auto theft Sean had worked on recently. They were total contrasts in personality, Sean being gruff and no-nonsense, Hobbs smiling, even now, his voice animated and hands doing half the talking.

"Do you miss home?" Tabitha immediately regretted her question, remembering what Hobbs had said about an abusive boyfriend, but there was no putting the words back once they were out.

"I miss my mom," Hannah said. "And Victor. He's my other brother."

"I met him. He came into Delaney's motorcycle shop, where I work. He needed new gloves."

Hannah nodded and poked her food around her plate. "That's Victor. Always riding."

"Do you ride motorcycles, also?"

Hannah's eyes crinkled up. "No, thank you. I'm as tame as they come."

"I've never ridden, either." Tabitha watched Hobbs go for a second grilled cheese. "But riding one is on my Badass List."

"What's that?"

"Just this birthday list I made." Tabitha waved it off. No use talking about a list she still hadn't made more specific and attainable. "Hey, do you want to do a massage soon? My log is almost complete for the semester but I need a couple more sessions. You'd be helping me out." Tabitha recalled the strategy Red had used on her the first time she'd offered Tabitha a massage. She'd told Tabitha she could be a guinea pig for new massage techniques, and whether or not that had been true, Tabitha never figured out. But she'd yet to pay Red for a massage. Now Red considered their massages professional "swaps," even though Tabitha was nowhere near a pro.

"Definitely. As soon as you want. Just let me know when you're free." Hannah leaned back in her chair and patted her midsection. "That sandwich was so good. My brother's food is so plain. Always just chicken and broccoli and protein shakes. Healthy, but it gets boring. I miss my mother's junk food. Good old-fashioned bread and cheese."

Tabitha laughed. She hadn't peeked in Hobbs's cupboards, obviously, but she didn't imagine he ate a lot of junk food with that six-pack of his. "I heard your dad died recently. That must've been hard." Tabitha glanced at Hobbs, but he was deep in conversation with Reverend Stokes about football.

Hannah faced her with a seriousness in her gaze that her brother never seemed to have. "I didn't know him very well. He's been in jail up until recently. And when he got out, it was just so he could die humanely. He had dementia really bad, along with other health problems from years and years of drinking and just poor living."

Tabitha let that roll around in her mind and found that it didn't really surprise her. She already knew that Hobbs hid from his past. She already knew that he didn't have a good relationship with his father. Now the man who had ended their massage when Tabitha had got too close to who he really was, deep down, made a whole lot more sense.

The doorbell rang. Everyone paused and looked at each other. Tabitha shrugged. "I don't have enough grilled cheese for the neighborhood," she joked as she pushed back her chair and headed for the door.

After she opened it, she stood there, blinking in shock.

"Surprise!" Thaddeus grinned over the large bouquet of fall flowers he clutched against his chest. "Aren't you going to invite me in?"

Hobbs had to admit, the guy was perfect. Maybe not his name. Hobbs stuck to his guns on that one—who named a kid Thaddeus?—but everything else about him. Handsome. A lawyer. Impressed everyone with his manners and occupation. Had a history with Tabitha, which the guy was not shy about cashing in on. All during dessert, he'd slide an arm around Tabitha's waist or bring up something from their past. *Remember that time we skipped prom and read books on my living room sofa instead? We sat in our nice clothes and drank hot cocoa, you read* Moby Dick *and I read prelaw while all the other idiots got drunk?*

Hobbs didn't realize how much he'd been staring, wondering who the real idiots were in that scenario—the people reading *Moby Dick* in expensive clothing or the inebriated morons vomiting in the bushes, of which Hobbs was one—until Tabitha caught his eye. She gave Hobbs a smile and brushed Thaddeus's hand from her hip.

"Where do you work, Thaddeus?" Hobbs polished off his pecan pie and took a slice of chocolate cream. "Is that what people call you, by the way? Thaddeus? Or do people call you Tad? Taddy?" *Tabby and Taddy* bounced through his mind.

"Just Thaddeus." He pressed his fork into his pumpkin pie and took a bite that was almost delicate. "I work for Sneldon and Schultz."

Hobbs had heard those names before. He racked his brain until it came to him, early mornings in the kitchen while he fixed himself some bulletproof coffee and had *Good Morning Football* playing in the background. The commercials during that show were always about waterproof goo, invincible cookware and ambulance chasers. "Are they personal injury lawyers? I've seen their ad on TV." Hobbs made his voice sound like a commercial narrator. "If you or a loved one have had problems with your hernia mesh, Sneldon and Schultz are here to help!"

Thaddeus smiled indulgently. He dipped the tines of his fork in his whipped cream and licked it off. "Yes, that's us.

We do a lot of malpractice litigation for our clients who have suffered from bad surgical mesh. The effects can be quite devastating. It's no laughing matter."

"I wasn't laughing about it," Hobbs insisted. "I just have the ads in my head, you know? Like a jingle? Hard to get out." Hobbs looked around the room. Delaney shook her head. Sean looked away, fist over his mouth, a smile spreading beneath. Hannah and the reverend were outside in the fenced yard, playing with the dogs.

Nora laughed outright and toyed with the cigarette behind her ear. "What the hell's a surgical mesh, anyway?" she said.

Tabitha quickly changed the topic. "I am so sleepy. I'm going to need a nap."

"Maybe you're working out too hard," Thaddeus said, settling his empty plate next to the sink. He'd eaten his hastily assembled grilled cheese without complaint, but also hadn't offered to help Tabitha when she'd raced to make it. "There are more injuries at your type of gym than any other."

"My type of gym?" Tabitha said. Everyone in the room turned to look at Thaddeus.

"Right. People try to lift too much. Do things they shouldn't. They get hurt." Thaddeus poked his tongue around his teeth. "It's sad."

"Those are people who aren't listening to their coaches," Hobbs pointed out. He'd heard this criticism many times during his years of coaching at Rhett's gym, and he was weary of it. People who didn't know what they were talking about were always quick to do an internet search of goofy videos and slanted statistics just to bolster their arguments against something that scared them or they'd never tried. "Truth is, more people suffer significant health problems by doing nothing than by lifting weights. A car breaks most when it sits in the driveway, not when it's on the road. Yes, you might get in a crash, but if you practice safe driving, odds are you won't. Same same." Hobbs dug into his chocolate cream pie.

"I disagree," Thaddeus said, his voice as calm as Sunday afternoon.

Hobbs waited, but nothing more came. "That's it? You disagree?"

Thaddeus smiled. "That's it. I get along just fine running and hiking. I don't need to sling weights around or climb up walls."

"Running and hiking are great," Hobbs agreed. "But why limit yourself? The more you try, the better. You should come to the gym with Tabby." He nodded at her, just as she was settling her plate in the dishwasher. She peeked over her shoulder with surprise in her eyes.

"Well." Thaddeus cleared his throat, the first time he'd looked rattled since he'd arrived. "*Tabitha* has never invited me."

"No problem." Hobbs smiled. "I'm inviting you right now." Hobbs was mildly aware that Thaddeus's unfounded hate of functional fitness was not his problem. Neither was the fact that he thought he had dibs on Tabitha because they'd dated in high school. Or because he was a fancy lawyer who chased ambulances full of people with surgical mesh disasters. "C'mon." Hobbs smiled again. "Put your money where your mouth is. What's the worst that happens? Delaney here out-squats you?" He gestured toward Delaney with his fork. She shook her head, but Hobbs thought he spotted a smirk beneath her disapproval.

"I don't succumb to childish dares." Thaddeus handed his plate and fork to Tabitha, who still stood near the dishwasher. She accepted the dishes in silence, stared at them a moment, then rinsed them off and stowed them with the rest.

"Well, if you change your mind." Hobbs shrugged. "Invite is always open."

"Thanks." Thaddeus smiled tightly. "Well, I hate to rush off. But I told my parents I'd be by for coffee. Besides." He offered what sounded like a forced sneeze. "My allergies are catching up with me." He glanced into the backyard, where the dogs were streaking around. Everyone out there was laughing and having fun, including the reverend. "Tabitha, please make my manners to Auntie El. I'm sorry she's not feeling well."

"I'll walk you out," Tabitha said. She cast Hobbs a glance as she walked past, but Hobbs couldn't read it.

Once they had all left the kitchen, Nora popped her cigarette in her mouth, though she didn't light it. "Subtle," she said, the cigarette waggling in her mouth as she spoke. "How bad do you have the hots for Tabitha? Because you're acting really jealous."

"Nora." Delaney shook her head. "You can't say anything that comes into your head, you know? We've talked about this."

"What?" Nora pulled the smoke from her mouth and clutched it between her first two fingers. "We're not at the store, talking to customers. I'm just telling it like it is. Besides, you don't even like him." She pointed at Hobbs with her cigarette.

"We should go." Delaney grabbed Sean's hand. "Wyatt's got to be worn out by now." She peeked out the window at the dogs and Hannah, who carried a pissed-off-looking George.

"Just one more piece of pie," Sean said, eyeing the assortment. "I only had chocolate and apple." He grabbed a knife and cut a huge hunk of coconut cream.

"Well, if you're going to eat more pie, I'm going to eat

more pie." Delaney thrust her plate under the slice he'd cut and took it for herself.

"Pie thief." Sean went to cut himself a new slice, but Delaney thrust a forkful of her pie into his mouth. The two pressed a little closer, laughing.

"That's my cue," Nora grumbled. "You guys are actually making me miss my boyfriend, back in Williamsburg. I'm going to go call him." She went out to the porch and slipped her cigarette to her lips, still not lighting it, then pulled out her cell phone.

Hobbs was left in the kitchen with the adorable couple and their pie, which felt like a crowd, so he strode to the dining room table and started clearing dishes just as Tabitha appeared.

"Why did you invite Thaddeus to our gym?" she asked.

"I thought I was being nice."

"Right."

"All right, he was talking smack, so I called him on it. Sorry. I had a macho moment."

"Don't you think that if I wanted Thaddeus at our gym I'd invite him myself?"

"C'mon." Hobbs gestured to the front door, where Thaddeus had disappeared. "You don't want to see him try the gym?"

"I'm not sure I do, no."

Hobbs suddenly wanted to reach out, hook an arm around her waist and draw her in close. He wanted to be possessive, kiss her, feel her arms go around his neck and her legs go weak beneath him. He wanted to feel her body soften under his, to open up, yield to him, like she had before. But he also remembered what'd it felt like when she massaged his hands—the uncanny ability Tabitha somehow had to delve deep inside him and witch up everything he held tight, like a magic wand, stirring the pot. Hobbs was pretty sure she wouldn't be a fan of what she found there, at the bottom of that pot. And then things would be over before they even got started. "I'm sorry for throwing the gauntlet down with Thaddeus. I should have been more mature. I hope he comes to the gym and you show him the ropes. And that he has a good time."

Tabitha cocked her head to the side. "You really hope that?"

Hobbs's lips parted, to tell her sorry again, to let her know that Thaddeus seemed like a really great guy, even if he was a really great guy that Hobbs secretly hoped she didn't like very much, when Gracie came streaking into the room. She ran in circles, her cold fur filling the room with the scents of the backyard—fallen leaves, chilly air, grass. George came trotting in after her. He jumped on the back of the beige sofa and settled there, alert and watching as Wyatt came running in after Gracie.

"Come, Gracie." Hannah appeared, leash in hand. Gracie ignored her, but Hannah chased her down and affixed the leash to Gracie's collar. "I think we should go, Chris. We don't want to wreck Tabitha's house."

Hobbs broke his gaze with Tabitha and turned to his sister. Despite the chaos, she looked happy. Full of something other than loneliness, regret and fear. "Sure," he said. "Thanks for inviting us, Tabby. Everything was great. I hope your aunt feels better."

Tabitha drew a deep breath. "Thank you. I'll go check on her once everyone is gone." She turned to Hannah. "Next week, right? I'll come over for massage."

"Yes, please," Hannah said. She petted Gracie's head until the puppy settled at her side. "I can't wait."

"Night, Tabby. Thanks again."

"You're welcome. Thanks for coming. And thanks for helping with the sandwiches." She offered a sad smile, then headed for the dining room.

Hannah glared at him. "What did you do, Chris?"

"I'm not sure," Hobbs said.

Even though that was a lie.

Once the last guest left, Auntie El came pattering out of the bedroom in her pink housecoat, hair a mess, glasses crooked on her nose. "I've been awake about half an hour," she admitted. "I just couldn't bring myself to come out."

Tabitha wasn't used to seeing Auntie El looking lost and ragged. She opened her arms and they embraced. "I made grilled cheese," Tabitha said, her head on Auntie El's shoulder. "But I used your brioche, so they were technically Thanksgiving sandwiches. And the turkey's on the counter now. All cooked. The ham, too."

Auntie El rocked her for a moment, even though Tabitha was the one trying to offer comfort. "You did good, T," she said. "Tell your friends I came down with a cold and didn't want to share it. I'll talk to the reverend myself. Make my manners."

"Everyone had a good time." Tabitha and Auntie El parted. She thought about asking about the doctor visit, the sleep meds, Casey. But she kept quiet, sensing Auntie El needed time and space.

"Did I hear Thaddeus?" Auntie El said, her face brightening. "I thought you said he wasn't coming."

"I didn't think he was," Tabitha admitted. "He popped in late and ate a sandwich." She thought back to Hobbs's interaction with Thaddeus and didn't know whether to laugh or be angry. Maybe because Hobbs was being so confusing himself. The other night he'd kissed her with a passion Tabitha had never felt before, one that had made her physically ache and yearn for his strong arms and soft lips ever since. She didn't ache like that for Thaddeus, now or in their youth, or for any of the men she'd dated so fleetingly over the years. Sex hadn't even been something she craved or enjoyed much in the past. With Thaddeus, she'd played along, acted the part that she knew to be normal, based on stories from girlfriends and scenes in movies, though she'd never really enjoyed their short, tidy interludes that included a carefully placed condom, some thrusting and grunting and a predictable finish of Thaddeus clenching, silent as the grave, then relaxing all of his weight on top of her. She'd lain there, bored, wondering what all the fuss was about, until he'd finally rolled over and driven her home. Dating other men had been different versions of that same game, and interactions with men since Afghanistan had been strictly platonic cups of coffee and tired excuses on her part. Captain Dorsey's harassment had made her leery of physical intimacy, and up until that first kiss with Hobbs on Halloween night, Tabitha hadn't been sure she ever wanted to get close to men again.

She definitely wanted to get close to Hobbs again. But he certainly seemed to have reasons to keep slamming on the brakes.

"Oh, I am so glad," Auntie El said, her pallor brightening. "Thaddeus is a good catch. An excellent catch. You keep your eye on that one."

"Times are different now, Auntie El," Tabitha broached gently. "Women aren't rushing out to find partners. We're learning to be happy with ourselves."

Auntie El snorted. "Well, while you're being happy with yourself, just remember that the good ones get snatched up early. Men like Thaddeus aren't going to wait around forever while you're taking your sweet time being liberated. Take it from an old lady who knows a thing or two."

"I see you're feeling better."

Auntie El smiled a little bit. "Soon as I get this insomnia

sorted I'll be just fine. You wait and see. Now I'm going to have some coffee and do my puzzle. Fix your old auntie a plate of ham, would you? On that brioche you sliced up." Auntie El settled at the table, where Tabitha had replaced her puzzle once she'd cleaned up after the guests. "Toast it, please. You know I like it toasted."

"Yes, ma'am."

Once Tabitha had laid a toasted ham-and-cheese sandwich in front of Auntie El, she sat down to the table, drew out her Journal of Invincibility and flipped to the back. It was about damn time she fixed that Badass List.

Help Auntie El.
~~*Don't act like a freak when you have coffee with Thaddeus on Friday.*~~
Learn about motorcycles.
Possibly ride one.
Ace massage quizzes.
Excel at massage.
Run a race with Clementine???

She read through the list again and drew a sigh. Hobbs had been right. Everything was vague, soft and light. There was no commitment here. Leave it to Tabitha to have created a timid Badass List. Oh, the irony.

She flipped the page. It was one thing to tell Auntie El that she was "finding herself" in lieu of hooking up with a fabulous catch like Thaddeus. It was another to actually put in the work. Time to start over. Time to do what Hobbs had suggested. This time, her goals needed to be bold. Specific. Achievable. Tabitha chewed on the tip of her pen a moment before writing.

Help Auntie El.
Choose a book at Delaney's shop next week and educate self on motorcycles.
Massage Hannah and take detailed SOAP notes.
Massage Candy 2x/week, noting changes, advancements.
Use Rx weights at gym for a workout within the next week (when safe).
Ride a motorcycle on a warm day.

Tabitha put empty checkboxes next to each goal and smoothed the page with her palm. These were things that she could start on right away and make clear progress. The only goal that was still vague was the one about Auntie El. Tabitha didn't know, as of now, how to make it more specific. The goal was staying on the list, anyway.

"Nine-letter word for *unflinching.*" Auntie El brushed bread crumbs from the front of her housecoat and peered over the rims of her glasses. "Starts with *D.*"

Tabitha clicked her pen closed and closed her eyes. After a moment, she rose to go finish what she'd started in the kitchen. *"Dauntless,"* she said. "The word you're looking for is *dauntless.*"

nineteen

The week after Thanksgiving, Tabitha showed up at the gym, riding shotgun in a sleek Range Rover Velar, complete with SV exterior pack and split-spoke wheels. The driver took the time to make two other cars around him wait while he backed the vehicle into the closest spot to the gym, showing off his quad tailpipes and vanity tag: lawman7.

"Who's this?" Rhett muttered, squatting near Humphrey's bed, his hand lazily petting over the old beagle's ears. Humphrey looked out the big glass windows and grunted his agreement.

"Man, that's a nice ride." Duke, who'd just finished the 1730 class, slipped his shirt over his sweaty chest. "Is that our Tabitha? Getting out of that Range Rover? Who's she with?"

"Clearly she's with Lawman Seven," Rhett said.

"Hang on to your hernia mesh, boys," Hobbs said. "That there is Thaddeus. He thinks our gym is dangerous."

"Thaddeus?" Duke, a giant of a man with a gleaming shaved head, wrinkled his nose. "Was his mama born in 1850?"

Thaddeus had just slammed the driver's-side door. Toting a pretty red gym bag, he walked ahead of Tabitha and held the front door open.

Hobbs watched them in silence, noting Thaddeus's confident aura and impeccable fitness attire. Every bit of his apparel was brand-named and fresh, the red color matching his gym bag to a tee. Tabitha, on the other hand, wore her usual simple black leggings, an old blue tank top she wore every week—Hobbs liked blue tank top day because the color made Tabitha's eyes pop like Valentine's Day chocolate—and her ratty sneakers that Hobbs had told her more than once to replace.

"This should be good," Rhett muttered.

"Ten bucks says this guy craps out halfway into the metcon." Duke spoke out of the side of his mouth.

"I give him five minutes," Rhett countered, rising to his feet and towering over everyone, including the massive Duke.

"Deal."

Hobbs nudged Rhett with his elbow as Thaddeus and Tabitha walked in. Unlike Thaddeus's confident strides, head held high, Tabitha appeared nervous, rubbing her hands together, like she was here for the first time and didn't know what to expect. "Can I change up the workout a little?"

Rhett glanced at him. "What'd you have in mind?"

"Nothing special." Hobbs mulled over today's menu, which included rowing and pull-ups. "I was thinking, just for this class, we run Nancy." A benchmark workout, Nancy consisted of five rounds of four-hundred-meter runs and fifteen overhead squats. "I met this guy on Thanksgiving. He's a runner. Just throwing him a bone."

Rhett stared at Hobbs in silence for a while, his jaw working his gum like a patient father, assessing his son and trying to decide whether to let him fall on his face or not.

"Oooh, Nancy." Red came up behind Rhett and slid her arms around his waist. Rhett covered her arms with his own instinctively, without breaking his stare with Hobbs. "I love Nancy."

"Okay," Rhett finally said. "You can run Nancy for 1830. Only because Stanzi wants to." He rubbed his fingertips along Red's arms. The whole scene gave Hobbs pause, since Rhett wouldn't alter his programming for anyone, including his girlfriend, but he wasn't about to question it when he'd just got what he wanted.

"Yesss," Red hissed. Then she waved at Tabitha and headed over to greet her. "Hey, Tabitha. Did you bring a friend? Hi, I'm Red." Her voice was smooth and encouraging, which was why, ever since Rhett and Red had become a thing, Red had been in charge of drop-ins, guests and new members. As good a coach as Rhett was, his abrasive edge wasn't always the most welcoming.

Hobbs listened to Red work her magic with Thaddeus as he headed to the whiteboard to make the change in the workout. After he had "Nancy" written up, he turned to see Rhett standing there, watching him, arms crossed over his chest. He said nothing, but Hobbs got the message, loud and clear: *I don't know what's going on with you and Tabitha but do not make a spectacle of my gym in the process.*

By the time Thaddeus was done talking to Red and filling out the waiver, it was time to start the class. Tabitha's gaze briefly connected with Hobbs's right before he started the whiteboard talk. She offered a polite smile. Thaddeus gave him a nod and pumped his fist when the running was mentioned, but, as Hobbs had expected, he had zero reaction to the overhead squats.

Warm-ups commenced, Rhett jumping into the group at the last second like he was still that father, letting his son's experiment play out as long as he was right there to watch it unfold. Thaddeus beat everyone back to the gym during the four-hundred-meter warm-up jog, but Hobbs could tell he'd sprinted by the way he bent double, grasping his quads. Rhett came in shortly after, not even breathing heavy, and the rest followed, one by one, with Tabitha bringing up the rear.

"There you are," Thaddeus said as she trotted inside. "Thought I lost you out there." He smiled and slung an arm around her shoulders. Tabitha's return smile was tight and controlled.

"What's this workout, then?" Thaddeus continued, oblivious to Tabitha's recoil. "Five rounds of running a four-hundred and some squats?" He rubbed his palms together hard enough to start a fire. "I thought this gym was supposed to be tough."

Tabitha ignored him and stepped up to Hobbs. "How do you feel about me using the Rx weight today?" She clasped her hands in front of her and waited, breath held.

"Can you manage sets of five, at least?"

Tabitha thought about it, but only briefly. "Yes." Her voice came clear and confident.

"Then absolutely, Tabby."

She smiled and turned away.

"Okay, everyone!" Hobbs shouted. "Grab a PVC!"

The class dutifully went to the bin of long plastic piping and snagged one for the overhead squat warm-up.

And now, Hobbs thought, *let the fun begin*.

It took Tabitha until the end of the workout, with Thaddeus on the floor, staring at the ceiling, eyes open in an odd, non-blinking stare, like he'd been blindsided, to figure out what had just gone down. She knew that Hobbs had changed the workout, because what was written on the whiteboard was not what had been listed in the gym's app on her phone. On paper, it appeared that Hobbs had done Thaddeus a welcoming favor by giving him a workout in his wheelhouse—five rounds of four-hundred-meter runs. But Tabitha had been at Semper Fit long enough to know that the workouts here were designed to keep the body guessing on a daily basis. If your body got thrown a dose of something it wasn't expecting, or was not acclimated to, it would have to adapt to overcome. These adaptations were the reason change was made, growth occurred and the athlete got fitter and faster and better at everything, while specializing in nothing.

Thus was the beauty of "Nancy." A runner would understandably be delighted with five rounds of four hundred meters. The distance was a short burst, and only added up to just over a mile total. But then came the overhead squats—the great equalizer. As Tabitha had heard more than once from her Semper Fit coaches, if you had a weakness, the overhead squat would find it. Weak core? Poor mobility in any of your joints, including shoulders, hips, ankles? Poor balance? Weak stability?

Cue the overhead squat, peerless in developing athletic movement, to come in and cut you at the knees.

That was exactly how it went for Thaddeus, who flew through his first four hundred meters as if his shoes had been fitted with wings. Nobody had been able to catch him, including Rhett, who had longer legs than anyone in the gym. But by the time Tabitha made it back inside from her own run, she'd found Rhett already done with his overhead squats and back out the door, while Thaddeus was struggling to get his hips below parallel with nothing more than the PVC pipe. On top of having never done the exercise, Thaddeus had classic tight runner's hips. He'd struggled all hour long with caving knees, weak glutes, chest falling forward and Hobbs's enthusiastic but firm guidance through the movement.

For once, Tabitha had not been last in finishing the workout. Despite the fact that she'd used the Rx weight for her own squats and had endured Hobbs yelling at her to *be more aggressive* several times, it gave her no joy to look down at Thaddeus, his expression wounded like a little boy who was used to getting his way but most certainly hadn't today. "You okay?" Tabitha held her hand up for a high five.

Thaddeus ignored the gesture. His eyes closed. "I'm fine," he muttered.

"Hey." Hobbs, making the rounds through the class, stopped over Thaddeus's sweaty, bemused form. "Great work, dude." He didn't offer his fist for a bump, perhaps having seen Thaddeus reject Tabitha's attempt. "How about them overhead squats? Kept you safe, though. Couldn't risk putting any weight over your head with those tight hips and ankles."

Thaddeus shot him a glare. "I'm not sure of their purpose in real life. You've had your fun, though, I suppose."

"Purpose?" Hobbs's eyebrows went up. "Overhead squats increase flexibility, mobility and strength." He ticked off each benefit with a swipe of his finger over his palm. "Builds your core. Helps identify weaknesses in your overall fitness, which will reduce the chance of injury in everyday movements or in those you enjoy most, such as running. That's what you were worried about most, right? Avoiding injury at my super-dangerous gym?"

Thaddeus rose to his feet and scrubbed some sweat from his brow with the heel of his hand. "So you did me a favor today?" He offered a grin devoid of warmth. "Is that what you're saying?"

"We provided you with a free workout that introduced you to a new movement in a safe environment." Hobbs shrugged.

"So, yeah. Seems like a favor to me. And bonus—you got to work out next to a beautiful young lady." He nodded at Tabitha.

Thaddeus's grin closed into a tight-lipped stare.

"And you—" Hobbs turned to her, his usual jovial demeanor in full force "—did excellent. Your first Rx Nancy!" He held up his hand for a high five. "How does that feel?"

Tabitha grinned, despite the tension in the room. She couldn't help herself. Not only was she proud, she could now check off her first accomplishment on the Badass List. She went to return the high five and Hobbs surprised her by catching her hand, lifting her up against his chest and spinning her around.

When Tabitha shrieked, Trinity came running over and jumped up against her leg.

"Whoa, girl." Hobbs settled Tabitha to her feet. "It's all good."

"Off, Trinity," Tabitha said, still laughing, glowing in her accomplishment, and a little bit from being in Hobbs's arms, too.

Trinity dropped but landed against Thaddeus's legs. "Jeez," he muttered. He stepped back and Trinity spilled over. "I just don't see the point in bringing this dog everywhere. She's like your purse or something."

Everyone around them went quiet. Red had just appeared, standing behind Thaddeus, probably prepared to ask him what he thought of the workout. Her smile fell. "What did you just say?"

Thaddeus regarded the sudden quiet, along with Red's hard stare. "Hey, I was only joking." He reached down and patted Trinity on the head. Trinity flinched.

"It wasn't funny." Hobbs had a hard expression that Tabitha had never seen on him.

"Oh, I get it." Thaddeus straightened up. "You're the funny man around here, right? Nobody else gets to make jokes."

"At least my jokes are actually funny."

"He's right," Red said. "You're out of line." She cast a glance at Tabitha.

Tabitha swallowed down the acrid taste in her throat, all of her joy gone. She thought back to this morning, when Thaddeus had texted her, short and sweet, that he had some time in his schedule and would love to take "her gym friend" up on his offer to try out Semper Fit. He could pick her up at six, if she was agreeable.

Tabitha had almost passed, but Auntie El had read the text over her shoulder and said, "Oh, how nice. See? Thaddeus is such a good young man. He's even willing to indulge you and try out that gym of yours. Go ahead, T. Say yes."

"Forget I said anything," Thaddeus said with a grunt. "You ready to go, Tabitha?"

Tabitha's cheeks were so hot she was afraid to meet anyone's gaze. She looked at Trinity instead, the little black pit bull in the service vest who spent all her days working hard for Tabitha.

The dog settled into a sitting position and waited, her sweet eyes big and bright. She was so cute the first thing people usually wanted to do was pet her. The first thing Thaddeus had said when he picked Tabitha up today was "The dog's not going to shed fur all over my car, is she?"

"No," Tabitha said. "Trinity and I will get another ride home, thanks."

Three people within earshot made instant offers to be Tabitha's taxi.

"Fine," Thaddeus said. "That's just fine. I've got a marathon to train for, anyway. I don't have time to be playing with these sorts of silly workouts." He glared at the rack of barbells.

"Clementine runs marathons," Hobbs said, pointing at the little blonde who was brushing chalk off her barbell with a wire brush. "In fact, I think her marathon time went down since she started working out here. That right, Clem?"

"That's true," Clementine said. "I also used to have horrible overhead squats. But, with time, they got better."

"Well." Thaddeus looked her up and down, sizing her up. "I run a three-thirty marathon. I don't play around."

"Wow, that's impressive," Clementine said, her tone genuine.

"But." Hobbs cradled his chin in his thumb and forefinger. "Didn't you just run Greenview Park in three-twelve, Clem?"

Clementine gave Hobbs a mom glare, sort of a *tsk-tsk* kind of look for stirring the pot, but then her gaze fell on Trinity and traveled up to Tabitha, whose cheeks were just starting to cool off. "That's right," Clementine said. "I sure did."

Silence passed, and then Thaddeus just collected his gym bag and left without another word. Once he was gone, sympathetic looks and words were exchanged, but Tabitha waved them off. She collected Trinity's leash and stepped outside the open bay door. She needed to be alone, away from everyone and the heat of her embarrassment.

After a minute or so, a warm hand planted on Tabitha's shoulder. She turned and saw Red, wearing a baggy men's T-shirt beneath her coat—The Hick from French Lick printed across the front—which Tabitha had been told was her standard gym attire when she first started Semper Fit, slowly ceding to her customary fitted tank tops and shorts. Her ponytail was all but undone, and one hastily clipped barrette, meant to hold back her bangs, was sliding out of her hair. She said nothing, just stood there with her hand on Tabitha's shoulder.

After a while of silence, Tabitha tried her voice. "I keep thinking I get a handle on things. Find a direction. Then, in true Tabitha fashion, something goes wrong. I start massage school…and give everyone erections or almost kill someone at the marathon. I catch the eye of a handsome lawyer…and he turns out to be a jerk. And the person I really like is completely unavailable. I just don't know anymore."

Constance smiled, slid her arm around Tabitha's back and squeezed. "It's like that tricky birthday candle, isn't it? You think you got this and then suddenly one pops back to life. But really—" Red cocked her head, making her strawberry ponytail list to the side more than it already was "—when you think about it…do we really want all the candles to go out? How exciting is that? We all need a little light. We all need a little surprise in our lives. We all need sparks to make us grow."

"The sparks hurt like hell right now," Tabitha admitted.

"Let's look at this problem like a massage therapist would. You're telling me something hurts, but what's my real job?"

Tabitha didn't feel like being quizzed but she also wanted to feel better, so she went with it. "Your job is to find out *why* I hurt."

Red smiled. "Exactly. So you have all these aches and pains but I need to figure out the root of the problem. Where it all started. In your case, maybe what's bothering you the most. You're talking about massage school and men, but those are just sparks. That's just where you feel the pain. Where's the real problem coming from?"

Tabitha mulled that over. Even though it shouldn't have been a surprise, the realization hit her hard. "I'm really worried about Auntie El," she admitted. "She raised me. She's always been there for me. She saved my life, really. And now something's wrong and it kind of bleeds into everything else.

Makes me feel like my foundation is crumbling. Even though I left home at eighteen to join the navy, when things went wrong, I came back home and Auntie El was there. And now something's wrong and I want to be there for her, like she was for me." Tabitha's voice choked up at the end.

"Now we're getting somewhere." Red rubbed Tabitha's back, between the shoulder blades. "What's going on with her? Has she been in for a checkup?"

"Yeah. They ran blood and found nothing. She's tired all the time but has insomnia and it hurts all over."

Red's hand stilled. She got quiet for a second, then said, "I'm not a doctor, obviously, but...has anyone suggested fibromyalgia? I have a few clients with this disorder. It's marked by widespread pain, fatigue, sleeplessness, brain fog. It's very hard to diagnose. They think that the brain and spinal cord amplify painful sensations in people who suffer from it."

Tabitha felt a little spark of hope. She turned to face Red. "How does this happen? Auntie El never had this before. Is it hereditary? Old age?"

"Research indicates you can be predisposed by hereditary, but the trigger is usually a stressful event. Either physical or psychological."

Casey, Tabitha thought. Could that have been Auntie El's trigger? If she even had fibromyalgia, though everything Red was saying rang true. "How do you fix it?"

"Some doctors prescribe antidepressants," Red said. "But you know what also helps a lot?" She got a little smile on her face.

"Are you going to say massage?"

"Not just massage." Red bent down and stroked behind Trinity's ears. "Massage with a lighter touch."

Now she knew what the smile was all about. "You mean... what I'm best at?"

Red's eyes sparkled with amusement. "Kind of funny how that works out, isn't it?"

Tabitha was quiet, her mind racing. Would Auntie El even let her give her a massage? Was Tabitha even ready? She'd only had one semester of school.

"I have an idea." Red glanced inside the gym, to where Rhett, Duke and Hobbs were in a discussion that involved a lot of shrugging and punctuated laughter. There had been a wager and now somebody owed someone else money, but they couldn't decide who. "I have a place where you can get some practice, before you go to your Auntie El with this. Are you interested?"

Tabitha thought about that sneaky candle, just waiting to pop back to life. What Red had said, without spelling it out, was that Tabitha had a choice: she could either be the kind of woman who blew out the wonky candle and got on with slicing up that yummy cake, or she could be the kind of woman who stared at the fire and wondered who the hell had tricked her into the flames. The choice was hers.

"Definitely," Tabitha said.

"Okay. I'll send you a couple of emails with the details. But about that other thing."

"Which one?"

Red glanced inside the gym again. "The one about the person you really like being unavailable."

Tabitha's cheeks got hot, despite the fact that her sweat had dried on her skin and she felt chilly now. Was it that obvious?

"Sometimes, life is like massage." Red offered a soft smile. "And despite what a lot of people think, depth doesn't always equal pressure and healing doesn't always equal pain. A lot of people would be surprised to know how deep a light touch can go. And how good it can feel."

Tabitha let that sink in. She offered a shaky smile. "Thanks, Red."

"Anytime."

Fist bump.

twenty

The things that we love tell us what we are.

~St. Thomas Aquinas

When Tabitha arrived at Hobbs's place, she noted that his truck was gone, which would give her and Hannah all the privacy they needed. Hannah greeted her at the door, holding a tiny green quilt with a pine tree in the center. Gracie did circles in the foyer, her natural playfulness heightened as she spied Trinity through the glass.

"I think it's a little small," Tabitha said, smiling as she hauled her massage table and rolling suitcase over the threshold. Trinity followed, and Tabitha immediately told her to break and go play with Gracie. As the dogs bounded away, Tabitha added, "I'm clearly no expert, but you know that won't cover anyone, right?"

Hannah laughed as she closed and locked the door behind her. "It's for George," she said as she followed Tabitha into the living room. "I made it." She held it up between her hands. George appeared out of nowhere, like he'd heard his name, screeched a meow, then did what could only be described as a gallop as he raced across the kitchen and into the room with the dogs.

Tabitha set her table down and took a second look at the miniature blanket. On close inspection, it was rather impressive. The quilt was made of squares that alternated in light and dark greens. Right in the center was the pine tree, in a different shade of green, which had been pieced with triangles, including a rectangular brown trunk. "This is really cute," she said. "You made this?"

Hannah nodded, clearly excited by her gift for the cat. "I've always been into sewing," she said. "My grandmother taught me. She made a lot of blankets and even clothes, whenever she had the time. I did stuff like this with her before she died." Hannah's excitement fell a little bit, like she was thinking back to her youth. "My mom let me bring her sewing machine with me. Along with George and Gracie, it's keeping me sane."

"Does George like his blanket?"

"He's hairless," Hannah said, like nobody had noticed. "So he definitely needs his sweaters and blankets. Especially in the cold weather. When he lies down with Gracie I put the quilt over him and he doesn't move."

"That's adorable. Lily certainly nailed it when she chose you to foster that pair." Tabitha unzipped her bag and hauled out the table. She'd decided to try a full massage for Hannah, and not just a quick chair treatment. She got the table set up, then plugged in the heating pad she'd splurged for. Red had told her the pad was worth the investment, especially in winter. The salt lamp followed, then the spa music on her phone. Tabitha located the switch for the lamp that burned on the end table and clicked it off. There. The room was perfect now.

"What should I do?" Hannah hugged herself, like she was nervous.

"You'll undress to your comfort, then get under the blanket. I'll go wash up and when I come back we can decide what you'd like to focus on."

Hannah smiled, but still looked nervous. "Okay."

Tabitha went into the bathroom to wash, to give Hannah privacy. The room smelled like cinnamon, which likely came from a small potpourri on the sink, plugged into the wall. The sink was spotless, the faucet shining. Small, perfectly folded blue towels lined the towel rack over the toilet. The matching blue rugs on the floor were fluffy, the tile clean. As Tabitha washed her hands with a foaming soap that smelled just like the potpourri, she briefly wondered what this bathroom had looked like before Hannah got here. The last time Tabitha was here she'd washed in the kitchen sink because Hobbs hadn't undressed beyond his shirt. It was possible, though doubtful, that Hobbs was a neat freak, but the odds of him having a mini-Crock-Pot full of cinnamon potpourri were minimal.

As Tabitha dried her hands, she took a look at herself in the mirror and drew a deep breath. Her eyes looked tired, but also bright. The black scrubs she'd bought looked comfy and professional. Her nails were trimmed and smooth. Her conversation with Red at the gym yesterday came back to her. Everything from the birthday candles down to the job Red had suggested for her over the upcoming holiday—to volunteer massage for the wounded service members at Fort Belvoir, where Red had spent a lot of free hours. "It's a matchless experience," she had said. "It's a different kind of massage, but one I think you are particularly suited for. It's entirely different from massages at a spa, or on your fellow students. And my contact told me there's a recent client who has fibromyalgia. You'll get good practice."

Tabitha hadn't registered for Semester 2 of massage school yet. How things went with Hannah and the wounded service members would determine whether she was cut out for this or not. She eyed her reflection one more time and reminded herself that Hannah had suffered some kind of recent trauma. An abusive boyfriend, Hobbs had said. That, Tabitha felt particularly suited for.

She left the bathroom and found Hannah faceup, covers up to her neck. Tabitha realized she hadn't directed Hannah to lie facedown, but in hindsight, this was a good mistake. Without direction, Hannah had chosen to lie faceup, probably because it was a less vulnerable position.

Trinity had settled near the couch, on the floor, but Gracie was doing circles around the table. She stopped near Hannah's face, put her paws on the table and pulled herself to her hind legs. She licked Hannah's nose and Hannah gave a gentle laugh. "I'm starting to win her over," Hannah whispered, as though in reverence to the quiet room. "She still prefers Chris but that's the real reason I'm making quilts for George. If I win George over, I'll win Gracie over. Kind of evil, huh?"

Tabitha laughed. "Definitely. Smart, though." She almost called Gracie down, who was nuzzling into Hannah's neck, but then thought better of it. This wasn't a clinical setting. This was Hannah's home, and Gracie made Hannah feel good. If anyone could understand that, it was Tabitha.

Tabitha moved to the head of the table and closed her eyes. She took several slow, deep breaths and just let Hannah get used to them all being in the room together. By the time Tabitha opened her eyes, Gracie had settled on the floor, near Hannah's head.

"Oh." Tabitha stifled a laugh as George appeared out of nowhere, his pink, hairless body looking creepy by the orange glow of the salt lamp. He gave a long, drawn-out meow, then leaped to the floor and settled behind Gracie's back. Tabitha spied the quilt Hannah had made lying on the couch, so she fetched it and draped it over George's body.

Hannah watched quietly, her face slowly relaxing. "Look how cute they are," she murmured.

Tabitha made a decision where to start, grabbed Hobbs's ottoman and pulled it over behind the head of the table. She sank down, diminishing her height so she wasn't looming over Hannah, and laid her hands on Hannah's shoulders, still under the sheet and blanket. She squeezed with light pressure. Hannah's shoulders relaxed.

She moved her hands up over Hannah's shoulders, then to her upper traps, then slid them beneath her back. Hannah sighed and sank deeper into Tabitha's hands. The music in the background was a soothing mixture of harps, flutes and birdsong that filled the room and softened the edges of everything. Hannah's breathing deepened, and as Tabitha glanced down, she could see that Gracie's ribs rose and fell in tandem with Hannah's, as well as George's, like the entire room was connected, feeding off the same pulse.

"Chris told me you were in the navy." Hannah's voice was almost a whisper, her eyes still closed.

"Yes, for a while. I enlisted when I was eighteen."

"So did Chris. In the marines."

"What a coincidence."

"Why did you join?"

Tabitha deepened her pressure around Hannah's cervical spine as she thought about the question. "It was a good opportunity. I wanted to see more of the world. Auntie El doesn't have a lot of money and I needed to start relying on myself. You know what they say—three hots and a cot. And now the GI Bill is paying for massage school."

"Chris wanted to get away." Despite the heaviness of her

words, Hannah's voice was dreamy, her body softening, giving in to the massage. "First time he came home he looked like a completely different person. He was this scrawny little kid all his life. Well, not to me. He was always my big brother. But after basic training and his first tour, Chris was so buffed up. So tough. I almost didn't know him."

Tabitha tried to picture Hobbs as a kid, and was kind of surprised to learn he'd been skinny. That made a lot of sense, though. Maybe joining the marine corps had been his way to turn himself into someone different. Someone bigger, stronger. Someone who couldn't be bullied.

"I was mad that he left me." Hannah sank deeper into her relaxed state, her voice like she shared secrets in the confessional at church. "My father was in jail by then but my mother didn't have anything left for me. I was alone a lot. Victor was working all the time, giving most of his money to Mom. Chris, who pretty much raised me, was gone. I guess I just got stuck there. Year after year. Kind of frozen. Living with Mom. Cutting people's hair. When I met James I thought..." Hannah's voice trailed off, choking at the end.

Tabitha's hands slowed, trailing down to Hannah's shoulders, where she let them rest. Tiny vibrations, just like the ones that had risen up out of Candy, were trembling out of Hannah's body, into Tabitha's palms.

"I was so stupid," Hannah whispered. "I thought he was so nice. I cut his hair. He has really nice hair. I thought he was so handsome."

Tabitha continued the massage as she listened, letting the voice of Hannah's body be her guide as to where to touch and how much pressure to use. She paused every now and again when the trembling came up to her palms and the sweat beaded Hannah's skin, despite the coolness of the room. Hannah's story, of slipping into a relationship with an abusive man who slowly broke her down over time, tricking her, making her forget herself, flowed out while Tabitha moved up to her scalp and her temples. The music washed over them and the room smelled of eucalyptus and the cinnamon potpourri in the bathroom.

"I'm mad at myself for letting this happen," Hannah said as Tabitha finished up her head, neck and shoulder routine. "If anyone should've known better, it should've been me."

Though their situations, and their pasts, were different, Tabitha understood what it meant to feel trapped, to have someone stronger than you—whether physically or in rank or both—take advantage of that power in cruel and abusive ways. "Have you seen anyone about this? Like a therapist?"

Hannah shook her head. "Chris suggested it. I didn't feel ready to talk to anyone."

"You've been talking to me."

Hannah smiled. "You're easy to talk to. I can see why my brother likes you so much. You're warm and open. There's something about you that makes the room calmer."

A flush ran up Tabitha's cheeks. "Thanks." She finished up the scalp massage and ran her thumbs down Hannah's forehead, then circled her fingertips at her temples. "I'll refer you to my own therapist before you leave. I have her card. Her name is Hope."

"Hope," Hannah echoed. "I bet she gets a lot of business."

They laughed together for a moment before Tabitha said, "You just close your eyes and relax now. Let the rest of the hour be all about you, just relaxing."

"Okay." Hannah's voice sounded small as her eyes closed.

After that, the room went quiet and Hannah's body quieted back down, sinking into rhythm with the music and Tabitha's strokes. At some point, she fell into a gentle sleep. Tabitha didn't bother making her roll over, just did what she could with Hannah faceup. When she finished, she touched her shoulder gently until she woke. "I'll go into the bathroom to wash so you can get dressed," Tabitha whispered. "Get up slowly. You might be a little light-headed." Once she was in the bathroom, Tabitha looked at herself in the mirror again while she washed her hands. Her eyes were less tired, a little invigorated from the energy exchange with Hannah. Even though most of Hannah's story had been depressing, Tabitha couldn't help but linger on her words: *I can see why my brother likes you so much.*

Back in the living room, Hannah was dressed and stretching her arms over her head. "I feel amazing," she said. "Thanks for this. And for listening."

"Anytime." Tabitha grabbed her coat and dug out her wallet. Inside she drew out Hope's business card and handed it over. She was proud of herself for listening to Hannah talk without offering any kind of advice that went outside her scope of practice. There were so many things she had wanted to say, but Hannah would be better off with Hope's words and only Tabitha's hands.

"Thanks." Hannah read the card and slipped it in her jeans pocket. "I hope I didn't make you uncomfortable. Telling you all those things."

"Not at all," Tabitha said as she packed up. "I'm glad you feel so comfortable with me. And I'm glad you're here. Safe with your brother."

"I hope so."

Tabitha zipped up the carrying case around her table. "What do you mean?"

"I hope I'm safe," Hannah said. "You can never be sure, can you?"

Tabitha's movements slowed as she packed away her MP3 player and salt lamp. She looked up at Hannah, noting that the room seemed almost too quiet. All the animals were still curled up, asleep, despite all her banging around. "What are you saying, Hannah?"

Hannah crossed her arms over her chest, hugging herself. "I've gotten some texts," she admitted, her voice going thin, like she was controlling the pitch. "I don't recognize the number, but they sound like him. I blocked his number but I didn't think about him using a different phone to text me. I'm not very smart about that kind of stuff."

Tabitha's skin sprang with gooseflesh. She froze. "What do they say?"

Hannah looked up at the ceiling. "Things like, 'You shouldn't have left me.' 'I know where you are.'" Hannah met Tabitha's gaze. "'You'll be seeing me soon.'"

Tabitha wasn't sure how long she stood there, hand looped through the handles of her carrying bag, the silence falling in on itself. She snapped out of it when Trinity bumped her hand with her nose. "You have to tell your brother. You have to show him those texts. Go to the police." Tabitha stroked Trinity's head.

"The police are no good," Hannah said. "They couldn't help me in Omaha when he was actually hitting me. They won't be able to help with a few texts from some unknown number. The texts don't even directly threaten me. They sound perfectly nice, out of context."

Tabitha contained her surprise at how much Hannah had thought this through. Well, of course she had. Her survival was at stake. She knew what this man was capable of. "You have to tell your brother," Tabitha repeated. "So that he's prepared, at the very least. We can show Sean, too. Detective Callahan. He'll know what to do."

"Chris is on a date." Hannah's expression darkened. "Someone from the gym named Serena. Just drinks, he said. He wanted to give us space for the massage."

"Oh, I see." Tabitha tried not to let the gouging feeling in her stomach show on her face. So much for the magic of her light touch. But now was not the time to dwell on her own problems. "As soon as he's home, then," Tabitha insisted. "You need to show Chris those texts."

"Tabitha." Hannah stepped closer and lowered her voice. "James is really good at mind games. This could all be just to mess with me. Do you think he really knows where I am?"

Tabitha looked directly into the eyes of the woman she'd just spent an hour relaxing with a massage and knew she couldn't lie. "I don't know. But you have to tell Chris."

twenty-one

"What happened to the mother again?" Sunny sat on the floor, covered in gold-and-brown puppies, two asleep in her lap and one attacking her shoe. The little aggressive one had her shoelace undone and was making good work of the rubber toe on Sunny's pink Chuck Taylor.

"Hit by a car," Lily said. "She was in the road and the puppies were in a ditch, a few feet away, which was filling up with rain." Lily glanced outside at the cold, gray sky. It'd been raining for two straight days, with the weather getting colder as time wore on. The gloom, along with the rush of the heater in the stuffy classrooms, had made school a six-hour challenge in not falling asleep. She'd popped home for a quick snack before heading to work to check on the new pups, who had come in last night.

Sunny stroked along one of the sleeping puppies' ears. "What did she look like? Did they say?"

"Lab mix, maybe?"

"That explains the ears," Pete said, quiet up until now, watching the puppies with that expert eye that told him whether or not a dog might be a good candidate for service training. "And the coloring. Maybe black Labs mixed with something? They're all dark brown with little caramel eyebrows."

Lily laughed as the one puppy that was awake did a flip over Sunny's shoe and landed against her shins. "They look about six or seven weeks, don't you think?"

"I would agree," Pete said.

"Normally they'd be somewhat weaned, but with Mom being a stray, they were probably getting most of their food from her," Sunny said. "Did you guys give them formula?"

"We mixed up some Esbilac," Lily said. "Fed them right after they got here last night. Nancy said she gave them a little bit of hard and soft food mixed throughout the day. They're all eating well, even though they're thin and mangy. Dr. Winters just took care of them all. She left right before you got here."

"Thanks for calling." Pete lifted the little rascal who wouldn't settle down and kissed him on the head. "Let's do some tests." He held the puppy in both hands and extended his arms. Sunny started to count to ten. When she hit number six, the puppy wiggled, then settled. He wiggled again as Sunny hit number nine. At ten, Pete set him down. The puppy immediately went after Sunny's shoe again.

"I think we oughta call him Sneakers," Lily said. "They can be the shoe litter. Sneakers, Boots and..." Lily squinted one eye as she watched the two snoozing in Sunny's lap. "Wellington," she finished. Lily shrugged as Sunny laughed. "We did find them in the rain," Lily pointed out.

"You're good at this, Lily," Pete said. "Definitely working in the right job." He knelt down and collected Sneakers again. This time he gently flipped the puppy on his back and held him there. Pete counted under his breath and Sneakers started wiggling like a turtle about four seconds in. "Sneakers is a feisty one," he said, setting him free.

Sunny lifted a rope bone that lay near her leg and tossed it to Pete. He caught it, then dangled it in front of Sneakers's nose. "Let's see if you really are a Lab." He tossed the rope bone and Sneakers immediately went after it. The puppy leaped on the bone and toppled over with it. Then he sat up and regarded the toy with a cock of his head.

"Well, he didn't bring it back, but he sure jumped on that bone quickly," Sunny said. At this, Wellington opened his eyes and gave a great big yawn.

"Welly is bored with talk of his brother," Lily suggested. "He's like, 'I can retrieve rings around that guy.'"

Everyone laughed. Despite the ruckus, Boots kept her eyes shut. She rolled over and stretched but then lapsed right back into deep breathing. All the puppies had patchy fur and smelled like demodex after Dr. Winters had treated their mange. "Aw, bless her little heart," Sunny said, lightly stroking her fur.

"Sunny and I will definitely take these poor orphans home." Pete winked at his girlfriend. Sunny winked back.

Lily had always liked the army vet who turned rescue dogs into service dogs for military veterans, like he had with Trinity. Pete had a quiet, firm sort of warmth, which seemed like the makings of a good dad. Lily's own dad, what she remembered of him, was similar in temperament, if a little on the wilder side—which, in Lily's opinion, made for a good father, too. Pete might be like Wellington but Lily definitely remembered her dad being like Sneakers. Whenever he was home, they were always off doing something exciting, usually outdoors—hiking, sledding, playing football in the backyard or climbing trees. "Go as high as you want, Monkey," Dad used to say. "I'll come get you if you get stuck. Just don't fall, or your mama will have my hide."

"Hey, can you two watch the pups while I take out the trash?" Lily got a whiff of dog poo and remembered the bin was full and ready for the dumpster outside. "Sally will be in any minute and won't be happy if it smells like poop in here."

"Like you have to ask," Sunny said. She rose up to stretch out her legs and laid Boots on the little dog bed on the floor.

Lily slipped on her rain jacket, decided against the umbrella that leaned against the wall by the back door and ducked out into the drizzly night. The cold hit her immediately, revealing the temps had dropped a lot since she got here. The sky was black, lit only by one streetlamp across the way, and the drops felt like needles against her skin. Lily heard the unmistakable pelting of ice balls against blacktop and decided this rain was definitely turning to sleet. She jogged the trash over to the dumpster, sliding a little bit, the plastic handles biting into her palms with the weight. Lily gave the trash bag a good swing, gathering momentum to toss it up and over the rim of the receptacle. Just as she was about to let go, beneath the pattering sound of the ice pelting the metal container, Lily heard something.

She dropped the trash bag and stepped closer to the dumpster, waiting. At first, she heard nothing. Lily was just about to grab the trash bag once more. Then she heard the sound again. She closed her eyes.

There it was. Something soft and primal. A low, mournful whimpering that seemed to come directly from the dumpster.

Was that...? Could it be...?

Lily slid to the edge of the dumpster and hooked her foot into a groove on the side of the tall metal bin. She grasped the edge and hauled herself up to get a peek. The bin was a huge pit of blackness, so Lily dug her phone out of her back pocket and turned on the flashlight. She shone it around the inside of the container, passing over trash bags, old wood, rotted blankets, until her light hit something that definitely shouldn't be in there. She passed over it first and had to double back. Then she froze.

There, right inside the beam of light from Lily's phone, was a small black, brown and white puppy. He lay on top of a black trash bag, his dark face and back blending in with his surroundings. But he had a white tail and a little white spot between his tan eyebrows that shone against the dark bag. He blinked in the bright light and went silent.

Lily stuffed her phone in her pocket and rushed back to the building, going so fast she nearly bit it on an icy patch and slammed into the back door. Both Pete and Sunny looked at her in surprise when she burst through. "I need help," she gasped.

Pete came out in the rain with Lily while Sunny stayed with the puppies. Sally was just showing up, coming through the front door, her brows knitting in confusion, but Lily didn't slow down to explain. "Where did you see him?" Pete was saying, following behind her. "The puppy is actually in the trash can?"

"Yes." Lily's throat filled with an acrid taste that made her gag. "Somebody put a puppy in the dumpster. There's no other way he could've gotten in there."

They reached the edge of the bin and Pete held up a silencing hand. Sure enough, the puppy was whimpering, soft and low, like he was crying only for himself.

"You have to boost me in there to get him out," Lily said, panic rising, the urge to get to the puppy so strong it tore at her stomach and made her throat burn.

Pete laced his fingers together and nodded, indicating Lily should put her foot there for a boost. That was what Lily loved about Pete—he didn't say stupid things most older people did, like, *You can't climb into a trash can. You could get hurt.* Or, *What would your mom say?* No, Pete immediately knew the score. One of them had to get that puppy out of the trash *now* and it'd be much easier for him to boost Lily inside than the other way around.

Lily footed Pete's hands and slung one leg over the trash. She tried not to think about all the disgusting things in there, including those rotted blankets, bags of poop, discarded, moldy food and maybe even rats. Instead, she pictured big, hairy rodents the size of the ROUSes in *The Princess Bride* getting to the whimpering puppy before she did, and that was all it took for Lily to drop down. Her landing was surprisingly soft on top of all the bags. If she remembered right, the trash people came tomorrow to collect, which meant that if she hadn't brought the trash out tonight she wouldn't have found the puppy before he got dumped into the back of a refuse vehicle tomorrow morning.

Lily shuddered, pushing away the thought. She clicked her phone light on to center herself and spot the puppy so that she wouldn't step on him. Once she had him located, she stuffed her phone away and followed the sound of the puppy's low cries, her feet crunching down trash bags and punching through one of them until she got to him. Her own Chuck Taylors—gray, not pink—got slick beneath her and a bad smell wafted up. Lily knew she'd tromped through crap and rotten food but her hands were on the puppy now, his fur cold and covered in ice balls. As soon as Lily touched him, the puppy's cries got louder, almost frantic, like when a person freaked out once they knew they were going to be okay rather than the other way around.

"It's okay, baby," she cooed. Lily scooped the wet puppy— about the size of Lily's minibackpack—into her arms and held him close. He was slick and stinky. "You're not trash, are you?" Lily murmured against his ear. "No, you're not. You're not trash." She carefully made her way back to the edge of the dumpster, where Pete was waiting. "Pete!" she called. "Climb up here and get the puppy. I'll hand him off. Then we can worry about getting me out."

"Roger that." Pete banged against the dumpster and his head popped over. He held the edge with one hand and extended the other arm.

Lily pressed the puppy, slick and shaking, into Pete's embrace. He tucked the puppy tightly against him. "Take him inside, to Sunny. Then come back for me."

Pete jumped down as carefully as he could, his footsteps and the puppy's cries getting farther away until they vanished altogether. Lily waited in the dank rot, the smells of poop and decay heavy in her nose. Even though she was soaked with rain and sleet, she felt itchy, like her body crawled with bugs. The acid in her throat was gone but her stomach was turning over in a big way, a thick feeling forming under her tongue like she was going to puke. "Don't do it," she muttered to herself. "Don't puke or you'll make me puke."

Humor kept her sane until Pete got back, clambering against the dumpster as he called out, "Hey. Lily. Grab my hand."

Lily reached up until she felt Pete's cold, wet hand grab her wrist. She scrambled against the side of the oily dumpster, her sneakers squeaking over the metal as she struggled for purchase. Between the little bit she could climb and Pete's surprising gorilla strength, he was able to haul her up until Lily fell forward on her stomach, the urge to puke compounded now that her gut hit the edge of the dumpster. She slung a leg over and from there Pete grasped her waist and braced her back against his chest until her feet hit the ground. Lily's body throbbed all over and she stank like rot. But she was out. And so was the puppy.

"Good work," Pete said. He had to have noted the putrid smell, but his face held nothing but admiration. "Let's get you inside."

As they took cautious steps toward the building, Lily imagined it all going down, the whole sequence of events of some soulless asshole driving out here and actually tossing a puppy into a cold, smelly dumpster. "People suck," she declared.

"Not all of them," Pete said softly. He slapped a hand on her back and kept her steady as they tiptoed over the ice to the safety of the shelter.

Clementine pressed the back of her hand to her nose and held her breath. "Somebody actually threw a puppy in the trash?" She regarded her daughter, clothes covered in goo, hair streaked with something dark, which Clementine didn't even want to *know*. Lily's shoes had come off at the front door. The icy rain might clean them or they just might become garbage themselves, depending.

"They did." Lily's voice was a harsh whisper. She had the puppy in a blanket from the shelter. All Clementine could see was his face, peeking out from the old quilt someone had donated. "They put him in the trash."

Clementine pitied the fool who had thrown away that puppy, if he ever ran into Lily in a dark alley.

"He's clean," Lily said. "We gave him a bath at the shelter. But I couldn't leave him there, Mom. He's too traumatized. He's still shaking, even though he's warm. He was probably in the trash for hours."

"He's way cleaner than you," Clementine agreed. "Here. Let me have him and you can go shower."

"Soon." Lily sank into a kitchen chair and tucked the puppy

tighter against her middle. "I can't leave him just yet. It's not good to pass him off from one person to the next so soon after his rescue. He already feels vulnerable. The people who had him probably breed puppies for a living and throw out any puppy that isn't perfect."

Clementine didn't suggest that this sounded a bit dramatic, because Lily always had a full backstory for every animal she rescued. Most of it was created in her own mind, suppositions that filled in the gaps of what little information the shelter had on the animals people tossed out, turned in and discarded like old clothes at the Salvation Army. This wasn't a practice Clementine discouraged and she'd got used to it over the years. Lily even had a backstory for her father's death, built around the few facts they'd been provided from the United States Marine Corps, and Clementine had been assured by the family therapist they used to see that this was healthy and completely normal.

"I can't believe Pete let you climb into the dumpster."

"Mom."

"I mean, why didn't he climb in? You don't let a sixteen-year-old climb into the dumpster."

"Mom."

"Okay." Clementine couldn't take it anymore. "I know you're used to how you smell by now, but, babe, you're rank. Go shower." She held out her arms for the puppy. "And take the quilt with you. It needs washing, too. I'll get him a new one."

Lily cautiously handed over the puppy. "His name is Terrence," she said. "We might work up to calling him Terry eventually, but right now he prefers his full name."

"I see." Clementine snuggled Terrence into the crook of her arm, and hell if the puppy didn't whine when Lily headed for the stairs.

Lily looked back over her shoulder. "I told you it was too soon."

"Go." Clementine pointed.

Once Lily was gone, Clementine went to the hall closet and dug out an old baby blanket Lily used to sleep with. It was covered in colored bunnies and had a ragged hem. Clementine took both Terrence and the blanket into the living room and settled him in front of the fireplace on the dog bed that had been shared by more than a dozen other strays Lily had brought home over the years, both before and during her time at the shelter. She let him lie there, in front of the warm fire, for a few minutes, before she spoke to him. "Hello, Terrence."

He wiggled a ways out of the blanket. Clementine could see that the puppy wasn't just black, white and brown. He had a blue-speckled appearance across certain patches of his back and haunches. On first glance, he'd seemed like a beagle, but Clementine had never seen a beagle with speckles before. The puppy sat up on his haunches and started doing a little yip-cry that tore right into the heartstrings.

Lily rounded the corner from the stairs, breaking the record for world's fastest shower. "I'm here, Terrence," she said. She crossed the room and settled on the floor near the puppy. She let him sniff her fingers. He slumped onto his side and Lily ran her hand gently over his head and ears. She drew the bunny blanket over him. Terrence laid his head down, drew a deep breath and sighed. His eyes closed.

"Well, I never," Clementine said.

"Dr. Winters is coming tomorrow," Lily said. "He'll need to be dewormed and checked out."

"Of course." Clementine stretched and glanced at the clock. It'd been a long day and the thought of an early bedtime sounded like heaven. "Should I get the crate out? The small one?" They'd collected dog crates in multiple sizes, but since the house had been empty for a couple of weeks now, they were all in the garage.

"No." Lily's head snapped around. She fixed Clementine with Tyler's gaze. "Terrence is sleeping with me. He's too vulnerable to be alone. He'll wake up, thinking he's back in the dumpster, and the shock will be too great."

"Lil. He's not going to think he's in the dumpster. The dumpster reeks and is freezing."

"Mom."

"Okay." Clementine sighed. The last thing she wanted to do right now was go in the frigid garage and dig out a metal dog crate. "He can sleep with you tonight."

"I'm going to lie right here next to him a little while." Lily curled behind Terrence on the dog bed. "When I'm sure he's out, I'll make the transfer to my room."

Clementine went to protest but tomorrow was Saturday. Lily didn't have to get up for school and her next shift at the shelter was Monday. "Don't fall asleep there." Clementine headed for the stairs, more than ready for her own bed. She'd get in a quick journal entry to Tyler, then turn on the TV. If she didn't hear Lily head for bed soon, she'd come looking.

"I won't." Lily's eyes were already closed. Little Terrence started snoring, the coming and going of his breath like the sound of a miniature zipper on a teeny tiny jacket.

"Sleep tight, Terrence."

Something told Clementine the little puppy was going to have the best night's sleep he'd ever had in his short life.

twenty-two

Hobbs felt an unusual weight pressed against his side. In his dream, he was stuck in the bottom of a pit, half-buried in dirt. Pops stood at the edge of the hole, staring down at him with a drunken squint in his eyes, his old work boots kicking a shower of sunbaked dirt to rain down on Hobbs's face. The dry dirt sounded like pebbles hitting glass, which made no sense. It was one of those dreams where, at the last second, Hobbs knew he was dreaming and gasped awake with a relief so fierce it left him shaking.

The back of his neck was sweaty. In fact, his whole body was sweaty. Hobbs tried to roll over, but bumped into something soft. Gracie, molded against his side, peeked up at him and whapped her tail.

"Why are you in my bed?" Hobbs grunted.

Gracie gave a little whine from the back of her throat.

"I don't even like you," Hobbs insisted.

She stared at him with those tawny eyes that looked just

like Gemma's. The image of Pops in that dream, standing over the pit and glaring down at him, flooded his mind. As his mind cleared, Hobbs saw the gray sky from his window. He hadn't pulled the shade last night and the little balls of ice pelting the glass should've been rhythmic and soothing. Reluctantly, Hobbs ran a hand over Gracie's head. Her wagging got more eager, her tail whapping in double time.

George's big moony eyes suddenly appeared, looming over the top of Hobbs's head. Hobbs made a startled *gah* sound and sat upright. George scattered. No wonder he was sweating bullets, with a dog on one side and a cat wrapped around his skull. "You two are out of your mind," he muttered, scrubbing his hands over his face. "You've got a perfectly good woman in the other room who actually wants your sorry butts and yet you keep annoying me."

At the mention of Hannah, Hobbs remembered what she had told him last night and the dream about Pops made more sense. A weight bogged down Hobbs's shoulders, heavy as the dirt Pops had been kicking into his dream grave. Remembering the flurried text exchange with Victor did nothing to lighten Hobbs's mood. Victor had set out to immediately hunt down Timbley and make sure he was still in Omaha, and Hannah, who had waited three days to tell Hobbs, had locked herself in her bedroom from the stress of their rapid-fire questions. Through the door, Hobbs could hear the sewing machine humming all evening.

Found the SOB. Still in Omaha. Didn't approach. Will keep tabs.

That was the text waiting on Hobbs's phone from Victor. Jesus. What time had Victor got up this morning? Nebraska was two hours behind Virginia and Hobbs's watch read eight thirty. He'd slept in, without meaning to. He blamed Gracie.

He petted the dog's head again and the weight on his shoulders eased up a little. If Timbley really was texting Hannah, at least it wasn't too late. If he was still in Omaha, he could be stopped. Victor would make sure of that.

Hobbs found his sister in the nook off the kitchen, alone at the table, her chin in her hand while she gazed out the picture window at the ice that had coated the grass and trees. They sparkled like a fairy tale. A steaming cup of tea sat in front of her, the tea bag squished on a spoon, the smell of cinnamon in the air, the box with the bear on the front open on the table.

"George and Gracie miss you," Hobbs said, noting that the pair had followed him down the hall.

Hannah looked up at him with big, sad eyes that reminded him of her youth. How many mornings had he sat her at a round oak table, much like this one, her fine hair uncombed and standing up with static and her big blue eyes full of protest about going to school, a bowl of half-eaten Froot Loops in front of her, the milk turning pink from the food dye? "They sneaked into your room again, didn't they?"

Hobbs sighed. "They can't very well sleep with you if you keep your door shut. What were you sewing all night?"

Hannah nodded at a stack of blankets that Hobbs had missed somehow. About five of them, in various colors, the size of baby blankets, folded up in a stack. They looked bright and soft. "I got a bag of scraps at the Salvation Army. I used up a lot of the flannel."

Hobbs grabbed his gym hoodie, slung over the back of a kitchen chair, and pulled it over his head. Gracie was dancing by the back door to go out and Hannah hadn't made a move to acknowledge her. "What are you going to do with them?"

Hannah shrugged.

"I see." Hobbs stuffed his feet into his sandals, but at least he had socks on. "Finish your tea. We're meeting Sean at Delaney's bike shop this morning. Tabitha's working the counter, so he can talk to you both and get all the information he needs about those text messages."

"He's not going to be able to do anything." Hannah kept staring out the window, maybe watching the cardinals that were all over Hobbs's bird feeders. Hobbs didn't do much in the way of landscaping, but he did like to watch the birds outside this window. The cardinals—either the bright red males or the cinnamon-and-honey-colored females—and the dogwoods in bloom in the spring, with their creamy white or pink flowers, were his favorite things about Virginia.

"It can't hurt to talk to him. He's a really good detective. And a friend."

Hannah finally tore her gaze from the window. She looked Hobbs up and down. He'd jumped into the gray sweats that were tossed at the end of his bed and an old sweatshirt. "Great outfit," she said, her eyes resting on the socks and sandals.

"At least someone is dressed to take the dog out," Hobbs shot back, eyeing Hannah's bare feet. "Finish your tea."

Hannah made no move to lift her cup, and as Hobbs stepped out into the icy rain with an inseparable dog-and-cat pair that he didn't want, he couldn't help but have that dream enter his mind, the glare of his father as Hobbs lay in the bottom of a pit, dirt pouring like desert sand over his face.

The shop was empty of everyone but Tabitha when they arrived. The streets had been deserted and the drive over slower than usual as Hobbs felt his truck's tires slide a little over the ice. He'd texted Sean and gave him the opportunity to reschedule, but Sean had been unmoved by the weather's show of strength. Triple M Classics was warm inside and smelled like fresh coffee. Tabitha was sitting much like Hannah had been at the breakfast table, chin in her palm, but with her face in a book that lay spread out before her on the counter.

"What're you reading?"

Tabitha glanced up, smiling at Hannah, big and genuine. She stuck a register receipt in the fold of her book and flipped it closed, so they could see the cover. *Proficient Motorcycling: The Ultimate Guide.*

"Working on that Badass List, I see," Hobbs said. "Too bad it's so slick outside or we could maybe take that ride."

"Yeah." Tabitha offered a somewhat sad smile. "Maybe someday."

"Are you alone? Delaney's not here?"

"She and Wyatt are in the back." Tabitha pointed toward the door behind her, which led to a larger workspace that had a couple of lifts and lots of storage space, which Victor had told him about after he'd checked out Delaney's '33. "Working on a bike."

Hobbs almost made a joke about that being a relief, but just then Sean pushed open the front door of the shop, bringing an icy wind with him. "Morning," Sean said, his strides long and authoritative, despite his friendly smile. "How's everyone today?" He wore jeans and boots and a sweatshirt that read All Caps, the letter *l*'s shaped like hockey sticks.

Everyone chorused good-mornings, but Hannah pressed herself closer to the counter, maybe getting as near to Tabitha as she could. Hobbs got it immediately, the fact that Hannah had been around the police many times growing up. They always looked a lot like Sean—strong, well-built, tidy hair, hard jaw, a glint in the eyes that indicated power and control. They were never at the house for good reasons, and Hobbs probably hadn't given much thought, up until this moment, to what kind of memories that had made for a young girl. He'd only known what kind of memories the police had created for him, which was that his father had been violent again, and the cops were there to mitigate things, maybe take Pops away in handcuffs, maybe just talk him down, spray him with the garden hose and order him to sober up. Even though Hannah had met Sean at Thanksgiving, he'd only been there in the capacity of someone eating dinner. This time was different, and everything about Sean's demeanor demonstrated that.

"We're just going to have a friendly chat," Sean said, like he sensed Hannah's sudden nerves. He drew out a notepad and pen. "In fact, let's pour some coffee first." Sean set his pad down on the counter and went to the coffeepot Delaney had behind the counter. There was a stack of paper cups, turned upside down, next to the glass carafe. "Anyone?"

Hobbs and Tabitha shook their heads, but Hannah said, "I'll have some."

Hobbs had never seen Hannah drink anything but tea, but he bit his tongue.

"Cream? Sugar?" Sean said.

"No, thanks."

Great. Now her first go at coffee was going to be *black* coffee. Still, Hobbs said nothing. Sean took his time pouring, then fiddling with the cream and sugar until he had what he wanted. The addition of condiments seemed to calm Hannah, as though she could stomach a hard-nosed cop who took cream and two sugars. "Hey," Sean said, once he'd finished and came back to the counter with the coffees. "Why don't you two let me have a little time with Hannah alone." He looked first at Tabitha, then at Hobbs, his eyes indicating he wasn't really asking.

Hobbs opened his mouth to protest, but then saw Hannah nodding in agreement. It slowly dawned on him that Hannah's nervousness might not be just about Sean's cop persona; it might actually have more to do with Hobbs being there, looming like the overprotective big brother. It kind of stung, to realize Hannah might have things to say she didn't want to share with him.

"Come on." Tabitha had already come around the counter and was staring at him. "Let's give them some space." She tilted her head toward the rows of shelves Victor had lost himself in looking for his gloves. "I have some inventory to stock. That way I can still mind the storefront while they get their privacy."

"I'm not sure if—"

"I'll leave Trinity with her." Tabitha looked down at her little pit bull, who sat there agreeably, ready to do whatever work Tabitha had in mind. "Trinity, stay," Tabitha said, pointing down as she took a few steps away.

Trinity settled on the ground and wagged her tail. Hannah gave Tabitha a grateful smile. "We'll just be over here." Tabitha pointed toward the shelves off on the left side of the shop.

Hobbs followed Tabitha around the corner, until they were deep in the rows of merchandise. Tabitha chose an aisle that was full of cardboard boxes, the top one on the stack undone, flaps sticking up in the air. She went to the carton, drew out some smaller boxes that lay inside and started stacking them on a high shelf. The boxes rattled, like they held small parts, and Tabitha had to tip on her toes to reach the shelf where the merchandise belonged. She wore jeans and a tight green sweater, both of which hugged her, curving and flaring just enough in all the right places. Her hair was pulled back with delicate gold clips that showed off her dark curls. Hobbs thought about commenting on her quads—they were definitely stronger than when she'd started at Semper Fit, back when she could barely back squat eighty-five pounds—but he found himself strangely unable to speak, to comment, to joke, to do any of the things he was used to doing with ease. Maybe it was the scent of her, all around him, something pretty like jasmine. Hell if he knew, but Tabitha seemed like the kind of girl who'd smell like jasmine, which was either a flower or a tea, Hobbs thought, but both suited her, so it didn't matter.

"Here, let me help you." Hobbs found his voice, but it came out scratchy. He leaned in and took the box from her hand, settling it easily on the shelf. He held out his hand for another, could see now that they were restocking bolts.

"Thanks." Tabitha handed him the next box.

"How've you been doing?" It took everything Hobbs had to force out the small talk. "Haven't seen you since that visit with Thaddeus."

"I'm doing good." Tabitha's voice was soft. "You?"

"Good," he echoed. "Other than the stuff with Hannah, of course. Thanks for helping her, by the way. The massage. And getting her to open up about those texts. Without you, I don't think she would've said anything."

"You're welcome. I just want to help her, that's all."

Hobbs opened his hand for the next box, and the next. Their fingers brushed once, then again, more each time, like they both might be doing it on purpose, until the shelf was full and the carton empty. When they were done, neither of them moved. They stood less than a foot apart, the air warm around them, the shop quiet, with only Sean's voice stabbing in the background. The scenario took Hobbs back, to all those times the cops would come to the house. He and Victor and Hannah would hide and the cops would grill Mom in that same voice—patient, but hard. Mom had never wanted them there, no matter how badly anyone had been hurt. Hopefully Hannah would be more forthcoming.

Tabitha parted her lips, like she might have something to say, but then she closed her mouth again. She pulled at the cuffs of her sweater, straightening the sleeves that had ridden up from stretching to reach the high shelf. Hobbs's heart started a steady thud in his chest, making him feel even hotter inside his old Semper Fit hoodie, one of the originals that was thinning and worn but was the best color and fit, so he refused to toss it out. Originals were always the best.

Hobbs knew he should say something, or grab the box knife and cut open the next carton, but that feeling was still there, the one that had silenced him earlier, kept him from joking or making small talk. Tabitha didn't talk or open another carton, either. In fact, she moved closer, apparently overcome by the same unspoken feelings Hobbs was having. Her fingertips brushed his as she fumbled for his hand. Cool, slender fingers traced gently inside his rough palm, sending a shiver over his body. He got that same feeling, just like the night she'd massaged him and had worked on his hands. Like she could see right inside him and know everything that was there, everything that he'd worked so hard to bury down as deep as the pit from this morning's dream.

Tabitha leaned in, not waiting for him to make a move, maybe buoyed by the magnetic draw that sizzled both ways. Hobbs's eyes closed and her soft lips touched his. The jolt of electricity woke him, his arm going around her waist, drawing her against him, his palm sliding over the enticing curve of her hip in her tight jeans. Tabitha made a little gasp as Hobbs pinned her against the shelves and deepened their kiss, knowing it was rough, that he ought to be gentler, but he'd been aching for more ever since that night at his house. Every time he was near her now he felt on edge, just this side of losing control.

Tabitha's arms went around his neck, pulling him tighter, greedy, encouraging his lust. Her hands went to his shoulders, then down his back, squeezing and tracing over his muscles, like she was frustrated with the fabric. Those slim, cool fingers lit on his bare skin as she slid them beneath his sweatshirt. Every touch felt like fire, searing into him. Hobbs tried to catch her hands as they moved around front, but the intensity of her kiss kept him dazed, off his game.

"Wait, wait, wait." Hobbs grasped her wrists and stilled her hands. He pulled back gently, but pressed his forehead to hers. "Wait."

"I'm tired of waiting."

"My sister is just around the corner."

That seemed to snap her out of it. Tabitha slackened in his grip, and he released her. Her hands fell away, which was both blissful and excruciating. The sound of Hannah's voice reached them, faint but unmistakable, and Hobbs's blood started to cool. They stood there, breathing heavily while they stared at each other.

"I'm sorry," Hobbs said, his brain still mush.

"Why are you sorry?" Tabitha arched an eyebrow. "I kissed you."

"Well, I don't mean I'm sorry. I just mean that I—"

"What do you mean, exactly?"

Hobbs scrubbed a hand over his face, then through his hair. "I don't know."

"Now who's the one pushing time around?"

"What?"

Tabitha smirked, but it was joyless. "You told me once, at Open Hour at the gym, that I was just pushing time around. Just kind of fumbling and making excuses. You were right. And you're doing the same thing now."

Hobbs parted his lips to protest, even though she was absolutely right.

"Excuse me."

They both whipped their heads around to see Sean, standing at the end of the aisle. He looked like he might've been trying to get their attention for a second or two.

"I've got what I need from your sister." Sean held up his

pad. "There's not a whole lot I can do, but I will look into this guy. His background and his movements. If nothing else, it might make Hannah feel better to know someone is keeping an eye."

"Great." Hobbs and Tabitha spoke in unison. They glanced at each other, their faces guilty. Not only was Sean no idiot, he was a detective.

Sean pointed over his shoulder. "I'll be out here." He tapped his notepad against his palm, then turned and disappeared.

Once he was gone, Hobbs turned back to Tabitha. "We should get out there," she said. She brushed past him, but Hobbs caught her hand.

"Tabby." He waited until she faced him. Her eyes sparkled. "I just… I wish I could explain. I can't… I don't know how to explain. I just need some time."

"You don't seem to need time with other women."

"I—"

"Like Serena."

How did she know about Serena? It'd only been drinks. She'd invited him back to her place, and Hobbs had gone, but as soon as Serena had gone for a kiss, Hobbs had turned his head and made an excuse, actually pretended there was a text from Victor on his phone that he couldn't ignore. And he'd bolted. Hobbs hadn't understood his actions then, but he did now. "Look, I know. I know how it seems. But they aren't… they aren't…" Hobbs trailed off. He knew what to say. He just couldn't say it.

Tabitha shrugged, the corner of her mouth curving down, a little tremor there that she tried to hide. "You don't have to explain anything." Then she pulled away and was gone.

Hobbs stayed hidden in the shelves for a moment longer. He sighed and rubbed his eyes with the heels of his hands. He saw Pops behind them, standing over that hole, his old boot on top of that rusty shovel, dirt raining down on Hobbs's face and the whole world collapsing around him. Hobbs had been so smug, thinking he'd had the last word, thinking he'd pulled the trigger and finally won the war with that abusive old man.

Oh, how wrong he'd been.

twenty-three

The quieter you become, the more you are able to hear.

~Rumi

The room was dim, lit only by some battery-operated candles one of the therapists had brought. Chinese flutes filled the air, pouring out of a small speaker that was set on a table in the corner, along with disinfecting wipes and hand sanitizer. A folded Ping-Pong table was tucked away in one corner and a large whiteboard hung on the wall, "The SRU welcomes Chef Spencer!" written on it in dry-erase marker. The room was warm to the point of stuffy, the building it-self large and nondescript with four levels of long, carpeted hallways that turned like a maze and were lined with door after identical door. Tabitha had been buzzed into the locked building by the event coordinator, and she'd taken an eleva-tor to the top.

There were four other therapists in the large, open room,

all of them set up in their own rectangle of space. One of them was Red, who hadn't done a shift here in years but had been welcomed in by the coordinator, Jenny, like a long-lost friend. They'd embraced and caught up on their lives while they set up their tables. Tabitha got busy with her own table, and once the sheets and drape were set, she'd looked around the room and assessed the environment.

Red was right next to her, with Jenny on her other side. A man in the corner, wearing a baseball cap with the navy insignia, had set up a reclining chair, instead of a table.

"He only provides reflexology," Red said, in answer to Tabitha's unasked question. She pointed at her feet.

In the other corner was an older woman with gray-streaked dark hair. She paced up and down the side of her table while she read over a piece of paper, which provided a list of names of wounded service members who had signed up to receive forty minutes of free therapy. Tabitha had her own list, but obviously didn't know any of the names. Red had explained that a lot of the men and women who came for the therapy were repeats, had been coming for weeks, months, even years. Red hadn't worked here in so long she didn't recognize any names, either, but she'd patted Tabitha on the shoulder and said, "Remember, for most of these people, you're just here to bring them down." Red had made a motion with her hands of flattening the air. "You might get someone who asks for deep pressure or a specific area of work, but many of the men and women who come in here just need some hands. They just need someone to make them feel human again. And that, my dear—" Red had leaned in close "—is your specialty."

But what if I don't? Tabitha thought. *What if I make them feel worse?* At that thought, Tabitha glanced down at Trinity, who wore her service vest and waited patiently by the chair Tabitha had put there in case she had some neck routines to do.

"You're going to be great," Red said, like she was giving words to Trinity's expression. Red's own face was set and certain. "Nobody will understand them like you do. Remember that."

Tabitha took a deep, cleansing breath and turned to face her table. She contained a startle when she found the older woman who'd been pacing standing only a couple of feet away, the client sheet clasped in her hands. "I've had your first guy a couple of times." The lady, whose name tag read April, pointed at the sheet, to the spot on the chart where Tabitha's first client was listed. "He's got fibromyalgia. So you'll have to use a light touch."

"Oh." Tabitha glanced over at Red, who gave her a thumbs-up. "Definitely." This was the whole reason she was here, right? Or at least one of them. After her conversation with Red, Tabitha had suggested to Auntie El that she go back to the doctor and bring up fibromyalgia, to see what they had to say. Auntie El had listened patiently and, despite her reluctance, made another appointment for the following week. Now Tabitha would actually have the chance to try massage on someone with this condition before she attempted anything with Auntie El.

"Just thought I'd share," April said.

"Thank you." Tabitha felt a lump form in her throat but she swallowed it down. She glanced at the clock. It was time to start. She couldn't bring jitters to the table, that was for sure. Just as April returned to her station, the automatic doors swung open and five people came through, a mix of men and women, some with walking support, others moving just fine but carrying unseen or invisible injuries. The therapists crossed the room to their clients as they settled into a row of chairs against the opposite wall and started taking off their shoes.

One guy, approached by no one, slipped his shoes off, but

sat there, looking around, his hands gripping the fabric of his sweatpants at his knees. Red pointed to him and nodded.

Tabitha approached, ready to take on her first official wounded service member massage. "Hi, Paul," she said as she reached his chair. He looked up at her with heavy eyes, the energy around him like he carried a great weight, his expression anxious, weary, confused and frustrated all at once. Tabitha knew that expression. Tabitha understood that expression. "I'm Tabitha. How are you feeling today?" She took his sheet from his shaky hand and read over his list of conditions and medications. Sure enough, fibromyalgia was listed there. His pain level, when given the choice to circle a one through five, was a four.

"Okay," he said.

Tabitha smiled. "Based on what I see here, we'll use a light touch. How does that sound?"

Paul nodded. "Yes, ma'am. I'll probably fall asleep. This is the only place I get good sleep." He smiled ruefully.

Tabitha's heart broke a little bit. Paul looked no older than midtwenties. *Younger than me*, she thought. She led him to the table and, given the choice, he opted for facedown. After he settled, Tabitha covered him with a light drape, then stood over him and closed her eyes. There was definitely a lot of pain here. Fatigue. Uncertainty. But also…hope. Tabitha wasn't going to let him down.

She reached out and laid her hands on Paul's shoulders. Immediately, he tensed. Tabitha felt a trembling, from deep inside—the same trembling that she'd felt when she laid hands on both Candy and Hannah. He probably wasn't even aware of it, and odds were, neither were his previous therapists. The tremble was so slight, rushing hands or jabbing elbows would miss it entirely. Tabitha stood there, hands rested, and just waited. She took a couple of deep breaths, in and out slowly, and waited until the tremor had somewhat eased. Once Paul seemed a little calmer, Tabitha slid her hands over his back and shoulders, slowly, with barely any pressure. She did this a few times, creating a rhythm.

After the third pass, Paul sighed audibly and settled deeper into the table.

After about ten minutes had passed, Paul's breathing slowed, the rise and fall of his back deep and even. A tiny snore came from the headrest. Paul was out.

Tabitha continued with her rhythm, going by feel, often closing her eyes and getting the invisible feedback that she seemed more in tune with than anything her eyes told her. The forty minutes went by fast. Paul's massage was the first massage that Tabitha hadn't wanted to end. She saw the clock click over to the final minute and she felt sad that there wasn't more time. She didn't want to uncover him, rouse him, tell him it was time to go. But she had to.

She leaned forward, near his ear. "How you doing, Paul?"

Paul muttered something that was half word, half sigh.

"Don't get up fast," Tabitha said. "Take your time." She waited another minute, giving Paul time to absorb the change, before she came around the side of the table and offered her hand. Paul took it and hauled himself up. Once he was upright, legs dangling over the side, he drew a deep breath and let it out slowly.

"How do you feel?" Tabitha said. "I wish we had more time."

Paul nodded. He smiled down at Trinity. "She's yours?"

"Yeah, that's Trinity."

Paul nodded again. "Thank you," he said as he rose up. He stretched and yawned. "What was your name again?"

"Tabitha."

"Thanks, Tabitha. Am I allowed to ask for you next time? Does it work like that?"

Tabitha's heart sank a little, even as it was filling up. What an odd sensation, to want to cheer and cry all at the same time. "I'm just a student," she said. "They let me in with special permission. But I'll be back when I graduate. For sure." Her own words surprised her. The mixed sensations of joy and sadness bloomed inside of her, like two sides of a coin that could never be severed.

"A student?" Paul's eyebrows rose. "Could've fooled me. Well, thank you, Tabitha. Your hands were like magic."

Tabitha smiled, speechless. She handed Paul his intake sheet. As he walked away, Red appeared by Tabitha's side. "You did amazing," she whispered. "April just told me that Paul never settles in that fast."

Tabitha smiled. "I feel like we connected."

"Really?" Red smiled. "So you're not completely scared off the massage profession now?"

"No," Tabitha said, only realizing it as she spoke. "Just the opposite, in fact."

Red squeezed her shoulder. Something like pride and joy and unabashed happiness spread over her delicate features. "Told you so," she said. "You're made for this."

Tabitha nodded, no words coming to her that worked or made sense.

Red nodded toward the door. "Number two, coming up," she said. "Better wash your hands and change your sheets."

Right. Tabitha had got so wrapped up in her first session she'd forgotten there were three more to go. April slipped up next to her just as she was finishing up. "Good job with Paul," she said. "Good luck with the rest, too."

"Thank you." Even as she spoke, Tabitha realized she didn't need luck. She didn't need magic shoes, and she didn't need a set of fully blown-out birthday candles. She just needed to work hard, register for Semester 2 and—as Hobbs had said—stop doubting herself.

I got this.

twenty-four

A week later, Terrence the puppy had definitely made progress. His fur, once patchy with mange, had filled in and his skinny ribs were less visible. His blue-speckled haunches had intensified, which was the marker Dr. Winters, the mobile vet, had used to suggest bluetick hound as part of his lineage. "Bluetick and treeing walker hounds would be my bet," she'd said. "And something small. He's not big enough to just be those breeds. I'd say he's about four months old."

What Terrence lacked in size, he made up for with an energy level that could only be described as *extra*. When let out back, he'd streak up and down the fence line, chasing squirrels and eyeing the gaps in the slats for any sign of life. He was doing that now, while Clementine and Lily watched from the window.

"He's doing suicides again," Lily said, giggling at the way he streaked, stopped on a dime, then turned and streaked in the other direction. Once the legs started, the voice was soon to follow. Terrence tilted his head back and loosed a string of hound barks that promised to be deep when he was fully grown.

"What a racket. He's going to need a home with a big yard. And some really patient owners," Clementine mused.

Lily let the curtain fall. The crestfallen look on her face was unmistakable, but she recovered in a flash. "It's not his fault. He's just chasing down the hoodoo there," she said.

Clementine almost laughed but it didn't come. It was rare for Lily to make jokes when she was trying to hide her feelings. To her, that would be like putting a bright red arrow over buried treasure.

"Don't worry—I've got prospects." Lily grabbed her backpack and headed to the front door as her friend Dana pulled up in her dad's old El Camino and honked the horn. Clementine had asked Dana more than once not to do that, but she didn't say anything today. This was the last day of school before Christmas break, so Clementine wouldn't have to hear the horn for a couple of weeks, anyway. "And if nothing else, Pete has expressed interest. He's not sure Terrence is suitable, but he's willing to try."

"All right." Clementine decided against trying to have a discussion about Terrence right before school. "Have a good day. Tell Dana to drive carefully."

"Sure." Lily rolled her eyes. Just then, Terrence jumped against the sliding glass door, his paws going one after the other, like he was trying to dig it open. Lily headed over and let him inside. The dog barreled into her arms, laying his paws over her shoulders for a trick Lily had taught him called "the hug." He'd learned it in only a couple of sessions. Lily stroked along his back before he slid down and rolled onto his back. "This is why Pete is interested in him." Lily rubbed Terrence's belly. "He's extremely intelligent. Aren't you, boy? Aren't you?"

Terrence wiggled from side to side, enjoying his pets.

"That's right. You're not trash. No. You're my good boy."
One more stroke and Terrence was up, on all fours, racing
into the kitchen and back again, at lightning speed. "And that's
why Pete is also not interested," Lily said with a laugh. "Terrence is a wee bit crazy. You'll feed him, right?"

"Sure. Go. Don't make her honk the horn again." Just as
Clementine said it, the sound of the El Camino came long
and hard from out front.

Lily grinned. "Sorry. Thanks. 'Bye."

Once she was gone, Clementine looked down at Terrence
and sighed. He stared up at her, his brown eyes moony, the
little white patch between them like a drop of cream someone spilled on his head. "C'mon, Nugget." Clementine tilted
her head toward the kitchen. "Let's get you fed."

She fed them both, a bowl of puppy food for Terrence and
a prerun smoothie for herself. She pulled out her latest journal while she sipped it.

*I'm watching this dog your daughter brought home. Some-
one put him in the dumpster at the animal shelter. A week
ago he was sick and mangy and smelly. He's a little spit-
fire now. Weirdest little puppy you'd ever meet. You put his
food in front of him and you'd think he'd inhale it, right?
No. He approaches it slowly, like it might bite him. Kind of
walks at it sideways, sniffing the air. He's a hound, so he
smells things nobody else can smell. He'll walk all around
the bowl, sniffing. Eventually, he'll try a piece. Then he
eats the food one little nugget at a time. It can take him half
an hour to finish off half a cup of food. It's maddening. If I
get impatient, Lily tells me to chill. Says he can't be rushed
or he'll "form a bad relationship with food." I just don't
know about that daughter of yours sometimes. She really*

*loves this dog, though. He sleeps in her bed, even though
she thinks I don't know it. The crate is in her room and she
thinks that I think that Terrence goes in there every night,
but I've seen him in her bed in the mornings. He looks a
LOT like Digger. A lot. You'd really like him.*

Clementine paused her writing to watch Terrence select one
of the last three pieces of food in his bowl. Once he'd chosen which pebble was next, he sat back and crunched it up.
Then he went in for another, poking around both remaining
pieces until he'd decided the final order. Clementine huffed a
laugh and went to find her running shoes. Once she'd come
back to the kitchen, Terrence had finished and was now licking his bowl clean.

The sound of the front door opening made Clementine's
hands freeze on the shoelace she was tying. She didn't even
have time to jump up and see what was going on before Lily
appeared in the kitchen. Her backpack was missing and her
face was tight, anxious, but determined.

"What's wrong?" Clementine glanced out the window and
saw that Dana was out there, idling by the curb, the exhaust
coming from the tailpipe indicating the engine was running.
"Are you okay?"

"I'm fine." Lily kept her arms at her sides, hands fisted. "But
I wanted to tell you now, before it eats me up all day." She
touched her chest. "I love Terrence and I want to keep him."
He rushed to her side, done licking his bowl, and jumped
against her thighs. "Down, boy." Lily waited until he settled,
then squatted down to stroke his ears.

"Lil, this isn't the time. You'll be late for school." Clementine peered outside again and could see Dana slouched in the
driver's seat, sipping on a Big Gulp, looking bored behind her
expensive sunglasses.

"I don't care. There'll never be a good time for you. You'll keep thinking up excuses to put it off until I find a home for him, but I'm not going to do that this time."

Clementine sighed. "We've been over this. If we keep one of the dogs, it'll make it harder to foster the others."

"That's just your excuse." Lily shrugged, her fingertips lightly tracing the cream spot on Terrence's head. "You don't want me to keep a dog because Dad loved dogs and Digger died right after Dad did. You think replacing Digger will replace Dad. Or something like that. And that's the real reason you don't want me to keep him."

Clementine's throat felt like it sealed over, making it hard to draw air. "That's not true."

"It is true. It's the same reason you keep writing to him in those journals, instead of getting back out there, opening yourself up to another chance." Lily's voice was calm and direct, held the surety of a therapist. "And I'm not telling you how long to grieve, Mom, or when you should date again, if you ever date again, but I am saying that I want this dog. Somebody put him in the trash and I took him out. Terrence was meant to be mine and I was meant to be his person. Your refusal to move on shouldn't be my weight to bear." Lily rose back up, standing stick straight at her full five feet ten inches. It wouldn't matter if Clementine stood up, too. They'd never be eye to eye.

Clementine glanced at her journal and pushed the cover closed, over the pen that still lay inside. "You'll be late for school." The words came out soft, gravelly.

"I'm sorry if I hurt your feelings." Lily's voice was sincere, but still firm. "But I had to tell you the truth. If I get detention for being late, I might not be home on time. I'll text you."

Then she kissed Terrence on the head and left.

Clementine listened to the front door click shut, then sat

in the quiet kitchen, waves of emotion rolling over her in soft, torturous splashes. She put her face in her hands and cried freely, the sound of her own sobs in the emptiness a sad, ghostly song.

After an indeterminate amount of time, pressure touched her knees and something wet bumped her arm. Clementine peeked out and saw Terrence, his eager muzzle trying to find a way into her steepled hands. Clementine reached out and petted his head, then both ears. The puppy licked her face, drying up the tears.

"Okay, Nugget." Clementine sniffed, sucking up her tears and remembering what Lily had said about not giving Terrence a nickname yet. That he wasn't ready for it. "Too bad," Clementine said. "You're a nugget. Aren't you?"

Terrence's little tail went so fast it was a blur. Clementine laughed through her snotty nose, then rose up to get a tissue. She blew into it, then looked down at the notebook on the table. She considered opening it, then sat back down and laced up her sneakers. She glanced at her watch, not really feeling like running, but there was still time for a quick five miles before she had to get to the shop. As soon as she stood up, Terrence started spinning. He woofed at her.

"What?" Clementine narrowed her eyes at the hound. "What're you dancing and barking at?" *He's chasing down the hoodoo there.* Clementine laughed under her breath.

Terrence spun in circles again, then offered another woof.

"Are you saying you want to run with me?" Clementine had seen people running with their dogs, but had never done it herself. None of Lily's fosters had shown interest and Clementine had certainly never encouraged it. Her running time was her own, a place she could get lost, let her mind go free, all her troubles and worries forgotten about for at least one blissful hour.

Terrence made an excited growling sound in his throat, like he actually understood Clementine's question. As she thought about it, Clementine realized this was the first run she'd dressed for since Terrence had got here with Lily not around. When Lily was here, they were an inseparable pair. When Lily was gone, Terrence either slept or Clementine put him in his crate if she had to go to work. That had been her plan this morning. Put him in his crate and go run, then let him out while she showered, then back in the crate when she had to leave for work.

She stared down at the little hound mix, his blue speckles looking lively, his eyes twinkling. Clementine's face felt hot and puffy, reminding her of her emotional outpouring. "Okay. We can try it." Clementine pushed her journal away and hunted down Terrence's harness and leash. She barely got them on him before he was straining for the front door. They stepped out to the front porch, where both of their breath turned to steam. The morning was cool, the sky overcast. She looked down at Terrence and offered a smile. "I hope you can keep up, Nugget."

Those were her famous last words, right before Clementine spent the next forty minutes running as fast as she could, trying not to fall on her face.

twenty-five

When Hobbs woke to the smell of pine, he remembered Hannah's insistence that they buy a real Christmas tree. Christmas was less than a week away and she'd got tired of Hobbs putting it off. They'd gone to a tree farm yesterday, had even taken Gracie and George, and Hobbs had told Hannah to pick out whichever tree she wanted. She'd chosen the most expensive Douglas fir on the lot, and despite Hobbs's protest that it might not even fit in his living room, she'd stood firm on her choice.

George, wearing an ugly Christmas sweater knitted in green and red with what looked like melting snowmen all over it, had seemed to take Hannah's side in the matter. Perched in a little stroller, George had glared up at Hobbs when he suggested Hannah go for a much smaller—and much cheaper—pine tree.

"Don't look at me like that," Hobbs had said. "Go chase Gracie." He'd waved his hand toward the tawny Lab mix, who'd grown quite a bit over the last couple of weeks, filling out her paws, her fur getting a shade darker. She roamed the tree lot freely, in no danger of taking off because she never got too far from Hobbs. She followed him around the house, sometimes tripping him in the process. She was always waiting for him inside the front window when he got home from work, her furry face behind the glass, her tail wagging as soon as she spotted him.

She was with him now, wrapped around him like a body pillow. The only way Hobbs could keep Gracie out of his bed was to shut his door at night, and then she'd cry out there in the hallway, which Hobbs couldn't take. The only thing out of place this morning was George. Hobbs sat up and glanced all around; he even dug under the pillows, just in case, but the hairless cat was nowhere to be found. "Where's George?"

Gracie gave a big stretch, making her body long, legs flattened behind her as she opened up her shoulders. She yawned, totally unconcerned about George's whereabouts. "Well, that's a first," Hobbs said. "Are you two finally able to separate? At least for a little while?"

Hobbs did his business, washed and splashed his hands and face, gave his teeth a quick brush—he'd read that you should brush your teeth before you drank coffee, then swish afterward, to avoid stains and the acidity of the brew harming your enamel—then jumped into his sweats and began a search for the little cat. Hobbs didn't have a lot of rooms or a lot of things, so even though George could fit pretty much anywhere, when a sweep of the living room and kitchen turned up nothing he got a nervous pit in his stomach. He even looked under the new Christmas tree, which dominated the corner where one of his end tables used to be, the smell of pine strong and merry. As soon as Hannah, who was aghast that Hobbs didn't own a tree skirt, had thrown a blanket under there,

George had curled up under the branches and made himself at home. This morning, though, the spot under the tree was bare.

Hobbs measured out the coffee grounds and flicked on the pot, hoping George might come running to the sounds of life in the kitchen. When he didn't, that left only one place to look.

Hannah's bedroom door was ajar, so Hobbs lightly pressed it open and peered into the darkness. Gracie, at his heels, poked her head in, too. Sunlight from the hallway spilled over Hannah's sleeping mound—she'd been sleeping later ever since Tabitha started giving her massages—and there was George, right next to Hannah's head on her pillow. Hobbs might not have spotted him if it weren't for his yellow eyes, because he was covered in one of those dumb quilts Hannah kept making. George lifted his little face and glared at them.

Hobbs pulled the door to its original position and headed back to the kitchen, where the smoky scent of coffee was overtaking the piney Christmas tree. He glanced down at Gracie, who'd followed him every step of the way. "You see that?" Hobbs pointed in the direction of Hannah's room. "Your buddy didn't sleep with you. Or follow us. And I know he saw you."

Gracie tossed her head and went to the front door, where her leash hung. This was another daily routine that had somehow become Hobbs's chore, not for lack of Hannah trying. Gracie just wanted to be with Hobbs. He leashed her up and forewent the cat stroller, which typically made Hannah poke fun at him for being this big, buff guy walking his kitty stroller, but today, George did not come running to join them.

"You know you're supposed to be hanging out with the lady, right?" Hobbs said as they headed up the sidewalk, Gracie walking politely at his side, eager to get to her favorite patch of community grass that was just over the rise, across the street from the kids' playground. The air was dry and on the warmer side for mid-December, no wind and the faint scent of a wood-burning fireplace on the air. Gracie trotted happily, not looking the slightest bit guilty, or like she missed the presence of her hairless cat. "You know that someday, unless someone else adopts you, you'll go live in Omaha with Hannah. It's flatter. With more snow. So you should kinda sorta start to get to know her, if you know what I'm saying."

Gracie tugged only the slightest bit when they crested the hill and she spied her grass patch—an open lot maintained by the homeowners' association—dotted in cherry trees, a few park benches and a receptacle specifically to dispose of dog poo, complete with a metal container that was supposed to be filled with bags for this purpose. Right now, it was empty, but Hobbs had his own bags, in a little plastic thing Hannah had bought that clipped to the leash. "She went to town on you with all this stuff," Hobbs said, dropping the leash as Gracie raced to her patch and squatted down. Nobody else was here, so he wasn't worried about being yelled at about leash laws. "And you don't even give her the time of day." He briefly wondered if that mattered, now that George had suddenly taken Hannah in his favor. Was it the stupid blankets? The thought made Hobbs smile.

His phone buzzed in his pocket. He drew it out to reveal a text from Sean.

Checking in. Anything new? How's Hannah?

Hobbs had to admit, despite not being able to do much, Sean had gone the extra mile for Hannah after their conversation at the bike shop. He'd looked into Timbley's background and talked to Hobbs after his workout the next night. "Those texts she got are from a burner phone, just like we thought. So that's no help. But I know this guy's type. They're the worst kind of bad news because they always look pretty good on paper. At least for a while. Everyone thinks they're charming and could do no wrong. But I can see the patterns. Frequent job changes, which is usually due to issues with authority. He's moved around a lot, too, which by itself isn't anything, but based on what happened with Hannah, it makes me wonder. There are probably other scared women out there."

Hobbs typed back. The texts went quiet after she changed her number. So far, so good.

Good. So Delaney wanted me to pass on that she stocks some personal defense stuff at the shop, like pepper spray and brass knuckles. She said Hannah can come by anytime and she'll drop her some for free. Not that we think she'll need them. Just being safe.

Hobbs smiled to himself and almost typed *What, no Taser?* but decided not to joke around.

Thanks. Will do. Hobbs didn't add that he hadn't heard from Victor in a few days, which made him kind of nervous. Victor had been checking in daily, oftentimes giving a report of where he'd tailed James to, whether to his job or a bar, if he'd seen him with a random woman, etc. But there'd been nothing since the weekend. On one hand, Hobbs thought Victor's obsession with tailing Hannah's ex around town was over the top, but on the other, Hobbs liked knowing where the scumbag was, that Victor's eyes had been on him in Omaha.

All right. See you tonight at the gym.

Hobbs cleaned up after Gracie and got her back home. The house was quiet and stayed that way while Hobbs fed Gracie, enjoyed his coffee and watched *Good Morning Football*. "Look at that," Hobbs said to Gracie. "Does that look like an angry run to you?" He watched as a quarterback broke a sack and plowed his way down the field, mowing over a guy twice his size and leaping over another like a ballerina. "Angry Runs" was a self-explanatory segment of the show that Hobbs enjoyed the most. "I bet you can out-angry-run that guy in a heartbeat."

Gracie crunched her kibble in reply, but actually did look up at the television.

"Right?" Hobbs finished his coffee and laughed at the dog, who really seemed to enjoy the segment. "Nobody could catch you. You could make the draft next year." He glanced at his watch and decided that if he left now, he could swing by Triple M Classics and see what Delaney had in mind for Hannah. That was his excuse, anyway. In truth, Hobbs was hoping that Tabitha would be there and maybe they could talk a little bit. Ever since the kiss at the shop the other week, she'd politely avoided him at the gym and Hobbs couldn't blame her. In fact, he'd invited that. That had been what he wanted, right? Just casual fun, nothing serious. Which would be great if he could stop thinking about her. But now, even when he'd tried to have a casual thing, like with Serena, there Tabitha was, in his head. Always in his head. The way she felt when she slipped her hand into his. The way her lips tasted. Those deep, warm eyes...

Hobbs sighed and shook himself free. He pulled his hoodie on, grabbed his gym bag and his keys. Gracie followed him to the door.

"You know you can't come. I have too many clients to keep an eye on you."

Gracie sat politely, legs straight, head held high. She whined from the back of her throat. Just then, Hannah shuffled down the hallway. Her hair was a mess and she still had her pajamas on. She carried George, wrapped in his blanket. "Morning," she mumbled.

"Go to Hannah." Hobbs snapped his fingers and pointed. Gracie glanced at Hannah, but turned back to Hobbs and whined again. "Sorry, girl. I've got to go."

"Gracie, come." Hannah's command was lackluster, like she knew it would do no good. "You walk her?"

"Yep. Again."

Hannah waved him off and headed to the kitchen with her cat.

"Coffee's still fresh," Hobbs called. "See you later."

Hannah mumbled something Hobbs couldn't make out. Gracie settled down on her stomach and put her head between her paws. She sighed. For the first time, Hobbs considered taking her with him. But no. She'd get in the way and Hobbs couldn't risk her getting hurt by a stray barbell. Besides, Gracie wasn't his dog, nor would she ever be. No use in Hobbs getting attached to her. "I'll be back later. Take care of Hannah."

As Hobbs shut the door behind him, he saw the curtains near the window move. Gracie had pushed in front of them so she could watch him through the glass. As he walked away, he looked back over his shoulder and felt a wave of sadness wash over him so strong he hurried to his truck and didn't look back again.

Tabitha basked in the quiet morning vibe of Triple M Classics. The shop was open but empty, Delaney in the back working regular maintenance on a newer Harley. Tabitha had spent the morning decorating the shop for Christmas, winding red garland around the front counter and setting up a Charlie Brown–style mini Christmas tree in the corner. It listed sadly to the side, but it had been 50 percent off at the tree lot due to the fact that it was patchy and droopy. She started a new pot of coffee and settled at the counter with her journal. She flipped to her Badass List, pen in hand, excited to check things off.

Tabitha made checks on all but two items—*Help Auntie El* and *Ride a motorcycle*—her veins sizzling with satisfaction at each mark. Help Auntie El was in the works. She'd finally seen the doctor again and brought up fibromyalgia. A helpful nurse had agreed with Auntie El's research and the doctor had offered medication. Auntie El had taken the scrip but hadn't filled it yet. This was when Tabitha made her move and suggested Auntie El let Tabitha practice massage on her to see if it helped.

"I've never had a massage," Auntie El had protested. "I don't like excessive lotions. Plus, I think it would annoy me, the way I feel these days."

"Well, you're in luck, Auntie El. We're trained not to use excessive lotion. And I am known for my featherlight touch, which is perfect for your condition."

Auntie El had sighed, not given a yes or no, but Tabitha could tell she was wearing her down.

That left only one item on the Badass List, the one that made her prickle under her skin to look at it. *Ride a motorcycle.* That one might just have to wait. Not only was spring far away, Hobbs would probably forget about it by then. He'd get caught up dating Serena or whoever else and forget all about their pinkie promise. Which was just fine with Tabitha. If Hobbs needed time, he could have all the time in the world.

The bell over the door jangled and a hulking dude in denim and flannel walked into the shop. As soon as she spied the blond curls, she recognized him. "Hi, Victor. I didn't know you were back in town." Tabitha hadn't seen much of Hobbs in the past week, but she'd massaged Hannah a few days ago and there'd been no mention of Victor coming.

"Morning. Tabitha, right? Hey, doggo." Victor waved at

Trinity, lying in Wyatt's dog bed. Her ears had perked at Victor's arrival. "Got in last night." He motioned to the outdoors. "Rented a Jeep this time, but I wanted to drop in for another pair of those gloves you sold me—brown, if you got it. They're the warmest gloves I've ever worn." Up close, Victor had faint circles under his bright eyes and an overall fatigue to his handsome, rugged face that suggested he'd done his drive from Omaha with minimal stopping.

"Sure thing." Tabitha rose and headed for the shelves. "I remember what you bought. Largest size available, right?"

Victor laughed and waited for her by the counter. When Tabitha returned with the gloves, she saw him checking out her Badass List. She resisted the urge to rush over and cover it. Tabitha had nothing to hide. Besides, she could've closed the journal when she went for the gloves but had left it open for the world to see, like wearing her heart on her sleeve.

"I'm surprised this one isn't checked yet," Victor said as she approached. He tapped his finger near *Ride a motorcycle*. "You're here all the time, and hell, y'all are still open. In December." Victor's accent was subtle but decidedly country—completely unlike Hobbs's. Tabitha suddenly wondered how much country Hobbs would have in his voice if he didn't try to hide it.

"We have a long riding season in Virginia," Tabitha agreed. "Especially for the diehards. The shop's hours are limited right now but Delaney still gets plenty of work." She hitched her thumb toward the back room, where Delaney and Wyatt were. "Some of her regulars ride their bikes year-round into the District for their jobs. Motorcycles are allowed in the HOV lanes, so it's economical."

"Good deal."

"Somebody offered to take me riding," Tabitha admitted as she rang up the gloves. There was no way in hell she was going to tell Victor that the *somebody* was his brother. "But we're waiting for a warm day." Tabitha shrugged. "Plus, I'm not gonna lie. I'm scared of them."

"Of what?" Victor raised his eyebrows as he handed over his credit card. "Motorcycles?" He made a *pish* sound. "You'd be fine. Just go on some back roads. Relax and enjoy yourself. Nothing like it."

"Yeah, well." Tabitha ran the card and finished up the sale. "Maybe in the spring. Or…" She mulled over her last interaction with Hobbs, right here in this shop, and decided she couldn't count on his committal, pinkie promise or no. "Maybe I'll take that one off the list altogether. I've achieved the important stuff." Other than helping Auntie El, of course. "I don't really need to ride a motorcycle." Especially if she was going to stick with massage school. Eventually Tabitha wouldn't even work here anymore.

"Bull crap." Victor snagged the gloves from her before she could slide them into a bag. "Of course it's important. You put it on the list, right?"

"Well…yeah."

"Aside from the fact that riding a motorcycle *absolutely* is important," Victor said, "if it's on the list, you should do it. You put it in writing. Now you got to follow through."

"He's right, Steele." Delaney's voice came from behind Tabitha's back. She whirled around to find her just coming out of the back room, wiping her fingers on a shop rag. Wyatt trailed behind, looking sleepy until he saw Trinity on his dog bed. He gave a woof, then trotted over and hunched down, ready to play. "In fact," Delaney continued, her voice taking a sly tone, "I got a Fat Boy back here that needs a big dude to give it a test run. Need some weight on it, if you know what I'm saying." Delaney eyed Victor up and down. "Welcome back, cowboy," she said. "Long time no see."

"A test run, you say?" Victor ignored the greeting and

leaped right on the offer. "Well, little lady." He grinned at Tabitha. "Today's your lucky day."

Tabitha spent the first half of the ride focusing on Victor's instructions to *lean with me, not against me,* which she figured might've been better accomplished if they'd not taken these winding back roads. Her body screamed at what felt like a counterintuitive order, not wanting to lean toward the road rushing beneath her when Victor took the curves, but she did as she was told and soon got used to it. Tabitha was glad they were pretty much solo out here, soaring down a single-lane road surrounded by farmland. She was surprised how chilly the air felt once they were flying, when back at the shop she'd been wondering why they were layering her up in a thick jacket and gloves for what was pretty calm weather in December.

"Trust me, you'll want all this," Delaney had said. "Even with this big lug as a windshield."

Tabitha clung to that big lug, her arms tight around his solid body and, for a while, her eyes closed tight behind her helmet's visor. Eventually, though, Tabitha opened her eyes and relaxed her grip. Victor was a smooth and assured rider, solid and confident. After a while she figured out that riding had a rhythm to it, just like massaging. Tabitha had to let go in order to become one with the bike and Victor and the road. Once she did that, something inside of her opened up, blooming and filling her head to toe. Leaning toward the road on curves felt more natural, like the slither of a snake, and the road rushing beneath her wasn't scary but exhilarating. Tabitha wondered if this was how a bird felt when it flew.

Hobbs's words from back on her birthday suddenly filled her mind. *Feels good to let go a little, doesn't it?* She'd overthought it back then, as usual, and missed the point entirely.

Tabitha eased her grip on Victor and sat up straighter. She

breathed deeply and enjoyed the cold seeping into her bones. When she got back to the shop, she would have another box to check off and only one more item on her list to achieve. But for now, none of that mattered. Nothing else on the list mattered, whether it had been checked or not. Right now, only this mattered.

Victor took a hard curve. Tabitha leaned in.

Tabitha let go.

Hobbs told himself more than once that he should let Hannah go to Triple M Classics herself to talk with Delaney and pick out the self-defense items. But then, Hannah didn't have her own car and the shop was on his way to work.

Also, there was that sneaky thing about maybe Tabitha being there. Typically she covered the shop floor on weekday mornings unless she had classes, and classes were over until spring semester. Odds were good she'd be there. Why Hobbs wanted to see her was another question altogether. More than once he'd put to bed the notion of pursuing anything serious. Tabitha deserved way more than Hobbs had to give. A woman like her deserved someone like Thaddeus—or, at least, a version of Thaddeus that wasn't a stuck-up ass. Someone successful, emotionally available and the monogamous type.

So why was he going to the shop to see her?

As Hobbs pulled up to Triple M, he saw that Tabitha's old Chevy was indeed parked in the lot. Right next to it was a Harley Fat Boy. A woman shaped a lot like Tabitha was climbing off the back. She wore jeans, cute little boots with a heel and a motorcycle jacket. That couldn't be Tabitha, though. Tabitha didn't ride. And when she did, she'd promised to ride with him.

As soon as the woman pulled off her helmet and shook out her hair, Hobbs's stomach sank. The beast who'd been driv-

ing the bike swung one long leg over and hoofed the pavement. Then he pulled off his helmet and Hobbs's breath froze.

What the hell was Victor doing here?

"What the hell is he doing here?" Victor's gaze was trained
on Hobbs's truck as it pulled swiftly into a parking spot. "He
doesn't ride." Victor turned to Tabitha, eyed her up and down.
"You his girl? I kinda got a vibe, last time I was here."

"Um." Tabitha watched Hobbs exit the truck, slam the door
and rush in their direction. They'd just finished their ride and
Tabitha had been basking in the afterglow. The sight of Hobbs
rushing toward them made her feel like a kid caught in the
cookie jar. "Not exactly."

Victor grunted. "That sounds about right for Chris."

"What's going on?" Hobbs was speaking before he even
reached them. "Did I miss a call or text that you were coming back out here?"

"I didn't bother." Victor stared down at Hobbs, whom he
towered over. "I just decided to come out. Slow your roll, bro."

Hobbs's gaze kept going between Victor and Tabitha, and
sometimes to the Harley Fat Boy. "But why are you here? I
haven't heard from you in days."

"I don't mess around with my phone when I'm on the road."
Victor settled his helmet on the Fat Boy seat and stretched his
arms over his head. "I decided I needed to spend Christmas
out here, with Hannah."

Hobbs's eyes narrowed. "And that's all? You drove all the
way out here, and left Mom back home alone, just because
you decided to spend Christmas with Hannah?"

"All right, look." Victor lowered his tone. "I lost sight of
the scumbag. Three days went by where his car was gone from
in front of his apartment building and not at his work, either.
I decided I better get out here, just in case he makes good on

his word and he's hunting Hannah down. It's not like it'd be hard. I'm sure Hannah mentioned you to him in the past. All he'd have to do is look you up. I just never really thought the bastard would do it."

Hobbs took a while to process this, indicated by his sudden quiet and the expressions that kept crossing his face. Tabitha felt silly, at this point, standing here in silence. Still, she didn't go inside. "Do you really think he came out here?" Hobbs finally said.

Victor shrugged. "I don't know. But if he did, I'm going to be here to stop him. And even if he's not here, just up and left or went and died in a ditch somewhere, no skin off my nose to be with my sister at Christmas. Work is slow this time of year, anyway."

"You could've told me." Hobbs's jaw clenched. "You should've told me. Especially if you expect to stay at my place."

"Settle down, Chris. I didn't want to panic anyone. I've texted Hannah every day and I know she's fine. And I have my own place to stay, so don't worry yourself."

"I see." Hobbs went quiet again. He looked out at the gray sky, a blank canvas of clouds that promised snow in the near future. "So what's this, then?" He waved his hand at Tabitha.

"Hello to you, too," Tabitha said. Up until now she hadn't been annoyed that Hobbs hadn't even greeted her. He'd been surprised and scared, and rightfully so. But now he was just mad. A new look on him, for sure, and kind of interesting to watch.

"I popped in the shop to get another pair of those motor-cycle gloves I bought last time. In brown. They're great gloves." Victor nodded at Tabitha. "Miss Tabitha here was working on a list. I saw something I could help her with. She just had her first ride." Victor held up his hand in a high five. "What'd you think, Tabitha?"

Tabitha had to work hard not to look in Hobbs's direction as she slapped Victor's palm with her own. "It was amazing," she admitted. "Thank you."

Victor smiled. "The pleasure was all mine. And now I'm going to go check in," he said. "I'm beat and need a nap. I'll be sure to text you later so you, me and Hannah can talk."

"Where are you staying?" Hobbs's voice was hard as concrete. "At the Dogwood Inn?"

"I was going to, but then I found this cabin for rent. It's more private. Out in the woods. Which is just my style. I called up and was lucky enough to snag a cancellation that happened this morning. Apparently she books up really fast at Christmas because there's this whole big party for her dog rescue or something like that. Party's this weekend. Christmas Eve."

"Oh, wow," Tabitha cut in. "That must be Sunny's place. She rescued my service dog."

"Good deal," Victor said, and gave Tabitha another high five.

Hobbs went quiet again.

"All right, then." Victor nodded at her. "Pleasure riding with you, Tabitha. You have a pleasant day. See you later, Chris."

"Text, like you said. It's really easy. You just take out your phone and..." Hobbs imitated the gesture by pulling out his own phone.

Victor barked a laugh and climbed in his rental Jeep. Once he'd pulled away, Tabitha eyed Hobbs up and down. He was dressed in coaching attire, but didn't look like he was ready to head to the gym anytime soon. He just stood there, flexing his jaw, his eyes bluer than usual, glittering with anger. This was so different from anything she'd ever seen, she forgot herself and said nothing, even though the air was getting chilly and was starting to work its way into her bones.

"So you went on your first bike ride," Hobbs said, his voice almost too quiet.

"I didn't plan it," Tabitha said, even though she didn't feel like apologizing. "It just sort of happened."

"That's fine." Hobbs shrugged. "But we had a deal, that's all. We were supposed to take your first ride together."

"I know." Tabitha shifted her weight from foot to foot. "Guess I figured I was doing you a favor. Now you don't have to worry about it."

Hobbs's gaze snapped to hers. "Why would I worry about it? We made a promise."

Tabitha swallowed down the cotton in her throat. "You told me to give you time. I'm giving you time. You seem to have time to date people like Serena, or whoever, but no time to be real with me. So yeah. When I had a chance to ride a motorcycle, I took it. I'm not going to apologize."

Hobbs looked down at the pavement and shook his head. "Well, I did ask you for more aggression," he said. "So I guess I deserve this. Though I gotta say, this doesn't suit you."

A flush took over Tabitha's whole body that made her feel like she was on fire. "What doesn't suit me?" When he was silent, Tabitha took a step closer. "What is this all about? I get it that you're annoyed at your brother and scared for your sister, but that's not what this is, right here. This is something else. I can feel it." A heartbeat passed. "Are you jealous? Because I rode with your brother?"

Hobbs finally looked up. He shook his head while loosing a humorless laugh. "I gave up being jealous of Victor a long time ago."

"Why are you even here, then?"

"I came to pick up some stuff Delaney has for Hannah."

He turned, as though getting ready to head back to his truck. "But it can wait. Now's not a good time."

"Or—" Tabitha seized her opportunity, clinging to whatever courage had bloomed inside of her after that ride "—you can just let Hannah come herself to get whatever Delaney has for her."

A flicker crossed Hobbs's face, but was gone in a flash. "Right." He turned to go.

"Really?" Tabitha called after him. "That's all?"

Hobbs sighed and stared up at the sky. When he looked back down, he shrugged helplessly. "Yeah, that's all."

"How truly disappointing." Now it was Tabitha who turned to go.

"What do you want from me?" Hobbs's words snapped at her back.

Tabitha whirled back around to face him. "I want you to be real with me. I want you to stop hiding. I want you to stop making excuses."

"No, Tabitha," Hobbs said, grinding over her full name. "You don't. You really, really don't. I already told you, I give you guys the best version of me. You should be glad for that."

And Tabitha did understand that. She understood about not being able to share all of yourself with the world, about having to keep a lot of it hidden in order to protect what sanity you had left. But there was more to this. "I'm not 'you guys.'" Tabitha's voice softened. "I mean more to you than that, and you know it. I can feel it, every time you touch me. Every time you've kissed me. But you hold back. You pull away. You hold back about everything real. Has it ever occurred to you that I don't want the best version of you? I want the *real* version of you. I want the real version of you, because the real one *is* the best one."

Hobbs stepped closer, erasing almost all the space between

them. His voice softened as his words turned to steel. "You think so, huh? You think my sob stories are going to make me more real, Tabitha? All my jokes and fun and good intentions aren't enough? You want the real me? You want it all? Well, you got it. What do you want to know?" Hobbs didn't give her time to answer, pushing ahead like a steamroller. "Take your pick. You want the stories about my drunken, abusive father? Like you haven't heard that one before. Boo hoo. You want the stories about how I was Pops's favorite target because I was just some skinny middle child that he could push around at will? That when he was done beating on Mom he came for me instead? Yeah, you've probably heard that one, too. Hey, I know." Hobbs's whole face was red now, his words starting to thin out as his voice turned raspy. "Maybe you want to hear about the Fourth of July. You want to hear that one? You want to know why I hate the Fourth of July?"

Tabitha's brain was scrambling now, her heart hammering in her chest. She was no longer cold; her skin had flushed all over, but her body was trembling, anyway. She remembered what Hobbs had told her last Independence Day, when she'd had that panic attack at the gym at the sound of the fireworks and she'd woken to Hobbs holding her hand. "It's a stupid holiday," he'd said. Tabitha had never asked him why.

"No," Hobbs said, when Tabitha had stood there, shaking in silence. "You don't want to hear that story. I can see it in your face. And I don't blame you, Tabby." His voice grew light and soft. "Nobody wants to hear that shit. Nobody should have to hear that shit." He reached out and touched her face, running his thumb along her cheekbone.

Tabitha wanted to flinch, but she leaned into it, like a cat.

"I'll tell you one thing, though. When I joined the marine corps at eighteen years old, it was because I wanted to be the biggest, baddest, toughest motherfucker on the planet. I wanted to get away, and I wanted to go somewhere that would turn me into a killing machine, so that nobody could ever lay hands on me again. And when I was in combat, the only thing that scared me was the thought that I might get hurt enough to get sent back home. I either wanted to be healthy enough to stay as far from Omaha as I could, or I wanted to be dead. Now, how fucked up is that?" Hobbs closed any remaining space between them and whispered right against her ear. "Is that story real enough for you? Do you want more? Because I have a lot of them, just like that."

Hobbs drew away and Tabitha reached for Trinity, but she wasn't there. She'd left her in the shop, where it was warm. "I understand about stories," Tabitha said, when she'd found her voice. "And I'm not asking you to share them all. But there's a difference between not sharing your stories and hiding behind them."

Hobbs's face flushed so bright Tabitha worried he'd have a heart attack. Any sign of the jokester who laughed his way through everything had been smeared away and plastered over with raw, sizzling emotions. The face that stared back at her was one Tabitha had never seen before. "Oh, I'm the one hiding, huh? Grow up, Tabitha. I'm not the one who has to make a little list to prove to the world I'm good enough."

A gasp escaped Tabitha's tight lungs.

"Yeah. Hurts, doesn't it? You wanted the real me. Well." Hobbs spread his arms open. "Here I am." Then he turned and walked away, without looking back. He got inside his truck, slammed the door, revved the engine and peeled out of the parking lot on squealing tires. Tabitha waited until he was gone, refusing to move one inch until he'd disappeared. She'd turned away from too many confrontations. This one, she would face down until the end.

Once Hobbs was gone, she raced into the shop, grateful that

Delaney was in the back room and wouldn't see her as she ran to Trinity, sank to the floor and held on tight. The service vest was abrasive against her cheek, but the warmth of the little pittie filled Tabitha up, quieted her pulse and slowly returned the world to a bearable state.

Only after some time had passed did Tabitha rise. She swiped away her tears and collected her journal from the counter. She grabbed the Badass List, crinkling the page in her palm, tore the paper from the metal rings, balled it up and pitched it in the trash.

twenty-six

"**I** haven't heard from him," Hannah insisted. She finished eating up to the very edge of her pepperoni pizza slice, then handed Hobbs the crust. She'd done that since she was a kid—only ate the good stuff and discarded the bread. Hobbs had always favored the crust, so even though he'd chastise her, he never minded the habit. These days, Hobbs didn't eat much bread. He took the crust, anyway, and stuffed half of it in his mouth.

"You just tell us immediately if you do," Victor said. He gulped down the rest of his water and set it on the table with a thunk. "No waiting for days, like last time."

"I won't." Hannah never argued with Victor. "I'm going to the restroom." She pushed back her chair and headed through the busy dining room of Nonni's Italian restaurant. Since it was near the bike shop, and Victor knew where the bike shop was, they'd all agreed to meet for dinner here and catch up. Hannah had been just as surprised to see Victor as Hobbs had, which meant Victor really hadn't told anyone of his plans. Just made a decision and flew by the seat of his pants. Typical Victor.

"What's your problem?" Victor demanded as soon as Hannah left.

"Who says I have a problem?" Hobbs's mood hadn't improved much over the course of the day. He'd been able to get through his coaching duties with only a few clients suggesting he "wasn't himself," but as soon as he was home, the mask came off. Even Gracie had sensed Hobbs's dark cloud, not her usual chipper self on their evening walk before dinner.

"I say." Victor balled up a napkin and pelted Hobbs in the head. "I know we aren't the closest of pals, but it's Christmas. And Hannah doesn't need any more stress."

Victor was right, but that only irritated Hobbs more. He grabbed another slice of pizza, even though he was full. His body, unused to the grease and preservatives in pepperoni, was sure to make him regret this later.

"Is it the woman from the bike shop?" Victor leaned back in his chair, one arm draped over the back, his long legs out in front of him, crossed at the ankles. He looked like a cowboy ready to tip his hat over his eyes and nod off in front of the campfire. "Tabitha?" When Hobbs was silent, Victor grunted. "Spill it. Maybe I can help."

"Yeah?" Hobbs's sarcasm came through a full mouth of pizza. "When's the last time you had woman trouble? You've avoided women since Sandra divorced you. Besides," Hobbs added quickly, knowing he was on thin ice invoking Sandra like that, "you did enough already."

Victor was silent awhile, his gaze steely and concentrated. "You're mad she rode the bike with me," he said finally. He even pointed a finger, as though to punctuate his claim.

Hobbs didn't attempt lying. "We were supposed to go together. For her first ride. Then I get to the shop and find that my brother, who doesn't even live here, who isn't even supposed to be here, who didn't even bother to tell anyone he was coming here, has stepped in like the big hero he always has to be and whisked Tabitha away on a cherried-out Harley Fat Boy." Hobbs applauded with a golf clap. "You win again. You going to eat my Christmas chocolate this year, too? Go ahead, then. Just take it. Take it all, Vic."

Victor was once again silent, unmoving. Finally, he laughed. A deep, resonating belly laugh that made the people at the next table glance over. "You gotta be kidding me." He sat up and leaned across the table. "You're blaming me because I gave your girl her first ride? Worse—you're blaming me for losing your Christmas chocolate back in 1985? Get serious, Chris. Who you really mad at? Ask yourself. Did you have to let me wrangle that chocolate away every damn year? No. It's not like I pinned you down and snatched it, which I could easily have done. I didn't exactly force your girl on the bike, either. If you were supposed to take Tabitha on her first motorcycle ride, why didn't you?"

"We were waiting for a warm day." Hobbs's voice was thick, angry.

Victor shook his head. "You didn't take Tabitha on a ride for the same reason you let me hustle that chocolate away from you every year. You'd rather keep on smiling than feel the pain. I get that and it's a good personality trait to have—you keep everything positive and everyone happy—but you got to know when something's worth fighting for every once in a rare while. If that little lady were waiting on me for a ride, you best bet I'm not going to let another guy get there first." Victor pointed his huge caveman finger again. "The only person you've got to be angry with is yourself."

"Oh, really? And not Pops? Not at all Pops? Not even a little?"

"Shit." Victor's voice boomed enough for the same table of people to glance his way. A young mother in a high-neck sweater covered her toddler's ears. "Sorry, ma'am." Victor nodded at her, then turned back to Hobbs. "Why waste your anger on that man? Even when he was alive. But now he's dead, so it's even more of a waste. I know life was hard, little brother." Victor's tone softened now, along with his expression. There was something in his steely eyes Hobbs was sure he'd never seen before. Something contrite. Something sad, yet resolute. "And I'm sorry I wasn't there for most of what you suffered. Maybe I should have done things differently, but I was a kid, too. But Pops is gone now. Don't let him paralyze you in death like he did in life. If you got a soft, warm something just waiting to ride with you, you gonna let that old prick hold you back? Hell, no." Victor slammed his fist on the table. Eyes turned his way yet again. The woman in the sweater glared. Victor didn't apologize this time. "You take that little thing for a ride. And don't look back."

Hobbs went quiet. Something loosened inside of him, like the unwinding of a tight ball of stress, fear and anger that'd been sitting deep in his gut. "Hannah's been gone awhile," he said, after the lightening of his insides made him realize the time.

Just as Victor rose to his feet to scan the crowd, Hannah pushed between two large men at the bar and headed their way, her feet quick. "Everything all right?" Victor said as she neared.

"I think so." Hannah sounded a little out of breath. She scanned the crowded room. "I thought I saw James," she admitted. "But I was wrong," she added quickly, when Hobbs jumped up. "I came out of the bathroom and, for a second, I was sure I saw his face. But then…" She shook her head. "I searched all over. I just imagined it. I think I'm just panicky because you told me you lost sight of him in Omaha."

Victor and Hobbs both studied her awhile before they exchanged a look with each other. Hobbs could tell Victor thought the same thing—Hannah had seen the scumbag.

"All right," Hobbs said. "Let me get the check and let's go."

"Soon as I check this place out," Victor said, heading off to search the restaurant. "You stay with her."

"Don't have to tell me twice." Hobbs watched Victor go and took note of Hannah's stricken face. Just like always. As soon as Hobbs started feeling good about something, all the abusers in his life reared their ugly heads to smack him back down again.

twenty-seven

Even though Tabitha had spent the day shopping with Lily for clothes for tonight's Christmas Eve party-fundraiser at Pittie Place, Tabitha was still in loungewear come six o'clock. Auntie El had been struggling with the different meds the doctors had prescribed—the antidepressants making her flat as a robot and the sleep meds making her dopey and not at all rested. By evening, Auntie El was in her robe, parked in the reclining lounger in front of the living room television. She stared at a sitcom, eyes bleary, face unsmiling.

"I was wondering," Tabitha said, lotion in hand, "if I could do your feet."

Auntie El shifted her gaze, the sitcom reflected in the lenses of her glasses. Everyone was laughing and smiling. "Don't you have a party?" She waved her hand. "Go. Leave this old lady to her misery."

Tabitha sighed, torn for a moment, before she finally went to the light dimmer switch on the wall and turned the lamp down to a soft glow. Hadn't she decided a long time ago that if she wanted to be a badass she was going to have to make it happen and stop waiting for magic? She pulled the ottoman over to the edge of the recliner, then sat down and removed Auntie El's slippers. Just because she'd destroyed her Badass List, and just because she'd been moping around about her fight with Hobbs for days, that didn't mean she wasn't going to finish what she'd started. *Help Auntie El* was the only unchecked box on that list and Tabitha was not going to watch the only mother she'd ever known suffer just because Hobbs had ruined everything.

"This isn't necessary," Auntie El said, but she didn't pull away, either.

Tabitha started in on her work, her mind on Hobbs and everything that had happened. After the initial anger and shock had worn off, Tabitha was left feeling everything that was really there, underneath it all. She wasn't sure what he'd thought her reaction might be, that she might recoil or turn away—or worse, maybe Hobbs had thought she'd feel sorry for him—but in truth, her only reaction had been to want to know more. She could almost hear how Red would analyze this: *You know that Hobbs lashed out at you. He said some mean things out of anger. But what's really going on? What's the real source of his pain?*

As the days passed, Tabitha let go of her anger, as much as she could. She'd obviously got deep inside, down into some things that hadn't been stirred up in a long time. These were things that weren't going to heal overnight. Tabitha understood that. But the longer she thought about it, the more she realized that Hobbs's outburst hadn't pushed her away, like maybe he'd hoped. Now she only wanted to learn more. To maybe be that person who *knew*. Tabitha knew from experience that sometimes you didn't need or want opinions or sympathy for the difficult things. Sometimes you just wanted someone to know. If someone else knew, the load wasn't so heavy anymore. If someone else knew, the bad stuff wasn't hidden away, festering—it was out in the open, with twice as much medicine ready to help the healing.

"Is Thaddeus going to be at this party?" Auntie El's voice got a little dreamy, like maybe she was enjoying the massage.

"I'm not going to see Thaddeus anymore," Tabitha said. "He said some things I didn't like about Trinity."

Silence passed, and then Auntie El said, "What a shame. He seemed so nice."

"Appearances can be deceiving."

After more silence, Auntie El's voice came even softer, like she was starting to drift. "There's somebody, though. Somebody you wanted to see at this party. I can tell. You can't fool your mama."

Tabitha paused her work for a second. Auntie El rarely used the word *mama*, even though that was exactly what she'd been to Tabitha all of her life. Tabitha had always called her Auntie El, just like the foster kids, with *mama* reserved for special occasions. The last time she'd heard it was when she'd come home from Afghanistan. Auntie El had met her at the airport, opened her arms and said, "Mama's here," and Tabitha's head had sunk to Auntie El's chest.

"There is somebody." Tabitha spoke in a calm, smooth tone that matched her massage strokes. She'd come to have a pretty good routine with feet and found that her practice subjects lost their tension quite quickly once she'd started in. "But I don't think he's ready for something serious. He might not ever be. He's got a bad past."

Auntie El was silent, but her foot flinched slightly. Tabitha continued as though nothing had happened, and after a while Auntie El's voice came sleepily. "If he's got a bad past, then he needs somebody like you," she said. "Somebody sensitive. Somebody with patience and a light touch. You know? You need to go to that party. Tell him to stop being a fool."

Tabitha let Auntie El's words settle around her, like the snowflakes that were pattering on the roof. Then she went quiet and stayed quiet, massaging with methodical strokes and a clear mind. She let herself go, not thinking about Hobbs or anyone but Auntie El and how much she'd been suffering these past months. The air in the room changed as time passed. The television still ran on low volume and Trinity was still asleep on the couch, on the one corner cushion where she was allowed. But there was an unseen shift in the room by the time Tabitha had finished with the second foot and she knew that Auntie El had fallen asleep.

Tabitha rose quietly, collected the throw from the corner of the sofa and draped it over Auntie El's snoozing body. Her glasses had slipped to the end of her nose and a soft snore escaped her lips. Tabitha smiled and headed upstairs. In her bedroom she glanced at the clock on the nightstand and thought about turning in early. The party would be in full swing and Tabitha wasn't really in the mood. She should probably hang around and make sure Auntie El stayed asleep, anyway. This was the first night she'd nodded off at a decent hour in months and Tabitha needed to watch over her.

As she headed for the bathroom, ready for a shower and then bed, something glittery in the corner of the closet caught her eye.

The ruby-red slippers.

Tabitha stared at the shoes and remembered Hobbs's words on Halloween. *You got the kicks. You want to make a wish, just click your heels three times and it's all yours, baby.*

She smiled. Even when he wasn't here, Hobbs could still make her smile. She realized, in that moment, that Hobbs's clown act wasn't just an act. There was a part of that boister-ous, happy demeanor that was all his, wasn't just a cover-up for the pain, but was also a remnant of the person he truly was without all the bad things weighing him down.

Tabitha's gaze shifted to the bag of clothing, unopened, at the end of her bed. Lily had spent half the day shopping with her to find the perfect party outfit. Auntie El had told Tabitha that she should go. What was she waiting for?

"Wow." Lily's eyes widened as they pulled into the park-ing lot of Pittie Place. "It looks like the inside of a giant snow globe."

Clementine silently agreed. The monster-sized pine wreath that hung on the Pittie Place sign leading to the entrance should've been her first clue that Sunny pulled out all the stops at Christmastime. As Clementine angled into one of the few remaining spots left, she had to remind herself to keep her eyes on the road until she killed the engine. She didn't let herself fully take in the decor until she'd safely exited the vehicle.

She and Lily both stood there, staring at the sparkling white lights tastefully wound around the enormous pine trees that flanked the long, winding drive. There were oversized pink and silver balls in the branches and a matching garland that sparkled in the dark night sky. The moon was a thin crescent peeking behind the Queen Anne roof, the turrets giving the house a fairy-tale vibe. As they headed up the drive and got closer to the dwelling, Clementine could see as much care had been taken on the home as the surrounding trees. There was an electric candle in each window, as well as a wreath with a bright red bow.

"She does all this herself," Lily said as they reached the front door. "Well, Pete helps her, but..." Lily shrugged. "She told me the other day, when she was at the shelter, that she uses the same decorations every year until they fall apart. She was pretty proud of what she accomplishes with old decorations." Lily looked older than her sixteen years in the party outfit she'd chosen—black, shiny leggings that looked like leather, matching black boots with little bows on the top and a slinky red top that hung off one shoulder and accentuated her long lines. Her lipstick matched the hue of the blouse and the small amount of eye makeup she'd worn made her hazel eyes pop. She'd styled her cinnamon-colored hair with a curling iron, giving it just enough wave to look like a movie star's.

"Sounds like Sunny," Clementine said, feeling a little old next to her knockout daughter. Lily was gorgeous on an average day, just climbing out of bed. The clothes and makeup kicked her up a notch, making her hard to look away from. Clementine smoothed out the "ugly sweater" dress she'd worn, a red-and-black gingham that was kind of loud, if not quite ugly. Made of a light nylon/poly blend, it wasn't really a sweater at all, and clung a little more to her curves than she'd expected from the picture in the online shop.

"This wouldn't have happened if you'd come to the mall with me and Tabitha and actually tried on a dress," Lily had pointed out, when Clementine had come out of her room and complained over the clinginess. "But you look great, Mom. You work out all the darn time—you might as well show it off."

"Yeah. Thanks." Clementine had checked herself out in the hallway mirror. "But does it look like I'm advertising? I don't want to look like I'm advertising."

"Why not? Women are allowed to dress how they want and be proud of it."

Clementine had gone back in her bedroom for her shoes and had glanced at the journal on her bedside table, which she hadn't touched since the morning Lily had confronted her about Terrence. Was she worried about betraying Tyler? He'd been dead for eight years. How stupid was that?

The thought had bugged her all the way here, but now that they faced the house, so cheerful and bright, Clementine let those thoughts slip away. She could have a little fun if she wanted. Tyler would want that, especially after all this time. They didn't bother knocking, as a sign on the door, under a big wreath of braided holly, bade them to enter. The party was in full swing, the sounds of voices and music spilling out into the night as they pressed their way inside.

"It smells so good in here," Lily said. "Like cinnamon and pine and fresh baked bread."

Clementine could also smell roast beef, but she kept that to herself so Lily wouldn't gag. First to greet them was Fezziwig, Red's three-legged pit bull, who hopped over and wagged his tail. "Hey, boy." Clementine stroked his head, but as soon as Lily squatted down to face him, Fezzi went to her. It happened every time. Lily was an animal magnet.

"Hey, you two!" Sunny appeared from the kitchen, her smile big, her body long and lithe in a red dress that was even tighter than Clementine's. There was nothing about it that indicated an ugly sweater, even though those had been the party attire directions. "Food's in the dining room. Get it while it's hot. There'll be dancing downstairs pretty soon. Ooh, Lil, I love your pants."

"Thanks."

The dining room was packed, and most of the people there were Sunny's donors for the dog rescue, as apparently this was her biggest fundraiser of the year.

"There," Lily said, indicating the only familiar faces in the whole joint. At a table in the corner were Red, Rhett, Pete, Delaney, Hobbs, Hannah and a man who Clementine had never seen before. He was sort of set apart, his chair farther from the rest, kind of tucked in the corner, his face half in shadow. They were all sitting down, so it was hard to say, but the guy looked like he rivaled Rhett for tallest man in the room. Unlike all the others, who had on dress slacks and button-down shirts, this guy wore blue jeans and a flannel, similar to the lumberjack costume Hobbs had worn to Halloween. Everyone had plates of food in front of them and engaged in lively conversation above the Christmas music playing through hidden speakers. The lumberjack sat quietly in the corner, speaking to no one.

The only people missing were Sean and Tabitha, but Tabitha had texted an hour ago saying she probably wasn't going to make it tonight after all. Clementine kept that to herself since Lily had spent so much time helping her pick out a party outfit today.

Red spied them and waved them over. Clementine and Lily exchanged relieved glances, made their way to the table and greeted everyone all at once. Even though there was only one seat left, Rhett stood up and offered his to Lily. "I need to get more food, anyway." He rubbed his flat middle and grabbed his plate. He stopped next to Red, bent over and kissed the top of her head. "Need anything?"

"I'm fine, thanks." Red smiled up at him and he stopped to kiss her on the lips this time before heading to the buffet.

Clementine sank to the seat on the other side of Red and looked her up and down. She wore leggings and a generous-sized black shirt with a golden reindeer on the front. She was pecking her way through a plateful of rib roast and Christmas pudding and had a glass of water next to her plate.

"Anything good?" Lily turned to Delaney, her fellow vegetarian.

Delaney, who wore a black sweaterdress adorned in reindeer riding motorcycles, pointed her fork at her plate, which held something that looked like a potpie, with a rich stew inside a crust. "It's a vegetable galette." She spoke through the bite she had in her mouth. "It's amazing."

"Awesome."

"Where's Sean?" Clementine looked around the room, even though the crowd was so thick she probably wouldn't be able to spy the detective.

"On shift," Delaney said.

"Bummer on Christmas Eve."

Delaney shrugged. "He's off tomorrow."

"Go get some food." Sunny, who was circulating the room, appeared at their table. "And some drinks. Then we can have a toast."

Clementine and Lily rushed to fill their plates. Lily helped herself to the galette and a sparkling water flavored with rose and cucumber. Clementine took some of everything and grabbed one of those rose-and-cucumber waters for herself.

Once they were back at the table, they all held up their glasses while Sunny toasted friendship and the coming year. Everyone clinked glasses and took a sip or a slug of whatever beverage they had, except for the tall stranger, who didn't participate at all. Clementine tried to study him without being noticed. She didn't think she'd ever met him before, but it was hard to say because he was hiding in shadows. He had thick curls of honey-blond hair, a day's worth of stubble that was significantly darker, a chiseled jaw and a full mouth. Looking at him was like seeing someone you recognized inside a bigger body with a harder personality. No one had as of yet introduced him, and Clementine was not about to ask, though she was hoping an opportunity would come up so she wouldn't appear rude.

He turned and noticed her staring at the last second, so Clementine quickly looked away, her gaze settling on Red and that glass of water she was nursing. Things suddenly fell into place. The big clothes. The nesting. Clementine knew Rhett and Red weren't married, but all the signs were there. She waited until Red's bright blue eyes met her own and said, "Spill it, Red."

Red's hand, absentmindedly rubbing her middle, slowed. A smile worked its way over her lips. "Okay," she said, her voice rising to climb over "Baby, It's Cold Outside." "I'm pregnant," she announced. "Twelve weeks." As the table erupted into surprised reactions, Red narrowed her eyes at Clementine, the smile still on her mouth. "How'd you know?"

"Clothes changed," Clementine said. "You're drinking water. Your beau is superattentive." She nodded at Rhett. "Congrats, you two. That's wonderful."

"Thank God." Sunny expelled a great breath and slugged down the rest of her champagne. "I don't think I could keep that secret any longer."

"I'm really proud of you." Red nodded at her sister. "You did far better than I thought."

"Congrats, man," Hobbs said. He'd been largely quiet up until then. "I can't believe you're going to be a dad." He chuckled a little bit over his beer.

"He'll be amazing," Red protested as the rest of the table joined in Hobbs's laughter.

"Speaking of babies…" Pete's voice rose above the others. Once the table had fallen completely silent, he smiled and waved a hand. "Just kidding. I was only going to ask Lily how Terrence is doing."

Everyone laughed again, especially Sunny. "You're lucky you're talking about a puppy," she said, and everyone *oohed*.

"Terrence is great," Lily said. "I've been training him, as well as I can. He's very, very smart, but because he's a hound, there's a lot in his breed that'll be tough to tame. His nose and instinct to hunt are wicked strong."

"Definitely," Pete agreed.

"I can bring him by soon if you want to see what you think about taking him." Lily's voice softened and she kept her eyes on her plate. She quickly stuffed a bite of the galette in her mouth.

"Sounds great," Pete agreed. "Maybe sometime next week we can—"

"You can't have him."

The table fell even more silent than when Red had announced her pregnancy. Lily's head snapped up, her eyes wide. "What?"

Clementine searched for words, her mouth biting over them but unsure where to land because she hadn't planned to say what had rushed out of her mouth. "You can't have Terrence," she repeated. "He and Lily belong together. He called out for help from the dumpster at the shelter and she dived into that stinky mess to rescue him. I'd say they're made for each other."

Pete got a big smile on his face and pointed it at Lily. "I couldn't agree more."

Lily smiled back at him, hers gentle and restrained. Clementine knew that her daughter, not a fan of public displays, was trying to hold back the emotions she felt. She glanced up at Clementine and a conspiratorial look passed between them that suggested Lily would get all excited about this later, in the privacy of her own home.

"Wow, what a great year." Sunny sighed to punctuate her words. "We've rescued hundreds of pups, with Lily's help." Sunny gestured toward her, even though she'd buried her face back in her food. "My big sis is pregnant. Tabitha has come so far with her fitness and her massage schooling and... Hey.

Where is Tabitha?" Sunny looked around the room, like she might spy her hiding in a corner.

Clementine had just parted her lips to mention the text message when suddenly Tabitha appeared, scanning the room as though looking for familiar faces. Everyone went silent again. Clementine actually had to look twice to make sure the woman who faced them was Tabitha. Rather than the quiet, modestly dressed woman they were all used to, she wore the same tight, black, shiny leggings as Lily, along with a snug black top sporting a shimmery red wreath made up of sequins. On her feet were matching red pumps and her curly black hair was styled to frame her face, which was adorned in smoky, bold makeup. The one giveaway was Trinity by her side, a bright red bow tied on her service vest.

"Holy crap," Rhett said. "Is that Tabitha?"

Clementine turned to Lily, who was grinning from ear to ear. "You didn't tell me you pulled a Frenchy-dresses-Sandy-for-the-school-carnival ending," Clementine hissed, but she couldn't help but smile with the others.

Tabitha's gaze finally fell on their table—or, more accurately, fell on Hobbs, whose chin had dropped—and that was when she strutted over, teetering a little in her heels, and stopped right next to him. "Hey, guys." Tabitha was now meeting everyone's eyes but Hobbs's. "How's it going?"

Clementine had half expected *So, tell me about it…stud!* to pop out of Tabitha's lips. And that was when the new guy, the mysterious stranger who'd uttered not a single peep since Clementine had arrived, busted into deep, hard laughter.

Hobbs wasn't going to lie. He hadn't been enjoying this party at all up until the moment Tabitha walked in, looking like some sleek, fast version of herself that had been bottled up too long and had burst like confetti from Christmas crackers.

He gathered from the giddy conversation going on between the women that Lily had spent some time dolling Tabitha up for the occasion, but Hobbs's attention was too rapt to really hear everything they were saying.

As the chatter died down and everyone got up and began moving downstairs for the live DJ and dancing portion of the party, Tabitha's eyes connected with his. Hobbs knew she would read everything he was thinking, because he was shit about hiding it, but she'd be wrong in some of her assumptions. Tabitha would think that Hobbs finally found her attractive because she was wearing sexy clothing, hair and makeup like so many of the women he went for. Tabitha would think that Hobbs was glad her shyer, more conservative side had been put away for the night so the party animal could come out and play.

Truth was, Hobbs could still see the other Tabitha, bright and curious behind her dark eyes. She was as surprised at herself as everyone else was, wondering just as much where this other persona had come from as the people who knew the more common facet. Tabitha had no idea where this other person might take her, but she was excited to find out, just so long as she didn't lose herself. Hobbs could see all this, and he could tell, by her tenuous smile, that she didn't want to change all that much. She just wanted to try things out a bit, like all those little tasting spoons they used to have at ice cream shops. When Hobbs was a kid, he'd ride his bike over and try for a spoon of every flavor until the shop owners got annoyed.

"Tabitha."

She had just reached the bottom of the stairs and was about to melt into the party and become this other person for the rest of the night. At the sound of Hobbs's voice, she turned back, her expression revealing that she was straddling a wall, one that she could easily drop down on either side. Once she chose, it would be a lot more effort to climb back up. This was the moment. Hobbs needed to decide right here and now to either leave Tabitha alone or finally let her in.

twenty-eight

"Will you dance with me?"

Tabitha's lips parted in surprise. She looked around herself, like a stupid girl wondering who the cute boy was talking to. Rhett and Red had already paired up and were pressed close. Delaney and Lily were in an animated conversation in a far corner, away from the speakers, Clementine was at the punch bowl and Victor sat by himself at the table, gaze flitting around like a bouncer at a club. Hobbs's warm hand closed over her own, snapping her attention back to him.

"Um." Tabitha looked down at Trinity, who was patiently putting up with the party music and crowded room. "Go to Fezzi." She spied Red's old pit bull over by the food table and pointed at him. Trinity knew Fezzi well from their many massage visits, so she trotted over and pushed him down, flattening him beneath her weight. Tabitha covered her mouth with her hand, stifling her laughter. "Trinity is giving Fezzi deep pressure therapy. It was my command. *Go to Fezzi.*"

Fezzi didn't appear to be struggling, though. He lay happily beneath Trinity's weight and started to lick her face.

Hobbs smiled back. "They'll figure it out." He drew her in, sliding an arm around her waist, the other cradling her hand in his palm. Hobbs took her around the room, his feet surprisingly graceful. Tabitha had learned proper dancing from Auntie El and could hold her own, but she found herself distracted by Hobbs's warm body and sweet scent. He still smelled like his buy-one-get-one-free bodywash, but riding atop the delicate lilacs was his aftershave, spicy but not overbearing. Unlike his brother, who'd worn jeans and a flannel shirt, Hobbs wore a pair of dress slacks, a crisp white shirt and a necktie covered in curvy Betty Boops in elf hats.

"I was hoping you'd be here tonight." Hobbs's breath tickled against her ear, making Tabitha go so weak in the knees she almost tripped. "I've been moping around like a total jerk until I saw you walk in."

Oh, yeah? Tabitha wanted to say, *Why is that?* But she couldn't speak. She had no voice. She'd worked so hard with Lily to dress like a confident, powerful woman who was in charge of every single one of her emotions and here she was, reduced to muteness as soon as Hobbs had her in his arms.

The arm around Tabitha's waist tightened as Hobbs slowed his steps and edged her into a corner, where the music was softer and they had more privacy. He pulled back to face her. "Were you hoping I'd be here as much as I was hoping for you?" His expression was open, prepared for anything she might say.

Tabitha swallowed down the lump in her throat, the one created by the sweet smells of his body and the strength in his arms, holding her up. "You're the only reason I'm here," she admitted, deciding to go for broke. "I wore all of this for you." She watched the surprise ripple in his eyes and pressed on. "I took up half of Lily's day and left my auntie asleep in her armchair just to wear this outfit, and I did it all hoping you'd think I look pretty. Because I just can't get you out of my head. I mean…" She drew in a deep breath and let it out slowly. "I just can't get you out of my heart."

The smile that had been playing around Hobbs's lips fell, but his grip on her tightened. "Tabby Cat," he whispered. "Will you go for a walk with me?"

Tabitha waited out back with Trinity, snow rolling from the sky in big, wet flakes that looked like a feather pillow had exploded under the Christmas lights. Her body was too warm to worry about shivering in the cold, her head full of Hobbs's scents.

"Hey, I'm here." Hobbs appeared by her side, shutting the door behind him and closing out the sounds of the party. "Sorry about that. Victor saw me heading out and told me he'd drive Hannah home. She's tired and he volunteered to do it because he saw me drinking a beer. I've had exactly two sips of a beer, but Victor doesn't mess around with alcohol."

They headed down Sunny's flagstone path, lit by colored lights that edged into the trees. They passed the building that housed the rescues, Roger's quarters and the puppy playground, and when they got to the gate, Hobbs unlatched it and they continued their walk into the woods that ran beside the cabins. The snow made a pattering sound on the leaves of the trees, and as their path darkened, Hobbs slipped his hand into hers.

"Your brother is a teetotaler, isn't he?"

Hobbs's pace slowed. "You noticed, huh? We each had different reactions to my father's alcoholism," he said. "Victor won't touch the stuff. I refuse to let my father's problem dictate me."

Tabitha squeezed Hobbs's fingers, which were warm and thick.

"I think it was the Fourth of July that got him," Hobbs said, his voice dropping an octave.

Tabitha stopped walking and turned to face him. Trinity's nails stopped clicking on the flagstones as she settled next to Tabitha.

"See, Victor had started drinking a lot, too, by the time he was a teenager. It was always available, it was all he'd ever seen and it was a coping mechanism—even if it was a bad one. I was fifteen, which means Victor was eighteen. He'd been moved out for some time by then but had come home for the Fourth. To hang out with me. I'd begged him. I'd scored these great fireworks from Missouri and was going to set them all off at night. As usual, my dad was drunk. He was never a fall-down drunk. His tolerance was too high. He could drink all day. Make his buzz last all day by just never stopping. The more he drank, the meaner he got."

Flakes of snow fell on Tabitha's upturned face as she watched Hobbs's eyes change in the moonlight.

"So there we were, setting off fireworks, having a grand old time. Even Hannah was having fun for a while. She was about seven, but she was mine by then. I took care of her all the time. My father kept losing jobs and Mom was the one paying the rent, which meant she was never home. Pops had been drinking all day but at some point he sobered up enough to come find out what all the racket was. He saw Victor, which set him off. By then Victor was like six-two, two-twenty-five, and Pops couldn't really pick on him anymore, which he hated. But Victor was so drunk he'd passed out. Which, you know—" Hobbs shrugged "—left me."

Tabitha's throat tightened up and the chill she'd been warding off began to seep inside, giving her a hard shiver.

Hobbs got quiet for so long Tabitha thought he was going to stop the story there. But then his voice came thick from the snowy dark. "There was this stray that showed up one day at the house. Our land butted up to several farms and she just popped into the yard one day when I was throwing the football around. I switched to a baseball and she liked to chase it. She kept coming back, as the days and weeks went by, probably because I fed her, so I named her Gemma. She'd come and go. I have no idea where she went, but it was clear she was a stray. She looked a lot like Gracie does, but way more scraggly." Hobbs paused to swallow. His hand tightened on hers. "I have no idea where Gemma came from that night. She wasn't around when we were setting off the fireworks. Maybe once they'd quieted down she popped out. But suddenly, there she was." Hobbs stared into space, like he was reliving the moment in his mind. His expression was blank and joyless. "Gemma didn't like the fact that my father was beating on me. He had me on the ground, whaling on me. She went at him. Was on his back, biting at his neck."

Tabitha's hand tightened on Trinity's leash. She had the urge to lean down and hold the little pittie, but she restrained herself. She didn't want to do anything that would stop the story flowing out of Hobbs.

"He threw her off," Hobbs said, his voice gravel now. "Then my father turned his attention on her. I was on the ground, nose bleeding, ribs bruised, but he was hurting Gemma. I heard her yelping. I…" Hobbs trailed off. He stared at the sky, flakes falling on his face like they could cleanse him. "I snapped." Hobbs faced Tabitha again, his eyes steely. "Pops had come into the yard with his shotgun. He'd laid it down to beat on me. That was his mistake."

Tabitha sucked in her breath. Her lungs went tight.

"That was my limit, Tabitha." Hobbs looked her square in

the eye, as if this was a moment of truth for him. "I watched my father beat on my mother for years. I watched him beat on Victor before he got big. I had endured my father beating on me for as long as I had memory. But when I saw him hurting that stray dog, who had done nothing but try to be my only friend, I lost my mind. I picked up that rifle and I cocked it. Aimed it right at him. The noise made him freeze. He turned to me. Looked me in the eye and said, 'Christopher. You don't want to shoot your old man, do you?'" Hobbs, who'd been staring off in the distance, like he was watching the memory happen all over again, slid his gaze to Tabitha. "And then I fired."

Tabitha's brain was racing with Hobbs's words. She'd been so prepared for Gemma to die she hadn't expected to hear what had happened instead. She felt no sorrow for the man who got shot, but the trembling of Hobbs's hands in hers forced her to think about how that action had affected the boy who'd pulled the trigger for the rest of his life.

"I didn't kill him, obviously." Hobbs's voice was colder now, like he'd borrowed some false courage from his cache of tricks. "Got him in the shoulder before the kickback knocked me on my ass." Hobbs touched his right shoulder. "It was enough to stop him. Gemma limped away. Victor woke up. Literally sat on my father, letting him bleed and scream, until the police arrived. Hannah had run into the house and called 9-1-1."

"Did you get in trouble?" Maybe the question was stupid but Tabitha knew the way of the world. Abusers not only got away with their cruelty but came out unscathed when they drove their victims to return violence.

"No." Hobbs shook his head. "The police were used to coming out to our place for my father's bullshit. They knew the score. He actually spent some time in jail for that one. After that, he was in and out for the rest of his life. Spent the last chunk of his years in for manslaughter after he caused a car accident by driving drunk. Killed an old lady out shopping for her grandkids' birthday party. They let him out on compassionate release when he got full-blown dementia and was going to die soon. And then he finally did. And I got to watch it happen. I was literally looking at him when he took his last breath. He looked right in my eye and spoke to me. Said the same words he did on the night of the Fourth. Asked if I was going to shoot him."

Tabitha blinked at him in silence. She had no words, so she slid her arms around Hobbs's waist and laid her head on his chest, squeezing him tight. She expected him to remain limp, but his arms went around her and he squeezed back, hard.

"Gemma never came back," Hobbs whispered above her head. "A neighbor around the corner took her in. I saw her walking Gemma on a pink leash one day, from across the street. Gemma looked well-fed and happy. She saw me and started wagging her tail really hard. She was pulling toward me. But I... I turned around and walked away." Hobbs's voice broke a little bit. "A lot of good things actually came out of that night. My father got put away for a while. Victor never touched alcohol again. I decided I was going to join the marines as soon as I was old enough and nobody was ever going to hurt me again. But that dog has stuck with me all my life. I can't get her out of my head. The way she pulled toward me. And I walked away. But I knew she was safer with that woman than she was with me. I still feel like I abandoned her. Is that crazy?"

Tabitha felt Trinity's weight against her legs. "No," she said. "Sometimes I think Trinity's the only reason I made it through the last year. Semper Fit helped, too, but—" Tabitha raised her head and looked into Hobbs's sad eyes "—without Trinity

I'm not sure I'd have been able to put myself back together. So if you're crazy, I'm crazy."

Hobbs traced the side of her face with his fingertips. "Crap. I'm in trouble."

They laughed together, until that died off, the necessary humor ceding to the heaviness of Hobbs's story. There was nothing for a moment but the sound of the snow pattering in the trees. "I guess you need to get home," Tabitha finally said. "Watch over your sister."

"Actually." Hobbs's voice changed, lifting up, like he was ready to put his past away, at least for tonight. "Victor gave me this." He drew a key out of his jacket pocket. "We switched for the night. I'm in his cabin. He's staying with Hannah."

"Oh."

Hobbs shrugged. "He said it was easier this way. I'm already here. He's already there. Why come all the way back?"

"Makes total sense."

Hobbs nodded at something over Tabitha's shoulder. She turned and saw that one of the cabins was directly behind her, just off the path, nestled in the trees. The porch light was on, showing off the rustic logs that made up the walls. "It's right there," he said. They stared at each other a moment before Hobbs tried a smile. It was a much more tentative smile than Tabitha had ever seen him wear. "Do you want to come in and get warm?"

At some point, Victor had layered logs in the fireplace. All it needed was a flame to get going. Hobbs silently thanked his brother as he lit the paper beneath the logs and watched the sparks catch. From the corner of his eye, Hobbs could see Tabitha shed her coat and wander around the small cabin, which had just two rooms: the main space, with couch, table and lamp in one corner and a bed in the other, the fireplace, equidistant from both, and a bathroom with toilet, sink and shower. Victor had left little sign of his occupancy, other than a toothbrush and razor in the bathroom and duffel bag on the floor by the bed.

As soon as the flames grew, Hobbs replaced the grate and Trinity cozied up on the rug right in front of the blaze. Hobbs ran a hand down her back, her vest removed and tossed next to Tabitha's coat. Just as he was about to stand, he felt hands on his shoulders. The touch was light, but it rooted him to the spot. Tabitha's body pressed against him as she massaged his upper traps, her fingers and thumbs working over the soreness and fatigue, her palms sliding down over his shoulders and back again. Hobbs closed his eyes as she moved up the back of his neck, into his hair. His relaxation slowly ceded to a deep, primal stirring. He turned, without rising, and buried his face in her midriff, inhaling the scent of her skin, feeling the damp of the melted snow.

Her fingers stroked through his hair, tender, fluttering. Hobbs turned his face up. The light from the fire danced over her face, highlighting her smooth skin and glossy curls. Her hair looked damp, her skin dewy.

Hobbs pulled Tabitha down, against him, into his arms, the warmth and sweetness of her radiating all around, like the fire had lit her from the inside out. It made him dizzy, intoxicated. She straddled his lap, her arms going around his neck.

The stirring in Hobbs's body grew, his breath quickening with his pulse. "Listen. I don't want you to think I set all this up. That I only invited you in here so that you'd sleep with me."

"I don't know which I prefer." Tabitha's voice was light and innocent. "That all of this was some kind of serendipity, or that you wanted me so much you really did set it up."

Hobbs nuzzled into her neck, kissing along her jawline.

"The fact that I want you is not in question." Tabitha's legs tightened deliciously around his hips. "It's never been in question. I'm just not used to someone getting to me like you do. I don't know what to do with it."

Tabitha's slender fingers undid the buttons on his shirt, pushing the fabric open. "You can't hold back this time." She leaned in close, stopping just short of kissing him. "Don't close up on me, Chris."

Hobbs rose and took her with him. He brushed the damp curls from her forehead and leaned in to kiss her temple. Then her cheek. By the time he made it to her lips, her body was trembling. She tasted sweet, like snow and lip gloss. "I don't think I can anymore," he admitted, his voice coming out rough. Just the thought of being inside her made Hobbs want to tear her clothes off, but he forced himself to slow down, calm his hammering heart. But as his own movements slowed, Tabitha's quickened, her hands impatient, her lips greedy against his.

She had him undressed and on his back on the bed before Hobbs realized she was still wearing her underwear, a lacy white set that glowed against her skin. As beautiful as she looked, Hobbs only gave the undergarments a moment in the spotlight before he reached behind her back and undid her bra. The silky panties were pressed right against him, making him throb so much he prayed for stamina. As though sensing his struggle, Tabitha released him and rid herself of the rest of her clothing, which joined the pile on the floor. She lay back on the bed and grabbed his hand, pulling him toward her.

Hobbs rested on his knees a moment, resisting, so he could take a moment to admire Tabitha, naked, warm, glowing in the flickering light. He expelled a long breath as he took in the woman in front of him, bare on this rickety bed in an old cabin buried in the woods. It was like finding a rose growing in the weeds out back.

"Chris," she whispered.

The word was as quiet as the snow, whishing into the trees. It also tore through him like a wildfire.

"What did you mean when you said kissing me wasn't what you expected?"

Hobbs almost laughed. There went that brain of hers again, never letting up. But laughter wouldn't come. "When I kissed you on your birthday," Hobbs said, "it felt like you got a peek at something I didn't have a chance to hide. Like you saw me before the curtain fell." He cleared his throat. "It was really uncomfortable. But…also really amazing."

Tabitha regarded him with sultry silence. After a while she whispered, "Well, what are you waiting for?"

Hobbs's eyes changed, went from unguarded to completely renegade, a hearth fire that had conflagrated outside its assigned space, dark magic that had broken the protective warding and rolled out, gathering her in, smothering her. He drew her against him, hard, his lips once again seeking hers, their hands a fumbling mess. He suddenly pulled back. "Wait," he gasped. "This should be gentle. I'm messing this up. Hold on, Tabby, and let me wind down a sec."

Tabitha reached for him. "I don't want to wait," she said. "I want you now."

Hobbs paused for only a second, frozen either by her words or her touch or both, before he grabbed his wallet from the coffee table, fumbled inside, muttered something about never making fun of himself again for having a condom in there, some tearing open with his teeth and a package tossed to the floor. As soon as he was ready, Tabitha drew him in again, her hands on his hips, forcing him closer, up, in, until there was nowhere left to go. The sensation hit her with such force she threw her head back, against the pillows, the explosion going off inside her drowning out the memory of fireworks, the memory of explosions, the memory of anything that had taken her down in the past, brought her to her knees, until there was nothing left but the sweet blackness of this, a midnight sky that rolled on forever, dotted with stars, reminders of ancient things so much bigger than their bodies, their problems, their worlds.

A million different curses tumbled from Hobbs's lips as he buried his face in her sweaty neck, his body a reaction to hers, moving in a rhythm she had created and he willingly followed. Tabitha felt herself building again, her body a delicious, painful traitor, sensations she hadn't known existed shaking her from the inside out.

"That's it, baby." Hobbs's voice was warm and tender against her ear, his body somehow moving exactly how she wanted it to. "Let it go."

The fire inside her was hotter now, the sparks shooting like a meteor shower, Hobbs's voice the fuel and his body stoking her, driving her higher. Her heart beat so hard, her lungs both tight and full, the intensity hooked her, shook her, made her cry out.

Hobbs's eyes opened, his gaze searching, his hips moving while he braced himself around her. "Stay with me, Tabby," he whispered, like he saw right into her, felt everything she was feeling, knew the intensity was almost unbearable, was new, was a little terrifying, like flying, like jumping into that midnight sky without a parachute. "That's it. Right there."

His voice was all around her now, his gaze locked in, holding her, his body moving with hers but also holding her up, until the world imploded, the sky bloomed, the fear strangled itself and Tabitha jumped.

Together, they both let go.

twenty-nine

Tabitha woke to a cold, dark room. The smell of the woods, and a dead fire, filled her nostrils. At first, her foggy brain took her back to Girl Scout camp at Bonnie Lake. But then the night came back to her, the scent of Hobbs's aftershave still inside her and the feel of his hands on her body still on her skin. She sat up in bed and saw that Hobbs had covered her with a blanket, even though they'd fallen asleep on top of the covers.

But the spot next to her was empty.

"Chris?" As her eyes adjusted to the dark, a quick scan revealed that he was not in the room. "Trinity?" Dog tags jangled, and a moment later, the pittie was staring at her from the floor. "Good girl." Tabitha kept the blanket tight around her body as she got out of bed and stepped onto the cold floor. "Chris?" she called again, going into the only other room in the cabin.

The bathroom was empty.

Tabitha's heart started a quick thud in her chest. She found her jacket on the couch and fumbled her phone out of the pocket. It was after midnight. There was a text from Hobbs.

Stay tight. Keep the door locked. I'll be back.

Tabitha's throat felt thick. She called Hobbs, waiting with tight breath for him to answer. After five rings it went to voice mail. She shot off a quick text. What's going on? Then she scrambled into her clothes.

Just as her hand lit on the doorknob, Tabitha thought about the text. If Hobbs had just said, "Stay tight. I'll be back," she might not be having this reaction. Why the line about keeping the door locked? She thought about doing just that, but then she got that gnawing in her gut, her radar going crazy. Tonight, Tabitha's intuition was telling her to go to Hobbs's house. Maybe he was there. Maybe something had happened with Victor or Hannah.

Hannah.

Tabitha fired off another text, this one to Hannah. Everything okay?

Stupid, maybe. If everything was okay, Hannah was probably asleep. If everything was not okay, she probably wouldn't be able to text.

Tabitha poked her head out the door and was met with the dead silence of the forest. The snow had stopped and there were no sounds coming from the trees. She called Trinity to her side and made her way down the path, which was covered in a light dusting of powder. As they passed by the house, Tabitha could see that the party had ended and all was quiet. Christmas Eve had become Christmas Day, and everyone had gone home to bed. The parking lot out front was empty except for a handful of vehicles. Hobbs's truck was not among them.

Tabitha checked her phone again as she reached her car, but there were no new texts or missed calls. She opened the trunk, dug her trainers out of her gym bag and swapped them out for the glittery heels. Then she got in the car and drove as quickly as she could with the fresh snow on the road, sliding only twice, and made it to Hobbs's house in twenty minutes. His truck was not parked out front, the driveway empty. Tabitha's instincts told her to park at the curb and kill the lights, which she did. There were too many other cars around to tell if anything stuck out; they could all be neighbors' vehicles. She sat there in the darkness, unsure what to do. She could knock on the door, but if Hannah was inside, asleep, Tabitha would be waking her for no good reason. She tried Hobbs's number one more time, but again, she got voice mail. She was just about to head home, where she'd wait with twisted nerves until she heard from Hobbs, when her phone rang.

"Chris!" Tabitha snapped out his name. "Where are you?"

"On my way home." He sounded out of breath. "Victor and I both got sent on a wild-goose chase. We got texts from an unknown number, telling us to come out to Oakwood Park to talk about the texts Hannah's been getting. We ran into each other in the parking lot, but nobody else ever showed. Now we're worried about Hannah, who Victor left at the house. It has to be her ex. He's found her, just like he promised."

Tabitha put the pieces together. Someone had texted both brothers, hoping to empty out the house and get to Hannah. Whoever it was knew that they wouldn't risk taking Hannah with them on what might be a dangerous trip. And now here she was, all alone in the house.

"Stay put," Hobbs was saying. "Just stay in the cabin. I'll be back there as soon as I can. I'm about half an hour from the house."

Tabitha debated what to say next. Did she tell Hobbs she

had ignored his directive and now sat in front of the house? Just as she went to speak, something in the yard caught her eye. She rolled her window down and squinted into the darkness. Tabitha sucked in her breath. "Okay, be careful," she said, then hung up the phone. No point in telling Hobbs where she was. He couldn't get here any faster.

She opened her door and leaned down to pet the cold, shivering dog. "Gracie," she whispered. "How did you get out?"

Tabitha told Trinity to stay in the car, then toured the entire perimeter of the house, but couldn't find anywhere Gracie might've slipped out. When she reached the front again, she squished through the snow and underlying mud in the front yard to the windows that lined the living room and peeked inside, through a gap in the curtains. The room was lit and Tabitha could see Hannah, sitting in the armchair in the corner. Beside her was a giant Christmas tree, decorated with glass bulbs and white garland. She held George in her lap, clutching him to her midriff, her face contorted, and what looked like a large, fresh bruise spreading near her mouth. Across from her, perched on the edge of the sofa, was a man Tabitha had never seen before. He was slim and wiry, had a head of glossy, light brown hair and wore dark clothing. Tabitha could hear him talking, his words clipped and harsh, though she couldn't make out what he said.

Tabitha backed away, her first instinct to knock on the door and distract him. He'd obviously hit Hannah once already and seemed ready to do it again, the way he leaned forward in his seat, his body taut, his hands fisted. But after careful thought, Tabitha knew that wouldn't go well. A knock on the door would probably just be met with silence. Either way, it would give away her position, and that was not a smart move. She quickly did her tactical breathing, only one round, as that was all she had time for, and felt her heart rate slow. Then she dialed 9-1-1 and waited until the operator popped on.

"Nine-one-one. What's your emergency?"

Tabitha quickly explained about a break-in and gave Hobbs's address.

"Stay on the line with me, ma'am."

Tabitha was just heading back to her car when she heard Hannah's scream from inside the house. She was so startled she dropped her phone to the wet grass. She grabbed it but stuffed it in her pocket, the dispatcher calling out, "Ma'am? Ma'am? Are you there?" as Tabitha slunk around to the backyard for the second time. Gracie, who'd been at her heels the entire time, followed. The door hadn't been ajar on her first pass, but Tabitha was hoping it was unlocked. She knew she should get in her car, lock it and wait for dispatch, but what if Hannah was dead by then?

No. Not on Tabitha's watch.

She tried the handle of the back door, but it didn't budge. Tabitha did one more round of breathing while she looked around the cold, dark yard, in search of something to help get her inside. A rock through a window might work, but that would do more to alert Hannah's attacker than anything else. Tabitha had just let out her breath in a long exhalation when she spied it: a dog door.

A newly installed dog door for a large-sized breed.

Tabitha looked down at Gracie. "So that's how you got out."

And that was exactly how Tabitha was going to get in.

By the time Tabitha had shimmied through the flap sideways, ending up on the floor of the breakfast nook, streaked with snow and mud, Hannah gave off another scream. A second later, George came flying down the hallway, nothing but a blur, and disappeared. Tabitha could hear the attacker's words now as he shouted at Hannah.

"I told you, you're not going anywhere! Not until you talk to me. All I wanted to do was talk to you, alone. And you turned it into a fight! I came all the way out here—stop crying!—and all you got to say is I should leave. Well, I'm not leaving. And when I do, you're coming with me!"

Tabitha paused in the dark breakfast nook, assessing the rooms and her situation. The man who was after Hannah wouldn't expect anyone to stand up to him, particularly not a woman. She could use that to her advantage. She didn't know for sure if he had a weapon, but even if he didn't, he was much larger than Tabitha. Maybe a distraction was all she needed. After all, she didn't have to stop him, just slow him down.

She faced the cold, dark fireplace nestled on the far side of the room, which looked like it hadn't been lit in years. Tabitha had a fleeting thought about the difference between this fireplace and the beauty of the one she'd just shared with Hobbs. She grabbed the poker, nestled in a rack with other fireplace tools, in an iron grip.

She slid along the wall, toward the living room. Just as she rounded the corner, Gracie came flying in, barreling past. The dog ran right up to Hannah's attacker, who now stood, towering over Hannah, fists clenched. Gracie reared back and barked. The man kicked his leg out, but Gracie dodged it, dropped back on her haunches and barked again, this time adding a growl to the mix. The man spun in circles, trying to connect his heavy boot with the barking dog.

That was when he looked up and spied Tabitha, frozen against the wall, poker in her grip. "Who the hell are you?" The man's eyes were dark and dead, almost ashy, like the unused fireplace in the breakfast nook.

"Leave her alone." Tabitha lifted the poker to her shoulder. Her hand was steady and her arm felt strong.

"Tabitha!" Hannah gasped. Her face was streaked with tears, blood dripping from her nose and the corner of her mouth. Her left eye was swelling up fast. "Run!"

"Oh, no, you don't." The man strode toward Tabitha, even though she hadn't made a move. "You're not going anywhere."

Tabitha knew that first responders would be here soon, but how soon? She quickly took in the scene. The intruder didn't have a weapon in either hand, other than those cruel hands themselves. There was one exit, but she couldn't get Hannah and herself there before the man grabbed either one of them. She gripped her poker and adjusted her position, like a batter up to the plate. Tabitha used to love playing baseball in high school—her batting average coming back to her in a flash, something she hadn't thought about in years—but she hadn't batted anything since she was a teenager. She looked the intruder in his cold, dead eye and held his gaze. If nothing else, Tabitha had distracted him from Hannah, and if she could at least hold him off until the police arrived, that was all she needed.

The assailant, who'd been slowly walking her way, lunged, suddenly making his move. Tabitha wasn't surprised. She'd seen what he was going to do in his eyes before his body had jerked. She darted out of his reach, but at the last second he caught the hem of her blouse and yanked. The shirt made a tearing sound and Tabitha stumbled, then fell to the ground. The man loomed over her, his eyes dark slashes and his mouth a grim line. He reached for her, and a great growling sound followed, like a snarling pack of wolves.

The assailant cried out, then cursed. He swung his leg and reached for the dog, which, to Tabitha's surprise, was not a tawny Lab mix, but a black ball of fury. Trinity, in all her tiny pit bull glory, had her jaws clamped down on the assailant's calf. She must've climbed out the open car window and followed Tabitha inside. Even when Hannah's attacker kicked her, she yelped, but didn't let go.

The attacker cursed a second time, then brought his fist down against Trinity's face. The pittie yelped and fell back, blood on her jowls. The man's arm reared back again, and just as he was about to hit the dog for a third time, Tabitha heard Hobbs's voice in her head—*Get mad, Tabby!* She took a great swing and brought the poker full force to the back of the man's knees. He bellowed and sank down. Tabitha reared back and brought it down again, this time against his back. He screamed out in wild, choking pain, then curled up on his side in a fetal position. Tabitha swung and gave him a third blow, this time to his shoulder. He screamed and pulled himself into a tighter ball.

"Don't move," she growled, "or your face is next." Tabitha drew the poker high, poised to strike. She caught sight of Hannah, from the corner of her eye, her mouth agape, Gracie standing sentinel in front of her. Trinity hobbled over to Tabitha's side, dribbling blood along the way, and smashed herself against Tabitha's legs. Red and blue lights flashed outside as vehicles tore into the driveway.

Moments later, the police were inside. Tabitha dropped the poker and sank down on the floor. Trinity climbed on her chest, planting her paws over her shoulder, and that was the last thing Tabitha remembered before her eyes closed.

thirty

When Clementine got out of bed on Christmas morning, the house was unusually quiet. Lily was always the first one up for the holiday, coffee made, bread in the toaster, eggs on the stove. It'd become a kind of joke about who was the real mom around here.

Today, when Clementine peeked in her room, she saw Lily's hair splayed across her pillow, nothing but a mound beneath the covers, with Terrence wrapped up behind the small of her back.

"Hey, Nugget," Clementine whispered.

He lifted his head, stretched and wagged his tail. Then he laid it back down and closed his eyes.

"Loyal," Clementine observed with a laugh. She padded into the kitchen and started the coffeepot, knowing the smell of the rich brew would have Lily awake within the next twenty minutes. She went to the living room and opened the curtains, letting in the bright morning sun, which sparkled over last night's snow. Maybe an inch had fallen; just enough to make the world look like a fairy tale, gilded in crystal.

She settled on the sofa, waiting for the coffee, and eyed the handful of presents under the Christmas tree. Both she and Lily were practical. They only bought each other things that struck their fancy, avoiding the glut of commercialism and limiting themselves to a few special gifts. This tradition had started when they were on a tight budget but had blossomed over the years into a mutual respect for the notion of less being more, and their time together being the most important of all.

Clementine spied her journal on the end table and lifted it. She opened it up and realized that the last time she'd written to Tyler had been the day she'd gone for a run with Terrence. She hadn't signed off that day, and had never gone back in to do so.

She fiddled with her pen, clicking it open and closed, over and over again. Clementine looked closer at the journal and saw that it was down to the last page. After this entry, she'd have to start a new one. No use starting a new one, of course, until she'd signed off in this one.

"Hey." Lily suddenly appeared, bounding down the stairs in her pajamas. "Merry Christmas." Terrence followed at her heels.

"Merry Christmas, kiddo."

At the foot of the stairs, Terrence flopped over on his back. "You're not trash, are you, boy?" Lily said as she rubbed his belly. "No. You're my good boy." After a moment she stood back up and stretched. "Writing in your journal?"

Clementine looked down at the last entry and clicked her pen closed. "Nope," she said. She slid the notebook back on the table and rose up. "The journal's done." She paused, letting that thought sink in for a moment. Yeah. The journal was done. And she wouldn't be needing a new one. "I'm just about to pour some coffee. Join me?"

Lily eyed the notebook, then eyed her mother. A slow smile spread over her face. "Definitely."

After coffee and presents, they snuggled on the sofa and clicked on the TV, which was something they rarely got to do with their busy schedules. "Oh my gosh, look! It's George and Gracie!"

"Dad's old TV show," Lily said, her smile both sweet and sad, but mostly sweet. "I know Hannah and Hobbs are going to adopt them, by the way. They're in good hands."

"I think you're right."

They were quiet after that, their silence punctuated with laughter as they watched the show. "Do you think about him much?" Clementine broached, when the show was near to ending.

Lily didn't clarify *who*. "Enough," she said. "But in a good way." Her hand dipped down to Terrence's head, where he lay on the floor. She stroked his ears absentmindedly. "What about you?"

Clementine offered a quiet smile. "Maybe too much. But I'm working on it."

"Cool."

The show ended and Lily turned off the TV. "Time for T's walk," she said. She rose up and stretched.

"Hey, I was wondering," Clementine said, the thought suddenly coming to her. "There was a guy at the party last night. Tall, sitting with the group, but never said a thing to anybody. Do you know who he was?"

Lily looked toward the ceiling, like she was thinking. "I remember him. But I don't know, either." Her gaze locked into her mother's. "But I could find out."

"No, that's okay," Clementine said quickly. "I was just curious."

Lily grinned a little bit. "You sure?"

"Yeah, I'm sure."

"All right. Let's walk T."

"Let's do it. C'mon, Nugget."

thirty-one

Hobbs had actually spent many a Christmas morning at either the police station or the hospital. Today, he got to spend time at both. At one point in his life, he'd thought that was normal.

By the end of the day, though, everyone had been checked out and statements had been taken. Timbley was in custody and everyone else had come back to the house and collapsed in the living room around Hannah's spectacular Douglas fir. No one was in the mood for gifts, nobody really felt like eating, and after a mug of hot cocoa Hannah decided to try sleeping.

"Thank you again, Tabitha." Hannah and Tabitha clutched each other in an embrace. "You were so brave. I can't believe I let him in. When he knocked, I thought it was Chris, because he gave his keys to Victor. I'm so stupid."

Tabitha shook her head. She carefully touched around Hannah's wounded face. "Nothing about this is your fault. You go get some rest. It'll all look better in the morning."

Once Hannah had disappeared down the hall, with George following behind her at a quick trot, Hobbs turned to Tabitha. Her sexy outfit from last night was torn and dirty, her face gaunt and tired. He wanted to be angry with her for busting in here and putting herself in danger, but truth was, Hobbs was only angry at himself for being duped by Hannah's abusive ex. He and Victor had already hashed out their stupidity together before Victor had declared this Christmas a loss, though strangely also a victory. "It's actually one of the better Christmases I've ever had," Victor had said dryly. "You're one brave young lady," he'd told Tabitha. "He doesn't deserve you." And then Victor had headed down the hall toward Hobbs's room. "I'm sleeping in here like we planned," he'd shouted over his shoulder. "Enjoy the couch."

Hobbs sighed. Once they were alone, he faced Tabitha. "I'm so sorry this happened to you in my house. I'm sorry that you got mixed up in the mess that is my life and my past, Tabby Cat. I don't even know what to say."

Inexplicably, Tabitha smiled. "Well, I'm not sorry for anything. Except maybe giving Auntie El a heart attack when I called from the hospital." She laughed briefly at herself, then sobered up. "I'm just glad I was here. I'm glad Hannah is all right."

Hobbs drew Tabitha in and held her tight against his chest. She smelled like the stale sweat of fear, blood and old snow. "You sure thought on your feet," he admitted, even if he didn't like to think about her being in harm's way.

"All my old training came back." Tabitha pulled back and smiled again. "Besides, that man hurt both Hannah and Trinity. That was just the last straw. I've come to feel really protective of Hannah, and Trinity spends her entire life taking care of me. I had to do the same for her."

Hobbs looked down at the pit bull, who was asleep on the

floor, her breathing deep and labored, like she was recovering from her horrible morning. "Of course you did."

"You helped me, too," Tabitha admitted. "I heard your stupid voice in my head. Yelling at me to get mad. Get aggressive."

"See?" Hobbs laughed. "It worked."

Tabitha smiled and gave him a shove. Silence stretched between them. Tabitha cocked her head to the side. "I need to go check on Auntie El. Any chance you want to come?"

Hobbs almost said no on default. It didn't come up much in his world, but he didn't meet the parents, ever. *I don't even like my own parents*, he'd say. *Why would I want to meet yours?* But when he opened his mouth to speak, he realized that he didn't want to be here right now, in this house with Hannah and Victor. If Hobbs lay on the couch, he'd toss and turn, thinking about Tabitha and how much he wanted to be with her. So why let her go? "Yes," he said, surprising himself. From the look on Tabitha's face, she was just as shocked.

"Okay," she said. "Good." Then she smiled. "And bring Gracie. Trinity could use some company."

Auntie El was in the kitchen, fussing with bread and fish and pie and any other thing she'd busied herself with that day, once Tabitha had called and explained and convinced her that everything was fine now. She wore a long purple dress with bright red flowers all over it and looked rested, despite her obvious worry.

Her arms opened as soon as Tabitha came inside. Auntie El crushed her in a bear hug and rocked her side to side. "My little T," she murmured, her embrace so tight Tabitha struggled to breathe. "You're all right now. Mama's here."

After a while, Auntie El stepped back and held Tabitha at

arm's length. "I'm okay," Tabitha said. "It's Trinity who got hit. Trying to protect me."

Auntie El looked down at the little pit bull and made a rare motherly sound toward the dog. She stooped down and stroked her head. "Good girl," she said. Then she grabbed some meat from a plate on the counter and offered it to Trinity, who took the morsel politely and scarfed it down.

"Auntie, this is my friend Chris." Tabitha motioned to the man who, up until now, had stayed behind her, quiet, with Gracie by his side. His nice clothes, which he'd never changed, were rumpled, and his wavy hair was finger-combed into place. His eyes were bloodshot and his boisterous personality tucked away behind fatigue and probably more than a little respect. "And his dog, Gracie."

"Hello." Auntie El looked him up and down.

"He's Hannah's brother. The lady I helped last night."

"Oh, I see." Auntie El studied him, her demeanor kind of soft and open, her eyes curious behind her glasses.

"Nice to meet you, ma'am." Hobbs offered his hand for a shake.

Auntie El touched her fingertips to his and lightly clasped them. "You look like someone I used to know," she said, her gaze only once flicking away, to check out Gracie, who had flopped to the floor next to Trinity, both of them exhausted. "A boy I fostered, way back in the day. His name was Casey." Auntie El finally drew her hand away. She looked at Tabitha. "You wouldn't remember him, I expect. But he looked a lot like this boy, here." She pointed at Hobbs. "His hair was a little darker and he was a little smaller but something about the eyes. Same color. Same kind of look." Auntie El's voice got faraway and her eyes clouded over a little.

"I remember you talking about Casey," Tabitha said, even

though it was Reverend Stokes who had told her about him. "He was important to you."

Auntie El's face brightened. "That's right." She gave a little shake, like she was snapping herself out of her reverie. "Anyway, Chris, I hope you're hungry. I made all this food for Christmas and nobody's been here to eat it."

Hobbs smiled. In that moment, it was like somebody had pulled the plug on a tub full of tension and Tabitha watched it slowly drain away. "Thank you, ma'am. As a matter of fact... I'm starving."

On cue, Tabitha's stomach growled. Everyone looked at her, including the two dogs, then burst into laughter.

"C'mon, now." Auntie El slipped her arm around Hobbs's shoulders. "Don't just stand there in the doorway. Get in here out of the cold and we'll fix you up a plate." Auntie El guided him to the dining room table and motioned for him to sit. Once he'd settled, she rubbed his shoulder approvingly.

Tabitha was watching them, growing a little tearful, when she caught a glimpse of herself in the mirror on the wall at the far end of the room. Her first thought was *What a mess*, but that initial reaction slowly changed. Tabitha eyed the ridiculous cobble of sexy black pants, trainers and the scrubs top from the car she'd changed into before heading out here, and it dawned on her that she looked...just right.

"Hey," Hobbs said. "What're you grinning at?"

"Oh. Nothing much." Auntie El had gone into the kitchen to fix plates, so Tabitha settled at the table. "Listen. I know you don't do the whole 'happy family' thing with moms and aunties and home-cooked meals, but—"

"She's great," Hobbs interrupted. He smiled, but it was soft and tentative, a complete one-eighty of his usual big grin. "This is great, Tabby. Thank you."

Just then, Gracie came trotting in, Trinity at her heels. They both found the humans they were seeking and plopped down in their respective places. Gracie settled her head between her paws, closed her eyes and sighed. Hobbs laughed. "She's hopeless," he said.

"You're going to keep her, aren't you?" Tabitha suggested gently.

Hobbs reached down and ruffled Gracie's head. "I hate to say this," he mumbled. "But I kinda like her."

"You more than kinda like her," Tabitha teased. "You like her a lot. A whole lot."

"Yeah." Hobbs looked up, no humor in his face, and held Tabitha's gaze. "I really do."

After a silent moment, Tabitha's whole body got as warm as Auntie El's kitchen. "Well." Her voice was soft. "She really likes you, too."

After another round of silence, Hobbs's face broke into that charming grin of his. "Well, she better," he said. "Because she still owes me a motorcycle ride."

"Does she, now?"

"She does. Because this one is going to be so much better than her last one. The one she took with that big, hulking oaf." Hobbs waved a hand in the direction of the outdoors, to whatever direction might indicate Victor. "This ride will be off the charts."

"Long as he doesn't change his mind. Get stupid," Tabitha said.

"Well, he can't promise he'll never get stupid," Hobbs said. "But he's definitely not going to change his mind." The grin fell away. He set his elbow on the table and stuck out his pinkie. "Promise."

Tabitha set her elbow on the table, too. She hooked Hobbs's pinkie in her own. A soft tug followed, and then Hobbs leaned in. Tabitha's eyes closed and his lips touched hers. The kiss was gentle and sweet, but even after last night, Tabitha could feel a fire starting to prickle under her skin. Hobbs drew away slowly.

"Was it what you were expecting?" Tabitha whispered.

Hobbs shook his head. "No. You surprise me every time."

Then he leaned in and kissed her again.

★ ★ ★ ★ ★ ·

acknowledgments

Many thanks to my agent, Sara Megibow, to my editor, Margot Mallinson, and to the entire team at MIRA/Harlequin for their hard work on this book.

To my family and beta readers—especially Magpie, Mike, Mom and Chris—thank you for your support, your keen eyes, your suggestions and your contributions.

Thank you to all of our military service members and health-care workers—silent heroes who help keep us safe and ask for nothing in return.

And thank you to everyone who rescues, fosters and adopts. You help make the world a better place.